THE HEART SPECIALIST

Lan
Copy

DS 1/19

This book should be returned/renewed by
the latest date shown above. Overdue items
incur charges which prevent self-service
renewals. Please contact the library.

Wandsworth Libraries
24 hour Renewal Hotline
01159 293388
www.wandsworth.gov.uk Wandsworth

L.749A (2.07)

"The novel is a gem on many levels. A
well-formed, believable characters, insigh
the action along, a cohesive storyline th
descriptive detail that make the reader year

The Record

"I can pay a book no higher compliment than to say I didn't want it to end. With *The Heart Specialist*, I rationed my reading, permitting myself only a few chapters at a sitting so as to savour the writing and the story."

The Montreal Gazette

"*The Heart Specialist* is a fascinating novel that conveys both a sense of history and of the timelessness of human emotions. That Rothman also demonstrates the damage that prejudice can do, and the power of the human spirit in overcoming it, is simply an added bonus."

The Quill & Quire

ABOUT THE AUTHOR

Claire Holden Rothman has worked as a lawyer, teacher, newspaper columnist, and translator in her native Montreal. *The Heart Specialist* is her first novel.

THE
HEART SPECIALIST

CLAIRE HOLDEN ROTHMAN

ONEWORLD
OXFORD

Published by Oneworld Publications 2011

Copyright © Claire Holden Rothman 2009

The moral right of Claire Holden Rothman to be identified
as the Author of this work has been asserted by
her in accordance with the Copyright,
Designs and Patents Act 1988

ISBN 978–1–85168–794–7

Cover design by Jon Gray
Printed and bound in Great Britain by
CPI Cox & Wyman, Reading

Oneworld Publications
185 Banbury Road Oxford OX2 7AR, England

Learn more about Oneworld. Join our mailing list to
find out about our latest titles and special offers at:
www.oneworld-publications.com

For Arthur Holden

*Cardiac anomalies may be divided, according to etiology,
into two main groups: those due to arrest of growth at
an early stage, before the different parts of the heart have
been entirely formed, and those produced in the
more fully developed heart by fetal disease.*

— MAUDE ABBOTT, "CONGENITAL CARDIAC DISEASE,"
IN WILLIAM OSLER'S SYSTEM OF MEDICINE

*Still the heart doth need a language,
Still doth the old instinct bring back the old names.*

— FRIEDRICH SCHILLER, PICCOLOMINI

PRELUDE
THE SMALL WATCHER

Observe, record, tabulate, communicate.

— WILLIAM OSLER

My first memory of my father is of his face floating above me and weeping. The image dates back to 1874 during a particularly brutal winter in St. Andrews East, a town near the mouth of the Ottawa River in Quebec, about fifty miles from Montreal. The month was January. I would soon turn five.

What mechanism triggers memory, selecting images to press into the soft skin of a child's mind? Often it is trauma, although at that particular moment the word had not yet entered my lexicon. I had no idea why my father had come into my room or why he was weeping. All I knew when I opened my eyes was that something was wrong. Routines had been disrupted, rules broken. My safe, small world had come unhinged.

My father smelled of pipe tobacco, a delicious smell that made me think of chocolate. I stared at the moustache drooping from his upper lip. I could have buried my face in that moustache, but of course I did no such thing. He was an imposing man whose moods were occasionally unpredictable. I just lay still and stared.

Not long after he left us, when the fields and roads were still glistening with ice, I came across one of his pipes abandoned in the barn in back of the house. I didn't even pause to think. I picked it up and stuck it in my mouth. It was an experiment, an attempt to copy what I had seen him do hundreds of times, an attempt to bring him back. The result was a shock. It tasted awful, nothing like the sweet dark-chocolate smell of my memory. I spat until my tongue hurt and I had no saliva left.

That night, staring up at him from my bed, I was at a loss. I was only beginning to understand that there were people other than myself in the world, living lives separate from mine. To think that my father might cry confused me, so I shut my eyes, shutting out everything but his smell and the sounds of his quick and shallow breaths.

He spoke to me in French, which he did sometimes when it was just the two of us. I have no recollection of what was said. It was not about the trial or his dead sister, that much is certain. He never spoke of these things to anyone in the house in St. Andrews East. He probably tried to reassure me. I suspect I knew even then that he was lying. I could sense that things were very wrong, and suddenly, just like my father, I too began to cry. I must have gone on for some time because when I looked up he was gone.

He took only his clothes that night and the money he had scraped together for the baptism — Laure's baptism, although at the time he would not have known it was to be Laure. He had chosen her name, just as he had chosen mine — Agnès — picking it out with my mother months before the births. Paul if a boy, Laure if a girl, names that worked in both French and English. In the end, Laure had to wait several years for her baptism. Grandmother took care of it, as she took care of so much else.

For the longest time I felt that I had chased my father away. My tears had sent him running. His face had been there one moment and then, after I shut my eyes and wept, he was gone. A child's logic, I suppose, but logic nonetheless. What if I had kept still, I later could not help thinking. What if I had reached out my childish arms to embrace him? From that day on I lived with one thought paramount in my mind. I would find my dark, sad father and win him back. Though I could not claim to have known him well, and my first memory of him was almost my last, it did not matter. His face stayed with me through the years, as clear as on that night in January when he went away.

I
SAINT AGNES

Saint Agnes' Eve — Ah, bitter chill it was!

— JOHN KEATS

I

JANUARY 1882, ST. ANDREWS EAST, QUEBEC

All morning I had been waiting for death, even though when it finally came the change was so incremental I nearly missed it. I had laid the squirrel out on a crate and covered it with a rag to keep it from freezing. Blood no longer flowed from the wound on its head, although it still looked red and angry. A dog or some other animal must have clamped its jaws around the skull, but somehow it had managed to escape, dragging itself through the snow to Grandmother's property, where I had discovered it that morning near the barn door. It had been breathing then, the body still trembling and warm.

Now the breathing was stopped and its eyes were filmy. I blew on my fingers, which had numbed with cold, and went to my instruments bag. It was not leather like the one used by Archie Osborne, the doctor for St. Andrews East. It was burlap and had once held potatoes. Along with most of its contents, it had been pilfered from Grandmother's kitchen. I took out a paring knife, a whetting stone and a box of pins in a tin that used to hold throat lozenges dusted with sugar. The blade of my knife was razor-thin and nicked in several spots. It didn't look like much, but it was as good as any scalpel. I rubbed the whetting stone along the blade a few times then cracked the ice in the bucket with my heel and dipped in the knife to clean off the sugar dust.

My dead house left a lot to be desired. It was too cold in January for stays of decent duration. After two winters of working here, however, I was accustomed to it. I had organized it well, with microscope in the far corner hidden beneath a tarpaulin and twenty-one of Grandmother's Mason jars lined up on the floor against one wall, concealed by straw. Above the jars, on a shelf fashioned out of a board, was my special collection, which consisted of three dead ladybugs, the husk of a cicada beetle, the desiccated jaw of a cow and my prize: a pair of butterflies mounted with thread and glass rods in the only true laboratory bottle I'd been able to salvage from my father's possessions two years earlier, before Grandmother had them carted away to the junkyard. I took only three things for myself — my father's microscope and slides, a textbook and that bottle. Any more and my grandmother would surely have noticed.

To a person glancing through the door, my dissection room appeared to be ordinary barn storage. Grandmother had forbidden me and Laure to play here, claiming the floorboards had rotted and we would fall through and break our legs. I had to use the back entrance for my visits, accessed by a path in the forest that abutted Grandmother's land.

The squirrel's yellow teeth poked through its lips. Its paws, curled to the chest as if it were begging, resisted my efforts to open them. The animal was already beginning to stiffen, but whether this was from cold or rigor mortis I could tell. Its legs were also hard to manoeuvre, but somehow I managed to get the body done, laying him out on his back like a little man. My pins had a delicate confectionary smell that was incongruous with the odour of newly dead squirrel. I sniffed as I fastened him down, wincing as the metal pricks punctured his hide. The last preparatory step involved the microscope, which I lugged to the crate next to the dissection area for easy access.

My knife pierced the belly skin, releasing a gush of pink fluid that arced up, splattering the camel-hair coat Grandmother made for me last Christmas. I stepped back, staring stupidly at the line streaking my front, then reached for my apron. I had been careless. A fault I knew well, as Grandmother pointed it out to me every single day. She was right. I tended to forget about the most basic things: my hair was often half undone, my stockings sagged at my ankles.

Up until that day in the barn I had worked mostly with plants and insects. The closest I had come to anything alive were the tiny creatures inhabiting the scum of ponds or nestling in the bones of meat on the turn. This was the first time an animal with blood still warm in its veins had fallen into my hands. I cut again, this time down the middle, adding two perpendicular slits at the ends to form doors in the animal's belly. These I peeled back and pinned, exposing the dark innards. My fingers were wet and red. Behind me there was a gasp.

Laure was in the doorway, mittens covering her mouth, her eyes starting to roll up in their sockets. She swayed, her pupils expanding into black holes.

I swung my hands in back of me. "Laure," I said quickly. "It's all right. Nothing. I'll wash it away." I plunged my hands into the bucket.

My sister is a very particular case. She cannot watch the gutting of a chicken. We have to make sure the kitchen door is shut fast and she is safely off in her bedroom when we prepare flesh for dinner.

Laure had now stopped swaying, which I took to be encouraging, but her pupils had shrunk to pinpricks. She was standing as stiff as the squirrel on my table. While she stood there like a corpse, I rushed about, covering everything with the potential to upset her. I pulled the strip of flannel back over the squirrel, but immediately a ruby eye appeared on the abdomen and began to grow. I tore off my apron and once again plunged my hands into the icy bucket to scrub them.

Laure moaned. Tears always followed the trance phase, with a headache that could keep her in bed for days. I called to her, but of course she was past listening. After another minute or so she was able to move and limped off toward the house, weeping and mumbling for Grandmother. The doctor we consulted gave it a French name: *Petit Mal*. He said it was less serious than *Grand Mal*, which was a full-blown epileptic seizure, but nonetheless, it was a condition we had to watch. No one knew the cause, although trauma — a childhood fever or even an emotion — was often at the root. The primary symptom was absence. Laure slipped into a trance and nothing anyone said or did could shake her out of it.

The squirrel's body was growing stiffer by the second, yet all I had managed were the preliminaries. I felt like weeping myself, in pure frustration. Laure almost never came to the barn. Why had she picked this of all possible days to try and find me? The squirrel grinned in silent mockery. You see, it seemed to say. Stick your fingers in the belly of a corpse and see if trouble doesn't follow. I closed my eyes to shut out his yellow teeth. If I wanted to do any work at all it had to be now. Perhaps Laure wouldn't be coherent and Grandmother would simply put her to bed. It was a slim chance but it was not a crime to hope. I reached for my apron.

By the time Grandmother arrived I had managed to locate the heart and what I suspected must be the liver. Grandmother marched into the barn, her old eyes narrow and grim. She is a short woman, barely five feet tall, but people think she is taller because of how she walks. She would have made a great general in the Army, and not just because of her posture. She was wearing my dead grandfather's workboots, the ones she kept by the kitchen door for emergencies, and she had forgotten her hat in her haste. Her hair had come partially undone and a couple of silver strands were snaking, Medusa-like, down her back. I had never before seen her in such disarray, and we stood gaping at each other for several seconds, quite unable to speak. Worse still, she was not alone. She had dragged Miss Skerry along with her from the house. Miss Skerry was the new governess, brought in expressly to "smooth my edges," as Grandmother put it, and assist my passage into womanhood.

Their eyes took in my knife and the filthy butcher's apron. Then they saw the squirrel with its abdomen slit open.

"Agnes," said my grandmother. It came out quietly, a sigh, and suddenly she seemed to shrink. Her eyes, often hard, had something new in them, which alarmed me even more than the shrinking had. It was fear, I suddenly realized. My grandmother was afraid.

She took the corner of my apron least marred by squirrel gut and tried to yank it over my head, but it caught on my ear. By then she had glimpsed my bloody coat. She let go of the apron and covered her eyes with her hands.

I had never seen my grandmother cry. I had never imagined she was capable; she was so steady, so grim. I was the opposite, erupting into tears at the smallest provocation, slouching off to the barn or to the woods behind the house to vent my rage and sadness. Grandmother disapproved of these episodes, calling them "performances" and warning me that if I did not put such childish things away I was doomed to a hard and lonely life.

But here she was crying herself, right in front of me and Miss Skerry. My mind went spiralling back what seemed a hundred years, although it was really less than ten, to another day and another adult weeping. My emotional nature, I had always thought, came from him — my father. In fact, Grandmother herself said this when she was angry, calling it my "Gallic blood." I was the family misfit — dark and teary, with a mind that must have seemed disturbingly foreign in that small Presbyterian town.

"It's not what you think," I said. "I didn't kill it."

I was trying to reassure her, but I managed to do the exact opposite. It was the word "kill." I should not have used it, for my grandmother was thinking of her son-in-law — my father — and his poor dead sister.

I have never seen a picture of my father — we kept no photograph after he left so I could not see it for myself — but everyone in St. Andrews East said I was his spitting image. They were careful about saying it, not wanting to upset Grandmother, but sometimes it slipped out. Archie Osborne, the town doctor, said it almost every time he saw me. And I was keenly aware that I looked nothing like Laure, who was blue-eyed and fair, with the delicate bone structure of the White family women. My skin was like a gypsy's, and my body stocky and squat. The ladies who came for tea at the Priory always remarked how pretty Laure was. It was hard not to, she looked so much like an angel with her flowing, corn-silk hair. When they realized I was in the room, serving lumps of sugar, an embarrassed silence followed. "Agnes is so *intelligent*," they would add, trying miserably to make amends.

My intelligence, it was generally assumed, also came from my father — bookishness, an unfortunate trait for a girl, especially one who is not nice to look at. Grandmother's theory was that I spent so much time reading I'd ruin my eyes. I did not believe her because she herself had bad eyes and the only book she ever opened was the Bible, and then only once a week, on Sunday.

Grandmother believed my father was a murderer. She never said as much; in fact, she avoided all mention of him after he left. It was as if he had died, just like my mother. Grandmother even went so far as to change our name. Two years after my father disappeared, and several months after Mother's funeral, Laure and I officially dropped Bourret and became Whites, and the accent was dropped from Agnès so that I became Agnes. My grandmother became our legal guardian.

The squirrel was just too much for her. I only realized it after the fact or I would have been more careful, performing the dissection in the woods, where neither she nor Laure would ever have looked. It was like a sign that all my grandmother's efforts to guide me, to provide me with a decent Christian home and name had been for naught. Nothing could change the fact that I was a squat, dark person with a foreign brain and foreign ways. For what was a thirteen-year-old girl doing out in the barn on one of the coldest days of January slicing open a squirrel?

Bourret derives from the French word *bourreau*, which, strictly speaking, means "executioner." In Quebec, however, it has other idiomatic uses. There is *bourreau des coeurs*, "lady-killer." And *bourreau d'enfants*, "batterer of children." In the case of my father's family the name was prophetic. His youngest sister, Marie, was found battered to death and drowned on the shore of the Ottawa River, not far from the family's home in Rigaud, about a day's drive west of Montreal. It turned out, however, that the girl had actually been living in Montreal, in the attic of our home, for months before her death, although no one besides my parents and me had known this.

The violent circumstances of her death and the fact that she had been secreted in our attic directly before it were considered sufficient grounds to charge my father with murder.

Marie Bourret was a cripple and a deaf-mute, alone in the world once her parents died. I have absolutely no recollection of her, although I have since returned to my father's former house in Montreal and stood in the rooms in which she allegedly spent her last days.

The prosecutor argued that she would have been a burden to my father, who was her oldest sibling and the most successful of his large family — a doctor teaching at the University of McGill with a young wife and family and prospects shining brightly ahead of him. The prosecutor convinced the public of this motive but had insufficient evidence to prove it. My father was acquitted by the jury but not by general opinion in the City of Montreal.

He was allowed to keep his practice, an empty gift, for after the trial no patient would come to him. Then McGill gave him notice. The murder was the biggest scandal the city had seen for years and all kinds of people who had not met my father spent hours speculating about his guilt in the affair. We had to take refuge in

St. Andrews East with Grandmother White. Throughout that winter and spring rumours flew. Letters were printed in the newspapers. An anonymous poem appeared in the Montreal *Gazette*.

> *Here is the city of Mount Royal*
>> *Built on a river of strife.*
>> *Here is where Dr. Bourret once stood*
>> *Pledging to save human life.*
>> *Was the oath all noise like the rapids,*
>> *As empty and light as the foam?*
> *And what says the poor murdered inmate*
> *In the still upper room of his home?*

This was the story of my father, Honoré Bourret. In a way it is also mine. Although my grandmother clearly tried to do her best by me, it was in her mind the minute she saw the squirrel.

Miss Skerry, who had been at the Priory for only three days, looked on with narrowed eyes. The muscles of her face were pulled down in what appeared to be a permanent scowl, which was why I had dreamed up a nickname for her the day she arrived. *The Scary One.* So far she had managed only one lesson with me and Laure, which had been an utter bore. We had had to read aloud a random passage from the Bible and scribble out an explication. It was no different from lessons with Grandmother, who believed that the Gospels were the only reading material to reliably produce young women of virtue.

Grandmother removed her glasses and wiped her eyes. "I must get back to Laure," she said, straightening her shoulders and looking a bit more like her usual self.

"What an introduction to our home, Miss Skerry," she said to the governess. "One girl faints away at the sight of blood and the other delights in skinning squirrels."

"I wasn't skinning it!" I protested. No one looked my way.

The governess put a hand on Grandmother's arm. "Please don't worry, Mrs. White. Just tell me how to help."

Grandmother nodded, relieved I think that the governess was practical. "If you can bear it I would like you to stay here, Miss Skerry, and oversee. That would be the greatest service to us all while I tend to Laure."

Grandmother then turned to me. "And you, young lady, will clean all of this up, every last bit." Indignation had brought blood back into her cheeks. For once I was almost glad she was angry. "Miss Skerry will stay here, although I do not expect her to help you. This is your doing, Agnes White, and you must put things right. The carcass is to be buried. And I want every trace of squirrel blood removed. The barn," she said, looking around for the first time at my specimens, "is to be emptied of all these dead things." She paused, taking in my father's Beck microscope squatting beside me in the straw. "And that is stolen property. Am I correct that it's the property of your father?" She stared at me hard, her jaw trembling slightly. "I cannot imagine how you ever stole it away and kept it hidden this long."

As soon as my grandmother had left, taking three empty jam jars with her, Miss Skerry removed her spectacles, exposing squinty mole eyes. "Well," she said. "This is a surprise."

She walked over to the microscope and squatted. "You said this was your father's?"

I did not answer. It was my grandmother who had said it, and even if the words were true I didn't feel I owed anyone, least of all the governess, an explanation.

"I will take your silence as an affirmation," she said.

"I didn't steal it," I finally muttered. "That instrument is my birthright."

This earned me a look. "He was a doctor?"

I nodded.

The governess did not seem angry so I continued, enjoying the furtive pleasure of talking about my father. "Yes, but not a country doctor like the ones out here. My father worked at McGill. His specialty was morbid anatomy." I looked at her, hoping she would be impressed.

"Morbid anatomy," she said. "How gloomy sounding."

"Morbid means disease," I said, for I had looked it up in the dictionary right after I'd learned the term and my father's association with it. "It comes from the Latin, *morbidus*." I was showing off now, parading my cleverness and subtly putting the governess in her place.

To her credit she did not react. "So he studied diseased anatomy?"

"That's right."

"Under the microscope," she said, bending to examine my father's sleek Beck model. "May I?" she asked.

I nodded. I had not shown it to anyone. A mixture of pride and protectiveness surged inside me. "Do you wish to see how it works?" I picked it up by its three-pronged base and put it on the work table. "It is not all that difficult to manoeuvre once you get the hang of it."

"You know how to work it?"

"Of course." I showed her how to fit her eye to the eyepiece and explained about the slides and the focus knob.

"Your father taught you this?"

"Not really. He did not sit me down to give me a lesson as I have done for you. I was four when he left."

Miss Skerry became interested. "You could not have taught yourself these skills at the age of four, Agnes. It is not possible. This is a highly complex instrument. You could not have figured out how to use it and the slides and how to collect all these things in bottles on your own?"

I had not thought about this before. I was eleven when I set up the dissection room in my grandmother's barn, and at that point I had been a complete novice. I do not believe I had touched a microscope before, but somehow I had known what to do. What I had had not known I figured out by trial and error.

"No one taught me," I said firmly. "I guess I watched when I was young. My father had a room set aside for dissections in our home." I could picture it as clearly as my father's face, although this last part I did not tell her. "It was full of jars on shelves. Not pickling jars like the ones I use," I added quickly. "Real laboratory jars with thicker glass. Inside were his specimens — diseased hearts and lungs and such like. My father excised them. That was his job. There was also a skeleton, a real one, not much bigger than I was at four. It was pinned with metal staples and propped up on a pole. I used to play with it — until its arm broke."

"You learned simply by watching him?"

I nodded. "Not just him. There were others too, his students from McGill." I had not thought of this in years. There had been one young man who came quite often, I remembered. He used to eat dinner with us. I could not quite picture him, but I remembered that he was kind and brought me candies.

"And these students would dissect things under your father's tutelage?"

"Dissect and draw and mount things. It's what morbid anatomists do."

"It obviously made quite an impression on you."

I couldn't make out Miss Skerry's expression, but I nodded anyway. It was true that I had been impressed, but it was also true that excised tissue had been as natural to me as gabardine would be to a tailor's child, or leather to a cobbler's. It was only after we moved to St. Andrews East that it began to seem otherwise.

"These are all yours?" Miss Skerry asked, motioning to my collection of bugs and bones. She was not looking at me, but her face was dark and serious.

"Yes," I said. I had decided to deal with her straightforwardly. Perhaps honesty in this initial interrogation would lighten my punishment.

Miss Skerry's expression was still inscrutable. She did not look as though she liked my work, which I admit was improvised and rough, but at least she seemed interested. She approached my microscope and spent some time fiddling with it. She was not afraid of the instrument, handling it, I realized with a start, as if she knew what she was doing.

"You know the derivation, I suppose?" she said, one cheek pressed against the eyepiece. When I failed to respond she continued. "It's from the Greek, Agnes. *Micros* means 'small.' *Scopos*, 'watcher.' I don't suppose you've picked up Greek out here in the barn as well as all this science?" She straightened up, and it was only then that I saw the smile in her eyes. Next thing I knew she was asking for slides.

In St. Andrews East the only person who knew anything about microscopes was the apothecary. Ordinary people, and certainly the women in our town, knew nothing about them, nor did they wish to learn. I was an exception, and I knew I had to keep these leanings strictly to myself. It had not occurred to me that one day I might meet another person in St. Andrews East with whom I could share my interest. I knelt down in the straw and pulled out a small metal box containing my father's collection of permanent plates.

"Honoré Bourret," said Miss Skerry, taking this box and reading the name printed on its cover.

I nodded and blinked. It had been close to ten years since I had heard that name pronounced.

"He left you quite a legacy." She looked away from me then, gazing around the storage room. "And you have done him justice. In a sense, this is an homage."

Until she articulated it that day I had not been aware of it. But it was true. I had built a dissection room a lot like my father's Montreal anatomy laboratory in this unlikely setting. Miss Skerry was scrutinizing me. "Your father was a man of science. Am I to presume, Agnes, that you wish to be one too?"

I nodded again but then realized the mistake. "Not a *man* of science, Miss Skerry," I corrected her. "After all, I am a girl."

She broke into laughter, making me start. For the first time since her arrival her face was clearly friendly. "A girl of science, then," she said. "Of course. That's it exactly." She laughed again. "You are original, Agnes White. No one can deny you that."

Miss Skerry and I talked for some time that day. She explained that she, too, was the daughter of a man of learning. He had not been a scientist like my father but a school master at a private academy for boys. He had had a passion for natural history, which he'd shared with Miss Skerry as if she were one of his students. "He was constantly dragging me off to swamps and bogs to collect things," she said, smiling at the memories. "And the school had a microscope, although I must confess it was primitive compared with yours."

At some point that afternoon she discovered my jar of butterflies. "This is Honoré Bourret's work too, I suppose?" she said, rotating it in the light. They were monarchs, big and brightly coloured. Their wings were spread so the markings could be seen. They bobbed up and down as if actually in flight.

This was the accomplishment of which I was most proud. Until that moment no other living being had seen it. "No," I said firmly. "That is mine."

INSTEAD OF BURNING THE squirrel's carcass that afternoon, Miss Skerry and I completed the dissection. She was excited when I showed her my illustrated volume on human anatomy, with which we managed to confirm my identification of the heart. Miss Skerry thought we should pickle it in brine, along with the kidneys and liver for future anatomical study.

We found the pancreas, which, according to the book, regulated sugar levels in the blood, and the gall bladder, which helped digest fats. Miss Skerry let me do all the cutting, reading out passages while I snipped and pinned. She did not mind blood, which was an enormous relief. But most importantly my fascination with the dead squirrel didn't bother her. In her vision of things it was not morbid at all, at least not in the conventional sense of the word.

2

Around four thirty in the afternoon, when the sky outside the barn window began to dim, Miss Skerry and I took what was left of the squirrel and buried him under pine branches in the woods. Then we scrubbed my coat and the surface of the crate and cleaned up the barn. The microscope we put back in its hiding place, along with all my slides. Miss Skerry did not make me get rid of the specimens, although she confiscated the butterflies. I was not particularly worried as we made our way with them over the snow back to the house for tea. By then I trusted her. I knew she wished me well.

The Priory's windows were glowing, and I realized suddenly that I was happy for the first time in a very long while. Happy and tired and sufficiently hungry to eat a horse. I had no idea what would happen next but I had a feeling that the day would not end badly.

Over tea, Miss Skerry spent some time explaining what a useful teaching tool the microscope could be. The best finishing schools in Europe were offering courses in natural history. The implement in the barn was of excellent quality, she assured my grandmother. It was an achromatic compound microscope manufactured by Beck, the best company in England. All this was said while toast was buttered and tea was drunk, as if we were talking about the weather or food.

Laure joined us. She was sitting on the couch, wearing her night-dress and a robe. Her face was milky white like the tea Grandmother had prepared for her.

"And what will Laure do while you teach Agnes the mysteries of natural history?" asked Grandmother. "You saw for yourself how delicate she is."

"Laure does not need to study it. We can keep this work separate from what goes on in the schoolroom. Agnes has things arranged quite cleverly out in the barn."

We were using the ordinary teapot and bone-china cups. I had just started in on my second piece of oatmeal bread slathered with my grandmother's raspberry jam. "Chew," ordered Grandmother. "You are swallowing it whole, Agnes, as if you were a boa constrictor and not a human being."

She turned to the governess. "As you must have noticed, Miss Skerry, my granddaughter is still in many ways a child. My object in hiring you was to change this. Encouraging her to spend entire days alone in the barn, or worse yet, to trek through the country-side collecting things for microscopic inspection will not help her. Nor, I fear, will condoning the slaughter of squirrels."

"I didn't slaughter it," I objected.

Laure made a sound like a kitten, jerking her head and spilling tea down her bathrobe. Grandmother mopped her and took away the cup. "This one's got an excess of sensibility. The other's got hardly any at all," she said, sighing and settling back in her chair.

"From what I saw today," said the governess, "Agnes has plenty of sensibility. She has an eye for beauty and patience for handi-work." From beneath her chair she produced my butterflies. "Just look at these, Mrs. White. Your eldest granddaughter is a person of considerable gifts."

Grandmother took the jar and stared. "Agnes did this?"

Miss Skerry said nothing. Grandmother turned to me. "You stitched them yourself?"

I nodded, forgetting to chew and swallowing a chunk of toast more or less whole.

"But she hates sewing," Grandmother said. "She wouldn't mend her frock if I paid her."

"These are butterflies, not frocks," said the governess.

For the first time Grandmother smiled. "So they are."

"But sewing is sewing," said the governess. "And here's proof that she can do it."

Grandmother said nothing. She raised the bottle and rotated it, causing the butterflies to bob up and down. "You are a compelling advocate," she told Miss Skerry. "And you're right. The butterflies are beautiful, and superbly sewn." But her smile began to fade. "They do not, however, negate the squirrel. Bad enough, the scandal with her father hangs above us like a cloud. If word gets out what she was doing in that barn, Agnes will be done for."

"Done for?" Laure repeated. She had just turned eight and often failed to get the gist of adult conversation.

"It's a figure of speech," explained the governess. "Your sister will be fine, Laure. I can assure you, nothing bad will happen."

"Except spinsterhood," said Grandmother. A faint blush spread up the governess's neck and Grandmother lowered her eyes. "Forgive me, Georgina. That was uncalled for. But Agnes is unconventional enough without outside encouragement. What man will want her if I allow these studies in the barn?"

Laure was sitting very still, her slippered feet pressed together beneath her chair. "Perhaps the man she is to marry will appear tonight, Grandma," she said in her sweet, small voice.

Miss Skerry looked confused. Not even I understood until Laure asked for the poem. She was trying to be kind, feeling guilty perhaps for having been a source of trouble in my life.

Grandmother smiled and patted her youngest granddaughter's knee. "There's no trouble raising you, is there, Laure?" She turned to Miss Skerry. "She's just like my daughter when she was young. Same sweet disposition."

"Today is Agnes's name day," Laure explained. "January twentieth. We always read John Keats before we go to bed."

"Of course," said Miss Skerry, who had told Agnes on the path up from the barn that although she liked the sciences, the subject she loved most was literature. "'The Eve of Saint Agnes.'"

"You know it?" asked Laure.

Instead of answering the governess stood up and began to recite.

"She knows it!" cried Laure. Even Grandmother smiled. She took the heavy volume *Poems of Our Land* from the bookcase and opened to an illustration of an old man in robes rubbing cold fingers, his breath emerging in puffy clouds.

"Shall I read, Georgina, or will you do the honours?"

Miss Skerry took the book and we pulled our chairs in close around her. I had always loved this poem. I listened as Porphyro stole through the halls of the enemy castle to find his sleeping love, the beautiful Madeline. It was the middle of January, Saint Agnes's Eve, and when Madeline awakened, Porphyro was bending over her like the prince in *Sleeping Beauty*.

Miss Skerry did not need the book. She kept looking up and grinning at the three of us, pronouncing the last syllable of the heroine's name as if she were a French princess and not an ordinary English girl.

Grandmother closed her eyes as Miss Skerry recited the last lines. "Well read. You have outdone yourself." Then she looked at the clock in the hall and rose to her feet. I was studying the final illustration. In the light of a full moon two lovers raced on the back of a dark steed across a snow-swept field. Madeline was holding Porphyro about the waist, her hair streaming behind them like a cloak. I could almost feel my own legs gripping the horse, my front pressing hard against the boy's spine.

"Dishes before sleep, Agnes," said Grandmother, looking straight at me. "No shirking of chores tonight, no matter what your name is."

"Agnes is the patron saint of virgins," said Laure, beginning to giggle.

I looked at my lap. Of all the saints with whom to share a name.

"Hush now, Laure," said Miss Skerry. "I bet you don't even know what 'vir-gin' means."

The way the governess said it, mimicking Laure, made us laugh, but then Grandmother got up and left, displeased with the conversation. I stayed, eyes glued to Miss Skerry. I did not really understand what a virgin was myself, and I was hoping that she might enlighten me. I knew it had something to do with men and sex. A woman was a virgin before she got married, and after that she was not. If she never married she might remain a virgin forever, which I supposed was the governess's case.

Laure was in high spirits now that the unpleasantness of the afternoon had been resolved. "Agnes ate too much for it to work," she teased. "We were supposed to fast."

"Nonsense," said Miss Skerry. "Your sister's name means that tonight she is above the rules."

"Laure's right," I said, vaguely regretting all the tea I had taken. "You're supposed to retire early on an empty stomach and lie completely still, looking up at the ceiling."

"At the heavens," Laure corrected, although in our shared bedroom the ceiling was what we would see. "And then Saint Agnes comes with the man you are to marry."

"Does she now?" asked Miss Skerry. "You sound like an authority."

"I do it every year," said Laure.

"Well then, I should expect to hear your wedding bells ringing any day." Miss Skerry smiled at the pint-sized virgin who was already dreaming of her marriage. "And you, Agnes?" Miss Skerry asked. "Do you practise this rite too?"

I could feel myself reddening. It was superstition and I knew it. The kind my father had scoffed at. And yet, I liked it. It was a ritual Grandmother had taught us when we were very small. I looked up at our governess and nodded.

"Then I suppose I must try it too," said Miss Skerry. "If a mind like yours accepts it, it will not do me any harm. Has it worked?" she asked, eyes shining like a girl's. "Be truthful now," she urged. "Have you had a vision?"

I could not meet her eye. Someone did come, year after year, hovering like a ghost over my bed in the early hours of my name day, but he certainly was no suitor. His presence was not at all what John Keats had had in mind.

Grandmother reappeared just then from the kitchen with a tray for stacking dishes. "It worked for me when I was young, Georgina. Saint Agnes brought me the girls' grandfather." She handed me the tray. "It works for those who want it to. That is the key. It is a question of intention."

THAT NIGHT I LAY in bed next to my sister, who had the annoying habit of slipping into unconsciousness the moment her head touched the pillow. Laure was on her back in the position Keats had recommended so that her eyes, had they been open, would have been staring heavenward. Her hair fanned across the pillow like spun gold. She could have been Keats's heroine herself lying there, awaiting her secret lover.

Because my hands were cold beneath the sheets, I was thinking about the beadsman from the poem and his numb fingers counting beads on his rosary. I exhaled in the darkness, my breath emerging in puffy clouds. How had Keats put it? "His frosted breath ... seemed taking flight for heaven without a death." I liked that.

I would also have liked to have met John Keats, who had been a sensitive soul. He knew about desire, the kind that would push you toward dangerous things, to risk derision and reprimand. He had been a medical man like my father, a fact Miss Skerry had divulged when Grandmother brought out the book. So it was possible to be a romantic and also to steep oneself in science.

The moon was gleaming like a coin in the frame of my window. How could anyone sleep with such brightness in the sky? Ten years ago, almost to the day, my father had disappeared, leaving my mother, me and a second unborn child who turned out to be Laure. For me, January was, and always would be, the ache of absence. The ache had faded slightly but it still made pastimes like dreaming of suitors and wedding bells misplaced. That was my very last thought before I fell into a deep and visionless sleep.

3

When I woke up the next morning, the bedroom was already light. I had been curled on my side of the bed and rolled over onto something hard — my sister's doll. Three of them were crammed into the space separating Laure's side of the mattress from mine. They were from England and my sister loved them passionately. Their heads were carved out of wax and their bodies out of wood. Every night she tucked the sheets tight around them and kissed their translucent cheeks, now greying with age, and every morning the dolls were scattered. I awoke with a wooden hand or foot poking me in the back.

These pokes and pains were forgotten on that particular morning because of other quite novel sensations. Each time I moved my head I felt nauseated. Pain in my belly was forcing me to fold my knees hard to my front. I was actually holding my breath it was so pronounced. My back was turned to Laure and I was looking out the window. Grandmother was already down in the kitchen fussing with the woodpile and pans.

It felt as though someone were prodding around inside me with large, clumsy fingers. The squirrel came immediately into my mind.

I had dreamed about it, I realized. On Staint Agnes's Eve a dead squirrel had been my vision.

Laure gave me a kick. "Will you stop?"

I realized I was rocking and sat up, but it only made the pain worse.

Laure sat up too. "You groaned the whole night, Agnes. Are you sick then after cutting up that animal? Did it make you sick?"

I shook my head and even this small movement made me dizzy.

"What's wrong?" Laure's face was scared.

"Nothing." I was trying to remember what I had eaten the previous night, thinking it might be poisoning. I had been sick once before after eating pork, but the sickness had come right after my meal and I had retched violently and repeatedly until the poison was gone. All I had eaten last night was Grandmother's freshly baked bread — safe food to which I was accustomed.

Laure's face was the colour of chalk. "I'll get Grandmother."

I shook my head even though it almost toppled me. "I just need to do my business." I stood up, wobbling a little, then crouched beside the bed.

I dragged out the chamber pot and pulled it to a spot beside the dresser, out of my sister's sight. I felt like a river as I voided, gushing wildly and noisily. When I hoisted my nightie and peered down though I got the shock of my life. The contents were red.

Maybe Laure was right. Maybe I was cursed. Or maybe I had fallen ill. Blood was often a precursor to death. It had certainly been so with mother, although she had bled from the mouth, coughing up clots, staining the pillowcases. Laure and I slept on those pillowcases with their faint rusty halos that no scrubbing would ever remove. Pulmonary tuberculosis was the scourge of women in the White family. All three of Grandmother's daughters had died of it. But White women tended to be willowy and wan, nothing like me. And besides, my blood was coming from the wrong end.

I carried the pot to the window and tossed the contents into the yard. Cold air pushed into the room and Laure squealed. Throwing things from windows was not allowed at the Priory, especially when the things were the contents of a chamber pot. I knew the rules. Every morning I had to carry our chamber pot to the outhouse for emptying. Then I sprinkled ash from the stove into the hole to mask the smell. After that I had to scrub the pot so clean it felt like a sin to use it again.

A bit of blood dribbled down my leg and dropped, bright and wet, onto the floor. I smudged it with my toe then squeezed my legs tight and hopped to the wash basin.

Laure was sitting up in bed watching. "What are you doing?"

I did not answer.

"Why are you hopping like that?"

Just then Grandmother called up. "Gi-irls!" One word split in two and sung at the top of her lungs like a song. Her voice dropped midword, as if pronouncing it reminded her of all the effort involved in raising two granddaughters alone.

I wanted to get back into bed and tell Grandmother I was ill but that would have been impossible. Laure had flopped back down in the sheets for the moment, her face thankfully hidden.

I had to get dressed. My winter dress was dark blue, so it would not show the stains. I refrained from moaning for Laure's sake. I moved my clothes to the side of the bed farthest from my sister.

"How come you're over there?"

"I'm dressing."

"Why there?"

One leg was through a bloomer hole. The other leg I did not want to lift. I had used a towel to staunch the blood and was trying to squeeze it in place with my thighs. All of a sudden it was too much and I tumbled face first into the mattress.

Laure crawled over her dolls and stretched out a finger. "What is that?"

My bloody towel lay in full view on the floor. I picked it up and tried to hide it, but I knew that it was futile. Laure's pupils were already the size of pennies. Her chin was trembling.

"Nothing," I said hopelessly.

She let out a scream that brought Grandmother and Miss Skerry scrambling up the stairs and into our room.

All the attention went to her, of course. Even after they calmed her down and put her to bed with two teaspoons of brandy, Grandmother refused to talk about my blood. Laure had blathered about it until finally I had to reach under my dress and pull out the towel. Strangely, Grandmother did not blink. She simply folded it and my soiled undergarments in our bottom sheet and handed the offending bundle to Miss Skerry for the wash.

Eventually, after Laure was settled, she brought me to her bedroom and showed me how to use rags to protect my clothes. There were no explanations. The guidance was about rags, nothing else. Grandmother did not mention the need for a doctor, which could have been a good sign or a bad one. Either my condition was not serious enough to kill me or else I was so far gone that medical attention would be futile. This was what had happened to Mother. By the time the doctor was called to examine her, there was nothing anyone could do. I listened to my grandmother's instructions, allowing my hips to be moved this way and that by her old, dry hands. Her face was closed to questions.

That morning I sat by myself, rising only occasionally to check on the rags. I had retreated to the window seat in the schoolroom and picked up *Jane Eyre*, which I had already read but liked and found comforting. Around noon the door opened and Miss Skerry slipped inside. "I have been busy with the laundry," she said, making me blush. "How are you feeling?"

To my consternation I began to cry. I had not realized until that moment how alarmed I was at what was happening. I was lonely and scared, half-convinced that, like my consumptive mother, I was going to die. I had not wanted to cry and I rubbed my eyes furiously, but this only produced a new surge of tears.

"There, there," she said, offering me a clean hankie. Miss Skerry sat down beside me and took off her spectacles, which she rubbed several times with the pleats of her skirt. "Has your grandmother not explained about your menses?" she asked, holding the frames above her in the dim gaslight and then replacing them on her nose.

I looked up in confusion.

The governess was quiet. She reached for my sketch pad and a pencil and turned to a clean page. The sketches were not proportional, but to me they were better than the paintings in any museum. I had become a woman, Miss Skerry said. What she called "menses," from the Latin word for month, was not a malady. It was simply discharge from the uterus as it restarted the female cycle of fertility. I was fertile, no different than an animal reaching maturation, or a field become ready for sowing, or the wives and mothers who walked every day on the streets of St. Andrews East. I had come of age.

I did not feel "of age." I looked down at my body, which had altered drastically over the past year, rounding and softening where it had once been flat and hard like the body of a boy. Now there was blood and an ache in my belly Miss Skerry called menstrual cramps. I was not sure I wanted any part of it. The information was overwhelming, but at least I knew I would live. I was all right.

Miss Skerry communicated all of this as she would anything else she thought I should learn, in language precise and clear. The menses, she said, were a time to stay quiet and think about things. The female body was like a garden, with cycles of birth and growth and death. A woman had to tend and respect it in its various seasons.

The cure for cramps was heat, which, on that cold January day, came as much from the governess's smile as from the hot water bottle she prepared and pressed against me. "There," she said, tapping it lightly so the water inside jiggled. "Being a woman can be painful at times, Agnes White, but I assure you, it is hardly ever fatal."

✢

4

JUNE 1885, MONTREAL

It is sad but true that people tend to dwell on the troubles of their lives and forget the riches. I am no exception, for in this account of my early days I am skimming over the two years I spent in Miss Skerry's company out at my grandmother's farm, which I count among the happiest years of my life. Of course, I did not realize how happy I was while I was living them. Happiness is a strange thing. It is something I tend to recognize only after it has passed, when I realize I miss it.

In Miss Skerry I discovered a companion every bit as intellectually driven as I was. I had not met anyone like her, and it freed me in ways at which I still marvel. Although I could not know it at age thirteen, when she arrived at the Priory to take charge of me she was a mentor, dropping from the sky as Athena did in *The Odyssey* to guide the fatherless Telemachus. It was Miss Skerry's idea that I leave St. Andrews East. She instigated the plan and worked tirelessly to ensure its success, even though she knew it meant we would have to separate. The year I turned fifteen Miss Skerry announced she had taught me all she could. There were gaps in her own education — algebra and geometry — which would become gaps in mine if I did not get myself out of the Priory and off to a regular school.

She did not boast about how splendidly she had prepared me in other respects. I was exceptionally strong in natural history. It was our mutual passion. She had also taught me a great deal about literature and history. I read widely in both English and French and was fluent in dead languages — Latin and Greek — which Miss Skerry had learned from her father.

Just before I turned fifteen Miss Skerry discovered an educational institution that she thought would suit me — Misses Symmers and Smith's School in Montreal. She arranged a visit so I could write the entrance exam. She sat with me on the train, waited three hours in the corridor while I wrote the exam, and, after I had won a full scholarship, presented such a strong case for my enrolment that Grandmother had to accept.

I found myself in June of 1885 in a tiny room with a crack on the ceiling fanning out at one end like the River Nile, and a girl called Janie Banks Geoffreys snoring in the bed beside me. Janie was lying on her back with her limbs flung out in all directions and the covers kicked to the floor. She mumbled something and heaved a sigh. She was the prettiest, most popular girl in my year at Misses Symmers and Smith's. I could not stand the sight of her.

For eight long months Janie and I had tolerated each other. We had been assigned to the same room in September on the hopeful theory that she could assist my integration into the school's social life and that I, with my brilliant performance on the entrance test, could help with her studies. The road to hell is paved with hopeful theories.

Now it was June and both the crack and my roommate would soon be things of my past, a thought that cheered me. We were graduating at noon at a ceremony to which our families had been invited. Grandmother, Laure, and Miss Skerry, who had spent the year tutoring Laure back in St. Andrews East, would attend. Later that evening the four of us would board the six o'clock train departing from Montreal's Windsor Station, and close this bittersweet chapter of my life.

I checked my pocket watch, a heavy old thing inherited from Grandfather White, and saw it was ten minutes to six. I had slightly more than an hour before the wake-up bell rang, shaking everyone, including my roommate, into some version of consciousness. I put on my glasses, new since Easter, when Miss Symmers realized I could not see a foot in front of me. At first the frames had cut my nose, but I'd bound the bridge with cloth and yanked the ear rails loose. These days I hardly noticed them. And how the world had changed! I felt like Alice down the rabbit hole, stumbling into a garden of delights.

Janie's face jumped into focus. Even this was delightful in its way. Before my glasses I had always looked down when she was around. Now the face of my roommate, like every other face I came across, drew me like a flame, offering up all kinds of intriguing details. Acquiring glasses had been momentous, similar to the day I had first used a microscope. I would never forget the awe I had felt all those years ago, peering through the eyepiece.

Janie's mouth was sensual, but if one looked closely one saw pulled-down corners. In public, with her gang of similarly pretty, popular girls, she was always laughing. In the privacy of our bedroom, however, when she thought she was alone, her sadness showed. Janie's mother was in a second marriage. Janie was boarding at Misses Symmers and Smith's not to learn but to keep her stepfather's house child-free.

My bloomers and school uniform were on the chair beside Janie's head. I swung myself up and reached for them. Almost immediately Janie's eyes opened. "It's barely dawn, Saint Agnes."

The nickname was another thing I would not miss. I had endured it since October, when we had studied Keats and the Romantic period in English class. It was not a compliment. I was a newcomer, a country girl who in a few short months had beaten the school's top students, earning the highest average ever for a graduating girl. Janie had coined the nickname, predicting I would be a virgin till the day I died, just like my martyred predecessor.

"Why are you putting on that old thing?" Janie's lower lip hung open, revealing a row of straight, white teeth. "We're allowed to wear what we want, remember?" She rose on one elbow and grabbed her own uniform from where it lay crumpled on her bed. "Between you and I," she added, "this thing gets burned the minute I get home."

I gazed at the fractured ceiling. Janie Banks had been a pensioner at Symmers and Smith's for ten years and in that time had not figured out how to use an object pronoun. Like so many of the girls here she didn't care a fig for learning.

"Yoo-hoo," said Janie, pulling me back from my thoughts. "Where do you fly away to, Agnes? Sometimes you look so utterly vacant. I just said we can wear real clothes."

When I shrugged she leapt off the bed as if she had scented a mouse. "Give it here," she said, standing over me. "We're all wearing pretty things today. You must too."

Janie opened our closet, revealing a large collection of dresses that belonged primarily to her. She withdrew the exception — a plain white cotton frock. "Here."

I shook my head. White thickened me and the tapered bodice made me think of weddings.

Janie held it up, jiggling the hanger so it danced like a puppet. "Come now, Agnes. It is perfectly saintly!"

I slipped my tunic over my head. "I must go."

Janie stopped jiggling. "What do you mean, 'go'? You'll miss breakfast." Her expression changed suddenly from stupefied to sly. She sat on my bed. "What is this about, Agnes? I detect that something distinctly unsaintly is going on."

Janie's mind had one track. It was almost laughable how for her all roads led to boys. I fastened my sash, self-conscious with Janie's eyes studying me closely. "I have to run an errand. I will not have another chance."

"An errand," Janie repeated. She reached for my watch and squinted at it. "At six o'clock in the morning." She stuck out a shapely leg. "Here, pull the real one, why don't you?"

The tension broke and we laughed.

"Is it a man? Come on, confess."

Light was pouring through the flimsy curtain. Girls would soon be in the halls, lining up for the toilets. If I were going to leave it would have to be now. "You'll cover for me?"

Janie smiled. "This is rich. I never dreamed you had it in you."

"Just say I am practising my speech if anyone asks." I was to give the valedictory that day. It was a perfect excuse.

Janie grinned. "Is he handsome?"

I pursed my lips in a smile I hoped looked something like the Mona Lisa's, grabbed my sweater and left. Rumours would be buzzing like blackflies when I returned, discretion not being in Janie Banks Geoffreys's repertory, but frankly I was past caring. By tonight school would be done with. Let them have their fantasies.

THE CITY WAS FULL of snow. Not real snow of course as it was practically summer, but something so close it looked like snow as I stepped into the street — pollen from the cottonwoods. I grabbed at flakes of it floating in the viscous air. Every June this happened in Montreal, and in St. Andrews East too — a sort of winter out of season.

Misses Symmers and Smith's School was perched on the steepest part of Peel Street in the shadow of Mount Royal. I ran down the hill, stopping only when I reached flatter ground at Sherbrooke Street. I continued a little farther south and then turned east, into the commercial district. On the corner a boy was hawking newspapers in a clear, sweet voice. A tram clanged by under hissing wires. The odours of springtime in Montreal were stronger than ever that day. This was the city of my birth. It had informed me in my earliest childhood and I loved to explore it. Because the streets were considered dangerous for girls I had not had much chance to leave the school grounds. I knew the Windsor train station quite well and the route from it to my school. I also knew the Church of St. John the Evangelist down on St. Urbain Street, where most of my classmates and I went to worship on Sundays. The instant the service ended, however, we were marched up the hill to our dormitories.

I scanned the heads bobbing in front of me on the raised wooden sidewalk. Nearly every time I walked downtown I saw him. Today would likely be no exception, although my glasses had changed things a little. For it was not actually him that I saw, not that this dampened my pleasure or my pain. I would catch a glimpse of a dark head or a shoulder and stop dead in my tracks. Sometimes it was not looks but the way he walked, or even the rakish tilt of his hat. Those first seconds when hope surged were so good they made up for the regret when he finally turned around, revealing a face I did not know.

No one was paying me the slightest attention. They never did. It was my one consolation for being short and unprepossessing. I could walk unobserved through the city's streets pretending I was just a pair of eyes detached from my woman's body. No one would think to interfere with me.

I loved walking in Montreal, where people did not know my name. Many times over the course of this year I had wondered what it would be like to live here and make my home in so big a place. There was little chance of this, of course. Grandmother had made it plain that I was needed in St. Andrews East for the coming year, not to mention all the years that would follow.

While Misses Symmers and Smith's School had enabled me to leave my childhood home, it had been a mixed success. The curriculum included a daily course in domestic arts, in which I was made to cut and sew things. I was working hard in mathematics, but it was the only subject that challenged me. Science at this school did not involve empirical observation, dissections or microscope work. For most of the year we learned the names of distinguished men and the dates on which they had made discoveries. The Latin course was so basic that after four or five classes I was granted permission to sit outside in the corridor and read novels. Miss Symmers and Miss Smith tried hard but they were no match for my governess and I began to understand how lucky I had been in having Miss Skerry come to our home.

In early October, when the leaves started to drop from the trees, my grades began dropping too. Miss Skerry tried everything to rekindle my interest, but I was too disappointed to heed her. In November McGill announced that it was looking for women to enrol in its undergraduate arts program for the third year in its history. Miss Symmers told us that a purse would be given to the girl in the graduating class with the highest overall academic average so that she might continue her studies.

It was what I needed. I started to apply myself with as much effort to domestic arts as to memorizing stories about Sir Isaac Newton and his apple. In March I wrote my university entrance exam and was accepted.

There was only one hitch: my grandmother. Even after I had told her of the purse and assured her it would not cost a penny to send me, she would not accept it. The idea of my living alone without her chaperoning skills in the city of my father was beyond her ken. Miss Skerry told me not to worry. She said I must do my best at my studies and things would work out. I was not so certain. Once Grandmother formed an opinion she stuck to it.

The smell of baking bread pulled me from my thoughts. *Pain frais*, announced a hand-painted sign hanging in a bakery window. Fresh pain, I thought, playing with the language, as opposed to the stale kind I was so accustomed to. My mouth watered for a simple roll or a croissant, but I had no money.

St. Catherine Street was shabbier than I recollected. I squinted at addresses, repeating the one I was searching for like an incantation. I became so involved I walked right past the unassuming greystone. From the street it seemed small, but it was one of those buildings that makes up in length for what it lacks in breadth. The stones were stained black except for a small pale patch near the door where a little bronze plaque had once been affixed with my father's name engraved on it. A wooden sign now hung over the door with a picture of a needle and a spool of thread.

The windows on the lower storey were barred, giving the place a slightly forbidding air, but up above they were open. My gaze continued upwards to the topmost rooms just below the eaves and I wondered if whoever lived there knew the building's sad history. People were walking toward me on the sidewalk so I slipped past garbage crates into an adjacent alley.

The alley was so narrow that I could reach out and simultaneously touch the stones on either side. There were only two windows that looked into it from my old house, both lined with bars. I pulled myself up to the back window, but the pane was so filthy that all I ended up seeing was my own dusty reflection. A dog began to bark so I dropped back down and retraced my steps to St. Catherine Street. I was within a few feet of the light and noise when a voice called out for me to stop. A man had stepped out of the house. In the morning light he sort of shimmered, more ghost than human. I could not see much more than his profile. He was not tall but made up for this by his girth. I was straining forward, trying to make out his face, when he spoke again.

The words were French but the accent, I realized, was not. He stepped closer and I found myself staring into the face of a stranger.

"Mais qu'est-ce que vous faîtes là?"

He was as scared as I was. He had probably mistaken me for a thief prowling among the garbage cans. I did not answer right away so he switched to English, speaking again with a foreigner's precision. "This is private property." He was German, I guessed, recently arrived.

A dog came tearing toward us, barking. It reached us so fast I had no time to protect myself. I fell forward spectacularly onto my hands and chin, the impact sending my glasses flying. The alley was suddenly a blur.

The dog had slobbery pink gums — that much I could see — and made threatening sounds even after the man grabbed it by the collar and pulled it off me. I had never liked dogs. My grandmother had said it was because of Galen, the animal my father had kept when I was small. It had been nervous and bitten me. The man must have seen my fear for he raised his hand as if to strike the animal. After it quieted he turned back to me and for the first time seemed to see who I was.

"But you are a girl," he exclaimed, his eyes taking in my clean hair and school uniform. "A young girl. I am so sorry," He reached out his free hand but had to retract it to keep hold of the dog. "Come inside," he said, yanking the animal toward the front door. "She is a guard dog. You must excuse her. But please, come in and rest. My wife will prepare something for you."

His spine curved like a shepherd's crook and he was balding. He looked nothing like my father. He opened the front door and ushered me in, then tied the dog outside to a post.

Stepping over the threshold I felt like a thief. The old man had no idea what it meant to me to be inside his house. I remembered everything as if it had stayed inside me, intact, just waiting to be remembered. The smells were wrong but everything else was deeply familiar. I could have led him without difficulty to the kitchen, where his wife would fix us coffee. The corridor that stretched out before us was long and dark with a runner covering its entire length. I had dreamt of this hallway and of this very rug, I realized with a start. I knew the wide oak staircase leading to the bedrooms on the second floor and the smaller, darker set of stairs that continued to the attic. We passed the parlour first, where my parents had welcomed doctors and professors and their wives. I peered into it but did not stop. The place I was after was located at the back of the house in the more private interior.

It was a shock when we reached it. The room itself was the same but its contents were so changed that, at first glance, I recognized nothing. The window I had tried to peer into let in little light, which contributed to the difficulty. The shelves were still there, but instead of holding jars they were piled high with bolts of cloth, the round ends gaping like surprised mouths. There was a central table, perhaps the same one my father had once used for his dissections, but now it was strewn with dress patterns and strips of fabric. Two sewing machines sat in a corner.

"You like dresses?" the man asked.

"Yes," I lied.

"You want I should make you something? My wife can fit you."

Just then an older woman with worried eyes came down the hall. She examined me suspiciously, but after the tailor, who introduced himself as Mr. Froelich, said something in German her face softened. "The dog jumped on you," she said to me in English. "We are sorry for that."

I told her I was fine, even though I'd knocked my chin badly enough that it ached.

The woman noticed. "You are bruised," she said, touching my jaw. "It is swelling. Come to the kitchen and I fix you."

I did not want to leave the workroom but could see no way to object, so I followed her down the hall. She sat me down at her kitchen table, producing chips of ice in a hankie and then prepared me a snack. "Mandelbrot," she said, laying down a plate of egg-coloured cookies and a mug. "A little sweet won't hurt you."

The coffee was so strong my fingers tingled, but it helped. The woman smiled. "You are a student? We have a client from this school," she said, indicating my uniform. She turned to her husband and asked for the name.

"Something with banks," he answered.

"Banks Geoffreys," I said, horrified that Janie might have set foot here.

"That's it!" the woman laughed. "You know her? A sweet girl."

I drank my coffee and lowered my eyes. The mandelbrot, with its hints of apricot and almonds, was delicious.

"You need a gown for graduating, maybe?" she asked when the

conversation lulled. From her pocket she extracted a yellow measuring tape.

I shook my head. She and Mr. Froelich had been hoping I was a client. Now that I had indicated I was not they would expect an explanation as to why I had been prowling in their alley. "I did not come to buy anything."

Mrs. Froelich's eyes narrowed.

I could not think of a convincing lie so I ended up telling part of my story.

"What did your father work at?" the woman asked. She was still wondering if she should trust me.

"Medicine," I said. "He was a doctor who taught at McGill."

"Yes," laughed the tailor. "That is correct. When we moved in there were many strange things he left. Do you remember, Erika?"

The old woman shuddered. "Remember? I had nightmares for months. Things in bottles. Things cut from the bodies of the dead."

"That room just next to the kitchen," I said. "Your workshop ..."

I never finished my sentence, for Mr. Froelich interrupted, saying it had been the worst room in the house. "It was your father's office. My wife hated it. To this day she swears it is inhabited by ghosts."

I looked at his wife, but really I was remembering another woman who had also hated it. My mother had even given it a name — the Room of Horrors. I had not thought of it in years.

"What happened to the specimens?" I tried to pose the question casually, even though casual was not what I was feeling. My father had left many of our possessions here when we fled to St. Andrews East, including the contents of that room. I had no idea what arrangements had been made. Maybe the Froelichs had simply taken possession of everything, in which case some of my father's things might still be here.

Mrs. Froelich was looking at me with a queer expression. "It was all properly done. There was a deed from the notary." She was worrying that I might make a claim. I took a moment to reassure her.

"We are only renters," added her husband.

"Tenants," corrected the old woman, whose English was more precise.

"So you do not actually own the place?" I asked.

The old man shook his head. "Another doctor bought it from your father. William Howlett is this man's name. He is our landlord. Perhaps you know him?"

The name meant nothing to me. I was more interested in my father's possessions and directed the conversation back to them. I could not help picturing the little skeleton with which I had once played, wondering if it had ended in the rubbish.

"We packed them all away," the old man finally said. Then he looked at his wife and corrected himself. "I packed them. My wife refused to touch them."

The old woman shook her head. "I am sorry, but these things upset me. I was happy when it was done." She shrugged, shaking her head again. "I am a simple woman. I could not sleep with those things in my house."

"You threw them out?" I said, my heart sinking.

"No, no," said the tailor. "I packed them up, like I told you. The other doctor took them."

"The other doctor?"

"The owner. Dr. Howlett."

The old woman glared at her husband and kicked him under the table. It was obvious that she did not wish him to divulge any more.

"We did keep one thing of your father's," she finally admitted, either to divert me or perhaps out of kindness. "This we can give to you." She went to a drawer near the sink, which clinked when she pulled it open. From what I could see it was their junk drawer, a place for all the lost and misplaced things that collect in a lifetime. She rummaged for some time and finally extracted a blackened metal square. "I knew we still had it," she said, holding it up to the light. "It needs a polish, of course."

Mrs. Froelich sat down at the table and proceeded to rub at the soot until her rag was black. Four words shone through: *Honoré*

Bourret, Medical Surgeon. She handed me the door plaque. "He is still alive?"

I nodded, although I had no way of being sure. The old woman was about to ask me more, but now it was my turn to be tight-lipped. Perhaps they knew nothing about my family and I did not particularly wish them to find out.

"Thank you," I told her quite genuinely, taking the plaque and standing up. "You have been most kind."

The tailor asked one last time if he could fit me for a dress, but I shook my head. I could probably have used one that day, but this was beside the point. Mr. Froelich and his wife had given me some-thing far more valuable, which perhaps they suspected as they showed me to the door.

BY THE TIME I made it back to school it was past ten. What a strange morning it had been. I had hoped to lay something to rest but instead it felt more alive than ever. The Froelichs' shop had stirred memories I had not even known I had and a longing so sharp it made me feel weak.

I entered the school from the back. In the yard girls were arrang-ing tables and cutting lilacs to place in pots on the auditorium stage. The girls in my class had all fixed their hair and dressed, and for the first time in my life I noticed what they were wearing. I wondered if any of these dresses were the work of the bent old tailor. When I entered the auditorium a girl by the door stopped me and said I was wanted at the main office.

Grandmother, Laure and Miss Skerry were standing in a group, looking starched in church clothes. Running was out of the question so I walked fast, eyes latching onto the figure whose letters had bol-stered me for the past eight months. It was strange to see Miss Skerry outside of the Priory. She was smiling warmly, but on her head was a derby hat with an elastic under the chin that made her look ridiculous.

"Good heavens," said Grandmother as I approached. Laure stood beside her, her mouth frozen in an awful, forced smile.

"I cannot say that they are flattering." Grandmother's eyes were the colour of forget-me-nots, with pinprick holes at the centre. "Do you wear them all the time?"

She had not even said hello. "I take them off when I sleep," I said. My glasses had been a point of contention from the start. Grandmother had a country woman's preconceptions on the subject of eyes.

"Surely it is unhealthy to keep them on so long," Grandmother said. "I have heard it warps the eyeballs." The headmistress, who was standing with us, tried to explain that this was not the case and that no damage would come of it, but Grandmother would not be swayed. "She will not wear them on the stage today. She must look her best, Miss Smith. People will be watching."

Miss Smith said she thought the glasses were flattering, but that it was entirely up to me and my family what I should wear. "She is our top girl, after all," Miss Smith said, putting a hand on my shoulder. "She has a duty to look her best."

The discussion over the glasses and my appearance did not end there. Grandmother, Laure and Miss Skerry followed me to my room, which was empty, I discovered with relief. The thought of Janie Banks Geoffreys watching me while I dressed was more than I could bear.

Laure immediately started rummaging in the closet, cooing over my roommate's dresses. She found the white Sunday frock Grandmother had made for me and laid it on my bed. "How do you want your hair, Agnes?" she asked, turning me around and eyeing me thoughtfully.

I hated every second of it. I had many positive attributes but my looks were not among them. No new dress or hairstyle was going to hide this fact.

Despite my protests Grandmother confiscated my glasses and manoeuvred me into the white frock. Laure, meanwhile, began twisting and braiding my hair. Miss Skerry took no part in these operations, but occupied herself by flipping through my year's worth of exercise books and scholarly manuals. I interpreted this as a subtle form of solidarity, although it was hard to say for sure. Miss Skerry's face was now as blurry as everything else in the room.

"My brain has won the prizes," I observed.

Grandmother shot a meaningful glance at Miss Skerry. "This school," she said, "has not been an unmitigated success, Georgina. Agnes's time here has done little to smooth her edges."

"That's unfair," I shot back. "What I need is a real place of learning, where substance is valued, not appearance."

"Form is as necessary as substance," said Miss Skerry, who in the four years that I had known her had never shown more than a rudimentary concern for her clothes. "The two are halves of a whole."

"A school tunic is fine apparel for an educated mind," I shot back. "Just as glasses are fine for eyes that like to read."

Miss Skerry shook her head. "As the French say, Agnes, there is no need to crash through open doors. You are at the centre of the honours today. I am afraid I have to agree with your grandmother. You must look the part."

Just before eleven they led me down the stairs to the main floor, where a crowd milled outside the auditorium. A couple of girls waved, but they were so blurred that I could identify only one of them — Felicity Hingston, the sole student at the academy who came close to being a friend. Over six-feet tall with skinny, hairy arms and legs, she was difficult to miss. She had been top-ranked in academics prior to my arrival.

The blur was a comfort in its way. It reminded me of childhood, when all I could make out were basic shapes and I had not suspected there could be more. My dress was now transparent in spots with sweat. We all trotted up to the front to get our diplomas, but then I was forced to rise a second time — and a third, and a fourth — until the sweat was running freely down my sides. I won all the academic prizes that year.

Each time my name was called I had to rise from my seat and walk up the centre aisle through throngs of girls. I was aware I looked ridiculous. My dress was too tight, exposing a body I usually hid in my loose-fitting tunic. The auditorium was as hot as my grandmother's kitchen on pie day, and people were getting audibly restless. By the time I was summoned up for my final prize and valedictory speech, a few of the girls actually groaned.

The audience began to applaud as they had for the other prizes, but mechanically this time, just going through the motions. I could hear rustlings and muffled laughter. I could not see, of course, which may have been a blessing, but by the time I made it to the front of the room it was obvious that most of my classmates were not feeling friendly. After all, I was responsible for holding them there in the sweltering heat, and most of them were not bookish or concerned with school grades. Miss Symmers registered none of this. She stood above me smiling. I was supposed to collect the purse, the one that would pay my way to McGill, and then give my speech. I had rehearsed it many times, but all of a sudden it did not seem so straightforward. I stood at the podium, gazing out at the sea of glistening, blurry faces and realized I could not remember a word of it. I had scribbled the main points on cards, and I read from these now in a pinched and little voice. Not the speech I had painstakingly planned, but a choppy, truncated thing that could not have made much sense to anybody bothering to listen. Miss Symmers smiled bravely through it all and then came forward to embrace me, but I was already lurching away, heading for the exit. I fled blindly, without a plan, my heart pounding so hard it drowned out all other sounds.

The first thing I saw with any clarity after the fiasco was Miss Skerry's face. She had raced after me, following me outside with my glasses. Laure came out next and gave me an unexpected hug. I had taken refuge under a willow at the far end of the school's playing field. During the school year I had come here to read. It was at the edge of the school grounds where few girls ventured. Its branches dipped all the way to the grass, providing a natural cover.

"Your headmistresses will worry," said Miss Skerry. "We ought to go and tell them you're all right."

I shook my head. My pride was still stinging so we stood together under the willow as the others began to file outside. Miss Skerry spoke softy to me, telling me it was all right, commending the speech, even though I felt I would die of shame for making such a hash of it. Eventually Miss Skerry sent Laure to tell Miss Symmers and Miss Smith where we were and to collect my purse.

"How will I face them?" I asked when we were alone.

Miss Skerry shrugged. "You've done nothing wrong, Agnes. I think you should go out there. Enjoy the graduation. Rejoice in the fact that you will be moving on to bigger and better things."

I shook my head, having none of the faith of my former governess. Grandmother was quite adamant that my future held a move back to the small and dismal St. Andrews East.

We stood for a while longer behind the branches. A canvas awning had been set up in the middle of the field, under which tea and sweets had been laid out on a table. Several girls from the next grade down were serving food.

I spotted Grandmother walking across the lawn with the two headmistresses. Laure ran up to them and gave them the news of where I was and they turned and peered in my direction. They crossed the field with Laure to seek me out. Grandmother was not quite as willing as my teachers to forgive my gauche departure. She walked over to the table and started a conversation with Mrs. Banks Geoffreys. I raked my fingers through my hair, pulling loose a braid.

"Your hair!" said Laure, who had just made it back to the tree with Miss Symmers and Miss Smith. She retrieved a fallen ribbon and approached to reattach it, but I shook my head. "Oh Agnes," she sighed. "I was just trying to help."

I pulled out the other ribbon and pins, letting my hair down just as my headmistresses ducked under the branches into our hiding spot.

"I can fix it," said Laure, more to the headmistresses than to me.

"I'm very good with hair." And right there in front of them she began to braid it again, smiling sweetly as if she really had it in her power to set every awkwardness aright.

"She's always been like this," my sister explained, tugging at me fiercely. "She's never cared about ordinary things."

Miss Skerry intervened. "Agnes is not an ordinary girl, Laure. That has been clear for years now, and frankly it is what I appreciate most about her."

Miss Smith laughed. And Miss Symmers, bless her, reached into her pocket and took out the purse for McGill. "It is true you are not ordinary, Agnes. Extraordinary is the word that best fits."

As soon as Laure finished we walked out into the sunshine. The playing field had been recently mowed and mounds of cut grass were giving off a fresh, hopeful smell. In front of us groups of girls were laughing and talking. Some of them looked my way and waved. I waved back, then lifted my hair so the breeze could reach my neck. Suddenly I felt much better.

Janie Banks Geoffreys and two other girls approached us. They had seen Laure with her golden hair and fine looks and wanted to meet her. "It's a pleasure, I'm sure," Janie said, nodding her head once as if not wanting to show more enthusiasm until Laure had been assessed. "Are you a genius too, like your sister?"

Laure blushed. "Heavens no," she said innocently. "Agnes is the clever one."

Janie Banks Geoffreys smiled, but Miss Skerry's expression turned fierce. Laure was just doing what girls did — downplaying her abilities — but Miss Skerry did not approve. Intelligence, she had told us repeatedly, was nothing to be ashamed of.

"Your sister is certainly special," said Janie.

"Oh yes," said Laure, not catching the underlying insult.

Janie was paying me back for forcing her to endure me as a roommate all year. She was not smart enough to think up a decent jibe. All she could manage was this sarcasm, a word whose Greek root, I had recently learned, meant to tear flesh like a dog. I longed for McGill, where a mind like Janie Banks Geoffreys's would be barred from entry.

Miss Skerry's hands twitched at her sides. She saw exactly what Janie was up to. She seemed about to intervene, perhaps to put Janie in her place, when Grandmother walked over. "Your mother pointed you out to me when I was at the tea table," she said to Janie. "I am so pleased to meet you."

Janie stepped back, eyeing her. Her friends exchanged glances.

"Your mother and I had a lovely chat."

Janie's eyes narrowed. The sensual mouth stretched into a practised smile as she waited to see where the conversation would go. She had not made up her mind whether she should be polite to Grandmother or dismissive.

"It is my understanding that you are to attend McGill this fall," said Grandmother.

"She is?" I said before I could stop myself. Janie Banks Geoffreys could barely spell. If she had not cribbed my notes, she would never have passed the year.

"I'll be an occasional," Janie said, shrugging, as if anyone or his pet dog could gain admission.

"So your mother said. Well I think it is marvellous. I had no idea so many girls from your class had applied. I thought Agnes was the only one."

"Oh no," said Janie. She nodded at the girl to her left. "Marianna's going too. There will be four of us including Agnes."

"Do not include me," I said, unable to lift my gaze from the lawn.

"As a matter of fact, Agnes," said Grandmother brightly, "you will be joining them. My mind was quite changed by my chat with Janie's mother." McGill, Mrs. Banks Geoffreys had explained, was safe for girls. They were sheltered in separate classes, and unlike the men there was no pressure to take a degree. Most girls took only a course or two. Of those who had applied the previous year more than half were now engaged.

Miss Skerry was standing behind Janie and her friends, leaning against a tree. When I looked over at her she grinned.

I grinned back. Life was full of irony, another word that happened to come from Greek. Janie Banks Geoffreys would attend university, and — irony of ironies — I would be indebted to her for life. I squinted into the sunlight, blurring the governess's small, oval face against the backdrop of leaves until her grin, like that of Lewis Carroll's cat, was the only thing I could see.

5

Puddles had sprung up all over campus, making the ground glitter. I was walking with Felicity Hingston, trying to listen to what she was saying, but I had to concentrate on keeping my feet dry, and Felicity's voice kept merging with the water rushing off the mountains.

"You have got to read them, Agnes," Felicity said, waving several newspapers that billowed madly in the wind. "*The Gazette* and *The Herald* have full-page stories. They even published your picture."

Felicity stopped to show me. My graduation photograph from Misses Symmers and Smith's stared at me with squinty eyes. I had been chubbier when it was taken and incapable of smiling. I immediately pushed it away. "I am so ugly!"

Felicity laughed. "It is quite the mug shot, isn't it? You look all of twelve years old!"

"There ought to be a law against school-graduation photographs. They are painful."

"Well," said Felicity. "Forget your mug. The articles are far more flattering. You have stirred up quite a controversy."

I groaned. Controversy was the last thing I needed right then. We fell silent as two young men came into sight, walking downhill in our direction. They gave us a wide berth, stepping to the very edge of the path. Instead of addressing us directly they started humming.

Felicity Hingston hunched her shoulders, looking up only after they had passed. Her cheeks were an angry red. "I cannot stand that."

I nodded. In and of itself the tune was innocuous, but the way McGill boys flung it at us was far from anodyne. "She walks abroad a dandy with no buttons on her boots." It was so catchy that sometimes I caught myself humming it.

It was sung when a girl was inappropriately dressed. I buttoned up my coat. I had attended McGill for four years now, with a year's delay at the start of my studies due to a smallpox epidemic that had swept through Montreal in the autumn of 1885. They were four of the most splendid years I could have imagined, but almost every week that song had been flung at me. Perhaps my stockings were snagged, or my boots showed flecks of mud, or my sleeve inadvertently revealed an elbow in the library. I had never attended much to these matters, but the McGill boys were like watchdogs, reminding me and the other women enrolled in the Donalda degree program that our presence was a privilege we must earn at every step. The "controversy," as Felicity called it, would not help matters.

I had excelled academically, which had not come as a surprise, but socially I had also blossomed. There were nine girls in my class. We were different from the occasionals, girls like my former roommate, Janie, who flitted around campus like butterflies for a session or two and then disappeared. The Donaldas, of which my year was the third in McGill history, were all as serious about learning as I was. And they liked me. Twice I had been voted class president. For the first time in my life I had friends, peers who understood me. I was active on campus and in the fall had become the first female editor of McGill's paper, *The Fortnightly*.

This spring I would graduate. I had packed my final term with science courses, supplementing Latin (Horace's *Epistles*) and philosophy (the presocratics all the way to nineteenth-century positivism) with zoology (a course taught by McGill's principal, Sir William Dawson), physics and math. These choices were not whimsical. I had a plan.

In February I had screwed up my courage and written the university registrar requesting admission to McGill's faculty of medicine. Three days later a written answer came back: a curt, unequivocal "No."

"Let us sit," said Felicity, pointing at the steps to the Redpath Building where honours classes were given. "We are early."

I squinted at the sun. "Is that not Laure up ahead?"

We advanced toward my sister, who was standing alone on the stairs, looking out over the city. She seemed taken aback to see us.

"She looks like a Rossetti painting," said Felicity. "Only the courtly lover is missing."

I laughed. Laure did look beautiful. No one would dare hum the buttons-off-her-boots song at my pale and golden sister.

"Done for the day?" I asked, arriving at her side.

Laure nodded. She was sixteen. Grandmother had enrolled her in a British-literature class offered by a fellow whom the students had nicknamed Easy-A Atkins.

"Your sister's a celebrity," said Felicity, huffing up the stairs. "Her name's in all the papers."

"So I heard," Laure replied. "Professor Atkins spoke of it in class this morning. He says she is overreaching."

"He is parroting the editors at *The Herald*." Felicity's face darkened. "He is not alone, although some of his colleagues have been daring enough to disagree. A number of the governors and professors feel it is high time that the McGill medical faculty let women in.

The medical schools of Europe have done it for years. There are hundreds of female physicians in Vienna and London. The University of Toronto now admits us. Even stodgy old Queen's University in Kingston does! It puts McGill to shame."

Laure was about to continue, so I checked her. "I must hear what was printed. Read."

Felicity folded the topmost paper so that the wind would not take it. "*The Gazette* is the best. They have predicted that you will succeed. There is a long quotation from Mr. Hugh McLennan, who is awfully influential in this city, waxing lyrical on your behalf. The headline comes from him. 'McGill must heed Modernity's call.'"

I raised my hand against the sun. "And *The Herald*?"

"Not so good, although I admit I only skimmed it. The *Herald* reporter interviewed local doctors, a disappointingly dour bunch."

"Read on, Felicity. I need to hear it, if only to plan my next move."

She smiled. "You would have been a good military leader, Agnes. Pity you will not get the chance."

"Hardly," I said. "I much prefer mending wounds to inflicting them. Now do your worst."

Felicity sighed, bending her head to the task. "It starts with a venomous profile," she said, skimming and synthesizing. "Your *Fortnightly* articles are strident. I quote, 'Surprising in a girl born and bred in the small town of St. Andrews East, whose great grandfather founded its Presbyterian church.'"

I flushed. The *Herald* man had engaged in some research. He had erred on my birthplace but he was right that my mother's grandfather, Joseph White, had been an early settler. Along with a handful of other Scottish families he had established the town of St. Andrews East, naming it after the patron saint of Scotland when he arrived off the boat from Glasgow in 1818. A year later he personally laid the cornerstone for the first Presbyterian church in the province of Lower Canada. This lore was well known to people in and around St. Andrews East. It would not have been difficult to discover. But what would have happened had *The Herald* stumbled upon the story of my father? I had considered this possibility and felt grateful, for once in my life, for the cloak of the White family name.

"'Miss Agnes White,'" Felicity continued, "'is attempting to enter the McGill Faculty of Medicine. Young women have attended the university since 1884, when Donald Smith (Lord Strathcona) endowed the institution with funds for separate undergraduate arts classes. Now, only a few years after this concession, Miss White wishes to extend her reach.'"

"There is the line Professor Atkins was parroting. Makes me sound like Lucifer."

"There is more," said Felicity. "They seem to have conducted a poll of prominent Montreal physicians. Dr. F. Wayland Campbell, dean of medicine at Bishop's College, thinks the introduction of women into the profession would be a fiasco. I quote, 'Can you think of a patient in a critical case waiting for half an hour while a medical lady fixes her bonnet or adjusts her bustle?'" Felicity made a sour face, then resumed.

"The man who heads McGill's physiology department says that bringing girls into the faculty would be 'nothing short of calamitous.' Oh Agnes, it makes me want to scream." As she skimmed the next paragraph her eyes opened wide. "Oh no." She pushed the pages away.

I picked them up and began to read. The longest and most damning quote was from Dr. Gerard Hingston, Felicity's father, who happened to be senior surgeon at the Montreal General Hospital and who swore he would die rather than see a daughter of his enter the profession.

"Oh Felicity," I said, laying down the wind-whipped page.

"He knows," said Felicity, biting her lip. "It was madness to think I could hide it from him."

"Maybe he just said it like that. He has no proof."

"It is likely because you two are friends," said Laure. "He must have heard you spend time in Agnes's company."

Felicity stood up. "I should go." Before I could say a word she scuttled up the stairs.

"So it is true that she wants to be a doctor?" asked Laure, once Felicity was out of earshot.

I nodded, sighing.

"I cannot imagine it," said Laure, frowning. "I heard one is forced to cut open bodies. One has to touch them bare-handed!"

I did not respond. Laure was so obtuse sometimes it was impossible to have a meaningful discussion.

"Frankly I find her disrespectful. I have never had a father, Agnes, but I should hope that if I did I would try to honour him."

"Following in his footsteps is a kind of honouring."

"Not when one is a girl. Read his words, Agnes. He would rather die."

I stopped listening. With Laure I was forced to do this when our views diverged too much. I knew I ought to go and find Felicity to comfort her but I had a suspicion that I might be the last person she would wish to see right now. I hunched down on the step.

The wind was tugging the pages, pulling them from my hands. I pushed my glasses farther down my nose and began to read. The ultimate quote in the article came from Principal Dawson, the man who was teaching me zoology. "Sir Billy," as he was nicknamed, would not upset McGill for the sake of a single, impatient girl.

"You *are* infamous."

A figure I knew well had stopped on the path below and was grinning at me. It was Huntley Stewart, editor-in-chief of *The Fortnightly* and nephew of Martin Stewart, *The Herald's* publisher. Many of the girls in my class envied me the chance to work with him. He was good-looking, I had to admit, surveying his tailored suit and the signature red tie. He looked more dashing and older than many of the boys on campus. But looks were no reason to like a man. Huntley and I shared a deep mutual mistrust. When it was first suggested that I serve on his editorial board he had fought it with every ounce of his strength. At present he tolerated me, especially when we were under deadline or the paper had to get to press, but he certainly had no love of me.

"So you want to be a doctoress?" he asked.

The sun was almost directly overhead and his figure pulsated, a dark shape burning into my retina. I did not know Huntley's views on women entering the professions. We had not discussed the issue, but I could tell from his tone that his words were no compliment.

"Who would have guessed your stockings were so blue?"

There it was. His own colours showing through. I couldn't resist a riposte. "Actually they are not," I said, lifting my skirts high and giving him an eyeful of lumpy beige leggings. "I'm in a brown study today."

He laughed and turned away just as Laure bent forward, trying to cover me.

"It is a lost cause," Huntley said, his face still averted.

"Don't be so sure." I rose to my feet, pushing Laure away.

"I was not addressing you," he said. "It is poor Laure my heart goes out to."

Time stopped on the Redpath stairs. The sun was high and so strong now that black holes opened in my vision. Huntley was grinning, poking his chin at me. Laure was studying her shoes.

"You know each other?"

Huntley nodded. "I only learned yesterday that you two were related. The resemblance is not obvious."

"Huntley asked to escort me home," said Laure, changing the subject. "Grandmother gave him permission."

"Grandmother knows?" The holes in my vision were growing steadily larger. I removed my glasses and rubbed them vigorously. "Forgive me," I said, leaning hard against the banister. "The sun's in my eyes." I mopped my forehead, gathered the newspapers and my books, and began to climb the stairs.

At the door to the Redpath Building I turned. Laure and Huntley were now halfway down the hill beside a yew tree. My sister's hand was tucked inside Huntley's arm and he was whispering in her ear.

Laure laughed, throwing back her head so that the sun caught in her hair. Felicity would have smiled to see the two of them, beautiful Laure and Huntley, in this familiar tableau.

6

The sun was spotting Felicity's nose with freckles. Neither of us had thought to bring hats, and our winter white skin was drinking the light as we walked up the hill from Sherbrooke Street.

"A robin," Felicity said, pointing.

A red-breasted bird was pecking at the soggy lawn. I should have been happy at this sign of spring. The snow had been gone for two weeks now and buds were vulnerable and glistening on the bushes and trees. Montreal was opening into life and all I wanted was to lie down in a corner, shut my eyes and sleep.

"It is my first one this spring," Felicity added, breathing harder as the climb up Mountain Street steepened.

I shot her a dark glance. She was trying to distract me from the fact that my life had just been gutted. We had come from Dean Laidlaw's office at the faculty of medicine. That morning we had left for the meeting so full of hope that the sky and sunshine and pungent spring smells had seemed like portents that we could not fail. Now they seemed like a bad joke.

Over the past three weeks I had worked harder than I had worked to that point in my life. Felicity Hingston and I were chief organizers of what the newspapers were calling the latest "women's campaign." It was ironic because when you came right down to it I did not much care for women. Apart from Felicity Hingston, Georgina Skerry and perhaps two or three women I had met at McGill, they were flighty, silly creatures on whom I determined never to depend. The fact that I was a woman was an accident so far as I was concerned.

In an initial meeting the dean of medicine could not have been more clear — under no circumstances would McGill allow me into classes with men. I had not been surprised. I had returned immediately with an amended request. Would McGill consider setting up separate classes for female students? Dean Laidlaw replied that while this was possible the cost would be prohibitive.

I requested a figure.

In three short weeks Felicity Hingston, a group of society ladies led by Mrs. W.H. Drummond, the wife of a well-known Montreal physician, and I had organized, raising one hundred and fifty thousand dollars. It was a substantial sum, surprising us even more than it would the dean. But it still fell short of the astronomical quarter of a million dollars demanded by McGill. Today we had gone to the dean to ask for an extension.

Dr. Laidlaw had kept me waiting for close to an hour. Eventually he sent his secretary out to inform us that one hundred and fifty thousand was still insufficient. If we did not bring the full quarter million to McGill by noon the following day the application would be considered null and void.

Several yards ahead, Felicity stopped in front of Mrs. Drummond's brownstone. "What time is it?" she called, gazing at me down the hill. "We are dreadfully late, I fear."

I took out my grandfather's pocket watch and snapped open the lid. I did not want to attend this party, which Mrs. Drummond and another society lady named Miss Rosa McLea had planned as a celebration and a rally of the troops prior to the final victory. How could I face these women who had invested so much time and effort in me?

"Quarter past three," I said. The party had begun over an hour ago.

Two men were squatting in the sunshine on the porch, having a smoke. Their faces were partially shaded by caps, but I would have recognized the broad shoulders and necktie of the taller one anywhere. Huntley Stewart waved a cigarette in greeting. "Agnes White. I was beginning to think you had chickened out." He threw his burning butt into the bushes and reached into his pocket for a pen.

I nodded at him curtly. Huntley Stewart would gloat when he heard of my defeat. He would not make it too obvious of course, because of Laure, but he would find ways to rub salt in the wound.

"Give us a quote," said Huntley. "How's the campaign faring on the eve of delivery day?"

I looked at him more closely. It made no sense. He sounded as if he were scrounging quotes for a story, and yet *The Fortnightly* had been put to bed for the summer. I had done the layout for our last issue.

"I am working for *The Herald* now," he announced, as if reading my mind, "covering the city desk. And this," he said, gesturing to the ill-shaven older man slouching next to him, "is Andrew Morely of *The Gazette*. I told him you and I are old friends."

Typical Huntley. His smooth talk masked a rougher reality. It was only because I was newsworthy copy that he was claiming a connection.

"A pleasure, I am sure," I said, offering my hand. I recognized the name. It was he who had written the piece interviewing certain professors and governors at McGill and suggesting my campaign might end successfully. Perhaps he was not all bad.

"I hear you are requesting an extension," Andrew Morely said.

Throughout the week the papers had been full of wagers as to whether I would be able to get the money by the May first deadline.

The sum demanded by McGill had somehow been leaked and rumours were now flying as to how much money I had gathered. On the street complete strangers approached me. Most of them congratulated me, but some, like the elderly gentleman who had cursed me today as Felicity and I left campus, were full of anger.

"How much have you collected so far?" asked Huntley.

That was a good sign. I had been careful recently with Laure, whom Huntley was courting, and no doubt was pressing for facts and figures.

"Much as I would love to stay out here chatting," I said quickly, "we are late for an engagement." I took Felicity by the arm and stepped toward the door.

"Wait," said the *Gazette* man, holding Felicity's other arm. "Perhaps this friend could stay and clarify some things. Could I ask your name?"

Felicity yanked free and continued walking. Throughout the campaign she had kept herself hidden, avoiding any meeting at which the press might appear. She had also left the visiting of donors to me, preferring anonymous tasks like drafting letters and planning strategy. Her father was keeping tabs on her. He had given her a single lecture during which he had called me "a nefarious influence" and had ordered her to stay away. This afternoon, however, convinced of success, she had dared openly to disobey him.

"Are you also a candidate?" Andrew Morely called after her. "There are five aspiring doctoresses, are there not?"

"Oh come on now," said Huntley. "What harm can it do to give us names? You ought to show pride instead of hiding yourselves away."

I lifted Mrs. Drummond's shiny brass knocker and brought it down hard. Then I spent what seemed an eternity staring at the door, willing it to open.

The room was absolutely packed. Everyone was dressed in party clothes and the table that Mrs. Drummond had laid out was nothing less than astonishing. Cut fruit, including sunny yellow discs of what appeared to be pineapple, gleamed on china plates. There were little triangular sandwiches, their crusts meticulously removed, and a vast spread of tarts, tea cakes and cookies. All in my honour. I could hardly bear it.

Grandmother was standing behind this well-stocked table in her familiar navy dress. What was unfamiliar was the smile beaming from her face. I lifted an arm to wave, but Mrs. Drummond appeared and clasped me in a clumsy, if well-intentioned, embrace. Mrs. D, as I called her, had been proprietary with me from the start, hugging me like a daughter, giving me tips on how to dress and what to say to Lady so-and-so or to her husband to win him to our cause. She even passed me clothes — discards from her own closet — which were slightly big but made from fabrics I could not have afforded myself.

"Mrs. Drummond," I began. I said nothing more, for she had already turned her attention to Felicity. Mrs. D's sister-in-law, Lady Dunston, now had me in her sights and Miss McLea was coming to shake my hand. No one mentioned the visit to the dean.

I was aching to cut through it all and unburden myself. "Mrs. Drummond," I began again, reaching around her sister-in-law and Felicity. "I have bad news."

Mrs. Drummond's large brown eyes turned my way. "Now Agnes. You have only just arrived. Business can wait, can it not? Take off your coat. I will get you both some tea. And if I do say so, the jam cakes turned out marvellously."

I looked over at Felicity, who at that moment was being dragged by well-meaning hands toward the table. Society women were odd. There was a protocol at these gatherings that they all mysteriously seemed to know. Each woman who walked in the door had to be greeted, seated and given tea before anything of substance could occur.

A short while later I was sitting on one of Mrs. D's delicate carved chairs, a teacup balanced on my knee, listening to my hostess chatter about a cat she had just acquired. I glanced miserably across the room and saw Grandmother wending her way toward me with Laure.

"Agnes," she said, walking up and clasping my hand. "You look splendid." There followed a discussion of the dress I was wearing, which Mrs. D had given me. Grandmother had altered it, but now she pinched my waist. "It is loose," she said unhappily. "My eyes are not what they used to be. I do not know how I missed it."

"It is not your eyes," I told her. "I think I have lost weight."

Grandmother had recently celebrated her eightieth birthday and had quite suddenly turned old. Laure and I were still accustomizing ourselves to the change in her, but strangely, as her body stiffened and withered, her spirit grew suppler. This past year she had shown me more love than I could ever have imagined possible. Of course it helped that I had been successful, and that women like Mrs. Drummond and Lady Dunston were now backing my cause. What would happen, I could not help wondering, when Grandmother learned I had failed?

Laure, who had been busy scanning the room, turned to examine my waistline.

"Huntley Stewart is here," I announced.

She blushed and looked away.

"He is with *The Herald* now," I continued. "You did not tell me."

"You dislike him." Laure's eyes once more began to roam.

"He was out on the porch having a fag."

"Agnes," said Grandmother in a warning tone. She disapproved of slang, but the warning went further than that. She was aware of my opinions of Huntley Stewart and thought them disloyal.

As if on cue Huntley and Andrew Morely poked their heads into the room. The maid followed remonstrating, but Mrs. Drummond rushed over and dismissed her, ushering the men in herself. I was dumbfounded. The rule at our meetings was to exclude reporters. What was publicized had been tightly controlled.

Huntley turned toward me and Laure and waved. Then he executed a theatrical bow for my sister's benefit, closing his eyes and making circles with his fingers in front of his bent forehead like a courtier.

He was creating quite a stir. All eyes, including my own, were on him when a clinking sound made us start. It was Mrs. Drummond tapping her teacup with a spoon.

"Attention," she called. I had grown fond of Mrs. Drummond. She was a hard-working soul with a great deal of common sense, but her voice went reedy when she made speeches and a British accent suddenly installed itself. "Attention," she said again. "Everyone must come to order."

My stomach turned. Mrs. Drummond was smiling as though the world were a happy place. Soon she would ask me to speak and I would be forced to admit my failure and disappoint at least half of the women on the island of Montreal. Felicity Hingston was standing behind Mrs. Drummond, looking strangely unconcerned. I tried to catch her eye but she would not look at me.

"We are gathered here in honour of an exceptional young lady," said Mrs. Drummond. Light applause rippled through the room. "She has set her sights high, and special though she is, she would not have been able to reach her goal alone." Murmurs could be heard along with modest laughter.

"Strength is found in numbers, ladies, in solidarity." The room erupted in delighted applause. Mrs. Drummond had to wave her hands like a conductor to quiet the crowd. "Without the help of every single one of you, whether you were part of the organizing committee, circulated to solicit funds, wrote letters or simply badgered your husbands until they signed a cheque, the dream of this young woman could not have come to fruition."

I looked over at the men. Andrew Morely was scribbling in a pad, but it was Huntley Stewart who worried me. He was leaning against the wall, examining his fingernails, as if nothing Mrs. Drummond said would be considered newsworthy. His hands were idle at the moment, but I hated to imagine how they would spring to action when he learned the outcome of my most recent discussion with the dean.

"Over the past three weeks," Mrs. Drummond continued, "we have worked extremely hard. Agnes White, especially, has had to contend with exams and a heavy load of meetings, solicitations and correspondence. She has given interviews to journalists" — here she made a gesture toward the male visitors — "and lived with what they printed, whether it was hurtful or flattering.

"And it has paid off," she concluded, her voice dropping an octave. "As of this morning a sum of one hundred and fifty thousand dollars has been collected. This is an astonishing show of support from the Montreal community in three short weeks. It is a credit to Agnes White and a sign that the women and men of this city are primed for change."

Applause erupted again, but I could not join in. I did not understand why Mrs. Drummond was so jubilant. She knew the sum was insufficient and that I had been forced to ask for an extension to find the remaining money.

Mrs. Drummond continued in the same animated tone. "We need another one hundred thousand dollars to meet the demand set by McGill." It was madness. Impossible. Especially since no extension would be granted.

"This is a tall order. One that even this committee, with its enthusiasm and commitment, must consider daunting. Fortunately, there are others in the wings waiting to help." She paused dramatically, looking around the room to make sure all eyes were watching.

"I have news, ladies. While Agnes was visiting the dean of medicine this morning, I dropped in on the solicitors of Lord Strathcona, whose name in Montreal is synonymous with women's education. Lord Strathcona is presently in London. He returns to Canada next month, but in the interim he is following our campaign closely via correspondence with me and others who support the cause. The McGill Donaldas are his spiritual daughters, as you know."

Mrs. Drummond paused again, this time to withdraw an envelope from her purse. "Lord Strathcona wishes to extend his generosity to aspiring female doctors."

Mrs. Drummond accepted an ivory-handled letter opener from her maid and slit the top of the envelope. Then she turned to me. "You will do the honours, Agnes dear?"

I had to look at the cheque twice, counting all the zeros to make sure I was not dreaming. There were five. "One hundred thousand dollars," I read aloud.

In the seconds of silence that followed I raised my head. Directly in front of me, still leaning against the wall was Huntley Stewart, jaw sprung wide open. Beside him was Andrew Morely, but his face was concealed by the black box of a camera.

In the next moment a flash exploded, blinding me. People began chanting my name. Felicity was beside me now, hugging me, hopping up and down. Grandmother put her hand on me, and even Laure squeezed me and said my name. I stood in the middle of this swaying, boisterous mass, speechless with surprise.

7

The doorbell rang just as Laure was jabbing the last pins into my hair. "Oh no," she said, snatching the small hand mirror from me and peering into it. "He's here!"

Laure's face was, as usual, just fine. Her hair too. The previous night she had spent two hours tying it up in rags, and this morning a mass of rich, honey-coloured ringlets spilled out from under her stylish hat.

"You look perfect," said Grandmother, moving toward the door. "Shall I bring him in? Is Agnes done?"

I reached a hand up to feel my hair and the bonnet lent to me by Laure. I certainly hoped I was done, but there was no way to tell because Laure had the mirror and was now running with it in rings around the kitchen. "Oh jeez," she kept saying, staring at her curls. "Oh jeezlumbud!"

The front door opened and we heard Huntley Stewart's brusque hello. Grandmother laughed then, girlishly, and there was a pause as Huntley removed his galoshes. He was here to take Laure and

Grandmother to meet his mother. It was an occasion as important to our family as my meeting would be at McGill. Neither Laure nor I had slept much the previous night. All morning we had been edgy, even though we both believed our meetings would be successful.

"Mister Stewart is here," Grandmother sang out, leading Huntley into the kitchen.

He stopped in the doorway, repeating his French-courtier bow from the day before. When he straightened his eyes were fixed on my sister. "You are as lovely as a spring day."

I bit the insides of my cheeks. Had he not noticed it was pouring outside? Spring days were not all the same, but Laure was blushing as if the simile were a wonderful compliment.

Huntley then looked at me. "I brought you these, Agnes," he said, holding out a soggy bag. "They got wet but I figured you would want to take a look."

Laure and Grandmother crowded in as I spread the newspapers out on the table. There were three of them and my face shone from the front page of each one. The photograph was the same, taken the previous day at Mrs. Drummond's party.

"Three pictures!" Grandmother exclaimed.

"She's front-page news on every single paper," said Huntley, "although our headline is the best."

"'McGill's quarter-million-dollar girl,'" I read aloud.

Huntley beamed with pride. "Thought it up myself."

I smiled back. As nicknames went, it was tolerable. He had always had a knack for one-liners. His writing, I had to admit as I skimmed the piece under his byline, was not bad.

"I hear you're meeting Laidlaw today," Huntley said when I looked up.

"At noon," said Grandmother. "The same hour as your mother's invitation."

Huntley grinned. "I am off work today, or I might have ended up accompanying the elder sister instead of the younger." He gazed at Laure, who lowered her eyes demurely.

I waved as though it didn't matter. "You've already written the scoop, Huntley. The rest is denouement." I lifted up *The Herald*, pretending to read Huntley's article, but really looking at my grainy face. I was not pretty by any stretch of the imagination, but unlike in my school photograph my face here was not displeasing. I liked my eyes, which looked alert even through my glasses.

We talked for a few more minutes. Huntley surprised me by offering to drive me to McGill in his trap before returning for Laure and Grandmother, but I refused even though rain was now pummelling the kitchen window.

"Your hair will frizz," said Laure.

"It will frizz whether I take a trap or a tram," I replied. "There's no saving me either way."

Huntley laughed and, to my surprise, I found myself laughing too. I could imagine for the first time a life that might include him if he and Laure married. I had been worrying about this possibility ever since he started courting her.

"Speaking of trams," said Huntley, "did you hear they are going electric?"

"Electric?" said Grandmother. "Whatever will they dream up next?"

"I'm writing a piece on it," said Huntley shamelessly. "I've been talking with the engineers down at the Montreal Street Railway. Right now they have a thousand horses. In five years not one will be left."

"But what will pull the trams?" Grandmother asked.

"Wires," said Huntley. "In the air above the tracks, conducting electrical currents."

Laure was looking at him doe-eyed, as if he had invented the plan himself.

"I don't believe it," said Grandmother.

"You said the same thing about privy pits," I broke in, realizing only once the sentence was out of my mouth that perhaps it wasn't the ideal subject to discuss in mixed company.

Grandmother glared at me.

"Well it's true," I said defensively. "You didn't believe in toilets that flushed for the longest time. Now almost everyone has one."

Laure made frantic little movements with her fingers to shush me while Huntley smirked at his boots. "Well," he said finally, pulling out his watch. "*Tempus fugit.* We must be off."

Grandmother and Laure collected their coats and umbrellas, bade me good luck and good bye, and allowed Huntley to herd them out the door. I took a minute to sit and appreciate the silence in the flat. It was rare for me to have the place entirely to myself, and I found myself thinking of my parents and trying to feel their blessing on this important day, but the rain distracted me, hammering rhythmically at the window. I could not hold them in my mind.

The rain was coming down in sheets by the time I made it outside. I could barely see the contours of the Catholic seminary across the way. I was beginning to regret refusing my future brother-in-law's offer of a lift. By the time I reached campus I would be as wet as a drowned rat. All the work of my sister and grandmother would be undone.

A strong wind blew from the north. I held my umbrella tight, pulling it close and turning it so the wind would push me along the sidewalk to the tram stop. Beside me the gutter threatened to overflow. My shoes were already several shades darker and making squishy sounds. The hem of my skirt slapped my shins.

If this were a scene in a novel, I thought, the storm would be significant. In books by the Brontë sisters, for instance, storms were always a bad omen. Thunder clapped above me and I laughed out loud. It was as if a mocking god were listening to my thoughts. I threw back my shoulders. The dean of medicine himself had given me a figure, which I had met thanks to the generosity of Lord Strathcona and a good many other prominent Montrealers. The weather today was irrelevant, except insofar as it was ruining my shoes.

I stood at the tram stop getting wetter and wetter until at last I heard the sound of hooves clattering in the distance. The lower third of my skirt was soaked through. My fingers, still clutching the hook of my umbrella, were waterlogged inside my gloves. My chignon was still in place, but straggles of hair were plastered to my cheeks and forehead. I was certainly no dandy, no matter what the men sang.

The tram stopped in front of me and I climbed aboard. There was only one other passenger, sitting far back in the car, but I didn't catch more than a glimpse of him before my glasses fogged up. He was likely from the suburb of Westmount. Older, more established families generally lived downtown in the Square Mile, but this was changing as Montreal grew more crowded and costly. Our flat was just outside the Square Mile, whose western border was Côte des Neiges Road. The rents were cheaper here, but we could still boast a downtown address.

I turned to look at my travelling companion. He was quite a dandy, in a light grey suit with wide lapels and a handkerchief poking out of his front pocket. His boots had spats. His face was partly hidden by a hat, but I could see that his skin was dark. And he had a moustache.

I was now staring quite openly. He was reading what appeared to be a textbook, which he had propped against the seat in front of him so he would not have to bend his neck. Suddenly he snapped the book shut and raised his eyes as if he had felt me watching. I blushed hard and turned to the front.

It was folly. I had done this too many times before to let myself believe it was really him. Part of me realized he could not be my father. The age was wrong. Honoré Bourret would be fifty-one this year and the man behind me was obviously much younger.

At Mountain Street there were problems with the tracks and we had to stop. I pretended to watch the driver, who went outside to poke around in the rain, but really I was trying to control my sadness. There was too much at stake that day for me to engage in flights of nostalgia. I was deep in thought, trying to cheer myself up when I realized someone was standing over me.

The man from the back of the tram was so close I could touch him. "I have just realized who you are," he said when I looked up.

I couldn't find my voice to answer.

"You're Agnes White, are you not?"

I stared. He was not my father, that much was certain, but so many of the details matched it was unsettling. He was stylish, as my father had been. He had swarthy skin and a moustache.

"You think me impertinent," the man said, laughing. "My apologies, Miss White. But you're a celebrity now. You will have to get used to strangers accosting you on trams."

I tried to smile.

"So it is you. I knew it. You're prettier than I thought you would be," he said. "Prettier than those photographs in the papers." He winked and grinned, and all of a sudden the face before me knocked loose a memory of a much younger man, dark-haired and dark-skinned with the same walrus moustache as my father, bending over me and grinning years ago.

I peered at him more closely.

"You're also a lot less voluble than the newspapers suggest," said the man.

I was still staring as openly and boldly as a child. He had been one of the students at our home. I was certain of it.

His tone grew suddenly serious. "Listen. You don't know me, but I am hoping you will trust me enough to listen to some advice. You have to take it on faith that I've given the matter thought and that I really am saying this in your best interests. I know that you are on your way to the medical faculty."

I was so taken aback I just stared at him, but what came next was even more unnerving.

"Turn around, Miss White. Forget this plan. It's ill-conceived and will only end in hurt and sorrow."

There was no malice in his face. He seemed honestly to think that he was helping me, but what business was it of his? What sort of a person would come up to a young woman on a public tram and address her in this way? If he was the person I suspected him of being he was a doctor, and I knew them to be a conservative bunch, at least in Montreal, with little faith in women. Was his so-called advice really just contempt? I was angry now, on the verge of giving a piece of advice right back, when he nodded, ending our conversation.

I could have stopped him I suppose, but the encounter had been so rattling and strange I sat wordlessly as he left the tram. Water streamed down the greasy windowpane, distorting him. He waved his umbrella at a passing cab, and as it drew up beside him he looked blurry, like a memory slipping in and out of focus. Before I knew it he was gone.

When I finally made it to the medical building on McGill's campus I was in a state. The tram man had upset me more than I liked to admit, and then crossing campus my umbrella had blown inside out in the wind. I walked the last quarter mile totally exposed.

"You poor thing," said the dean's secretary, who recognized me from previous visits. She relieved me of the mangled mass of rods and cloth that had provided such poor protection and put it in her trash can. She was a heavy-set woman, and the flesh of her arms jiggled whenever she moved. She led me down some stairs into the basement. Apparently there was no powder room for women on the main floor, only a men's lavatory. In the autumn, with five of us joining the faculty, this would have to change. The room to which she led me was no bigger than a broom closet, but it did contain a sink and mirror. For once I actually wished that Laure were with me to do something with the strands poking out rebelliously all over my scalp.

The dean's secretary congratulated me through the bathroom door as I dried myself. "You made it onto the first page of *The Gazette* today. Whoever would have thought."

I smiled at my reflection. I may be a little soggy but I was also the quarter-million-dollar girl. Nothing could take that away. We climbed the stairs again and I sat on the same bench outside the dean's office on which I had sat the day before with Felicity. On the wall opposite was a life-size portrait that I had studied rather carefully over the past few weeks. "Andrew F. Holmes, 1824," the caption read, "founder of McGill's Faculty of Medicine." Dr. Holmes certainly held himself erect. I straightened my own back and coughed. He would probably roll in his grave to learn why I was sitting there that day. Yesterday I had laughed with Felicity about his fierce-looking eyebrows. Today, sitting all alone, I didn't dare smile.

I tried to look Andrew F. Holmes in the eye. I would not be intimidated, not now, with cheques for such an enormous sum tucked away in my handbag. Damn the dean and his deadline, which had very nearly broken us. Damn that man on the tram for his curious words and insolence. All kinds of people now felt entitled to counsel me on my life, but that did not mean I had to listen. I was in the medical faculty, a place I had dreamed of all through my childhood and young adulthood. Honoré Bourret had once walked through these halls, passing under this very portrait.

A bell sounded and the secretary, whose desk was in an alcove just outside the dean's office, went to see what was wanted. I removed my glasses and gave them a vigorous rub, more to calm myself than because they were dirty. Seconds later the secretary reappeared. "They are ready," she said.

I wondered about the "they," but did not ask because the secretary had rushed off, urging me to follow. The alcove was a cluttered space, piled high with boxes and books, and my sleeve, still wet from the storm, brushed against a vase on the desk's edge. It wobbled precariously for a second then crashed to the floor, spilling tulips and a quantity of water.

Someone leaned out the dean's door but I couldn't see because I didn't have my glasses on. By this time I was on my hands and knees and the first thing I registered after I put my glasses back on were a pair of spats.

"Miss White?"

The tram man was bending over me, looking amused. Behind him three other men peered. For an instant I was somehow able to gaze down at the scene as if I were one of them and not a girl squatting on the floor in a mess of flowers. I knew I looked ludicrous with my fists full of dripping stems.

"Oh, don't bother with that," said the man in spats. "You have come to supplicate, but there's no need to do it on your knees." The others laughed politely, and as he bent to help me up I could see his own eyes were laughing too. I definitely remembered him now, even though he had less hair, and some of it was beginning to grey. Without his hat he looked older, but I could see his facial lines more clearly now. He had come often to see us at the house. He had been one of my father's proteges.

Dean Laidlaw finally came to my rescue, ushering me inside then introducing me with a certain grace, considering I had just shamed myself. These were the members of the faculty admissions committee. The air in the inner office was thick with smoke, but I had no trouble recognizing spidery Dr. Hingston, whom I had met on several occasions, first at Misses Symmers and Smith's School and later at Felicity's home. He nodded curtly but did not smile. A short man who looked more like a boxer than a doctor said his name was Dr. Mastro. He taught physiology and was by far the youngest man there. The last hand I shook belonged to the man from the tram.

"William Howlett," he said smiling.

My jaw must have dropped because he started laughing and gave me a squeeze. This was the man I had heard about at the tailor shop, the one who now owned my father's former home.

"We were not sure," Dr. Howlett said, "that you would show up in such inclement weather."

I glared at him. Nothing, I assured him in as calm a voice as I could manage, could have kept me from McGill today. I was on the point of mentioning the tram but thought better of it. The dean was watching me carefully. With his mutton-chop sideburns and beady eyes, he looked a little like a fox, which I found disconcerting. At his invitation I took the only available chair, which happened to be in the middle of the room facing the four men.

My gaze kept intersecting with Howlett's, partly because he was staring at me. It was making me even more nervous than I was already. What if he recognized me and made the connection with my father? In my dealings with him today he had shown himself to be someone who did not rein in his impulses. He might blurt out my identity right here, right in front of these medical men.

"I will start," said the dean, "by commending you."

I straightened in my chair. There was no time to think anything more about Howlett or even about the tulips and my bumbling entrance. I pushed it all aside, smiling, trying to concentrate on the honour the dean was about to bestow on me. On the desk were the morning newspapers, which he held up, inquiring if I had seen them. He said that I had accomplished a remarkable feat for which everyone on the admissions committee and in the entire faculty held me in esteem.

While the dean was saying all of this, Howlett studied me. It was unnerving. The other men were worse. Dr. Mastro had relit his cigar and was smoking. At one point he blew a ring in the air that hung suspended above him for several seconds before wobbling across the room in my direction. Dr. Hingston gazed out the window.

The dean kept talking, praising the grades I had earned throughout my undergraduate years and the initiative I had shown being the first woman to edit *The Fortnightly*. I was a credit to the university. He was not looking at me either. The words were laudatory but his eyes would not meet mine. They roved around as if searching for something more interesting. "And now you have set your sights on medicine," he said. His orange whiskers had faded to white in some places and I half expected him to lick them.

"The way you have rallied people in this city is remarkable," he went on. "Collecting such a sum of money with such constrained delays is without precedent."

"I have the cheque," I said, opening my handbag.

But the dean held up his hand, stopping me. "I know about that," he said. "Lord Strathcona telegraphed, warning me you would be bringing it. The gesture is appreciated, Miss White, believe me. The university could use the money. But money is not the only issue here."

I had found the envelope in my purse and was now clutching it to me like a shield.

"Experiments in mixed education have been," the dean continued, "mixed, to say the least. In Toronto, as you probably know, they have led to violence."

Dr. Hingston turned back from the window for the first time. "It is completely unthinkable."

The dean touched his arm. "Now Gerard," he said. "I'd like to finish here, if I may." He winked conspiratorially, as if he were about to deliver the punchline of a joke, but what came next from his mouth was not the least bit funny. "I cannot, in all conscience, subject McGill to upheaval because of the desires of a single young lady, no matter how clever or talented she happens to be."

I looked down and saw for the first time that my gloves were dirty. A dark smudge stretched from the tip of my left index finger down to the middle of my palm. The smudge grew suddenly, blurring and widening, and it struck me that I was crying. The whole room was now blurry, as if someone had lifted off the roof and let the rain in. Don't do this, I told myself sternly. I tried to breathe, which was difficult because my chest was tight and full. I could not let the men see.

"It's not just me," I said. "I am not just one young lady." To this day I don't know where I found the breath to speak.

My words were like a glove thrown in Dr. Hingston's face. "We are aware of that," he said, his voice and hands trembling with rage. "Your example has been infectious, Miss White. We know that all too well. But don't include Felicity among your lot. Don't you even dream of it."

The dean had to intervene again, and he had a good deal more trouble this time with his colleague. To my surprise William Howlett jumped in to defend me. "Miss White has done nothing wrong, Gerard. Friendship is a virtue. You have read your Aristotle."

"Friendship is one thing," said Dr. Hingston. "What this young woman has done to my daughter is quite another. She has bewitched her! And as for Aristotle, he never intended the *Ethics* to apply to girls. Where will this lead, Miss White? Have you thought it through? It's not just a few years of study, you know. You will have to practise afterward. Have you even considered the life you will have to lead?"

"That's the main objection," said the man called Howlett. He turned to me, his face quite serious. "What do you know of a doctor's life, Miss White? I dare say you cannot even picture it."

"Even men don't undertake it on a whim," said the dean, as if whim were my motive. "We have to deal with matters to which women ought not to be exposed. I am afraid," he said, lowering his voice as if this might soften the blow, "that even with the quarter million we cannot admit you. Our committee convened earlier this morning and the decision is unanimous." He handed me an envelope with my name typed neatly on the front. "To everything there is a season, Miss White. And I'm afraid your season has not yet arrived."

I stood up, not trusting myself to speak. It was all I could do to get my body out of the chair and out of Laidlaw's office, away from the intrusive eyes of these men whom I now understood had never intended to admit me, no matter what feats I performed. Dr. Howlett jumped up as soon as I rose and offered me his arm, but I did not take it. I could not stand any reminder of my gender. In the alcove the secretary looked up, but I walked right past her without speaking. One word and the floodgates would open.

The hallway outside the office was bright and empty except for Andrew F. Holmes, hanging smugly on his wall. I stopped for a second to collect myself, clutching my handbag with the cheques that I had once been innocent enough to believe would open the doors to this faculty.

William Howlett caught up to me. "Don't say I didn't warn you."

I could not look at him. He had voted against me. Nothing he said now could change that fact.

He began discussing the issue in the soothing, rational voice he probably used with his patients, and my tears finally came, spilling out all the grief and anger I had been trying so hard to keep inside. My handkerchief was soon useless.

"I do know the life," I said, when I could finally speak. "I do know it." I sounded like a child, but I was past caring. "My father was a doctor," I told him. "You used to know him. You probably even knew me."

William Howlett's eyes narrowed.

"White isn't my name," I said all in a rush. "Not the real one, the one that I was born with. I'm Agnès Bourret. My father was Honoré."

William Howlett went quiet for a moment. Then he began to laugh. "You're right," he said. "I do know you. Indeed. How remarkable. You were the little girl." He cleared his throat, raising a fist to his lips. "You look like him," he said, scrutinizing me. "I see it now. Of course."

We talked a little longer. He told me my father had been a good man, upright and sound. He spoke of the murder. Not in so many words, but telling me indirectly that my father was innocent. I could have fallen to my knees all over again.

He accompanied me to the main doors, and this time I did accept his arm. Outside the rain had stopped, but a wind was blowing, drying the leaves and tossing them into the air above the courtyard. We stood together in silence while I wrapped myself in my shawl.

"It is best you keep your ties to Dr. Bourret to yourself," he said as we were about to part. "Certainly within these walls."

I nodded. "My father's history is a complex one," I said, "even though I believe, as you do, that he's innocent."

"Keep it under your hat," he said to me, winking, "or your bonnet, or whatever."

"You will too?"

He smiled, nodding, and drew an imaginary cross over his heart. *Cross my heart and hope to die if ever I should tell a lie.* Laure and I used to swear this when we were small. It was childish but it comforted me. I smiled too, as if we had sealed a promise.

He swung the heavy front door open and it was only then that I realized how windy it was. The minute I stepped outside my shawl billowed like a sail. Dr. Howlett shouted something after me, perhaps another warning or perhaps simply a goodbye; the wind that day was too strong for me to tell. His parting words, like almost everything else about the man, would remain a mystery to me for years to come.

8

JUNE 1890

I do not remember much about how I made it home the day of the meeting with Laidlaw except that it was by foot. Grandmother said that every item of clothing I was wearing was soaked through. My boots and petticoat were mud splattered. I had lost my umbrella and somehow my shawl, but had managed to hold onto the purse containing the money and the dean's letter of refusal.

Fortunately, Grandmother was home when I arrived at the flat. She and Laure had just returned from Mrs. Stewart's house, a visit that had been more successful than either of them had dared dream. Laure was now officially engaged. Huntley Stewart had descended on one knee in the middle of his mother's parlour. The couple would wait until Laure turned eighteen to marry, but in the meantime she would wear a diamond on her left ring finger. It was actually several diamonds — one as big as a peanut in the centre and several smaller ones embedded in white gold surrounding it. It was an heirloom, Mrs. Stewart explained when Huntley produced it.

Back at the flat, celebration over the ring ended abruptly when I stumbled through the door. Grandmother stripped me and marched me straight to bed. And bed was where I remained until I boarded the train to St. Andrews East a week later. Life had shrunk to the size of my mattress and the one I was lying on in the Priory's guest room was narrower than the one on which I had been sleeping in Montreal.

"Breathe," said the doctor, exhaling as if I no longer understood English. I was sitting up and he had slipped the stethoscope underneath my nightshirt, placing the cold disc below my left clavicle. His breath smelled of mints, but there was a sadder scent of fermentation underlying this. Dr. Osborne was a drinker. This early in the morning his hands tended to shake.

"It's been how long now?" he asked. "A month?"

"Six weeks," said Grandmother, standing just inside the bedroom doorway, watching us.

"You should have called earlier."

Grandmother said nothing. She had been plying me with remedies of her own for quite some time — valerian root to help me sleep, spoonfuls of cognac to spark my appetite — but nothing had worked. My eyes were ringed with blue and my weight had dropped over a stone. My hair, unwashed for days, smelled like an animal's pelt.

"Cases like this can descend precipitously. But Agnes is a clever girl," he said, withdrawing the stethoscope's head with a vague, hostile smile. "We know that from the newspapers. She's going to listen to reason and stop exhausting her poor grandmother with all this fuss and nonsense."

Archie Osborne sat down heavily on the mattress. He had known us for years and known my grandfather too in his time, which gave him a certain right to familiarity. Seventeen years ago he had assisted at Laure's birth. He had also tended to our mother in her last hours of life. He was respected by the townspeople, even though they were aware of his weaknesses. He was old-fashioned; he used mustard plasters for chest colds, leeches for disorders of the blood and brandy for just about everything else.

"These'll cure what ails you," he said, pulling a bottle of pills from his pocket and uncorking it. He shook two into his palm and held them out with the glass of water from my bedside. "Come now, Agnes. Drink up."

I slumped onto the mattress, the mixture of mint and moral righteousness making me feel truly sick.

The doctor addressed me again, this time speaking to my shoulder blades. When I did not move he got angry. "Listen to me, Agnes. Your grandmother is no longer young. You've got to pull yourself together."

I pulled the sheet high instead and burrowed beneath it, my unwashed smell a relief after Archie Osborne's odour. I did not want to admit it, but he was right about Grandmother. She was over eighty. The last thing she needed was a granddaughter collapsing. I lay heavily, feeling the mattress moulding to my hip and trembling each time I inhaled. I had been strong for too damn long. That was the problem. I had borne so many blows, losing my step sometimes from the impact but always picking myself up afterward and continuing as if nothing had happened. Strength was a lie. I saw it now so clearly. I was so broken I couldn't imagine lifting myself ever again out of this pit of goose down.

An hour later, after Dr. Osborne had gone and Grandmother had retreated to finish her chores with Laure, I lay in my bed contemplating the small brown bottle on my table. Liver pills, a brand purchased from any itinerant salesman. They were probably just sugar and water with a salutary pinch of caffeine or other stimulant to perk up the sick and the weary. Next to useless.

It was a muggy June day. A Tuesday, I realized, because Grandmother and Laure were in the yard, twisting sheets and pinning them on the line to dry. Tuesday was our day for washing. I watched through my window as the two women tugged the sheets taut and wound them, spilling water until hardly any drips scattered. No words were spoken. They were engrossed, unaware of anything outside the task at hand.

Grandmother liked to work. It sustained her in some way. She washed the sheets on Tuesdays and on Wednesdays polished her silver. Thursdays were for dusting and Fridays she stayed in the kitchen, baking pies and cakes. For more than sixty years, she had kept this orderly housekeeping ritual. As a result the Priory was spotless, the pantry full and life so busy that Grandmother had never had to face for an instant the meaninglessness that had opened a month ago like a chasm beneath my feet.

Grandmother's white head bobbed in the sun. The June snowfall had begun. Bits of fluff floated lazily in an azure sky. Cows were lowing in the fields and a fly caught between the two panes of my window buzzed in short, sporadic bursts. It was summer, a season I usually adored in St. Andrews East because it meant a break from studies and the freedom to ramble for hours in the woods. But this year was not like the others. There was nothing to look forward to once summer ended.

In two days I was supposed to graduate. There were only nine girls in my class at McGill and every one of them would climb to the stage in Redpath Hall to receive a diploma. Every one of them except for me. I had told Grandmother I would not go. A long discussion had ensued during which Grandmother had urged me to change my mind. The irony was rich — the old woman who had once been so against my setting foot inside McGill was now practically ordering me to go. After Dr. Osborne's visit she let it drop.

I closed my eyes, letting the sun paint glowing red swirls on my eyelids. What did the future hold? Laure would marry Huntley Stewart and set up house in Montreal. Grandmother would eventually die. What would become of me, the ugly one with a useless degree, no marriage prospects and brains enough for three?

Friends had stepped in after the debacle with the medical faculty. In early May a letter had come from Miss Symmers suggesting I apply to normal school. Once I had a teaching certificate my former high school could offer me work. Felicity Hingston was doing this. She had already paid her normal school fees.

I kicked off my greasy sheets. One of the girls from my McGill class was planning to study medicine at Kingston. For me, however, this was not an option. Grandmother simply did not have the funds to set up a second household. Bishop's College, the only other English university with a campus in Montreal, had a small medical school that took in Jews and others restricted from McGill. Unfortunately their doors were still barred to women. The dean there had made noisy pronouncements against female doctors at the height of my McGill campaign.

I could, I supposed, find work as a governess. The thought filled me with such despair that I flopped over to face the window again, hugging my belly. The sun was warm against my skin. Grandmother was still outside, only now she was walking across the grass to the house for some reason, leaving the laundry half hung. She was calling Laure's name so she would come too. I watched with growing curiosity, then forgot all about this odd scene as soon as they were out of sight. When a knock sounded on the bedroom door I had fallen back asleep. I thought it was Grandmother coming for my sheets, but the head that poked through the doorway was brown, not white, and it sported a familiar derby hat.

"Miss Skerry!" I cried, forgetting for an instant all my sorrows. It had been four years since I had last seen her. When I started McGill she had left Grandmother's employ and moved to Ontario. At first we had corresponded regularly, but soon my life at the university had become so busy that our letters tapered off. The last I had heard she was in Ottawa working for the family of a judge.

"Agnes," she said, removing her hat and peering myopically. "I came as soon as I heard you were ill."

My smile fell. God only knew what I looked like after a month of confinement. The smell must be pretty bad too. I tried to smile again but it cannot have been all that convincing.

Without a word Miss Skerry set to work straightening my bedding.

She hoisted me to a sitting position and plumped the pillows, then gathered up hankies and writing paper lying on the floor.

I watched. I had once possessed energy like this — dumb animal energy that might have gone mindlessly on and on until infirmity or death put an end to it. Watching Miss Skerry flitting about restoring order was exhausting. All that effort — the bending and reaching, the straightening and sorting — how futile it seemed to me now. Order and purpose were lies, I had decided. People were rushing to go nowhere. Couldn't Miss Skerry, with her sharp eyes and sharper mind, see it?

"Don't you ever give up?"

The governess paused, holding a tray of untouched toast and tea. To my surprise she laughed. "I did once," she said. "And in my case that was all it took. Once and I learned."

"When was that?" I asked, shocked and more than a little curious.

"Right after my father died."

"You were in mourning," I said. "That does not count. People have a right to come undone after a parent's death."

Miss Skerry eyed me thoughtfully. "Yes, but it was not just the death. All of a sudden I had no place. I couldn't imagine what shape my life would take."

My breath stopped then, as if my lungs had ceased to function. "And then what happened?" I was like a child begging for a bed-time story.

"And then I came to St. Andrews East."

"To the Priory?" I asked, sitting upright. "To us? You mean to say that your father had just died? I had no idea it had been so recent."

"It wasn't something I wished to talk about at the time," she said, carrying the tray to the landing outside my room and thereby managing to hide her face.

"You did not seem sad," I said, thinking back to the wry young woman who had helped me dissect the squirrel. Few people could have matched Miss Skerry in that moment for energy or imagination.

"St. Andrews East was a blessing, Agnes. It was the best thing that could have happened to me."

I started. How could she use the word *blessing* to describe this bleak, little town? Was an isolated barn in winter and the charge of a couple of orphans all it took to make this woman happy? "Laure and I were your first pupils?" I asked.

Miss Skerry blushed. "That's right, although I never admitted it to your grandma. I did not want her to know how inexperienced I was. I had lived in my father's home until then, you see. I had never dreamed that I might become a governess. I was forced into it, much like Jane Eyre."

"But it turned out to be a blessing?" The question was spurred by personal concerns, although I did not think Miss Skerry could have guessed.

My former governess laughed again. "Your grandmother accepted me into her home and heart, Agnes. She gave me an allowance for books. There was your microscope in her barn and you and I were given free rein to ramble in the woods almost daily." Miss Skerry's eyes were shining. "My father had been sick such a long time. I think I had forgotten how to live."

"So you like being a governess?" I asked hopefully.

Miss Skerry shot me a glance. "That's putting it a little strongly, Agnes. St. Andrews East was, I think, a high point." She turned then and stood very still, looking out the window at the yard filled with undulating laundry. "It is a life," she said slowly. "There are pleasures there if you care to seek them out."

I sighed. I could not imagine putting myself at the mercy of others, tending to their children, eating at their tables and sleeping in their spare beds in a room beside the kitchen. Pity was what I felt for Miss Skerry — pure, unadulterated pity.

Miss Skerry turned toward me, her mouth curling in a cryptic and not entirely generous smile. "Don't worry about me, Agnes White. There are worse ways to make a living than wiping the bottom of another woman's child."

I fixed my eyes on the bedpost, cheeks flushing with shame. It was as if she could read minds.

"You yourself would make a splendid governess. I can just picture you hunting for squirrels and insisting your charges analyze the entrails. Their mothers would kick up a fuss but you would probably win them over. Your McGill diploma would place you in high demand. Apropos," she said, fixing me with taunting, owlish eyes. "Your grandmother tells me you have a graduation coming up."

I nodded.

"And you have elected not to go."

I closed my eyes. The mere thought of McGill made me sick.

"Go, Agnes. You owe it to yourself. Show you are not beaten."

"But I am beaten. That is exactly what I am."

The governess looked at me almost fiercely. "You underestimate yourself."

"You overestimate me."

Miss Skerry removed her glasses and rubbed them thoughtfully. "You are wrong, Agnes White. I think I see you quite clearly." She replaced them on her nose.

I began to cry. The governess did not reach to comfort me. Instead she actually smiled and started talking about her new station. She had just moved back to Montreal and she said how good it was to be back in Quebec.

I listened with half an ear. My tears had stopped but my nose was plugged and the skin around my eyes felt inflamed. I resented Miss Skerry, who was blathering on about her most recent charges — two girls, just like me and Laure, only *both* of them were budding scientists. She had been offered this governessship at least in part because of her knowledge of natural history. The girls' father had purchased a second-hand microscope for their schoolroom. "It is an enlightened family," observed Miss Skerry. "Their father is a well-known Montreal doctor."

I stopped rubbing my eyes.

"He knows of you, of course. Thought you were a regular little harridan until I set him straight." She patted my leg through the bedcovers, laughing as if she had told a joke. "I had to swear on my life you were the sweetest, most even-tempered girl."

"What is his name?"

The governess paused, leaning over my bed. "Campbell."

I took her arm, forgetting my fatigue and tripping over my words in my rush to speak. "You can't possibly mean the dean of medicine at Bishop's University?"

Miss Skerry cocked her head. "Oh, can't I?"

I threw back my sheets and leaped out of bed. "Do you mean to tell me that you work for the dean of Bishop's Medical School?"

"That is what I have been trying to say for a while now, yes." Miss Skerry broke into a laugh. "Dr. Campbell knows I am here today, by the way. He asked that I deliver this."

She handed me a small cream envelope. Inside was a note hand-printed by Dr. F. Wayland Campbell on stationery embossed with the school's name. Bishop's College, it said, would be pleased to offer me a place in the medical faculty for the autumn term of 1890.

"But he hates the idea of women doctors," I said. "He said so in the papers."

"Perhaps," said the governess, "but Dr. Campbell is no fool. It will be a boon to Bishop's right now to show itself more liberal than McGill. They are rivals, are they not?"

I suddenly became aware that I was wearing only a shift and ran to the closet for my dressing gown, banging out questions about Dean Campbell and how the offer had come about.

Miss Skerry stood rather stiffly, regarding me with her funny, close-lipped smile. The Cheshire Cat again. After a long silence she finally spoke. "Well!"

"Well what?" I asked, twitching with impatience for answers to all the questions I had.

"Is it possible, Dr. White, that we have managed a cure?"

II
ARS MEDICA

The rarity of cardiac defects, the obscurity of their
etiology and symptoms, together with the fact that the
cases are often of serious clinical import, make the subject
of congenital cardiac disease of the highest interest.

— MAUDE ABBOTT, "CONGENITAL CARDIAC DISEASE"

9

As I stepped into Mansfield Street light stung my eyes. The office I'd rented on the top floor of this downtown brownstone was so small and dark my pupils were in a constant state of contraction. The rent was low precisely because I hadn't insisted on a window. As long as I stayed inside I did not notice, but when I stepped out the extent of my deprivation became painfully clear.

My cloak, bought three years back for travels in Europe, was too heavy for the day. Yesterday, when clouds had scudded across the skyline like stampeding herds and the temperature had plummeted, I had been happy enough to have it. But today was different, soft and cajoling, full of promises it could not keep. On days like this in a Montreal autumn you could be lulled into thinking the fine weather would last forever.

The clerks were out on their lunch breaks in shirt sleeves and braces. A man passed me whistling and I quickened my pace to keep up with him, tapping his beat with my heels on the board sidewalk. He probably had an errand to run or was getting lunch before heading off to a meeting. The same was not true of me. No one would care if I wandered off for the rest of the day, or for the rest of the year for that matter. I had no appointments, no obligations that afternoon. The day stretched before me like an empty page.

This past spring I had returned from studies in Europe brimming with energy. The Continent had been good to me. Universities there were more progressive than in North America and they had welcomed me as they would any other young doctor out to polish her skills and knowledge. In Europe people took female competence for granted. In Zurich where I had resided the first year, the university had been admitting women to its medical faculty for over a decade. I studied obstetrics with Dr. Wyder, rising to the rank of his *Unterassistentin* at the Schanz-Gebar Klinik for women. I also worked in a pathology lab and attended lectures by Dr. Forel, a specialist in hypnosis who made his living treating the disorders of Swiss minds.

After Zurich I travelled to Vienna, the acknowledged centre of medical science, where I studied pathology with Albrecht and internal medicine with Ortner — men whose work I had read about but whom I had never dreamed I would eventually meet. My skills with the microscope had been remarked upon quickly, and before I knew it I was the star foreign student, valued above the men. Paying positions had helped to defray my travel costs.

I missed speaking German, I thought, slowing my pace so the whistling man was soon far ahead. And I missed the company of men. Most of all I missed the work, the sense of having something to which my mind could turn each day other than my own petty concerns and self.

At Sherbrooke Street the whistler turned west. I could barely hear him anymore. He had been whistling a simplified version of "Eine kleine Nachtmusik," which Laure played for us Christmases in St. Andrews East. It had been a while since Laure had touched a piano. She was not doing well. During the three years of my absence her letters had been cheery enough. They had been short, but Laure had always preferred music over words. It was not until I returned that my younger sister's state was revealed.

Right after her marriage to Huntley she had become pregnant, which had pleased everyone initially. But in her sixth month she had lost the baby. I knew what a miscarriage that late in gestation meant. It was a birth — the same pain, the same breathing and pushing, but at the end of all the labour and sweat, death instead of life. Laure told me I would have had a niece. She had seen the baby, a perfect creature, pretty as a doll, except for the grey skin.

Since then Laure had been in a steady decline. There were still good times occasionally. These were the days on which Laure must have written me, but Huntley had since confessed to entire weeks when his wife would not stir from their bed. And other weeks when she grew so agitated that he barely knew her. He began spending evenings at his club. Some nights, I learned, he slept there.

Grandmother said I shouldn't worry. Marriage could be tricky, especially in the initial years. Grandmother was sure that Laure and Huntley would find their way. I was not so optimistic. I was anxious about my sister, who was delicate as our mother had been. I also worried about Grandmother, living alone out at the Priory. The house was badly in need of repair.

No sooner had my ship docked in Montreal than did I call on Laure. She was too sick for company that day, and again the next. It was a week before I could see her.

I vowed to restore the Priory, which had been shamefully neglected, but scraping together the necessary funds turned out to be a daunting challenge — more difficult than raising the money McGill had required. Since I had hung out my shingle exactly three patients had come to my Mansfield Street office. The first was the woman who cleaned my office building, with whom I had bartered services. The second was faithful Felicity Hingston. And the third was Laure, who needed a cure of the soul, not the body.

I cut across Sherbrooke Street, dodging a streetcar, and reached the front gates of McGill. Huntley Stewart had been right about streetcars. They were now electric, although this did not make them any less dangerous than the former horse-drawn ones. With cars now taking to the roads, as well as electric trams, the horses were more skittish. Crossing Sherbrooke Street had never been so difficult.

The campus was like a small paradise in the middle of this vehicular traffic. What twists my life had taken since I had last walked through these grounds. I was a doctor now, no thanks to anyone in this place. The faculty of medicine at McGill continued to bar its lectures to women. It was a mean, small-minded institution, and yet I loved it against all reason. When I walked through its front gates my father's face came into my mind and I felt the pull of longing.

On the field in front of the Arts Building a group of men were tossing a football. I had not learned the rules of this game. It seemed to me the men lunged at each other with extreme violence and then suddenly, inexplicably, stopped. They took their play so seriously. One moment they seemed ready to kill, the next they were hugging men they had minutes before flattened in the mud.

My shoes made a shushing noise in the leaves. Up ahead a man was raking, but the leaves were falling so fast it seemed hardly to make a difference. I felt old. The students must be what age? Sixteen? Seventeen? Children with their hopes and dreams intact and untarnished before them.

I had achieved my dream, but what had it brought? Wealth? I glanced at my dress, worn too many days now without washing, and at the patched cloak bunched under my arm. Renown? I'd been a celebrity in my student days, but since then I might as well have died. Happiness? My eyes pricked with tears. The day I received my degree I thought my life would be completely altered. I had entered the forbidden land of my father. Nothing would ever be the same. But in truth nothing happened. I remained plain old Agnes White, no richer or more famous or happier than before.

Across the way a girl who looked vaguely like Laure put down her book and peered at me. The girl turned away abruptly and I realized I had been staring. Was I becoming eccentric, making the young uncomfortable with my hungry, yearning eyes? Grey shoots were beginning to show at my temples. Was it Jane Austen who had written that a woman was washed up at twenty-seven? Which book was it — *Emma? Persuasion?* Miss Skerry would know.

I was twenty-nine and I had two diplomas in black frames hanging on my dingy office wall to show. I started walking again. The girl now had her nose in her book. How I wished I were still in the safety of school, reading books and scribbling assignments for teachers. I was halfway across the cobblestones, absorbed in these self-pitying thoughts, when a driver shouted, his horse and buggy narrowly avoiding me. The horse's eyes bulged with terror. Flecks of froth dotted his metal bit. He was so close I could smell his breath.

"Watch where you're stepping," the driver yelled as I scrambled out of his way. "Almost cost you your life." He slapped the horse's flank and the carriage rolled on.

I was about to slink back to Sherbrooke Street to take refuge in the faceless crowds and my hole of an office when I heard my name.

In the distance a man in a grey suit raised his hand and waved. He had no hat on and the wind was blowing his hair up. It was Dr. Samuel Clarke I realized with a start, the man who had instructed me in general medicine at Bishop's. He stepped down onto the path and took my arm. "Dr. White!" he exclaimed. "Where on earth have you been hiding? Walk with me if you have a minute."

I was so surprised I fell into stride. I remembered this charm, how valued I had felt in his presence. This was classic Dr. Clarke, as if he were begging for my company when really it was just the opposite. I had heard months back that he was McGill's current dean of medicine.

"Are you working nearby?" His eyes actually seemed interested. Dr. Clarke was the only one of my medical professors who had shown interest in me in my student days. As the only woman in the class I had stood out like a sore thumb. The other professors had viewed me mostly as an insult and a threat.

I told him briefly about my residencies in Zurich and Vienna and gave him a card with my Mansfield Street address.

He made a comment about the need for women physicians, how they allowed mothers and children to feel more at ease. Others had said it before, but from Dr. Clarke it sounded sincere. I did not admit how few mothers had knocked at my door since I'd hung out my shingle.

"You should come by the Vic," Dr. Clarke said, pointing to the stone building on the southern slope of Mount Royal. The Royal Victoria Hospital had been constructed during my absence in Europe. It reminded me of a castle, couched in golden leaves that shimmered in the autumn sun.

Dr. Clarke turned to consider me. I suddenly saw myself through his eyes: the dull dress I wore every day as if I were a nun, the patched cloak, my scuff-marked shoes. I would buy blacking this afternoon on the way back to the office. How could I have let myself go like this?

Dr. Clarke continued to observe me. At Bishop's I had belonged to a band of students he'd watched over. We included Joseph, a coloured man from Jamaica, and several Jews. He brought me in as the only woman in the class. Dr. Clarke made a point of learning all our names and organized schedules so the Jewish students could leave early on Friday nights for their Sabbath. Once we graduated he helped secure positions for some of us. Rumour had it Clarke himself was a Jew. He was a member of the Presbyterian Church and he'd married an Anglican. His sons' names were Christopher and Luke. Yet the rumours persisted.

"I'm afraid I have to leave you," he said as we reached the entrance to the medical building.

I nodded. Who could blame him? Why would McGill's dean of medicine waste his time with the likes of me?

"We must get together."

I nodded a second time, grateful for his civility, but no longer really listening.

"What about tomorrow? Is nine too early?" His intense brown eyes were studying mine.

I was so surprised I didn't immediately reply. Dr. Clarke was serious. He was not merely being polite.

"Nine then?" he repeated and left me nodding on the path.

NOW I WAS SITTING in exactly the same spot in exactly the same chair I had occupied eight years back when Dean Laidlaw had called me in. His secretary, of the jiggly upper arms and effusive welcomes, had continued in her position and was now Dean Clarke's amanuensis. Strange to think that while I had taken a degree at Bishop's and travelled halfway around the world this woman had continued to fulfill the same role behind the same desk. How many young men had passed through McGill's doors since I had had last sat here? How many women? On the wall opposite Andrew F. Holmes continued to gaze down with fierce mockery.

Gowned boys walked by, chatting and laughing on their way to class. I did not recognize a soul. How awful it would be to encounter William Howlett or any of the members of the admissions committee who had refused me and the terrific sum of money raised for my cause. A bell clanged, the hallway emptied and became so quiet I could hear the ticking of a clock up in what appeared to be a reception room nearby. I was squinting at it when Dr. Clarke came out and found me. He opened his arms as if to hug me, then thought better of it and swung them behind his back. "Welcome, Dr. White."

In his office the windows were open wide, letting in the sound of pigeons cooing in the eaves. Dean Clarke had rearranged the furniture, pulling his desk to one side and allowing visitors a glimpse of trees — poplars planted in a row on the lawn outside, reaching into the morning light.

"I've ordered tea," he said.

How different this was from the time before, when the room was filled with Dr. Mastro's smoke and Dr. Hingston's hostility. The secretary, whose name I learned was Mrs. Burke, carried in a tea service. As I drank from a steaming cup Dr. Clarke caught me up on faculty news. Of the committee that had rejected my admission only one person remained. Dr. Mastro was now chairman of the physiology department. Dr. Howlett, whom he'd replaced, was in the United States, apparently amassing a fortune and garnering fame. Dean Laidlaw had retired and Dr. Hingston was dead. This last fact I had known. Laure had mailed the obituary to Vienna and I had written an awkward note to Felicity, who was still living at home with her mother.

Dr. Clarke was behaving as if I were a colleague, as if I warranted attention. It was pleasant but it was also unnerving. I had changed my dress for a clean one, but it was not flattering by any stretch of the imagination. My shoes were blacked, but I didn't deserve the care of a dean.

He was a good-looking man with the smooth cheeks of a boy and thick hair that was only now, late in his fifties, turning grey. "Disarming" was the adjective that leapt to mind. "Gentleman" was the noun. In that moment, however, he was making me nervous. In all of our conversation he had not met my eye. He glanced at the ceiling then out the window. "I have a proposition."

I put my cup down. For a crazy moment I was sure he was going to lean forward and suggest something indecent.

"For several months now," he said after an uncomfortable pause, "we've been searching for someone."

The breath I had just taken caught and I coughed. I thought I must have misunderstood him. McGill University still did not admit female students into medicine. Surely Dr. Clarke could not be offering me employment. The sun chose that moment to climb over the tops of the poplars and I pushed my chair back into the shadows.

"It's the medical museum," he said. "We need someone to take it in hand." He shook his head regretfully. "It's not the most enthralling work, I know, and the money ..." He trailed off, leaving the sentence unfinished.

"You are offering me this?"

"I am sorry, Dr. White."

It was all I could do not to burst out laughing. Dr. Clarke was apologizing as he was offering me employment at McGill, with pay. He was unlocking the doors to the institution for me. I had to restrain myself from reaching out to hug him.

"I'll do it," I said. I had to say it twice and then a third time, more slowly, before he understood.

THE ROOM WAS LIKE a tomb it was so dark; it was full of dust. Dr. Clarke covered his mouth with a handkerchief. There was no overhead light. "I'm sorry, Agnes," he said again after he'd opened the doors. They had not yet extended the electricity up here and he had to light a gas lamp, which lent everything a yellow glow. Faculty offices were below us, the lecture theatres were below that. Few people ventured up here. Chairs and broken desks sat abandoned in the hallway.

"Mastro was supposed to have it cleaned," Dr. Clarke muttered into his handkerchief. "He's the curator."

The name startled me. "Dr. Mastro?"

Dr. Clarke nodded. "It comes with the chair in physiology." He drew his finger along the surface of the main work table and held up its blackened tip for me to see. "Mastro's wife is in a sanatarium down at Saranac Lake. She has consumption. He has more to attend to than the medical museum."

My eyes were becoming accustomed to the dark. I made out high ceilings, walls lined with shelves. Once there had been order here. Someone had cared. I could now see why it was so dark. I walked to the far end of the room and tugged on a cord. A blind rolled up in a whirring rush, revealing a large, grimy window.

"*Fiat lux*!" said the dean. I could see him better now, grinning like a smooth-cheeked boy.

The jars and cavernous room pulled me back to another place and time. I stood still, inhaling formaldehyde. The smell of things preserved. I was remembering the barn at St. Andrews East and my own early attempt at curatorship, but these memories went even further back. I had seen these jars and shelves before. The room at the back of our house in Montreal.

Eventually the dean left, promising to send the janitor with a pail and any other cleaning materials that I might need. He was apologetic about this too, as if cleaning the place was somehow beneath a person of my station.

For the following half hour I did nothing but sit on a stool by the work table, watching the dust motes swirl. The sun was at its highest point in the sky and its light made its way through the grime of the window, which faced south over McGill's campus. I would get light all day.

Dr. Clarke had not described my duties but the first tasks were obvious. The museum was like an attic, things placed haphazardly and tumbled on their sides. Something white caught my eye. Bent awkwardly around a metal pole was a skeleton. It was undersized, too small for a grown woman. As I straightened it out the right arm detached at the shoulder, coming away in my hands.

I cradled this arm. My father's possessions had been preserved. William Howlett must have brought them here for safe keeping, and now I would be their custodian. Did Dr. Clarke have an idea of the gift he had just offered me? My eyes filled with tears.

Like the skeleton almost every item in the museum needed repair. But it would be a pleasure. I put down the bones of the arm I still held, which were grainy and surprisingly light. I began to inspect the jars. Some were from animals. One jar contained slices of pig's lung, culled for the parasites blocking the bronchi. "Strongylus," I read in handwriting I'd been deprived of knowing intimately. My own script is somewhat squat, especially if I hurry. His was tall and thin, spiking upwards as if it yearned to fly away.

One shelf held nothing but pickled human hearts. The first jar on it was labelled "Fatty Heart with Rupture," in my father's hand. These specimens were very old, with mossy surfaces you would not want to touch. Another specimen was labelled "Acute Purulent Pericarditis." It had belonged to a woman who, according to my father's notes, had produced a pint of "laudable pus." These things had belonged to him. He had excised them himself and then preserved them. It was overwhelming.

"The Room of Horrors," I said aloud, smiling at the memory. I looked about at the extent of the disorder. It would take time and effort to sort through it all, but I had days and months and Dr. Clarke was going to pay me.

When the dean returned after lunch he found me sweeping, my charcoal skirt knotted to keep the hem out of the dust, a bright kerchief wound around my head. A good number of the jars were already lined up on the work table for a preliminary sorting. He sneezed prodigiously.

"I'm afraid I've stirred things up," I said, waving my hand through the soupy air.

Dr. Clarke laughed. "Is that not your specialty, Dr. White?"

I was about to object when a second man appeared in the doorway and stopped me short. I recognized him immediately.

"I thought you two should meet," Clarke ventured affably.

Dr. Mastro did not step forward. He remained at the threshold, his powerful shoulders rounding slightly, hands thrust in his pockets.

"We have already had the pleasure," I said, bowing my head in greeting. I ensured my voice was cordial.

"I have just learned of your appointment," he said. "Forgive my surprise."

Dr. Clarke produced a small, embarrassed laugh. It was clear he'd overstepped the chair of physiology. It was equally clear that Dr. Mastro was not pleased. "Dr. White is eminently qualified ..."

"I'm sure she is," said Mastro, shifting his weight as if he might take a boxer's two-fisted jab at us. His gaze took in my presentation, which was closer to that of a charwoman than a member of the faculty of medicine, then stepped past me into the clutter. "Well," he said after a pause. "Someone had to do it."

"And you're away, Ed," Dr. Clarke pleaded. "You couldn't do it by yourself. I thought you would be relieved."

Dr. Mastro smiled. "Of course." He clicked his heels as if he were a soldier and made a dismissive gesture with one of his hands. "If you two will excuse me now, I have a lecture to prepare."

His shoes clacked on the tiles as he retreated. Dr. Clarke laughed again, but I could not bring myself to share his mirth. I had stirred up more than dust that morning. The museum was full of ghosts who were all awakening.

III
THE HOWLETT HEART

The heart may be prolonged into a hollow process.

— MAUDE ABBOTT, "CONGENITAL CARDIAC DISEASE"

10

I made it through that first winter at McGill, but with the exception of Dr. Clarke I had no friends on faculty. No one stopped me in the halls to chat, and the one time I ventured into the common room at coffee hour my colleagues stared with such intensity that I didn't dare repeat the experience. They were perturbed by my presence at McGill. I had not been hired to teach or do research and yet I was collecting pay. The hostility was never spoken. They were too respectful of the dean to show open defiance, but it was there all the same. No one besides Dean Clarke addressed me formally as "Doctor." There was no plaque on my door announcing my title or name. I was a class apart.

I pulled my scarf tighter around my neck. There was a crack down one side of the window, which skewed my view across campus and let in frost and drafts. I had complained to Mastro about it in November but nothing had been done. It was the least of his worries. He was away in Saranac Lake often; I was left to run the museum without him. And now it was April. It would probably not snow again but still the air was chilly.

The window shuddered. I was sure it would give way one day. I took a moment to survey my little kingdom. Today the exhibits seemed drearier than usual because it was overcast, but on sunny days the glass jars gleamed and their contents glowed. I had done a great deal of work since first setting foot in the building last September. I'd had to sort through each item, dusting and grouping it by organ or functional system. At first I'd had to undertake the basic housekeeping jobs of cleaning and painting the shelves. There was a prodigious amount remaining to do. Many of the seals on the jars were broken and decay had set in. In others the glass tubes supporting the specimens had slipped loose or snapped.

In my darkest moments I couldn't help thinking it was a mistake to have accepted this position. When Dr. Clarke had first proposed it I'd thought it was a dream come true; but I should have asked questions I now realized. A more experienced person would have made sure that the salary was satisfactory before flinging himself headlong at Dean Clarke's feet. I now understood why nobody else had jumped at the position.

On the table before me was a collection of hearts — three dozen in various sizes and shapes, collected at any time between the previous week and seventy years before. Cut from thick slabs of glass, the jars shone like crystal. In some the formaldehyde had yellowed, in others there were hints of blue. Some of the organs were whole, others sectioned. Whatever their state, each was strikingly beautiful, yet also defective. The irregularities were there — small tears in the septum, scar tissue on the valves hampering opening or closing, coarctation of the aorta, transposition of the aorta and the pulmonary artery. During the patients' lives the clues would have been subtle: breathlessness, recurrent pain, pallor and a cyanotic cast to the skin. To the initiated there would also have been sound. A stethoscope on their chests would have related an unearthly symphony.

The newer specimens weren't labelled. Precious little in this forsaken place had been labelled when I'd first arrived. I had cleared two shelves in a corner for these broken hearts — a heart corner like the one Father had had in the Room of Horrors. For now, however, the heart specimens sat in a mess on the work table, surrounded by chemical puddles and the stained pages of my notes.

I picked up the nearest jar. Inside was the largest heart of the collection, grey as a pigeon's breast, with feathers of disintegrating flesh blurring the contours. This one was labelled "Ulcerative Endocarditis." The handwriting was my father's.

There was a knock on the door and Dr. Clarke's head appeared. I checked my watch. It was eleven o'clock, the hour I'd said I would expect him. I had forgotten. My lab coat needed a wash, I thought suddenly. I smelled as if I'd been pickled in preservatives myself. I blushed, trying to disentangle myself from the coat as Dr. Clarke walked toward me across the room.

"How's the system?" he asked, taking my hand.

The "system" was something I had dreamed up when I realized the extent of the pathology collection with which I had been entrusted. The oldest items dated back to 1823, the year the McGill medical school had been founded. In the intervening years hundreds of specimens had been collected. With some regularity specimens arrived by the pail-full from the Montreal General or the Royal Victoria Hospital, compounding the chaos. There was enough room for everything, but the challenge was to organize the collection so that items could be retrieved with speed and efficiency.

In Zurich a physician had adapted the Dewey Decimal Classification system — devised in 1876 and used primarily to sort books in libraries — to anatomical specimens. My innovation, which had impressed Dr. Mastro and several other faculty men, was to add a pathological number after the decimal point. It had taken four months to devise this system and apply it. As of this week each of the identified specimens in the museum, save the hearts, had been tagged.

Incoming specimens were less problematic. They arrived with autopsy reports, and if these reports were unclear all I had to do was check with Mastro or the doctor who had supplied them. It was the older specimens that caused me anguish. Much of the time I felt like Sisyphus, pushing that boulder up the hill only to have it roll down and squash me. The anatomy was the easy part of my task. More challenging was to identify the pathological anomaly. I had to date these specimens, which led me to search through ancient hospital records to see what had been written about them. It was slow, painstaking work.

"Done!" I said dramatically.

Dr. Clarke laughed and shook my hand. "You're quite a girl."

The skin on my hand was rough from daily handling of specimens; I pulled it back quickly.

Dr. Clarke pretended not to notice. "So what have you unearthed, Agnes?"

The previous night I had left a note on his desk. As a rule I tried to avoid placing demands on him. He had too much work. On top of his administrative functions he published scholarly papers and ran a private medical office. He was also a mentor to students and younger colleagues.

I pointed to the jar with the large heart at which I'd been peering all morning. It was an adult organ, but such a strange, misshapen thing, it was a mystery how its owner could have survived infancy.

Clarke pulled the jar toward him and squinted at the heart in the uneven light. "Ulcerative Endocarditis?"

"The label's wrong."

"I'll say," Clarke agreed. "It's some sort of anomaly, but not one I've ever seen. Look at how dilated the auricles are."

My spirits began to sink. Working here was like trying to piece together an enormous jigsaw puzzle with parts missing and others that refused to fit. "You're not familiar with it?"

He rotated the jar slowly. "It has only one ventricle," he said, shaking his head in wonder. "Like a reptile!"

I nodded. When I first came across it I had thought it could not be human. The museum held a number of veterinary specimens and I'd suspected it might be one of those. I suggested this to Dr. Clarke.

"Too big," he said, scratching his chin. "All but the ventricle is clearly human."

"Not quite," I said, pointing to the heart's right corner, just off the pulmonary artery. "There's a cavity. Can you see it? I suppose it's to make up for the missing chamber."

Clarke rotated the jar a final time, lips pursed, deep in thought. "Do you know who could help you with this?"

My breath slowed. I didn't dare turn my head. The heart was old, perhaps even predating my father, although he had been the resident expert in morbidity when it had been acquired. He had, perhaps, autopsied it. I did not look at the dean, did not know what I would do if the name I both dreaded and hoped for rolled off his tongue.

"William Howlett," the dean said, bringing the tips of his fingers together.

I was surprised and turned to face him.

"He knew this collection better than anyone," Clarke explained. "When he was teaching here he used these specimens in the classroom. They were demonstrations for his students."

I tried to nod and smile. *William Howlett*. His name hadn't even crossed my mind.

"Yes," said Dr. Clarke. "Howlett's the man you want. You've heard of him, of course?" He put the mysterious specimen down on the table. "He's made quite a reputation for himself since he left Montreal."

I nodded weakly, which Dr. Clarke would interpret as he wished.

"You would do well to arrange a meeting with him, Dr. White, for many reasons, the least of which may be this heart."

II

What I first noticed about the city of Baltimore was the colour. Green leaves unfurling on the branches of elms and oaks lining the sedate streets, green buds on all the hedges, green grass on the large, well-maintained lawns. When I'd boarded the train two days before at Windsor Station, Montreal had been clothed in grey. Spring had only just begun in my northern city. On my journey south colour seeped incrementally into the landscape. By the time I reached Baltimore it was as if a hand had reached down from the sky and painted the land in lush colours of spring.

I was here because of Dr. Clarke. It was he who had instigated the trip and secured the funding in the face of opposition from Dr. Mastro and others on faculty. My primary destination was the Army Medical Museum in Washington, which housed, according to Clarke, the largest collection of pathological specimens in North America. It would do much, he said, to inspire me. On the way there he suggested I stop in Baltimore to visit the Johns Hopkins medical school and hospital. Dr. Mastro had put up quite a fuss when he had heard. He did not see why university funds — insufficient at the best of times — should be spent on someone who wasn't even a faculty member.

Clarke had arranged it, however, and here I was, on a tram winding through the Baltimore streets, heading toward the most renowned medical school in the United States. On my lap was a leather satchel stuffed with tissues and week-old newspapers. Nestled inside this wrapping was a jar containing the enigmatic, three-chambered heart that had obsessed me since I'd first laid eyes on it. I hoped I was about to solve the mystery of its origin. In addition to the heart my satchel held a letter of introduction to the physician-in-chief at the hospital, Dr. William Howlett.

I was excited to be meeting him again. He was sure to remember me as I had practically fallen at his feet in the dean's office at McGill and then sobbed out the confession of my true identity. I wanted to show him that I had succeeded.

The heart weighed heavily on my legs. It was proving to be a literal burden. I had carried it all the way from Montreal and hadn't left it unattended in all that time. Although the glass of the jar was thick it was still breakable. I was hoping I could stash it in Howlett's office for the length of my sojourn.

Below me stretched the harbour and a labyrinth of streets. Baltimore is an industrial city. There are wealthy residential neighbourhoods, including the one in which my hotel was situated, full of huge old houses of brick and stone, but the city also contained many more with crowded row houses and tenements. There seemed to be a large working class, made up, I understood, mainly of German immigrants. The servants, however, were uniformly coloured. This morning as I'd waited for the tram I had been passed by no fewer than five Negro ladies, each pushing a perambulator with a white child inside.

Johns Hopkins Hospital sits on a hill in the middle of Baltimore with a view of Chesapeake Bay. It was built in the 1870s, before Pasteur dispelled the notion that contagion was airborne. Back then the hill, which caught fresh sea breezes, had been considered conducive to health. Overnight theories had changed and the place had become an anachronism. I had read somewhere that not only was the sea-breeze theory wrong, the architect hadn't planned adequate sewage or ventilation. In spite of this the hospital and its medical school were reputed to be the best in North America. The buildings may have been constructed on a faulty premise but the people inside made up for it.

The tram wheezed as it travelled uphill. It was electric. There was nothing but a thin wire to keep us from plunging backwards into Chesapeake Bay. The two other passengers didn't seem to mind. One had her nose in a textbook. I was just near enough for me to discern pink organs embedded in a sea of print.

The other passenger was a man closer to my own age with cropped hair and a military bearing. He carried no books and paid no attention to me or to the girl, passing his time staring out the window. His colour was too good to be that of a patient, but he couldn't be a medical student as they lived up the hill. Why would he be in this tram at eight thirty in the morning? "Living in" was one of the requisites for enrolling at Johns Hopkins. One had to be single and willing to sleep in the hospital itself. These rules had been set down by Dr. Howlett, who believed apprenticeship was far more useful than book learning in training student physicians. The few women enrolled in the program were exempted from the rule; they took rooms in the city or slept in the nurses' residence, also located up the hill.

By the time the tram reached the hill's crest it was close to nine o'clock. The man was the first out. He didn't wait or offer to help me with my bulky carrying case, but proceeded quickly toward the hospital. The girl hurried after him, checking her watch and stumbling beneath a load of books.

I too hurried off the tram. When I had written William Howlett's office to request a meeting his secretary had warned me not to be late. "Dr. Howlett is a punctual man," she had written. "He will expect as much from you."

I wondered what he made of my request to visit and exactly how he would greet me. Nine years had elapsed since our unfortunate encounter in Montreal. I cringed slightly, recalling the committee's hostility. How humiliating the entire affair had been. Miss Skerry said that the most painful situations were the richest because you learned so much from them. This one had not taught me much. It had been an irredeemable fiasco.

Dr. Howlett had not contacted me in the months following that first meeting. Perhaps he had been put off, or perhaps the mention of my father had shaken him. Whatever it was within a year he had left Montreal, crossing the border to work first in Philadelphia and then a few years later in Baltimore. Now he and I would meet again. My grip tightened on the handle of my case. I would not have sought him out without Dr. Clarke's prompting; he was perhaps the only person in the world capable of solving the riddle of my heart.

The hospital loomed majestically above me. Most of its buildings were constructed of brick and there was a tower with a cupola making it seem more like a fairy-tale castle than a sick house. A couple of patients and what I presumed to be their families were standing near the entrance conversing. A guard sat at a desk, whittling with a penknife. Before I opened my mouth he gave several short, practised waves of his hand to indicate the route.

When I pushed open the door on the landing to the second floor I found a huge crowd milling about. I was hot from my climb and from lugging the satchel. I remained at the periphery, trying to decipher who all these people were and what exactly was happening. Everyone was talking excitedly. A hush fell over the crowd and everyone turned in the same direction toward an office door that had opened. Dr. Howlett stepped out. I could see him through the lines of people, smiling and reaching to shake hands.

Nine years had barely altered him. He was still carefully dressed, this time in a morning coat and top hat, which he declined to remove even though there were women present. In his left hand was a walking stick and in a buttonhole was a sprig of purple lilac, which he sniffed as he spoke. His face was thinner than it had once been, but the eyes were every bit as lively.

The people in this crowd had probably each written him, just as I had, requesting a private interview. It was likely that he hadn't read my letter. He might not know I was here. I watched him work his way through the crowd with smiles and light conversation. I recognized the girl from the tram, now carrying a notepad instead of books. She smiled shyly as Howlett whispered something in her ear. They could have been lovers the gesture was so intimate. The young man who carried himself like a soldier was also here. He now had a stethoscope hanging around his neck and was following Howlett's movements with a look of what I can only describe as yearning. This crowd was here only to see him, which explained why the guard had known without my asking where to direct me. When Dr. Howlett's secretary had arranged the appointment I had imagined it a privilege. I had tossed and turned on my hotel bed the night before, trying to picture myself in Dr. Howlett's office and composing speeches in my mind. As it was, I thought, surveying the group with whom I was to share the occasion, I needn't have lost sleep.

It was doubtful I would have the opportunity to discuss the specimen I'd lugged from Montreal. Dr. Howlett was about to start his morning rounds. Evidently it was his custom to invite many students and colleagues. I leaned against a wall, placing my satchel containing the heart on the floor beside my shoes, polished with care at five thirty that morning.

"Good Lord, is it you?"

I looked up and blinked.

William Howlett was standing in front of me. "It *is* you, yes. I didn't think I was mistaken. What a surprise, Agnes White."

His skin was still dark, as if a private sun had shone on him through the bleakest days of winter. He was more handsome than I remembered. The moustache had been coaxed upward and waxed at the tips. I stared stupidly then came to my senses and mumbled something about Dr. Clarke, McGill and Montreal.

Howlett smiled and took my hand. I was the first to break eye contact, glancing nervously about. Every eye was now upon me.

"Samuel Clarke?" Howlett cried. "Now there's a name to stir the embers of memory." He took the letter of introduction and opened it right on the spot as if it were a gift. "Well, well," he said when he'd finished. "*Dr*. White, I welcome you." He took my hand again, this time raising it to his lips.

People were staring with open envy, trying to guess my identity, wondering why I deserved the great man's attention. I felt Howlett's lips on my skin. What on earth had Dr. Clarke written? I had anticipated that Howlett would remember me, but never had I dreamed he would be so lavish in his welcome.

He released my hand and turned back to the crowd, allowing me to collect myself. With his walking stick he pointed toward the first of the wards and motioned the crowd forward. Then he clicked his heels, perhaps in salutation to me, or perhaps as a general sign that the rounds had begun, and strode down the corridor. When I next looked up no one was paying me the slightest attention. I straightened my dress, picked up my satchel, and followed. It soon became evident, however, that the treatment I had just received was far from unique.

William Howlett was the essence of social grace. With each person he encountered he stopped, offering a moment of such pure attention that they were overcome. I saw the same rapt look on every face.

Rounds were over in two hours. I had not dreamed a person could be so skilful, for Howlett had to satisfy patients and at the same time address the students and clerks and visiting doctors crowding about him. He did not exclude the patient, never once referred to anyone in the third person, at least not within earshot. His commentary was full of lively jokes and anecdotes.

The tone of the morning was informal; one had to listen carefully to ascertain the quantity of information communicated. As he joked and talked, Howlett was observing. When he put his hand on a sick man's foot, the gesture was more than kindness. From the foot Howlett discerned information about pulse and blockages of blood. When his gaze turned to the same man's face he was checking for pallor, the yellow tinge of bile, the blue of cyanosis. What he saw rolled off his tongue faster than the interns or clerks could record. The young man from the tram was taking notes, barely looking at the patients in his effort to catch every word.

The tour finally came to an end and the crowd began to disperse, students heading to their lectures and clerks to their hospital duties. A few of us lingered but Howlett evidently felt that he had paid us his dues. He tipped his hat and began to walk away.

I felt suddenly sick at heart. Had it all been an act, then? Charm dispersed so evenly that my presence had not in the end registered? Did he not wish to speak with me, to hear about Dr. Clarke or McGill or why I had travelled all these miles to Baltimore? I clutched the satchel to my chest.

I was standing in the doorway separating the first ward of patients from the professors' offices when Howlett passed by. He was barely an arm's length away but he didn't raise his eyes. He was looking at the floor. I put my left hand on the lintel for support. The other hand dropped to my side, still holding the dead weight of the satchel. I wanted his notice. I wanted to feel his eyes on me once again.

The young man from the tram pushed in front of me. He turned, gesticulating wildly, shouting something about the door. I stared into his eyes, the pupils of which were expanding so fast there was no division anymore between them and the irises. His voice was surprisingly high, as if it hadn't broken yet, as if it belonged to a boy. But perhaps it was squeaking with distress. Was he having some kind of a fit? I didn't think so because his skin was preternaturally white, lending him a delicate, calm beauty. Skin like that was the envy of any woman. For one strange and intimate moment before the door slammed shut, crushing my ring finger, I pictured myself reaching out and touching him.

The next thing I knew he had disappeared and I was staring up at another face. A dark face, brown as coffee with hardly a drop of cream, with a moustache drooping from its upper lip. I lay perfectly still trying to make sense of this. A smell was in the air too, familiar, yet so distant I couldn't immediately place it. Spice and chocolate together but with an underlayer of bitterness. I tried to lever myself up and immediately collapsed.

Howlett helped me lower myself flat. "She's come around," he said and it was as sobering a stimulant as smelling salts. The room stopped spinning. I stared into his eyes and felt the full weight of my mortification.

I had swooned like a girl in a fairy tale, gone down right at Dr. Howlett's fashionably shod feet. What would he think? I had so wanted to impress him, to show him my hard-won toughness and strength. My awareness gradually expanded to include whisperings in the air around me and a number of blurry faces.

"Hand me her glasses." This was Howlett again. The frames were placed on my nose and hooked gently behind each of my ears.

I was startled. Nurses, doctors, students, even patients in their nightshirts had formed a ring around me and were peering anxiously down. I tried to protest, waving my left hand for emphasis, but it didn't seem to belong to me anymore. The sight was awful. My ring finger was a pulpy mess. Blood was dripping on the floor, on my coat and on the fabric of my dress. And yet I felt nothing. I was looking at someone else's wound.

Howlett took the hand and placed it gently on my stomach. "Turn your head or we'll lose you again," he said gently. "It appears a lot worse than it is, just needs a bit of antiseptic. You'll be on your feet in no time." He motioned to someone behind me and the young man who had cried out prior to the accident stepped forward.

"I tried to warn her," he said in his squeaky voice. His eyes darted everywhere, avoiding my face.

"Couldn't be helped, Rivers. You did your best." Howlett hadn't flinched at the voice so perhaps it was always like this. He turned from the young man and addressed me. "Dr. Rivers is an expert in first aid. He'll tend to you. If you're up for it he'll also give you the royal tour. What do you say?"

My finger was throbbing. I couldn't tell by looking at it whether or not I'd lost the tip.

The accident gained me admission into the pathology department. I glanced gratefully at the young man named Rivers. He seemed not at all pleased, however, and it went beyond guilt over the door slamming. The corners of his mouth were pulled down in a pout.

Howlett spoke again, offering me an invitation to dine with him that evening at his home. It was the least he could do, he said, to compensate for my pain and suffering. He wouldn't want me to leave Baltimore with only negative memories of my visit. I was dazed, I barely managed to stutter a thank you.

Howlett dusted off his pants and retrieved his walking stick. "Ladies and gentlemen," he said, addressing the crowd still milling about the hall, "the show is over. This young woman has had the intelligence to injure herself in one of the best medical facilities in the world. She will be well-attended, of that you can rest assured. Now go back to your stations and your studies." He made a shooing motion and disappeared into his office.

Only the man with the squeaky voice and I were left in an otherwise empty corridor. He dispatched a nurse to fetch disinfectant and gauze, and while waiting for these materials chatted with me, trying to put me at my ease. He turned out to be nicer than he had initially appeared. He became almost garrulous, and the way he held my damaged hand was confident and gentle. It turned out he was a

Canadian born in Ontario. His medical degree was from Toronto, where he'd been a gold medalist but where the education, he confessed, had been second-rate, nothing like what he was now experiencing at Hopkins. He'd been down here for a year, working with Howlett as a resident in pathology.

When he talked about Howlett his eyes changed. One moment they were the dull brown of tree bark, the next they ignited and blazed. He didn't look at me when he spoke but fixed his gaze somewhere over my left shoulder. I kept turning, expecting to find someone behind me, but all I saw were hospital walls. His voice changed too. In his excitement he spoke more breathlessly. Every two or three words he wheezed, as if his mouth couldn't keep up with his multitude of thoughts. At one point, after a particularly eloquent bit of praise, he doubled over, gasping.

He had been holding my hand when it happened. We were still in the hospital corridor. I was lying on the floor, knees up in case of a faint and he had just bound me with gauze and tape provided by the nurse when suddenly he lurched away, struggling for air. Once I had seen an infant die of this — the inability to draw sufficient oxygen into the lungs — but it was rare in a grown man. Then, as suddenly as it had flared, the attack ended and Dugald Rivers collapsed into a chair. "Sorry about that," he said. "It's probably the tree pollen. I guess we're both hard on our health today."

Minutes later he was back at my side, tying one last knot at the base of my finger so the bandage wouldn't slip. "All done," he said, his voice cracking on the second word. "You look like a soldier with that thing. It'll make a marvellous conversation piece tonight."

I laughed. I had managed to sit up and my head had stopped spinning. I was getting used to Rivers's voice, but it was embarrassing to have seen him in such weakness. To break the tension I raised my finger, which was longer than usual because of the splint and bandages, and aimed at him. He smiled, lifting his hands like a prisoner.

Clearly Dugald Rivers was in Howlett's thrall. Equally clearly he was not alone. We were members of a large club. To have been singled out by the great man and invited home for dinner was an honour many coveted. But how would I manage? Almost every item of clothing I had brought with me was stained or dirty. I wouldn't be able to wash things in time, especially with only one hand free for scrubbing. I had a clean dress in my closet at the hotel, but what about shoes? And my satchel was ruined. "I must look shocking," I said gazing down. I was covered in drying blood.

Rivers smiled. "I have seen far worse. You are speaking to a doctor, don't forget."

His words were hardly a comfort.

"The chief won't mind," he assured me. On a couple of occasions during the tour people had addressed Howlett as *Chief*. "He's a medical man too. And you can count on Mrs. Chief to act proper."

I peered at him. "Mrs. Chief?"

Rivers nodded. "Kitty Revere Howlett. The wife."

So there was a wife. I should have expected it with a man as successful as Howlett, but for some reason I hadn't considered this possibility.

"She's not bad," Rivers said amicably, "If you ignore her obsession with dolls."

"Dolls?" I repeated, thinking I'd heard wrong.

"Their house is crammed with them. On the plus side she doesn't stick around long. As soon as the meal is done she's off. Can't abide medical talk."

I nodded and glanced surreptitiously at my bag. I would bring it along tonight but make sure to keep it out of Mrs. Chief's sight.

"The kid is sweet. Spitting image of his old man." Rivers paused and took a breath. "I don't know why I'm telling you this," he said, "except perhaps that you are lucky. This," he said, pointing at my finger, "is a hidden blessing. You can thank as well as curse me for swinging that door on you. The Chief hasn't had a dinner in weeks and we're all a little hungry."

So dinners with Howlett were a regular thing. It turned out he was in the habit of inviting the entire crew of clerks in on Saturday nights. "He's like a father to us," Rivers said, his breath shortening again and his voice breaking awkwardly.

It was time to change the subject, to divert poor old Rivers for his own good. I began questioning him about Johns Hopkins and his research work, but no matter how I tried to push the conversation in other directions it kept returning to the great man, Howlett.

"You'll see the house tonight," Rivers said breathlessly. "It means the world to us, you know, shut up in our dorms for months on end. He's the only one on faculty who does it. The rest dig under their rocks for the weekend, but not Dr. Howlett. He gives of himself ..." The following words were lost as Rivers doubled over in a fit of coughing.

12

Number One West Franklin had a wide lawn and a cobbled, curled driveway. It was not far from my hotel so I had come by foot in shoes wet from scrubbing. I had changed my dress but was still carrying the blood-stained satchel.

The royal tour with Dugald Rivers had lasted longer than anticipated. He took me to his laboratory and showed me the project on which he was working. In turn I revealed the heart.

"Phenomenal!" he cried after staring at it dumbstruck for a full minute. "An aberration of nature." He'd done nearly a hundred autopsies so far but never had he laid eyes on anything so singular. "Why are you carting it around with you if you don't mind my asking?"

I had been asking myself the same question. But when it popped so impetuously out of his mouth I laughed and sat down on one of his lab stools. "I thought I would show it to Dr. Howlett." He nodded as if this were perfectly logical.

Before moving to the States Howlett had taught at McGill, I

explained. He was from Canada originally. While at McGill he had been in the habit of using specimens from the pathology museum as teaching aids during his lectures. I was hoping he might know the origins of this aberrant heart. He might have autopsied it himself. It had come to me without a correct label or record and I was anxious to learn its history.

Rivers was nearly as intrigued as I and urged me to bring it to the house that night. "You must present it to him, Dr. White. Absolutely. It's the type of thing he loves. A young lady touting a heart in her bag all the way from Canada. It's rich, Dr. White. Truly rich."

As wonderful as Rivers's company had been, I now wished I'd cut the visit short. I was late getting back to my hotel, late arranging for my clothes and shoes to be cleaned, late attempting to scrub my satchel in the tiny hotel wash bowl, late obtaining directions to the Howlett house, and late leaving for dinner. I'd had to hurry a good part of the way and was now flushed and sweating.

I gazed up at the facade of the house. I had exactly five minutes in which to cool off and have a look around. The street was quiet. The sun was still high, although a hint of evening's dampness had crept into the air. The neighbourhood children must all be inside now, taking their baths or eating supper with their nannies. This part of Baltimore had a solid look to it. Men with respectable jobs lived here along with their respectable wives and children. They hired people to care for the lawns and hedges and regular painting of their porches.

Howlett's house was number one and the street bore the name of one of America's most illustrious historical figures. Everything about it was of a piece. It was an impressive structure of red brick with white trim around the windows and doors. The veranda was green with white verticals between each step. A picket fence surrounded a substantial, well-tended lawn. Beside the gate was a mailbox emblazoned with the name Dr. William E. Howlett.

I looked at my shoes, which squeaked damply with each step. My reticule had a dark, ugly stain down the middle. I did not belong here. A house such as this would not tolerate a marginal soul like me, living alone without husband or child, working to support myself, and proving dangerously prone to accidents.

Before my hand touched the knocker the door opened and a man pronounced my name. He was dark skinned as every servant in Baltimore seemed to be and did not lift his eyes to look at me. He took my coat and tried to take the satchel, ignoring the stain with great tact. I shook my head and pulled the bag close.

As I peered into the vestibule mirror to check my hair I had the strongest sensation of being watched. It wasn't the manservant. It had to be someone else. The mirror was positioned in such a way that I could see most of the hallway and a bit of red caught my eye. A child with a red shirt and a holster slung around his waist peered around a doorway. He held a toy rifle in a tight grip, aiming it right at me. Our eyes met for a second, he grimaced and slipped back into hiding.

Without pausing I raised my bandage to my nose and took aim. "Bang," I said loudly, alarming the poor servant if not the boy. "Bang, bang, bang." I could see him now. He poked his head out again and was fixing me with gleaming eyes. I focused on my finger, blowing the tip as if it were smoking. The boy gazed in wonder. So did the servant, whose eyes had risen to meet mine. In Baltimore, evidently, women did not pack pistols when invited to dine.

I was led up a curving staircase to the study where Dr. Howlett was waiting. No one seemed to be about. I could smell dinner cooking, which suggested there must be human life somewhere not too far off but I saw no one.

Halfway up the stairs was a landing with a window cross-hatched in lead. On the sill stood three large dolls, leaning together as if gossiping: Kitty's collection. It was just as Dugald Rivers had warned. These were made of beeswax as Laure's dolls had been. Kitty had taken pains with the costumes, which were both intricate and colourful. White gloves hid their hands and one of them had a fan covering her mouth.

In an alcove on the second floor were two more whey-faced dolls and a vase of freshly cut daffodils. A woman's touch. The pale pink runner and flowery wallpaper also must have originated from a woman's design. My hand closed a little more tightly around the handle of my satchel. What had I been thinking, a pickled heart in this place?

The servant made a noise in his throat to get my attention. He obviously did not appreciate the way I was looking with such curiosity at all the details of the Howlett home. He wanted to deliver me to the master and be done with it.

As I started walking again I smelled smoke. The end of the second-floor hall was pungent with it. I didn't really need to be shown the way after all. All I needed was to follow my nose to the closed door, which was the source of the smell. I stood on the threshold breathing in the pepper-sweet scent of pipe tobacco.

There was a rustling inside the room after the servant knocked. I could hear someone rising. "Enter, my dear. Enter," said Dr. Howlett, opening it wide. His scalp shone through thinning hair in the bright light from overhead. He looked more his age without the hat he had worn that morning. Was it vanity that had kept it on his head in public? His moustache was practically white in places, a detail I had failed to notice before. His eyes, however, were unchanged. They still danced playfully, giving him a youthful air. He dismissed the servant and turned to me, smiling warmly. "Was I hard to find?"

I shook my head. My hotel was only five blocks away, I told him. A succession of platitudes then jumped from my mouth like dry little toads. The house was lovely. The neighbourhood grand. What a perfect day it had been for a walk! I snapped my mouth shut in dismay.

He seemed to take in everything, starting with the nun-like charcoal habit I had put on at the hotel, thinking it looked dignified, going next to the now-grimy bandage swaddling my hand and settling finally on my sweaty face. With my good hand I clutched the satchel closer.

"Honoré's," he said quietly.

I stared into his eyes and to my complete mortification burst into tears. It was horrible. I had wanted so much to be strong, to show him the mettle of which I was made, and instead I'd burst out crying. Howlett had every right to dismiss me. Instead he came around the desk and offered me a handkerchief. He didn't touch me, probably because we were alone and the situation awkward, but I could feel the heat of him as he bent over me. He sat me down then fetched another chair and joined me. "Your father used to carry that to our lectures," he said, his voice reverent and sombre.

A fresh wave of tears rose in me. All the resentment I'd felt toward him for his role in barring me from McGill evaporated, insubstantial mist in the morning sun of his attention. It was too strange to hear someone speak of my father without rancour or shame. I bit the insides of my cheeks but this only served to increase my anguish. What must he be thinking? I must have seemed horribly weak.

When he next addressed me, however, his voice was kind. "You loved him, didn't you? It was easy to love Honoré."

He talked for a while about how my father had been his mentor and how he'd respected him almost to the point of worship. "It's because of him I started smoking, you know," he said, holding out his pipe. "We used to go at it like chimneys in the Dead House to mask the smell." That gave me a start and I wondered about his moustache. Perhaps it too had been inspired by my father. It took some doing to imagine William Howlett, the object of admiration to so many of his own students, holding my own fallen father in awe.

He inhaled deeply. "Enough about him, Agnès," he said, pronouncing my name as my father had. "You must tell me about yourself."

It was too much. My head felt like a pumpkin, the brain scooped out and tossed away. If I could have fled I would have, but I was stuck there, mesmerized by his gaze. I looked down at his ink blotter and its wormy blue patterns. I studied the shelves behind him sagging with books: Virchow's *Cellular Pathology*, Bigelow's *Discourse on Self-Limited Diseases*. I spotted the textbook he had authored, his name shining in gold print on the spine.

His hands were folded in his lap. After a few more seconds he said something to fill me with gratitude. "You are stronger than you look. You persisted." He paused and puffed on his pipe, watching the smoke dissipate with such concentration he seemed to forget all about me.

I began to speak. It was easier now he wasn't looking. I opened my mouth and out my story poured; it had been there through the difficult years of my young womanhood, waiting for me to remove the cork. I told about my disappointment over McGill. How that had been the absolute lowest point of my entire life. I did not enter into details, my breakdown and months in bed. I was ashamed of this and didn't wish to seem bitter or rancorous. He was unembarrassed about McGill, accepting the account of my hardships quite neutrally. At times he hardly seemed to be listening, which helped me get through my narrative. I recounted how I had ended up at Bishop's Medical School through the intervention of a kind friend with connections. The friend was, of course, my former governess, but this fact I did not disclose. I told him about my work as an intern at the Montreal General Hospital and then my travels to Zurich and Vienna, where I'd laboured in some of the best university laboratories in the world. I larded my account with the names of prominent physicians. I had studied with the pathologists Kolisko and Albrecht and with Ortner in internal medicine.

His eyes widened with respect. Yes, I thought silently. I had met these men and dissected specimens alongside them with no help from him or from McGill.

I told him about my return to Canada. This part came out disjointed, punctuated by the blowing of my nose. I had stopped crying but my mouth was dry from emotion and from talking so much. I didn't stop, however. I had never done this before, never put into words the story of my life as if it might be something worth listening to.

Howlett's eyes had been averted throughout most of my talk, scanning the walls and ceiling, fixing on his desktop. When at last I stopped for air he turned to me. "Commendable."

Commendable. A single word but it meant the world at that moment, erasing his complicity in the McGill fiasco, erasing the fact that he had not tried to contact me all these years, even after he learned I was the daughter of his mentor. *Commendable.* Compensation indeed.

He sucked on his pipe and struck a match, releasing a fresh cloud of smoke into the room. "And now?" he asked from under a hazy halo. "What are you doing with yourself now?"

It was imperative to keep his dark eyes on me. I could hardly believe how close we had grown in twenty minutes' time. It was as if he had known me forever. What could I say that might bring us closer still? He wouldn't want to hear about my clinical practice, of that much I was sure. I wasn't exactly a paragon of success. The museum was a better bet, even if my role there to date had been largely that of charwoman.

Howlett continued to draw on his pipe. He did not seem bored, although his gaze had remained oblique, settling now on a book-shelf, now on the skylight or the back of my chair. I talked about Dr. Clarke and the generosity he'd shown me. I told of the chaos of the museum in my first few days there, of the slow and difficult restoration of order. I spoke of the specimens: jars standing in row upon row, awaiting my attention. People thought it strange that a young woman would choose to spend her time in a room full of pickled remains. They couldn't understand it. What they didn't know I whispered in a voice so small he had to lean forward to hear was that these had been my playthings as a child.

Howlett laid his pipe down on a small white plate on his desk and smiled. "Honoré's study," he said.

"Yes," I said, picturing it.

He nodded solemnly but soon his smile returned. "You were always different, weren't you Agnès? You rather liked it there. That's why this makes such sense. It's as if Providence itself were guiding you. You've been lucky."

The dusty old museum at McGill was suddenly given dignity. Howlett pulled a journal down from one of his shelves. "There's a piece in here you must read about the pathology museum in London," he said. "I practically lived there during my stint in that city as a student. It was marvellous, a shrine to death and life both. The mysteries of nature revealed." He fixed me with his laughing eyes. "There's nothing like it in America, Agnès. Perhaps it's time we changed this, you and I?"

I nodded, only half believing that I was speaking with the great man. He was interested in my work to the point of suggesting a partnership. The sense of intimacy was palpable and I decided to show him the heart. The moment could not have been more propitious, but suddenly the bell rang, announcing dinner.

We both started. Howlett put his pipe on the plate and stood up. "We must go. Kitty will be waiting in the dining room and she likes me to be prompt. But we will continue this discussion, that much I promise you."

I could hardly breathe I was so happy. I picked up my briefcase and rose to my feet with him. Years ago this man had spurned me, shutting me out of the place I longed to be, and now here I was in his study, telling him the story of my life as if he had intended it all along, as if I were someone worth attending to.

As I proceeded toward the door his hand alighted on my hip. He was looking straight ahead, intent on moving us both into the corridor, so it wasn't really improper, but I was shocked. Sounds became amplified. The smell of pipe smoke was particularly strong. The floral print on the walls in the hallway jumped out in heightened gaudiness. Through it all I was aware of one thing above everything else — the burning spot beneath his hand where my iliac crest jutted out.

I repeated his wife's name over and over in my head like a prayer. Howlett was married. I was about to sit down to a meal his wife had overseen. At that very moment she was waiting for me in her dining room, perhaps trying to imagine me just as I was trying to imagine her. The hand was still on my waist, exerting its pressure and heat. I shut my eyes.

THE MAHOGANY TABLE GLEAMED. A five-pronged candelabra blazed in the centre. The silver place settings shimmered. At the head of the table stood Kitty Revere Howlett, watching us enter.

She was as stunning as the table she had laid for our benefit. She had fine golden hair. Her dress was elegant, made of pale velvet that drew attention to her perfect skin. I felt hunched and dumpy beside her. I was suddenly aware of my own hair, which was more ragged than usual as I had had but one hand with which to tend it back at the hotel. I wanted to hide my laughable excuse for a dress. My hand was bundled in gauze that was now a filthy ash colour. I was poorly coiffed, underdressed and entirely inadequate. How could I have thought Howlett would be attracted to me? I had been dreaming, that was all, forgetting for one delirious moment that a woman in my position could not afford the luxury.

While Howlett carved the meat Kitty showed me to my chair. She glanced more than once at my satchel, offering to have the manservant put it in the vestibule, but I explained that I did not wish to part with it. I placed it at my feet, leaning it against a table leg.

The little boy was to dine with us, which struck me as odd. He was no older than five or six, too young to endure the conversation of adults. His nose barely cleared the table. Revere they called him, after his mother's family name.

I smiled at him but he was too shy to look directly at me. I must have intimidated him earlier during the shootout in the vestibule. Kitty meanwhile hadn't a retiring bone in her body. She asked all kinds of questions, notably about my accident at the hospital. What a shame it was, she exclaimed, that I had injured myself on holiday.

"On business," I said reflexively. "Officially I'm here for McGill."

"Why yes, of course," said Kitty, slightly taken aback at the correction. "Willie mentioned that. You're a doctor in Montreal."

The little boy looked up at me, his mouth dropping open in surprise. "Like Father?" The words came out before he could stop them and he blushed with embarrassment.

"Like Father, yes," said Howlett, still at the sideboard carving.

"But she can't be," the boy persisted.

Perhaps he didn't know that women could be doctors. Or he'd believed me to be a sharpshooter. His reasons were to remain a mystery because at that moment Kitty intervened, shushing her son and warning him to mind his manners.

"I am a doctor," I explained, ostensibly to the mother but also for the benefit of the silenced boy, "but I run a museum as well. That's my principal occupation. Your husband knows our collection."

"A museum," Kitty said. "How marvellous. And what sorts of things do you have on display?"

I glanced at Howlett but he was at the sideboard, his back turned to me. I was on my own. Surely Kitty wouldn't want to hear about diseased organs at a table laid with such care. Rivers had warned me to avoid talk of medicine tonight but Kitty looked at me with anticipation.

"Things of use to students," I said vaguely, waving my good hand. "We're part of the medical school."

To my relief Kitty let the subject go. She was probably one of those women who had a list of things appropriate for discussion at mealtimes and pity the guest who strayed.

"Willie was at McGill as you no doubt know. He absolutely loved his time there."

Howlett chose that moment to interrupt with a platter of steaming chicken. You could see the order of his mind even in this simple task. Thin slices of breast were arranged in one corner, drumsticks and dark meat in another. Stuffing was piled neatly at the centre. "Here you go, ladies and gent," he said, laying the platter on the table and bowing theatrically. "One beautifully roasted bird, care of your most excellent hostess, Kitty Revere Howlett."

Kitty blushed and then recited grace. I could not pass plates and serving bowls on as well as the others. I had to take each dish in my good hand, place it on the table, take up the serving spoon or fork with the same hand, serve myself, return the spoon, then pass the dish on to Howlett on my right. The little boy watched intently, cringing when I raised my bandaged hand.

After we had all served ourselves silence descended. Howlett and his child were reserved with Kitty, as if the dining room were foreign territory. Howlett seemed to watch his wife for cues. The little boy remained wordless too, his eyes darting from his father to me and then to his own feet, which he swung back and forth beneath the table. He was not one bit interested in his food. I chewed bravely. I had as little appetite as Revere seemed to have and the bandage exacerbated my innate clumsiness.

What did one do at such a dinner? How did one behave? Unlike Laure and Grandmother I had been born without this sixth sense. I was capable of committing serious blunders without being aware of them. I praised the food. That was a safe bet, and Kitty seemed to appreciate it. I said how much I liked Kitty's house. Words tumbled from my lips. I sounded insufferably dull! How lovely, I heard myself declare, were the dolls that Kitty kept on the landing.

Surely Howlett would hurl something at me — a forkful of peas, a bun, anything to get me to stop? What I would have given to talk about medicine again, to learn about his work at Johns Hopkins and the differences he'd noticed between medicine practised in Baltimore and Montreal. He was writing a textbook. He was teaching. There were hundreds of thing to be discussed. I looked up but Howlett was chewing placidly. Kitty, to my astonishment, was smiling warmly at me. She was so pleased in fact that she decided to reward me by directing the conversation to a topic she thought might interest me.

"Willie is all for women studying medicine." This unwarranted comment sailed out of the blue and into the dining room. A candle dripped onto the polished tabletop. Kitty obviously knew nothing of my past and its intersection with her husband. While she reached to straighten the candle Howlett served himself seconds.

"We're fully capable," I said carefully. I wasn't sure of Howlett's views on the matter and did not know Kitty well enough to guess her opinions either. "We can be every bit as intelligent as men."

Kitty nodded, but her brow creased slightly. "Yes, but I worry about all that knowledge. I'm not sure I could bear to know the things you've had to learn."

"But that's the point of it," I said. Kitty had hit a nerve. "Knowledge is precisely *why* I do it."

Howlett moved his eyes from his plate, a slow, warning glance.

The candles threw shadows around the room. Kitty's face seemed suddenly older, more angular. She no longer looked at me. "There was a girl last year," she said. "You remember her, Willie. The Jewish one. Stein I think she was called."

"She was uncommon," said Willie.

"They're all uncommon. But this one was so completely and utterly brain. No heart, no grace. Nothing to her apart from intellect. She was quite aberrant."

"Now, now," objected Howlett. "That's a little strong."

Kitty laughed. "You're right. I sound old-fashioned, don't I? But Miss White is different. That's why I mention it. She's not merely brain. She is obviously well brought up."

I felt like I was at a tennis match, watching the ball volleying back and forth across the table. I did not dare to say a word.

"Dr. White is intelligent," Howlett said smiling. "That much I can vouch for."

"Of course she is," answered Kitty. "But she also likes dolls."

Blood rose to my cheeks. I checked Kitty's expression but it contained no hint of irony.

"Guinevere Stein failed to notice them when she came to tea."

"Gertrude," Howlett corrected. "Gertrude Stein." He turned to me and continued. "Bit of an odd duck with some rather strange opinions she insisted on airing at inappropriate times. She was asked to withdraw last spring."

"Yes," said his wife. "And guess who did the asking?" She pointed at Howlett, raising her eyebrows significantly.

Howlett shrugged. "She did not have the temperament to be a physician," he said, absently pushing peas onto his fork. "Far too unconventional."

"Your dolls are wax," I said, changing the subject.

Kitty nodded. "The oldest one dates back to 1760."

I mustered the delighted surprise Kitty expected. "From England, I presume?"

Again Kitty nodded. "Yes. Wax always means England. In France during the same period porcelain was used for the heads."

"My sister and I had wax dolls when we were growing up," I told her. This was not entirely true. Laure had owned them. I had merely tolerated them as a border dividing her side from mine on the bed. But the lie seemed to work on Kitty, who offered me a second round of peas.

I reached with my bad hand for the bowl, which was heavy and banged down on the tabletop, turning on its side, scattering its contents. I tried to wipe the mess with my napkin but Kitty stopped me. "It's nothing," she insisted. She was good in an emergency. Calm. A servant was called in and in no time the table was put to right. I resumed my seat. Kitty had just revived the conversation with a story about someone spilling gravy at her wedding lunch when Revere screamed.

He was no longer in his seat. In the confusion over the peas no one had noticed that he'd vanished. I stared at Kitty, then at Howlett, trying to make sense of it. Howlett bent suddenly to peer under the table and then disappeared from view. "Little rascal!" he said laughing.

"He's under there?" Kitty was also trying to bend but her dress was too starchy to manage.

By leaning back and twisting sideways I could see the boy. And what I saw made the blood stop in my veins.

"What have you got there?" Howlett said. "Give it over."

He crawled beneath the table to join his son. There was a sound of tussling. I could only see part of Revere's body, the part holding my satchel. He was trying to shove the bottle back inside, out of sight, but his father was too quick. The tussling stopped and there were several seconds of silence while Howlett registered what he was holding. He started to laugh.

"My son's been a snoop," he said, standing and brushing off his pant legs. To my horror he placed the laboratory jar in front of him on the table. "I presume this belongs to you, Dr. White?"

My face must have ignited. I looked at my hostess but Kitty had no idea what was happening. She was smiling, assuming we were still in the realm of normal social intercourse. Reluctantly I looked back at Howlett, whose eyes were dancing a wicked little jig. "It's from the museum," I said quickly. "I'm so sorry."

Kitty's face changed. She peered at the jar then quickly looked away.

Howlett was still smiling. "A remarkable specimen."

What could I have said? The worst thing that could have occurred had and there was no undoing it. What had I been thinking to bring this heart tonight?

Howlett called to his son, who emerged from under the table after a bit of coaxing. The thing in the bottle was a heart, he explained. The boy asked if it was dead and his father nodded. Yes it was dead, but it wasn't anything to fear. One could learn a good deal from studying it. That was, in fact, why it was in the possession of Dr. White.

Revere glanced at me warily, most likely thinking me a witch with my bullet firing finger and this heart I was toting in a blood-smeared bag.

Kitty Revere rose abruptly. "Enough, Willie. I do not consider this appropriate. That thing," she said pointing at the jar, "does not belong on a table where food is being served. I would be grateful if you and Dr. White removed it."

Howlett looked at me. His face was solemn now but his eyes gave him away. He stood, taking the heart in both hands and cradling it like a baby. "My dear," he said to his wife. "We have upset you. Perhaps it's best we retire to the smoking room with this offensive thing?"

Kitty took her son and stood with her hands protectively on his shoulders while Howlett and I took our leave. I tried to apologize but it was clear that our time together was over.

Unlike the other rooms of the Howlett house the smoking room was dark and almost claustrophobic. Stained wood panelled the walls. Burgundy curtains drooped heavily over the only window and the air smelled of cigars. Ashtrays, one still holding two blackened stubs, had been strategically placed on several small tables.

I collapsed in an armchair and covered my face with my hands. "Forgive me," I said. "I can't believe I was so stupid."

Howlett laughed. "It wasn't you," he said, standing in front of me. "It was my son. Revere has the annoying habit of sticking his nose in things, just like his old man."

He was trying to comfort me, trying to be kind. I knew it but this did not ease my shame. "Kitty must think me a monster."

Howlett held the jar beneath the lamp. "It's a beauty," he said, turning it slowly so that the bulge attached to the right atrium gaped at us. "Look at that compensation. What a miracle."

"It doesn't look quite human," I said, momentarily forgetting my shame.

Howlett laughed for the second time. "Oh it's human all right. I knew that the first time I laid eyes on it."

I sat forward in excitement. "So you know it then. You've seen it before?"

"Know it? Why I was there when its owner died." He replaced the jar in the crook of his arm, cradling it once more. "It became something of a personal trademark at McGill. They used to call it 'The Howlett Heart.' I never expected to see it again."

I told him that I'd found it in the museum. The label had been wrong, which had thrown me off, and there had been no record attached.

"My fault," said Howlett. "I used that thing so often in my lectures the records must have been misplaced. I can rectify things for you this instant."

Dr. Clarke had been right. I removed my glasses and gave them a rub. My fingers were shaking slightly with anticipation. "He was your patient?"

Howlett's face took on an odd expression.

I put my glasses on again and peered at him. "But you said you were there when he died." I sensed an uneasiness in him.

He eyed me slyly. "Can I offer you a cigar, Dr. White?"

I demurred, shocked at the offer. Cigars were strictly for men.

"A digestif perhaps?"

I demurred again. He wanted me to drink with him alone in his parlour? I had insulted his wife once already. I was not about to do it again and risk whatever remained of my reputation.

"I'm at a loss," he finally said, mirroring my own state.

"Please," I said, waving to the bottles and decanters on a nearby shelf. "Take some yourself. I am fine as I am."

He shrugged and poured himself a snifter. "Brandy is a tonic. Good for the blood especially," he said. "You know that Dr. White. Besides, you make me feel inhospitable. You're sure you will not change your mind?"

In the end he insisted on pouring me some brandy. It was the colour of burnt sugar; its fumes stung my eyes. At his urging I took a mouthful but then spat most of it back out into my glass.

Howlett burst out laughing. "Slow down. No need to down it all at once."

He created a swirling tornado inside his snifter. Then he inhaled, closing his eyes.

When I did the same he laughed a second time. "You're a quick study, aren't you, Dr. White? Open to just about anything."

He leaned forward over his knees, right up close so he could keep his voice practically in a whisper. And then he told me the story of the heart. It was as if I'd passed some sort of test. He'd taken my measure in some way that only he could judge and found me worthy. The patient, he said, had been a notary, a sedentary man, which may have explained his longevity. In his thirties he had developed chest pains and been admitted to the Montreal General. Howlett had been a student at the time. The year was 1872. He'd been taking classes but they'd allowed him to assist at the initial examination, which had revealed nothing but a hint of cyanosis upon exertion and chest pain. No strange rattlings or whistlings in the thoracic cavity upon auscultation. No abnormal breathing patterns. When the patient died a month after this visit Howlett rushed back in curiosity to witness the autopsy.

"No report of which was ever written," I reminded him. "I can't tell you the number of hours I've spent combing the literature."

"Waste of time," said Howlett. "There was a report but you won't find it."

I looked at him sharply but couldn't read his expression. He sounded defiant, almost proud.

"It was never published."

"But it's such an important case," I objected. "The journals would have leapt on it."

"Under normal circumstances, perhaps," Howlett said and paused, jiggling his brandy so it undulated in small waves. "The doctor who wrote it ..." he paused, looking up at me briefly, "was in difficulty."

The pieces fell together. Howlett had already told me that as a student he'd followed one mentor in particular, sticking to him like a shadow.

"My father," I said quietly.

Howlett nodded. "Honoré Bourret did the autopsy."

I sat up as if he'd touched a nerve. All these weeks I'd been consumed with something that had once belonged to *him*. I'd carted it for miles without ever once suspecting. I leaned forward to re-examine the specimen jar. In the lamplight I could only just make out the heart bobbing inside like a closed fist.

13

JANUARY 1900

When my needle punctured the heart it met with resistance. I had imagined it soft, a sponge-like mass that might disintegrate at my touch, but it was actually quite solid. When I had returned from Baltimore it had been at the top of a long list of things to do. Then a series of events and circumstances intervened, preventing me from attending to it.

There was work, of course, which was ever more demanding. Grandmother had fallen ill and required immediate attention in St. Andrews East. She was ninety-five, tough and independent; it was hard to imagine she would not live forever. She had slowed down over the years. Right up until the end she did the washings on Tuesdays, shined the silver on Wednesdays and baked Friday afternoons. The summer I returned from Baltimore was the first one in memory that she did not keep the garden. That had been one chore she truly loved and the source of excellent tomato ketchup and pick-led beets, which she was constantly sending back to Montreal with me in jars I had once used for my own entirely different purposes.

She did not complain about her health. It was the untended garden that finally gave her away. When we called the town doctor in, my suspicions were confirmed. What she had been dismissing as indigestion was actually an advanced tumour in her large intestine. Cancer in patients as old as my grandmother tends to grow slowly, but this one was already big enough to cause pain and blockage.

I did not shed many tears during the funeral, unlike Laure who cried so hard she'd had to leave the church on Huntley's arm before the eulogy. People probably thought me callous, toughened unnaturally by my professional training, but the truth was that I couldn't quite believe in my grandmother's death. The loss was not yet real.

The day after the funeral I had walked into the kitchen at the Priory to get some breakfast. It was a large room with earthenware pots on the counter for flour and sugar, and a set of copper-bottomed pots scoured to a brilliant shine. Everything was orderly and in its place. It was so familiar to me, so full of my grandmother, that I said her name aloud.

There were plenty of good reasons why I neglected the Howlett Heart until the winter. I kept putting the work off month after month. I knew I would have to do it eventually. It was my prize specimen now that my article had been published. William Howlett had suggested I write it up and even found me a publisher. The heart was indeed a prize. It was a complete anomaly, one of only two such specimens in the world. The other one was in London I had since discovered. A pathologist had written to inform me after my publication came out. In Montreal colleagues who had never so much as nodded in greeting stopped me in the halls to inquire about it. The recognition had spread farther than McGill's faculty of medicine. My name was now known to physicians in the United States, England and the Continent. Howlett had seen to it that my first publication was in a prestigious and widely read journal.

Each time I invited people in to look at the specimen I was ashamed. It was one of the largest hearts in the McGill collection, and perhaps because of this the glass tubes supporting it had slipped. It hung lopsided on a single thread and looked sinister and mouldy with age. The formaldehyde in which it soaked was cloudy and yellow like concentrated urine. For months I simply hadn't had time to do anything about it. Now time was not a problem. I had an entire week of bereavement leave. Laure and I had buried Grandmother two days before in the family plot in St. Andrews East, right behind the church founded by her father-in-law in 1822. My mother was buried there, as was my grandfather, whom I had never met. The snow was so high that the tombstones bearing their names were only just visible.

It was a relief to be back in Montreal away from the mourners. The funeral had been an exhausting, drawn-out affair. Laure was still in St. Andrews East, closing up the Priory where we had stayed together as in the old days, only now in separate bedrooms. Laure and Huntley took over our old bedroom while I slept in the room off the kitchen, formerly occupied by Miss Skerry. I certainly wasn't about to sleep in Grandmother's room, in the bed in which she had died. We'd left the corpse there for a day as an informal viewing before the undertaker came. She had seemed so small she looked like a child.

One of her cousins had come to tend her in her final weeks. This was for the best as Laure certainly couldn't have undertaken the day-to-day care and I could leave my work only for brief stints. St. Andrews East and the life I had once led there now seemed impossibly remote. I had a new home and a new life, a situation Grandmother's illness seemed to underscore.

A whole new era did indeed seem to be opening. In the last two weeks, while Grandmother lay dying, the twentieth century was born. There had been speeches and parades. The newspapers were full of retrospectives and projections of ambitious hopes. The excitement was contagious. In my own little corner on the third floor of the McGill medical building I too felt it stirring. The pathology collection was growing. I had identified and classified about three quarters of the specimens, a feat Dr. Clarke declared miraculous. Miracles had nothing to do with it. For the last six months I'd worked relentlessly, arriving hours before classes began and remaining late into the night. When the professors' common room was refurbished I inherited a chesterfield, and on a few occasions I slept there. Dr. Clarke and the others would have been scandalized to hear of it but they all arrived too late in the day to notice.

My responsibilities seemed to accrue like organic growth. There were the specimens to label, including new ones arriving daily from the Montreal General and the Royal Vic hospitals, which compounded my chaos. Since September I had been teaching.

It started without my full awareness. Two students came by inquiring about the Howlett Heart. They were Dr. Mastro's boys, enrolled in his physiology course. I showed them a few of the specimens, pointing out functions and anomalies, and the next morning they came again, this time with friends in tow. Soon I was meeting with half of Dr. Mastro's class. It had taken my attention away from my other duties, adding a substantial burden at the height of my grandmother's illness, but it could not have made me happier. I drew up a schedule so there would be no more than five students at any one time. I made them tea as the room was full of drafts and the conversations long. I even offered them biscuits.

At the end of term Dr. Mastro's students presented me with a purse. It touched me so deeply I wept right there in front of them for it struck me that I was now teaching at McGill, just as my father had done, and William Howlett, the man who had once considered my father his mentor.

I loved the work. It did not enter my mind to ask for pay. I had sufficient funds to meet my needs and, more importantly, I now had ample funds for the museum. Howlett was contributing money. He sent it to Dean Clarke, clearly marked for me, a cheque to be spent on the museum's maintenance as I saw fit over five years. In November I'd hired a man to fix the window and I'd had electrical lighting installed. My workroom was now warm and bright.

The shelves, once chaotic, were now orderly. Each jar had three inches of space around it and a typed, detailed label. The McGill collection held all manner of specimens, from an enormous hairball in the shape of a human stomach to the lumpy fungus-infected jaw of a cow. Both these specimens had been provided by my father, I had recently learned. The hairball was my favourite — an incidental finding in an autopsy he'd performed in the 1860s on a clinically insane woman who had been obsessively pulling out and consuming her hair. It was so bizarre he had bottled it for display. At least this was what I imagined must have happened because the pedagogical use of such a thing was limited. There had been no label or indication who the discovering physician had been. It was Howlett who let me in on the secret.

The written records that should have documented my father's contributions had been removed or his name excised. When the label on an older specimen was missing or obviously wrong I began to suspect the handiwork might be his. All I had was a hunch, but often enough consultations with Howlett or clues provided in the scholarly writings of other men proved me right. My father's name seemed to have been systematically removed from the faculty annals. Someone had deliberately erased all trace of him. Intellectually I understood what had happened — my father's name was associated with calumny and McGill wanted no part of it — but emotionally I could not fathom it. It seemed a cruel thing to wipe out all trace of his accomplishments, especially as he had been acquitted by the courts. My archival detective work began to feel deeply personal.

In contrast to my father William Howlett left traces everywhere. He had taken pains to document everything he touched as a pathologist. One of my early discoveries was his collection of autopsy journals: three volumes detailing every case he had worked on from his student days to his years as chief pathologist at the Montreal General. What a mine of information. The material from his student days had been the key to my father's work, the source unlocking many mysteries. Most of his early post-mortems, Howlett confessed to me in conversation, had been done under Honoré Bourret's supervision. My father had been his teacher, his mentor and, later, his friend. Howlett claimed he had taught him more about medicine and about life in general than anyone else in all his schooling. Howlett was a stickler for detail. Each case included a patient history as well as autopsy results, so links could be made between symptoms in life and lesions unearthed after death. The other thing he mentioned, almost equally important in my eyes, was who had been in attendance at the autopsy and who had actually wielded the knife.

As I laboured, mucking about with formaldehyde-soaked specimens and dusty books, sorting, searching and labelling, William Howlett and my father became closely associated in my mind. Most of the older material was theirs. Their hands had touched the jars I picked up every day. Their scalpels had probed the organs inside, peeling back membrane and fat, exposing hidden points of weakness. Every time I set foot in the museum I felt their presence. At night in my rented room just east of the campus on Union Street I also felt them. I spent my evenings sifting through Howlett's publications, digging deeper and deeper. I fell asleep with his words propped on my chest and his face in my mind's eye.

The heart was cupped in my left hand. The thread was through the pericardium now. It had been easier than I'd thought. I pulled the two sides even and pushed one end through a tiny puncture in the glass tube. It did not smell good, this heart. Not rotten exactly, but unclean. I filled the jar with fresh preservative, as clear and colourless as water. I'd read somewhere about people in Portugal going to dust the bones of their ancestors in family crypts. There was a special day for it and everyone in the entire country took part. This was more or less my current job, year-round.

I took the heart in my hands. It was as slippery as a stone pulled from a stream. I held it and with infinite, anxious care, lowered it into the jar. There was a second's hesitation when I feared it would not work. But then the tubes snapped into place. I heard the tiny, satisfying popping noise. I had done it. The heart hung evenly now, perfectly aligned.

14

On a Sunday in early February I was startled awake from one of my
first truly deep sleeps since the funeral. I had been dreaming of the
North River in St. Andrews East. It must have been autumn in
the dream because the trees were bare, the river was free of ice and
the valley was blanketed with a dense November fog. I was down by
the water's edge in bare feet and a nightgown trying to find Grandmother, who was calling my name. Her voice seemed to come from
the river but the fog was so thick I could not see a thing.

I sat up and realized I had overslept. It was five minutes to eight
and someone was knocking with great force at my door, calling me.
It was Peter, the man who worked for my sister. He stared with wide
eyes after I opened the door, as if it were strange that I was still in
my bathrobe with my hair uncombed at this hour on the Lord's day
of rest. Actually it was an unusual for me, but there was no way he
could know this. In the winter I was usually out the door to the
museum before dawn. Sundays were no different except that I allowed
myself a midmorning break to attend services at St. James's. Last

night, however, I had worked late. I glanced behind me at the chaos of paper littering the floor. A plate with a half-eaten tart sat in full view on top of the mess.

"Peter," I exclaimed with more brightness than I felt. "Whatever brings you here?"

He looked quickly left and right then mumbled his message, not daring to step inside. *My sister was unwell. Mr. Stewart requested I come immediately.* He offered no details so I told him I'd be there straight away and packed him off to Huntley.

In no time I changed, fixed my hair and was stepping out into the brilliant white street. It had snowed the previous night, but today it was melting. The sun beat down with such boldness I had to loosen my scarf and undo my coat. It was only February but this thaw had the unmistakable feel of spring. Water ran in the gutters. The earth was warming up. The weather did not improve my mood. I was still anxious from my dream, and more so from Peter's strange apparition on a Sunday bearing bad news. I was walking quickly now, my thoughts on my sister's household. Peter had been so tight-lipped it was hard to tell how serious this was. Laure didn't live far away. In fact it took barely fifteen minutes to walk from my rooms on Union Street to their home on Mountain. Of course the snow would slow me down. My boots were making a clopping sound, not unlike a horse's trot. They were heavily soled like those worn by the farmers in St. Andrews East. Huntley had laughed when he had first seen me in them, but I did not care. They were a lot more practical than the flimsy, tottering things he liked to buy for Laure.

My brother-in-law and I had never known quite what to do with each other. For Laure's sake we refrained from outright hostility, but mostly I tried to keep out of his way. If I visited it was while Huntley was out or else I asked Laure to come to me. Today was an exception. Circumstances must be serious for Huntley to send for me.

I hadn't seen Laure since the funeral. I counted back the days. Eleven. How could I have been so neglectful? I'd been grieving in my own way, hiding out in the museum with my hearts. I had just finished compiling one hundred of Howlett's cardiac cases, classifying them by anomaly and summarizing the findings. He'd been so pleased when I told him he had set off immediately to find me a publisher. But here was the price I would pay for the luxuries of work and solitude.

I walked west from Union along Sherbrooke Street and was now beginning to climb Mountain Street. Sunlight stroked my head; it glinted off the snow that covered the roofs and window ledges of the houses, giving them the appearance of gingerbread. It was too bright a day for calamities I told myself, much too bright, much too sunny.

Huntley's property was considerable, encircled by a fence. His father had purchased the land and the impressively improved house for the couple right after their wedding. Huntley and Laure referred to it as a "prize." On the top floor were six bedrooms and two lavatories with running water and toilets. The lighting was electric and the furnace burned oil. It was a house in which to start a dynasty Huntley had joked when he and Laure gave me a tour after my return from Europe.

After five years of marriage there was still no hint of a dynasty. No Stewart heir had been produced. Huntley's mother had talked with Laure, plying her with questions. Grandmother had advised prayer, that time-honoured tool for all troubles. But Laure's menstrual cycle had been spotty since girlhood. The difficulty could not be cured by prayers.

In the middle of the door was a heavily oxidized bronze knocker in the form of a fish, imported from London. Huntley was a collector of antiques. His house was full of ornaments that Laure spent much of her time organizing for maids to clean and polish. After my second knock with the fish Peter swung the door open, blinking in the glare off the snow. I peered past him into the house, expecting to see Laure, but the hall was dark and ominously still.

Huntley's voice broke the silence. He came into view, shaved and formally dressed. He did not smile or offer a greeting so I repaid him in kind.

"Where is she?"

"Your sister," he said, avoiding any mention of his own relation to Laure, "has locked herself in the bedroom and refuses to come out. The situation has degenerated to the point of absurdity. She has been in there ever since she got home from St. Andrews. At first I ignored it," he said, describing the strategy one might employ with a difficult child. "Your sister can be mercurial, as you know. I've found when I ignore her she comes around in a day or two. This time, unfortunately, she has not."

I removed my boots and walked to the stairs. Huntley blocked me. "I must warn you, Agnes. It's bad this time. Worse than it's ever been."

I shook free of him and ran, taking the stairs two at a time. Huntley followed close behind.

The bedroom door was locked so I rattled the doorknob and knocked. "She's in here?" I asked when there was no answer from within.

Huntley nodded. "It's day eleven."

"Eleven!" I tried the door again, this time frantically. "Does she have food in there, or water?"

Huntley shrugged. "Mary brings a tray three times a day and leaves it outside the door but she never touches it. Two days ago she chased the poor woman away with a knife."

"A knife?" I couldn't picture it. My wisp-thin sister threatening to stab a servant? "She faints at the mere thought of blood."

Huntley shook his head. "She's lost her mind, Agnes. I think she's finally gone."

Behind the door floorboards creaked. Someone was standing there and listening.

I bent to the keyhole but could see only black. "Laure?" Silence followed, punctuated by the sound of my breath. "It's me," I tried again. "Agnes. It's safe now. You can open."

There was a pause and then finally Laure spoke in a voice so small it could have been a child's. "Is Huntley with you?"

I glanced behind me. Huntley's hands were clasped at his back. He was chewing on his lip. "Yes," I said. "He's right here, Laure. He's worried sick about you."

There was a second's pause and then the sound of furniture being dragged over the floorboards.

"She's barricading," said Huntley.

"What is going on in there? Open up. No one is going to hurt you, Laure." The dragging noises stopped. I waited, counting breaths.

"Go away," cried Laure. "I'm armed."

Huntley shook his head and looked down the corridor. When he faced me again he was crying. I was shocked. "I never bargained for this. I should have listened to my mother instead of following my foolish heart. Where did it lead me?" he said, shrugging and looking at the ceiling. "To this awful, barren place."

I got up from my knees and pulled him out of earshot. He was obviously too distraught to think about my sister's feelings. His lower lip was sticking out.

He pulled his arm from my grasp and straightened his shirt cuffs. "All I wanted was a life with children and a wife who loved me. Instead, what did I get?" His eyelids fluttered closed.

"Hush," I said sternly. "That's enough."

But Huntley wasn't done. "I've worked to get where I am now. I studied hard. I excelled at McGill. You knew me there. Do I deserve this? I'm president of the Metropolitan Club, for God's sake. This can't be happening!"

"That's enough," I said again. It was all I could do to keep myself from shaking him. "She's in mourning, Huntley. Grandmother's death has shaken her."

Huntley tossed his head. "It's not just your grandmother. The balance of her mind was already disturbed."

I suspected that the mean-spiritedness Huntley had always reserved for me might be something he directed at others too. My suspicions were now confirmed. My poor sister had received this treatment at a time when she was utterly vulnerable. "You might show some compassion," I said sharply.

"I'm just telling the truth. You girls grew up motherless. A trauma like that marks someone. Your father abandoned you. The Whites seem like a stable lot but you two didn't start your lives as Whites, did you? You had another name once. A French one."

So Huntley knew about the past. It made sense that Laure would have told him.

"She is grieving, Huntley. It won't help matters to be hard on her."

He was past listening. He seemed to have forgotten I was beside him and addressed his next words to his feet. "I should have seen the signs but I was blinded by her beauty, distracted from what was obvious to anyone with eyes. Damn the day I first met her."

I sent him away. It took some time as he was determined to articulate fully the blame for this situation. What concerned him most was the blow to his reputation.

When the hall was empty I knelt down by the keyhole. I could see nothing but I felt my sister's presence, and once or twice the creaking floor confirmed that she was near. A long period of coaxing ensued until finally she spoke.

"Is he still there?" Laure's voice was like a stranger's.

Huntley was gone. I repeated it until she was calm. Finally she unlocked the door.

After I had squeezed through the narrow space between the wall and a heavy mahogany dresser with which she had barricaded the door I was struck by the whiteness of the room. A mirror on the wall where the dresser had stood was draped with a sheet. A bedside table was also covered, as was the little desk by the window. The bed, mattress and pillows stripped bare, was the only piece of furniture left exposed. It was as if the room had been prepared for a lengthy absence.

Laure stood in the middle of this strange decor in her nightdress. She was terribly pale, with eyes sunk in their sockets, suggesting dehydration. Her hair hung in unwashed strands. Her feet were bare. I gave an involuntary cry and ran toward her but she fended me off, waving what seemed to be a knife.

I froze. This was the procedure I had been taught in Zurich when I was a medical resident for several months in an asylum. Freeze when a patient turns violent. *Use only the voice. Remain calm and reassuring.* The knife was not a knife. It was a silver-tipped letter opener. Laure's arm was trembling. She was exhausted, on the verge of collapse. There were marks on her forearm, partially healed gouges. Self-mutilation. The letter opener was more dangerous to her than to anyone else.

I began to talk, using the skills I had learned in Switzerland. They seemed to come reflexively, which made sense in a way because the person I was using them on was Laure, my little sister, whom I happened to know better than my own self. I got the letter opener away then took her in my arms. It was surprisingly easy, for in the end every person, no matter how full of fear and aggression, wants comfort and support.

Laure's words were disjointed, the story she recounted revealed deep paranoia. Huntley had turned the household against her in a campaign to drive her insane. People had been sneaking into her bedroom and damaging the furniture. The damage was always just enough that she alone would notice. It consisted mainly of nicks in the wood, small gouges and scratches that appeared overnight. She had locked the door but obviously Huntley had the key for he kept up with his work. It was done while she slept. She was trying to outsmart him. That was why she had draped the furniture with sheets. "He wants to drive me crazy," she whispered, jerking out of my arms. "Then he'll send me packing to get rid of me."

"You mustn't listen to that nonsense. Huntley is upset. He is not thinking about what's coming out of his mouth."

"He knows what he is doing." She paused and looked up at me. "We're defective, aren't we, Agnes? We shall never fit in."

I did not answer. Unlike my sister I did not consider "fitting in" a worthy goal. Quite the contrary.

"I thought I could do it when Huntley started courting me," said Laure, "but I was wrong. We're stained. We stain others."

"Nonsense." I put a hand on her arm to steady her. "You have a medical condition, Laure, a condition that affects fertility. It is not your fault."

Laure began to weep. "He talks of sending me away."

When I took her in my arms it was like rocking a child. Over Laure's shoulder the room came into view: the letter opener abandoned on the mattress, the shrouded, wounded furniture. Huntley was right. There was more to Laure's state than mourning. These were the hallmarks of psychosis. He was rejecting her because of it. He claimed to be so solid and yet was bolting.

"It's all right," I said, rocking us both, comforting myself as much as her. "It's all right, Laure. I'm here."

I HAD NO IDEA how I'd manage but I knew that Laure couldn't live under Huntley's roof any longer. So I bundled her into a dress and a shawl and fixed her hair as best I could. I was keenly aware of the irony of doing my sister's toilette, haphazard as it was that day. She sat utterly disinterested, allowing me license with her combs and pins as if her appearance no longer meant a thing.

In the vestibule Huntley came to talk to us while I was searching for Laure's boots. He had been alerted by Peter that Laure was out of the bedroom. "You got her out."

I was on my knees rooting in the coat closet. Beside me Laure cringed, trying to get away from him. "Yes," I said, fishing out a pair of women's galoshes. "You can address her directly, Huntley. She still speaks English."

Huntley stared at the galoshes. "What are you doing with those?"

I handed them to Laure, who began putting them on. "She needs them to protect her shoes." I was now rummaging for a coat.

"Hold on," said Huntley. "You can't just take her."

I turned. "I'm not *taking her*, Huntley. She's coming with me freely, of her own volition. It's quite obvious she can't remain here with you. She's stopped eating and sleeping. She needs care."

"There are places for this kind of thing."

I was a full head shorter than he was but I stepped forward. I could smell the scent he'd applied after his morning shave. I could practically count his nostril hairs. "I won't allow that, I'm afraid."

Laure began to cry.

"She's ill," said Huntley. "She needs a doctor."

I stared at him in wonder. "And what in the name of God am I?"

"Look here, Agnes, you work full time at that museum. You're not really a doctor of the type your sister needs right now. And besides, I can't have news of this leaking out. If you take her from me and keep her like a pet in your flat the whole city will hear of it. I'll be the talk of the town."

So that was it. Huntley Stewart had scandal on his mind. He wanted to send Laure far away, out of sight and mind, where the stain could be hidden, or at least covered up, and perhaps, with time, forgotten.

A plan came suddenly into my head. "She needs a place that is calm," I said, choosing words calculated to soothe Huntley as well as my poor sister. "Why couldn't she move out to the Priory until she feels strong again? Is that far enough away? It will allay gossip more than any institution, Huntley. You can tell people she's organizing Grandmother's things. Out there we will hire someone to give her proper care."

Huntley seemed relieved. He summoned a cab for us and saw us off at the front door.

15

There were three of them come to visit me for the final tutorial of the term. I had opened my window wide, which under the circumstances turned out to be a mistake. Sunlight was streaming into the room and the air carried a smell of earth and rotting leaves. The chirpings of starlings threatened to drown out my words. Beside me at the table the young men fidgeted and sighed. Academically they were the three weakest boys in their year. They probably ought to have been plucked in their first year but for some reason had been permitted to remain.

The one named Hornby picked dried mud from his boot. Beside him Sean Falconbridge rolled his head on a stubby neck as if he found it too cumbersome to hold upright. Only the third boy, Derek Sloan, looked at his notes, but these were indecipherable so they weren't much help. Ordinarily I would have made tea but these three cared so little I didn't make the effort. What was I to do with students like these? Their exam was five days off and they were hopeless, no better now at diagnostics than they had been in September when they had started pathology.

Set out before us on the table were three lab jars, each one containing a heart. I nudged the smallest one toward them as one might push a bone toward a sleeping dog.

This heart was one of my prizes. No bigger than my thumb and mounted to reveal the hidden defect. Howlett's work. My best pieces came either from him or from my father. In fact, all three hearts we were looking at today had been supplied by them. The donor of this one was an infant who died the day she was born.

I looked at Falconbridge and requested the cause of death.

He shrugged. Derek Sloan said stenosis but didn't know what it meant. Hornby just stared blankly.

I gave hints. "Think of wires crossing. Think of the arteries."

They still didn't know so I explained. It was transposition of the vessels, a problem afflicting about a tenth of infants with congenital defects. The aorta and pulmonary artery switched places, emerging from the wrong ventricle. Newborns with this problem would be blue from head to toe, although their hearts would sound perfectly normal.

The boys were scribbling in their notebooks when Dr. Clarke looked in. They all stood up, showing more energy than they had all morning.

"Good day, gentlemen," said the dean. He smiled and dipped his head at me. "Sorry to interrupt your work, Dr. White."

Work was hardly the word for it but I kept silent, especially when I saw that he was not alone. Standing behind him was a dark-haired boy.

I sensed right away that there was something wrong with this person although at first I could not identify what it was. He looked far too young to be enrolled in the medical faculty. Tousled curls that looked none-too-clean extended to his shoulders. His clothes were several sizes too big, accentuating his look of a street urchin. The suit was a decent one, or had once been, but was now so worn

I couldn't help thinking he never took it off. His shirt collar was grimy and frayed. But what bothered me, I finally realized, was his face. It was expressionless, betraying no hint of feeling or emotion. His eyes were active enough. They took in the boys standing by the table and the glassed-in cabinets full of labelled jars. They did not rise to meet mine.

"I want to introduce you to Jakob Hertzlich," said the dean.

I took the young man's hand, which was dry and cool even on as hot a day as this. The tip of his middle finger was stained yellow and his jacket carried the stale smell of cigarettes.

"Jakob is joining the faculty," continued the dean.

I looked at him more closely. He wasn't as young as I'd first thought. Perhaps in his midtwenties. Too old for a student. Surely he wasn't a professor. His clothes had been slept in. I was sure of it. He smelled slightly rank.

"At long last, Dr. White, you will have help. Jakob is your new assistant."

I stared at the dean and then at the young man who was continuing to avoid my gaze. He had reached into his pocket and pulled out an oval tin, which he shook lightly. Then he popped something in his mouth. What a strange person he was. All the time his fingers worked the tin his eyes roved.

"Well," I said, breaking the silence. There was an irony to this situation, I had to admit. For months I had been pestering Clarke for an assistant but I had imagined someone entirely different from this morose, peculiar boy. I also remembered my own hiring and the way it had been announced to Dr. Mastro. The dean seemed to take pleasure in throwing together people who were clearly incompatible.

"He comes highly recommended," Clarke told me. "He's medically trained."

A muffled snort came from the trio at the table. In my shock I had forgotten them. Falconbridge was pretending unconvincingly to blow his nose into a hanky.

"Well," said the dean, echoing the only word I had been able to utter. It was a word of so many possible meanings that in the end it meant nothing. It was noise, that was all, in this case intended to cover feeling. Wells were for drawing water. Wells were for wishing. I smiled bitterly. Dr. Clarke had granted my wish.

He cleared his throat. "I'll leave you to your work, Agnes. Mr. Hertzlich has papers to sign in my office."

I sat down rather heavily in my chair when they left. Dr. Clarke tended to present matters this way. It had the virtue of avoiding arguments so common among academics but it also made people angry. I thought again of Mastro. Our relationship had improved recently, much to my surprise. After Grandmother died he had come to my office to offer condolences. More astonishingly he had commended my work with his students. Apparently the class average in physiology had risen that year, which he attributed in large part to my tea-party tutorials. He had spoken with the dean and insisted the tutorials be included officially in the curriculum for the following year. Thanks to him I had climbed to the ranks of a sessional lecturer.

My interactions with Dr. Mastro might be improved but I doubted there was hope for this lad in an ill-fitting suit.

"He's a Jew, Miss," Hornby whispered.

"Don't be small-minded, Horn," said Falconbridge, suddenly alert. "What you really ought to know, Miss, is that he's loony."

The other two burst out laughing.

"You know him?"

"Never laid eyes on him," Falconbridge said. "But I've heard of him. He's a legend."

Jakob Hertzlich had apparently been a prodigy in the class from several years earlier. He won every prize in his year. Then, in the middle of his training, without word or warning he disappeared. Rumour had it he was institutionalized. The faculty had driven him stark raving mad. Boyish laughter followed the telling of this tale.

"Sorry to be the bearer of bad news," said Falconbridge, puffed up with pleasure, gathering his books.

I shrugged, unable to hide my impatience with these students, not one of them capable of writing their final exam, let alone winning a prize.

"Good luck with the loony," Falconbridge said before slipping out the door. His laughter resonated in the hallway.

Luck, I thought. Yes. I had been rather short of it lately. I rose from my chair and walked to the window. The air smelled fresh and full of promise. I could not believe what Dr. Clarke had done, what thought process had led him to deliver young Hertzlich to me. I had told the dean about Laure. Had it been anyone other than Dr. Clarke I would have called this act sadistic. He'd felt sorry. That must be the explanation. Jakob Hertzlich was a misfit, a Jew, and a cut above most people in intelligence, just the sort of individual Dr. Clarke was in the habit of collecting. I had been a beneficiary of the dean's compassion. Why not this singular boy?

Because it affected me! Because I had quite enough lunacy on my hands at the moment without having to endure it in my place of work. The museum was my refuge. At home I was managing, but just barely. I had thought Samuel Clarke astute enough to understand my situation.

I had installed Laure at the Priory where she felt safe and where Huntley wouldn't interfere. Not that he was showing much desire in that regard. He seemed relieved to have Laure out of his hair. Miss Skerry had dropped a perfectly good job in the city to come back to St. Andrews East and care for her. Yet Laure was a trial; some days she was herself, others a complete stranger. Just last week she'd thrown a boiling kettle at Miss Skerry, who had had to call in neighbouring farm hands to subdue her.

Here Dr. Clarke expected me to accept this boy with no facial expression and a total lack of grace into my life. What was I to do? A light rattling sound startled me and I whirled around to find the very boy of whom I had been thinking standing less than three feet away.

"What are you doing?"

He didn't answer and stood with his head bowed. He fidgeted with his hands, working at his mysterious oval tin. At last he opened it and popped something in his mouth. He did not seem nervous. He sucked whatever it was he'd put in his mouth and gazed about in an odd, disconnected way. He might have been contented to stand there forever if I hadn't interrupted.

"What is that?"

"What?" His voice was lower than I'd imagined, definitely not a boy's.

"The thing you just put in your mouth."

"Oh," he said, extending the box to me. "Licorice bits. From Holland. Would you like one?"

I took the tin and shook one into my palm. It was tiny and hard, tar black.

"I'm trying to quit cigarettes. My mouth misses them."

"When do you start?" I asked neutrally as if we were talking about a job at the market and not a position in my museum.

"Now." He popped another licorice bit in his mouth.

There was no way out of it. The licorice bit made me realize I was thirsty so I offered Jakob tea, which he accepted and then lingered over as if it were a special treat to be savoured.

When I had recovered my spirits I assigned him a task. Nothing difficult: sorting work to start with. I'd test him over the next few days, I decided, build up the challenge in increments. If he slipped up even a little, even once, the dean would hear about it. Looney was one thing. Incompetence I would not tolerate.

After an hour or so he walked over to where I was sitting. He'd been so quiet in his corner I'd actually begun to get work done myself. "Finished already?" I asked, knowing this couldn't be the case.

He shook his head. "I've noticed something."

His bluntness was sweet but unnerving. He was looking at the wall. "Over there."

I looked too. His gaze was directed at a labelled drawing of a heart I had tacked up to hide a crack in the plaster. I'd never been fond of it. The aorta, pulmonary artery, atria and ventricles were painted a garish petunia pink.

"It's wrong," he said simply.

"Excuse me?"

With hands plunged into his pockets he now looked like a professor about to expound. "I was a student here once," he told me. "I know that poster and it's always bothered me. In my day it used to hang in the library."

"The colours are dreadful," I agreed in an effort to sympathize.

"It's not the colours, even though it is a crime to put that pink next to the green veins."

I laughed. Jakob Hertzlich had a sense of humour.

"It's worse than that. Look at the pulmonary artery."

I squinted.

"Not only was the artist colour-blind, he was standing on his head."

Sure enough. The thoracic aorta was where the pulmonary artery should have been. I looked back at him in wonder. How many months had I worked in the museum beneath this poster and failed to notice the glaring error? The illustrator wasn't the only one with eye problems.

$$\maltese$$

16

That autumn, just as the new term was starting at McGill, I bumped into Dr. Rivers outside the professors' lounge in the medical faculty. He'd won a fellowship in pathology, which allowed him to teach at McGill and work at the Montreal General Hospital. His bearing was even more military than the last time we'd met. His hair was shorn right to the scalp and his shoulders, surprisingly narrow in a man so tall, were ramrod straight. He had just come from a year fighting the Boers with the D Battery of the Canadian Field Artillery, he told me in his funny, high-pitched voice.

I had read about the Boer War in the newspapers and about protests among French students across Montreal. I had to confess that my sympathies were with the protesters. What did Britain think it was doing, sticking its nose into the affairs of a country as far away as South Africa? Why was it recruiting Canadians such as Dugald Rivers to risk their lives on such distant soil? Rivers saw no problem with it. When he announced his rank it was a boast, although I hadn't the foggiest notion of what it meant. "Battery" sounded violent and "field" made me think of the farms around St. Andrews East. I cut short the soldier talk and invited him to tea. He was welcome at the museum any day of the week, I said, any hour. "Please send what specimens you can from the Dead House. Keep an eye out for me."

Dr. Rivers's first visit came at the end of September, a particularly warm day, which made everyone forget winter was about to descend. I opened the upper half of the big window in the museum and sunshine poured in, turning the interior a dusky gold. Pigeons cooed from their perches beneath the eaves. Rivers showed up with a pastry box in one hand and a pail in the other. He stepped over my threshold and then took a step back when Jakob and I turned, realizing he hadn't yet been invited inside. I rose immediately to welcome him.

He stood in my doorway, illuminated by golden light. With his cropped hair and eager smile he didn't look at all like a distinguished pathology fellow. When he'd first arrived he'd caused quite a stir with the nurses. His looks were undeniable — the chestnut hair and skin so wonderfully unblemished and pale. He held himself with authority, which women tend to like. But there was something lacking, I couldn't help thinking. Looks weren't what made me sit up and take notice when a man entered the room. It was something else, a kind of energy that even a short, ugly body might possess. Whatever this energy was Rivers didn't seem to have it. I found I could be completely at ease with him. This may have been why, of all the women who flocked about him that first autumn in Montreal, I was the person he chose as a friend.

"I brought you something," he said, swinging his pail up on my desk.

Jakob Hertzlich and I peered inside. A freshly excised heart was sloshing in its juices.

"I've come from the Dead House," Rivers said. "I figured the fastest way to get it here was by foot."

Jakob usually ignored strangers, continuing with his work when someone dropped by for a visit. Today, however, he made an exception.

"You mean you walked like that from the hospital?" he said, much impressed. The Dead House was annexed to the Montreal General Hospital on Dorchester and St. Dominique Street, a good twenty minutes by foot.

I began to laugh.

"With one stop along the way," said Rivers, lifting his pastry box.

"You stopped to shop?" I asked. "And no one noticed the pail?"

Rivers flashed a boyish grin. "One lady did. She mistook it for a beef heart though and gave me a recipe for entrail pie."

I laughed so hard my ribs ached. Jakob smiled. I poked a finger at the gift, which was very large and red. A grown man's, given the size, neatly chiselled to show the lesion.

"Atrial septal defect," I observed. "A fine example."

Rivers accepted the compliment with grace. "I have the autopsy report and a patient history for you," he said. "I thought it was an especially clean one. It's a wonder he lived into his forties. I had no idea until a few days back when his pressure suddenly shot up."

"The atrial ones can be sneaky," I said, nodding. "It's the pressure that usually gives them away. The ventricular ones you can tell right off because of the murmur."

"How right you are."

It was my turn to show grace. "Enough to predict that this one will soon smell if we don't get to work. You'll excuse Jakob if he tends to it before tea? Thank you, Dugald."

The new fellow was surprised and visibly gratified when I pronounced his name. First names were my custom in the museum. I was Agnes, Jakob was Jakob, and now Rivers would be Dugald. Poor man. Patronymics were the only thing allowed in the Army and as a general rule hospitals were not less formal than military barracks.

I handed the pail to Jakob. Over the months I had come to trust him and was now convinced that he could do any job in the museum as competently as I. He was intelligent, hard-working, and had proven to be a brilliant choice on Dr. Clarke's part.

When I returned to Dugald's side he was examining the wall.

"Nice likeness," he said, pointing at a poster Jakob had brought in not long after he'd started working for me. It was a pen-and-ink drawing on bristol board, lightly coloured with water wash, depicting three hearts from various angles. The component parts were meticulously labelled.

"My assistant's work," I told him.

Dugald Rivers's head bobbed in surprise. "Him?" he whispered, turning to the corner of the room where my unimposing helper was rinsing our newest specimen. "That person?"

I nodded.

"He's talented."

It was one of the many surprising facts I'd learned about Jakob Hertzlich over the months of our association. He was an artist. A real one. He liked nothing better than to sketch the day away on his notepad. His spare time was devoted to drawing and his results were sometimes breathtaking.

I invited Rivers to take a seat. I liked a proper tea, and in order to make the occasion festive I spread a white cloth embroidered by Laure and Miss Skerry over one end of the dissection table. Rivers laid down his pastry box. While we waited for the kettle to boil we chatted about the faculty and his duties and I asked how McGill compared to his experience in Baltimore.

"Apropos," he said suddenly. "Did you end up learning about that heart of yours? You remember the one — that mysterious reptilian thing you brought all the way down on the train with you? I've thought of it many times."

I lifted it from where it now sat on a permanent, privileged corner of my desk. "This one you mean?"

Dugald Rivers nodded, sucking in his breath. "It really is a wonder."

"Wondrous or not," I said with a laugh, "it very nearly got me thrown out of Number One West Franklin." I proceeded to tell the story of little Revere and his pilfering.

Dugald laughed. He could picture it, he said, the old heart ticking like a bomb beneath Kitty Howlett's meticulous table.

"I managed to get the history, though," I said. "Dr. Howlett has such precise recall. The autopsy was performed twenty-seven years ago. October of eighteen seventy-three. The patient was in his thirties when he died." I paused to let him take this in. "That makes it nearly sixty years old."

Dugald whistled. "Well it's a damned nice job. Howlett's got more than recall, I can tell you. Look at the way he opened up the ventricle. What a light touch."

"The work isn't Howlett's."

He looked at me in confusion.

"It's misleading because for years everyone called it the Howlett Heart." I took down from the wall a framed copy of the article I'd published with Dr. Howlett's help in the *Montreal Medical Journal*.

"*Burritt*," he read, mispronouncing my father's name.

"Dr. Honoré *Bourret*," I corrected with French Rs and a silent T. The name rolled off my tongue with intoxicating ease. I even managed to meet Dugald's gaze. It was French, I explained, although like so many ambitious French Montrealers he had spent his adult years speaking mostly English.

Dugald's curiosity was piqued. "But where does William Howlett come in? Why the Howlett Heart?"

"Bourret was his mentor," I explained. "He was a professor here. They worked together a lot of the time. The patient was Bourret's and Howlett was invited to the autopsy."

"So it was this fellow Bourret's work?"

I nodded. "There was a scandal, though. Bourret was forced to leave McGill." I kept my voice neutral and avoided Dugald's eyes.

"Is that when Howlett was hired? When this Bourret fellow left?"

I did not trust my voice. I nodded.

"Lucky man," Rivers sighed. "I wondered how he was appointed to faculty at such a young age. He was a full professor and the sole pathologist at the Montreal General practically upon graduation."

My throat clamped. I needed tea.

"He's fortune's child," said Dugald.

I watched him withdraw from me, his eyes becoming slightly unfocused. Was I as transparent as this? Since returning from Baltimore I'd been floating. Dr. Clarke and Miss Skerry had remarked on it: how strong and full of spirit I was despite my grandmother's death and Laure's collapse.

Howlett was the reason. My work in the pathology museum, which I was now undertaking with his blessings and on his penny, and my correspondence with him were my lifeline. When his name was spoken my cheeks became hot. I was aware of my affliction but it was only now, watching Dugald Rivers, that I wondered if it might show. At the slightest reference to Howlett Dugald's face turned wistful. It was at once pitiful and funny. I glanced over at Jakob, who watched us from his corner. I could only pray that I was more opaque than the adoring Dugald Rivers.

I felt an urge to snap him awake. "It was not fortune alone." Howlett had worked with discipline and energy to attain his present stature. His list of publications was impressive. The number of autopsies he'd performed — 787 in fewer than ten years — seemed unimaginable.

I explained a little of this to Dugald. "I'm not even through my classifications yet but I'd say a good two thirds of the specimens are his. The quantity of his work is remarkable, Dugald. And everything was written up either in notes or for publication."

Dugald Rivers was completely still while I enumerated Howlett's accomplishments. He looked slowly around. "So you're saying that almost all of this is William Howlett's."

I smiled. "Some things come from Bourret. These days the specimens from the Royal Victoria and the Montreal General arrive with a frequency that makes it difficult for me to keep up. Now I suppose," I said, nodding at the pail, "there will be material from you too. The majority of the specimens, however, come from Howlett's autopsies."

Dugald laughed. "And that makes you his high priestess, like Apollo's oracle."

I laughed uneasily. "Don't come to me for truths, Dugald. Tea I can offer, but nothing as grand as the truth."

"What became of the illustrious Dr. Bourret?" asked Rivers, replacing the specimen bottle on my desk. "I don't believe I've heard of him."

I looked away. I had no answer to that particular query, and this happened to be the truth, as opposed to the rest of the story I'd recounted, which was riddled with omissions. I had besieged William Howlett with questions but he had not seen or heard from his former mentor. "He disappeared."

Dugald Rivers rubbed the stubble on his chin. "Must have been an awful scandal to ruin a career like that." He was looking at me, waiting for elaboration, but I couldn't. My throat was dry. Were I to utter one more syllable Rivers would understand the emotional depth of my involvement in this history. Seconds ticked by. I could feel colour seeping into my cheeks, and then suddenly Jakob was beside me with the kettle.

"It was about to sing," he said. "Do you know where I can find the teapot?"

I felt a surge of gratitude but hid it and joined in a hunt for the teapot. After I found it I busied myself setting out cups. With exaggerated care I measured two spoonfuls of smoky black twig into the pot. "Have you ever tasted Lapsang Souchong?" I asked Dugald in a voice that I hoped sounded close to normal.

Dr. Rivers shook his head.

"You're in for a treat." We had returned to safer ground with the subject of food. "If you don't like it there's standard fare on the shelf." I was feeling more in control now. I took up the pastry box and snapped the string with a scalpel. A pair of my favourite tarts stared up like rising suns. "Apricot!" I exclaimed. "I do believe we shall be friends, Dugald Rivers."

There was no milk but I did have a supply of sugar lumps and a baguette, half-eaten from lunch, so I put Dugald to work slicing while I peeled a cucumber.

"Cucumber sandwiches?" he muttered. "Civilized."

"One has to have standards, Dugald. Especially given the work we do."

Jakob joined us. He liked Dugald, which I fully understood. I cut the tarts in half so he too could partake. It was a pleasure to feed him. On his pittance of a salary he seemed forever hungry.

It was he who told Dugald that I was working for Howlett. "She's writing scholarly essays for that man in Baltimore you seem to admire so much."

Dugald Rivers stopped chewing. He put down his teacup and reddened.

Jakob was glancing back and forth between us. "She's writing a chapter in his forthcoming textbook."

Dugald looked at me. "Is it true, Dr. White?"

I nodded. I was the only woman of one hundred and four physicians invited to contribute to the multi-volume series Dr. Howlett was editing. Dugald's breath had grown slightly raspy, I noticed. It was hard not to feel sorry for this man who seemed so incapable of dissembling.

"What is the subject?"

"Hearts." I answered with pride, though it was sure to nettle him. The cataloguing work had quickly borne fruit. "It started with that," I said, pointing at the framed copy of my first published article.

With my first piece of research into the misnamed Howlett Heart, William Howlett had realized I could write. He had commissioned a statistical survey of one hundred of his other, less spectacular, cardiac specimens, which he also helped me to publish.

"Dr. Howlett is an expert in circulation, but he needed help with the congenital material," I explained. No one actually worked in the field of congenital heart defects. There was nothing one could do for these cases save to diagnose and then autopsy them. There was no money in it.

"You're damned lucky," Dugald whispered.

I shrugged this off. It wasn't as great an honour as he imagined.

It meant gruelling nights at the typewriter after equally gruelling days at my museum work table. The work itself was derivative. I would have traded places in an instant with Dugald Rivers, who worked at a hospital and performed the autopsies that I merely examined afterward and tabulated. "You're the lucky one. You won a McGill fellowship."

We set to the business of eating and drinking. Dugald Rivers loved my smoky Chinese tea and I loved his choice of tart. With the help of hungry Jakob Hertzlich we devoured every morsel.

IV
THE HEART'S REASON

Le coeur a ses raisons que la raison ne connaît point.

— BLAISE PASCAL

17

I had been working in the museum for seven years when Dr. Howlett arranged to visit. The museum had become a second home to me — a third one, really, if the Priory is to be counted — and a sustaining comfort in a life with what sometimes seemed like a disproportionate share of discomforts. Laure's case was not improving. I didn't know how Miss Skerry managed for there were fewer and fewer good days for my sister on the family property in St. Andrews East. Huntley had all but abandoned her, which was a relief in every respect but financial. The upkeep of the Priory, the payment of Miss Skerry's salary and the livelihood of both my sister and my former governess were on my shoulders alone. Miss Skerry was frugal, ingenious at doing much with little, but it pained me not to be able to offer more when her life and my sister's were so obviously circumscribed and hard. Money was a constant worry. I was underpaid by McGill. Thanks to supplements from Dr. Howlett I was able to scrape by.

And now he was to come. He had promised a visit several times before but there were so many claims on his time he had not been able to follow through. This time around the chancellor of McGill had commissioned a portrait of him to be hung in the medical building. Howlett had agreed to come for two whole days to "see my dear old Montreal friends," he had written in a letter several weeks back, "and sit for that damned portrait."

The portrait was hardly damned. I would have gladly hugged the chancellor and the portrait artist as well, for that portrait had succeeded where all my petitions and invitations had failed. An ocean now separated us from each other for Howlett was at Oxford, the regius professor of medicine. What was more, he had a new citizenship and name. He was Sir William Howlett, for he'd become a British citizen and been knighted since we last met. Now he was celebrated not only throughout Canada and the United States but in England as well. Dean Clarke had told me Howlett was the personal physician to the British prime minister.

The day of the visit was wet and cold. April is such a fickle month in Montreal, changing from warm to bitterly cold in the space of a few hours. That day happened to be punishing. A hard wind pushed me up the path through campus toward the medical building. I had slipped on the ice on Sherbrooke Street, ripping holes in my stockings. As soon as I was inside the door I raised my skirt to survey the damage. Both my knees were scraped and bloody. I could wash the knees but my stockings, purchased a week prior specifically for this visit, were ruined. They were silk, imported from London, far beyond my means.

Students streamed in for their classes, rosy cheeked and buttoned. A timid young man waved as he hurried past. The upper-year students all knew me from tutorials. During my first year at McGill no one had waved. Before Christmas break this year there had been an informal poll and the students had selected me as one of the best instructors on faculty. Students sought me out to chat before class on days without tutorials and on their lunch breaks. It was flattering, even if it meant I no longer had mornings to myself. It was my custom to arrive an hour before Jakob to put the kettle on and putter in sweet seclusion. These days if I wanted solitude I had to show up earlier.

On a day such as this I longed for my former invisibility. I hoped no one would knock on my office door for an early chat and tea. I could not afford the interruption. The previous night I'd stayed up working far too late, and this morning when my alarm had rung I'd slept right through it and had to run all the way here.

Three students were lounging by my door. One had his back against the wall, a knee jackknifing out. A second boy facing him was rising repeatedly on his toes. Up and down, up and down, as I approached, his head bowed in concentration. The third one saw me and alerted the others.

"I'm sorry, boys," I said, pulling out my keys. "I'm late, as you can see."

"We were wondering if you had a minute," said the one who had noticed me.

"No minutes today, I'm afraid." I swung the door open and inhaled the familiar, musty, museum smell.

"It won't take long."

I relented. I always did. Jakob said I needed to add the word "no" to my vocabulary. I was forever compounding my already complex life with favours such as this. "It's your one womanly trait," Jakob had observed. I still hadn't decided if this was an insult or a compliment.

The three young men hung their coats on hooks I'd hammered behind the door. They stood awkwardly beside the table. Ordinarily they would have sat down with me and opened their books to the matter they wished to discuss. Today this was impossible. The table was so cluttered there wasn't any space.

"Spring cleaning?" one of them asked.

I laughed. "In a manner of speaking." I wished they would go away. My right kneecap was throbbing and I knew I ought to rinse it. Instead I stood there tending to the three young men. I glanced at the pocket watch inherited from my grandfather that hung around my neck.

At eight forty-five there was a knock and Jakob Hertzlich appeared. My salvation. He knew his anatomy cold. He could take over.

Jakob's ears were bright red. He never wore a hat, probably because he didn't own one. He greeted the boys but they stayed silent and kept their eyes low. A lot of the students did this with Jakob. He let it pass and kept on with his business as if their behaviour were inevitable, like bad weather. I wasn't as fatalistic. I glared at the boys, cursing them inwardly.

Now my irritation shifted to him. His clothes were the same as he'd worn the previous day. The coat I could forgive. He had no money to replace it and besides, Howlett wouldn't see it. But his shirt was unchanged. His pants were several sizes too big, held up with an old belt. He was so thin he'd pierced extra holes in the leather. No tie. I had asked specifically for a tie.

"Mr. Hertzlich," I called. "Do us the honour of taking over this tutorial."

The boys simultaneously raised their heads, dogs catching a scent.

"We've got to go," said one.

"The bell's about to ring," said another.

I glared at them but Jakob gave only a shrug as they shuffled out. When the door closed after them he turned to me. "It's winter again." He blew on his red hands.

"A hat might help," I observed.

"So you keep saying."

"Not that you listen."

"I listen plenty," he said, glaring. "You've said yourself I never cover my ears."

Touché. I smiled but he wouldn't smile back. "Yes," I said. "Well today they're the colour of beets." He was moody today, perhaps because of the boys.

"You sound like my mother."

I laughed. Peevish or not, Jakob Hertzlich was refreshing. Especially after empty exchanges with my weaker students, such as the three who had just left. How dare they disdain him. It wasn't only that Jakob knew anatomy and pathology better than anyone on faculty or that he was so clever. It was that he was always himself. I could count on him for a straight answer.

He was on his knees now, rooting in the icebox near the window. Most mornings I brought buns and milk for him. I harboured vaguely maternal feelings not only for his ears but for his stomach as well.

"Slim pickings," he observed.

"I'm afraid I didn't buy milk. But there's no time for tea anyway." My sympathy was starting to erode.

He slammed the icebox shut. "When's he coming?"

So he hadn't forgotten. The failure to put on a tie and to fill his stomach this morning was not due to a lapse of memory. Jakob Hertzlich wasn't one to forget. He was one to let you know when he considered something a waste of time.

"Now," I said tersely. "I overslept so there's a lot of work to do, but first I've got to get to the lavatory."

"What time did you leave last night?" His voice was suspicious.

I didn't want to say because Jakob was sure to disapprove. He considered it unsafe for me to work unaccompanied in the building at night. He'd only left because I had promised that I would leave soon after him. To avoid answering I hurried away into the corridor, which at that moment was packed with students. McGill's medical school had grown so fast it had been forced up the stairs into what had once been my private wing. An adjacent storeroom had recently been converted into a laboratory.

It was kind of Jakob to worry about me. He was a good man, on the whole, who laboured without complaint for hours by my side, forgetting meals and sleep. He lost himself in the work, as did I. On the walls of the museum five of his drawings now hung. Over the winter I'd requested a series of anatomical illustrations, all paid for with Howlett's money. It gave me a means to ensure Jakob had sufficient funds.

I commissioned a drawing of the Howlett Heart, which Jakob had rendered beautifully. I had it framed. The piece now hung on my bedroom wall. I would have brought it that day for all to see but in my early morning scramble I'd forgotten.

I steadied my pocket watch, which was swinging in great arcs to match my stride. I had perhaps twenty minutes before Howlett was due to arrive. My knees were no longer bleeding but they needed a rinse, and my hair, which I'd pinned in haste at my flat, had unravelled. I felt disordered, unbalanced. My fall on the ice had been no accident. It was an expression of my inner state. Freud had published books on the subject in Vienna but I did not need to read them. I could write one myself about dark forces and compulsions. I was almost at the lavatory door when I saw him.

Time stopped. The nine-o'clock bell rang muffled and distant. The students faded into the background. It was like the films I sometimes went to see at the Salle Poirier, unfolding in silence. The roar of an ocean filled my ears.

"Dr. White!"

His voice was exactly as I remembered. But how short he was! This I had not recalled. When he came up beside me our eyes were practically level.

It had been six years but nothing about William Howlett had changed, even if he had moved to England and been knighted. He was fifty-six, an age at which most men turn old, but he was slender and quick, with eyes that seemed to devour every detail of the world around him.

He took my hand and lifted it. Was he going to kiss it? I looked around in panic. Medical students made fun of everything and a dowdy old girl like me being kissed in broad daylight would be great fodder. But Howlett had other things in mind. He scrutinized the tips of my fingers.

"Nicely healed."

He had remembered. He had not pushed me completely out of his mind.

"It's wonderful to be here," he said, gesturing at the hall. "The building hasn't changed one bit. Only now you are here to welcome me as your father once did."

For several seconds I couldn't speak. There it was. He'd had the courage to say it, to put it right there in the open. I looked around to see if anyone had heard.

"I ... we expected you later," I said stupidly. How awkward could I be? My first words to him made it sound as though he were not welcome. His face fell a little. "I'm sorry," I said. "You've caught me off guard. It's such a surprise after all these years, such a pleasure ... words can't express ... I've been looking so forward ..." Complete silliness. My stomach turned, my head spun. I steadied myself against the wall.

When we returned to the museum Jakob Hertzlich was sitting on top of the icebox, gnawing a heel of day-old bread. He did not stand when we entered, nor did he stop chewing. I could have thrown something at him. He looked far younger than his twenty-eight years with his surly, unshaven face.

"This is my assistant." I pronounced his name.

Jakob gave a curt nod and swallowed. He did not stand until I asked him to round up Mastro and Rivers and Dean Clarke, at which point he jumped off the icebox and, seizing another chunk of bread, moved to the door.

Howlett watched in silence. As the door closed he raised an eyebrow.

"A bit rough around the edges." I regretted the words as they came out. Jakob Hertzlich had told me that in one orthodox sect of his religion if you talked behind a person's back you had to seek that person out afterward and admit the transgression.

But Jakob was in the wrong here, wasn't he? He was often surly with people in the department, myself included. He did not know the meaning of good manners. How dare he subject Sir William Howlett of all people to such treatment?

My distinguished guest laid his coat and walking stick on a chair and began a tour of the museum, peering into my glass cabinets, which lined the room on all sides from floor to ceiling. As he gazed he stroked his moustache.

Dean Clarke was the first faculty member to arrive. He took Howlett's hand in both of his and shook it warmly. Dr. Mastro came next and shook Howlett's hand with great seriousness. He seemed nervous. Several times in the past week he'd dropped in on the museum to inquire about my preparations, fearing they wouldn't be sufficient. Dugald Rivers came in last, muttering apologies. "I thought we were convened for ten," he said, shooting me a dark and meaningful look, as though I'd plotted to keep Howlett all to myself. Howlett's warm greeting instantly improved his humour.

That morning we were five — Dean Clarke, Dr. Mastro, Dugald Rivers, Jakob Hertzlich and me. Five devotees, or rather four, as Jakob made it clear he was a conscript. I had primed him in the preceding weeks, recounting anecdotes and offering articles and texts, but it was obvious that these efforts of mine did not have the same effect as having worked or studied alongside the man. I had tried to convey Howlett's uniqueness but my descriptions had fallen on deaf ears. The previous day Jakob had stayed after hours to help me lay everything out: eighty-six specimens arranged by function with blank cards propped against them.

These were my mysteries, specimens that had so far eluded identification. I had managed to catalogue the bulk of Howlett's specimens but these eighty-six stymied me. From the table Howlett picked up a fat tome with a binding so old it left a rusty residue on his hands. It was one of his autopsy journals. I had thought he might want to see it.

He sighed, flipping through it. "It's like meeting an old friend." He reached for my hand. "The work this woman has accomplished," he said, gesturing at the shelves, "simply takes my breath away."

I couldn't move. His touch was a shock, stunning me momentarily as the praise surged through me.

Howlett took a pen from his breast pocket and uncapped it. "These, I trust," he said, pointing with the nib at the blank cards laid out so carefully by Jakob and me the night before, "are for me to scribble on?"

"If it's not too much trouble," I said with excitement. Dugald beamed a smile while Mastro moved in closer to see what the great man would write. We circled him like moons; each of us caught up in his magnetism, except for Jakob Hertzlich.

There was no time to think about anyone but Howlett. Although it had been twenty years since he'd laid eyes on these specimens he set to work. I had hoped he might identify the half of what I had laid out but in the end he managed seventy-three. He was a walking mine of information. Each jar he picked up and turned in silence. After a moment's pause there was an anecdote. The stories were fascinating medically, but also for the light they shed on Howlett's mind and personality. His powers of observation, his recall and his concentration were amazing. He displayed an endearing modesty as well.

"That fellow I remember well," he said, scribbling on the card propped against an aortic aneurysm. "There was no trace of clot, but strangely the aorta had ruptured into the right pleura. It took some time to diagnose. He kept complaining of fatigue. One day he came to the hospital with a pulsation in the second and third right interspaces, so I put him to bed and gave him potassium iodide. The dose: 120 grains a day. His pulsation vanished and I was about to discharge him in triumph when he died."

Jakob, who had been designated secretary, looked up from his notepad. I could see he was intrigued. This was vintage Howlett, admitting his own limits and the limits of the profession while at the same time suggesting that no one could have done more than he to save the patient. We all laughed. Jakob transcribed Howlett's comments and anecdotes.

Howlett turned to him. "Do you understand me when I speak of pulsations and interspaces?" he asked. "You see, of course, the aneurysm of the aorta?" Then he addressed me in my capacity of museum supervisor. "How much can I assume the scrivener knows?"

The tips of Jakob's ears turned red again, but this time not with cold. I cut in before he could say anything rude. "He has been trained in medicine. Here at McGill," I said a little defensively. "He knows exactly what is what."

The skin of Jakob's cheek had mottled. With his pink ears he appeared to be sunburned. He refused to look up from his note-book. For the duration of the session he sat this way, staring at his lap and smouldering. Howlett paid him no attention and seized instead a small, unlabelled specimen that had long bedevilled me. It looked like a healthy bit of thoracic aorta, but in its wall was a hole leading into a sac the size of a tangerine nestled up against the esophagus. "This," Howlett explained, "is an extraordinary case of mycotic aneurysm of the aorta, rupturing into the esophagus. She died without any warning at all." Howlett asked if I'd come across similar cases.

"Dr. Rivers supplied this just last week," I said, jumping up and retrieving a jar from a nearby shelf.

Howlett turned to him. "You'll report it, won't you? Resurrect mine at the same time and make a pair of them. I never wrote mine up. They'd make a first-rate article, don't you think?" He tossed the jar to Dugald, who caught it and grinned, so pleased he could do little more than nod his flustered head.

We proceeded item by item until just short of noon. One of the last items on the table was the Howlett Heart. Unlike the other specimens it had a typed card in front of it for Howlett had given me its full history six years ago.

He picked it up, smiling with recognition. "And this one, Agnes?

Your signature piece? What is it doing here among the mystery items? I've already supplied you with its story."

I smiled back at him. "And I thank you for that, Sir, for it started me on what has turned out to be a life's career. But there remains one issue concerning it that troubles me. It has to do with your autopsy journals, which I've been combing through to correlate with the collection."

I brought out the journal and opened it to the passage that had puzzled me. I had come across it a month previously and had been worrying about it ever since. Ordinarily I would have written to Howlett about it and cleared the matter up, but I had decided it could wait until we met in person. There was likely some perfectly good explanation that for some reason I couldn't figure out by myself.

I pointed at an entry from the autumn of 1872, a season that seemed to involve almost daily work at the Montreal Dead House for Howlett, who would have recently graduated from McGill. "This entry," I explained, "concerns the Howlett Heart. You say here that you did the work, Dr. Howlett, and that you worked alone. But I thought Dr. Bourret was responsible. You told me it yourself. I put it in my article."

Dr. Howlett pulled the journal closer. "That can't be right. There's a confusion of some kind." He scanned the entry.

"The description of the lesion fits," I said. "And the date. I'm certain it's the same heart."

"It is indeed," said Howlett, rereading the entry and frowning. "Of that there's no dispute." His face had gone quite serious, but then suddenly he laughed and looked at us. "I remember now. Something came up and there was doubt as to whether Dr. Bourret would be able to make it that day. He delegated the job to me as we were frequent collaborators. I thought I would be working alone but at the last minute he was able to attend."

"So it's a mistake," said Jakob, challenging him baldly. I cringed.

"That's right, old boy," Howlett said, smiling coldly. "It was a mistake. Being human I make them occasionally."

Jakob had a look in his eye I knew all too well. He stared straight at Howlett, his interest fully engaged. "But surely you wrote a report after the autopsy? By then you would have been aware who had presided."

I attempted to kick him under the table but my legs were too short. He had no sense of propriety. Not a grain. Jakob had degenerated our discussion to a court-room interrogation with our guest in the witness box. I turned away, wishing I had not introduced the issue.

Oxford's new regius professor of medicine was not, however, looking for a scrap. "Yes, well," he said, shrugging. "Mistakes happen, as I said, Mr. Hertzlich. It was an oversight."

"So you're saying that this fellow Bourret did the work?" persisted Jakob.

"Look here, Hertzlich," said Dr. Mastro. "I think he's made himself clear."

"Yes," I said, although I wasn't as certain as my intervention sounded. I too wanted an answer to Jakob's question despite its impertinence. "Mistakes happen. We all make them, Dr. Howlett. But your records are so meticulous. This is the first error of yours I believe I have come across."

I had meant this as a compliment to smooth the ruffled feathers but William Howlett did not take it this way. "*Mea culpa*, Dr. White," he said, refusing to look at me. "Now if you don't mind my proposing it we should move on."

The morning was not entirely ruined, but its tone had changed. I wasn't sure what to do. There were several more items to discuss, but the group's desire to look at them had evaporated.

William Howlett was the first to recover. He moved back from the table, loosening his tie, and began to talk about his days at McGill, nudging Dean Clarke for names or other details when his memory failed him. He had grown up in the province of Ontario and when he first arrived in Quebec he'd been shocked at how lawless the place was. "There were laws," he clarified, "but no one seemed to obey them." There was a law, for instance, decreeing that bodies unclaimed at death be sent to the medical faculties of Quebec universities. The Catholic Church wouldn't hear of the practice so there was a chronic shortage of cadavers for dissection. Some of the students became adept at body snatching, paying their way through medical school with the proceeds they collected for this service. Howlett told about tobogganing down Côte des Neiges Road from the Catholic cemetery one time in the dead of a winter's night, clutching a freshly exhumed corpse. On another occasion he agreed to present himself at Windsor Station to claim a stinking Saratoga trunk that had been shipped across the US border by rail. He also remembered the memorable night the medical faculty was searched by the Montreal police after bodies were reported missing from a nunnery. The corpses of the dead sisters were never found. Howlett and several other students had stuck them outside the medical building, which at the time had been on St. Urbain and Viger Streets, in a snowbank behind the nearby Theatre Royal.

Howlett was a gifted raconteur with a flair for adding just the right detail and soon I was laughing hard. But the stories gave me pause. This man I admired dearly had lifted corpses out of nunneries. He had been young, of course, probably encouraged by his peers, but my picture of him shifted that day, if only slightly. The mix-up over the Howlett Heart could not be put down to youthful exuberance. Something did not add up.

The magic of the morning was spent and I had only myself — and Jakob Hertzlich, my sorcerer's apprentice — to blame. Over in his corner Jakob waved his writing hand and winced. "Nearly fifty pages," he said to no one in particular. "I think I need a doctor."

We laughed uneasily. "We have to take care of this young man," I said with feeling. "Just look at what his hands can do."

Howlett was clearly finished with work for the time being, but I didn't want him checking his watch so I pointed at the drawings adorning the museum's walls.

"These are yours, Hertzlich?" asked Dr. Howlett.

Jakob's head was still lowered.

"I happen to be looking for someone like you," Howlett said. He turned to the rest of us. "I've received word from England. Our heart book is going into a second printing, Dr. White. Perhaps we could make use of Mr. Hertzlich's drawings as illustrations? Excellent exposure for him. We've just won a prize over in London, which they tell me is quite prestigious. That's something I wished to announce today."

I stopped breathing. The heart book, which bore my name right under Howlett's, was a prizewinner. He took me by the arms and looked me full in the face. "You are a laureate, my dear. I only wish I'd brought the laurel leaves with which to crown you!"

His hands remained on me for several seconds.

The prize was to be awarded by the London Pathological Society. "You must come to London in November for the ceremony," said Howlett. "We will accept the purse together." He told me I could stay with him and Lady Howlett up at Oxford, perhaps visit the London Museum of Pathology on a day trip and travel up to Edinburgh and meet curators there. Introductions would easily be arranged.

I nodded, agreeing to it all. The news swept away the morning's problems and confusions. Howlett's announcement and invitation so bowled me over that I could barely attend to anything, least of all my colleagues from McGill, who approached me with smiles small and forced. Dean Clarke looked genuinely pleased, but Rivers and Mastro both tried to conceal their envy. Mastro's face froze and Dugald coughed into his hand. I had neither the time nor the energy to look at Jakob and so failed to see him slip away. It was only when we'd moved collectively to the door to exchange goodbyes that I noticed he was gone. But by then there was even less time to think about it. Howlett was sticking his arm into his coat sleeve. Clarke was holding his walking stick, about to hand it over.

I couldn't let him leave. Seven years of waiting was too long to be offset by such a short visit. There was so much else I wanted to ask and hear. The promise of London beckoned for the autumn, but that was months away. I chattered aimlessly. At one point I even caught myself clutching his sleeve.

He took the walking stick from Dr. Clarke and adjusted his hat. "It's been enormous fun," he said, appraising each one of our eager faces. "And you," he said, taking my hand, not to examine this time but to kiss, "you've done a remarkable job here."

His eyes were on me. His lips were too, and at that moment I would have done just about anything to keep them there. Inspiration hit me.

"You'll come tomorrow," I said, surprising myself with my own forwardness. "I insist. You haven't heard about my teas, Dr. Howlett. They are not to be missed."

Dugald laughed. "She's famous for them. It's not an invitation to pass up lightly: high tea at the museum. You can pretend you're in England."

"We'll make a party," I said, excitement rising in me like a fever. "Everyone is welcome. How does four o'clock sound?" Dugald nodded immediately. Dean Clarke and Dr. Mastro were willing too.

Sir William Howlett reached out a gloved hand. "I'll see what I can do."

"I insist, Sir William," I said, my voice rising to something resembling a squeal.

He glanced at me. "My appointment book is full but I'll see what I can do."

"Four o'clock then?"

He bowed slightly, touched his cane to his hat, and was gone.

18

The next day I rose at dawn. Most of the night I had sat wrapped in a comforter drawing up lists of purchases, figuring out tasks and listening to the clock tick through the interminable passing of each hour.

At the moment, walking along the still damp street, a tote bag beneath one arm, I looked like a housewife, although perhaps more carefully dressed than some of the women I was passing. I'd taken pains with my hair, pinning it so tightly that even Laure would have been proud. Because the weather was good I didn't need to hide it with a hat. I'd put on fresh stockings as well — not silk like the ones I'd ruined the day before — but of good enough quality that they hugged my legs like a shiny new skin. My dress was green, punctuated with tiny wine-coloured buds. Laure and Miss Skerry had given it to me the previous Christmas, taking the pattern from a well-known Montreal couturier. It was the most fashionable item of clothing in my wardrobe. So fashionable in fact that I'd dared wear it only once before, on Christmas day in St. Andrews East, so the gift givers could see me model it. Miss Skerry must have done the lion's share of the handiwork. Laure's shifts of temper were such that these days it was hard to imagine her concentrating for long on a single project, but the dress was beautiful regardless of whose hand had made it. It made me feel almost beautiful.

St. Lawrence Boulevard was the first stop on my itinerary. Plenty of people were out already, crowding the muddy boardwalk. Just in front of me a boy sang out in a striking soprano, "*Herald*. Get your *Montreal Herald*!" A few steps on a man in a red sandwich board was competing with him, yelling about smoked fish.

I was part of this swirling, boisterous scene, swept up in the crowd energy. The sun was already high and I squinted up at it, feeling the warm rays touch my face. What a change from the day before. The ice had just about disappeared, exposing soggy squares of grass. In the gutters beside the wooden ramps the water ran freely.

At last I arrived at the fruit emporium. This was one of my favourite places to shop although I rarely made it down here. The size made me feel like a child. The first floor resembled that of a normal store, with barrels of apples and root vegetables harvested the previous autumn, but the real wonders lay below. I descended into the basement, a cavernous room with treasures imported from places so distant I knew them only as dots on maps. There were oranges, plums, and pineapples with spiky tops, picked green and carried north on ships in whose holds they slowly ripened.

What a sight for eyes dulled by six months of winter. What would it be like to live in a place where such extravagance existed year-round? The people living there probably didn't react at all to the sight of an orange in April. Maybe a certain degree of deprivation was necessary to the experience of pleasure, just as suffering was an integral part of joy.

The pineapples were right in front of me. I remembered the first time I'd eaten this fruit at the party Mrs. Drummond had thrown in my honour fifteen years ago. It had been like eating sunshine, taking that brightness right inside of me. I picked one up and sniffed.

The smell was faint but it was there: sunshine just under the skin.

I was not here for pineapples, however; the fruit I wanted wasn't available so early in the year. On a big table in the corner I found what I was looking for — jars of bright strawberries boiled in sugar and pectin to last through the winter. It was a poor substitute for the fresh fruit but it was the best I could do. On my way to the cash register I spotted cucumbers and slipped a couple into my bag.

After this I visited the cheese shop and bought a round of brie. Quebec was one of the few places in North America where you could buy good soft cheeses. Settlers from Breton and Normandy started making them here in the seventeenth and eighteenth centuries, educating palettes like mine in the English and Scottish communities. The cheese I bought that day cost me half a week's wages, but the man assured me it was ripe and of a fine quality. It came in a wooden case, which was a blessing as I still had several errands to run and didn't want to squash it. Next I visited the patisserie and finally the wine shop, empty at this hour of the day. I was ashamed to be seen there — a woman alone — but the clerk was respectful enough. He owed me that at the very least because I was buying a magnum of his very best champagne, thereby completely draining my coffers.

By the time I made it to campus, tote bag straining at the seams, the noon bells were ringing and the sun was high. I would have to air myself out and re-pin my hair before the party, but it was good to be out of doors at this hour. Usually I was shut away at work with my catalogues. I had forgotten what a rich, sensual world existed outside the museum's walls.

The main lawn on campus was newly melted. I breathed in the smell of mud and chlorophyll and excrement, decay that would feed the first delicate green shoots. I felt my entire self opening to the sun just like the plant life pushing through the steaming earth. Ahead of me a boy and a girl walked side by side. They were not lovers — I could tell from the way the girl stiffened when the boy's arm touched hers. He kept brushing her as if by accident when they both knew it was deliberate. The girl laughed while the sun poured down like honey, anointing us all.

My hands were too full to search for my key; luckily the door to the museum was ajar. I barrelled in, carrying the smell of outdoors with me and tracking mud. The air was so foul I almost walked right out again. Jakob Hertzlich was at the table, blowing smoke rings. I watched as one detached from him and wobbled up over his head like a lopsided halo.

"Good morning," I said to let him know I had arrived.

There was a pause but he did not look up or rise. "Afternoon if I'm not mistaken."

"Good afternoon then." He was always so punctilious! In his work for me I appreciated it, but at the moment it made me want to scream. "What do you think you're doing?" I asked, nodding my chin at the smoke.

"Working," he said, deliberately misconstruing.

I dropped my bags. "And the implication is that I am not?"

"No implication." He looked up at last, squinting through the haze. "You know what you're up to. Far be it from me to judge."

"Precisely," I said. I waved my hands, making ripples in the air. "What is the meaning of this?"

"You weren't here. I didn't think it mattered."

I groaned and went over to the windows. Opening them was tricky. At one end of the pole was a metal clip one had to fasten to a ring at the top of each window pane. It made me think of a harpoon as it wavered unsteadily in my hands. I was short, that was the problem. If I were a foot taller the task would have been easy. As it was the pole wobbled this way and that, grazing the ring on occasion, but never coming close to real connection.

Jakob did not offer to help. Not that he was doing anything else of value. He was finishing his cigarette. I laid down the pole and stripped off my coat. Sweat beaded on my lip. I could taste the salt, smell the rankness of my own frustration. I went after that window as if my life depended on it, as if the world would end if I were unable to open it.

The concentration demanded by the task calmed me. Work tended to affect me this way. It was like a meditation, a path to still waters. The hook caught and I pulled hard, up and back. The experience was much like fishing: the stretches of silence, the excitement as the rod's tip bobbed and jerked. The pane slammed down, stopped only by two chains nailed into the topmost ledge, bouncing three times before it settled. The air rushed in. The clean green smells of spring. For the first time since my arrival I took a deep breath.

"I gave the tutorial this morning."

That stopped me short. "Oh Lord," I said. My best student came on Fridays. A Jewish boy like Jakob. His name was Segall. It was believed he'd win the physiology prize that year. "I completely forgot. Was he upset?"

Jakob gave a snort of laughter. "No. Worried, if you must know. You're never late."

"I had to go to the shops. I've bought preserves, cheese, bread and champagne."

Jakob stared blankly and it was only then I understood. He had not been present when I'd announced the party for Howlett. He had already left the museum.

"We're having a party," I said quickly.

"You and I?"

I had to restrain myself from shaking him. "Don't be stupid," I snapped. "It's for Howlett."

Jakob returned to his work. His shirt, I couldn't help noticing, was the same one he'd worn the day before, and the day before that. He hadn't shaved or combed his hair. "You can leave that, Mr. Hertzlich," I said, pushing the specimens out of his reach and shoving his notes to the side. "We must clean up."

"I'm not a proud man," he said, swivelling to face me, "but making parties for windbags wasn't one of the requisites when I signed on." He retrieved his notes, went to my desk and sat down.

I took out my pocket watch. It was almost one and I didn't have time. If Jakob Hertzlich wouldn't help, so be it. I would remember his insolence, perhaps even speak to Dean Clarke about it, but the choice was his.

I transferred the jars in the process of being labelled to nearby shelves. I wasn't particularly orderly about it. There simply wasn't time. After the party we would retrieve them and restart the labelling process, but for now I needed them out of the way. I had to wipe the table down. It was stained and reeked of chemicals, highly unappetizing no matter how accustomed Howlett was to such things. Bad enough that he would be surrounded by excised organs as he nibbled and drank.

From one of my bags I pulled a folded bed sheet that I planned to use as a tablecloth. There was no embroidery or lace trim at the corners, but it was clean and starched and would be an improvement over the stained, nicked wood of the work table. The fit was perfect and the room grew suddenly more formal.

Jakob watched me sidelong, and at one point as I swept with a broom in the vicinity of his feet he addressed me. "It's not worth it."

I kept on sweeping. I was wearing a lab coat to protect my dress, but it did little to protect my feelings. It was humiliating to be working like a maid, breathing in dust while Jakob sat in my chair, looking on. I was his superior for heaven's sake. This would not have happened if I'd been a man.

"You'll exhaust yourself."

I could not believe his gall. I had been working for over an hour and he'd not lifted a finger. "I'd tire myself less if you'd help."

Jakob barely flinched. "Why are you going to all this trouble?"

"Your salary depends on him for one thing," I reminded him. "Much of mine does too."

Jakob snorted again. "So it's money? Is that what this is all about?"

I threw down the broom, scattering dirt and debris. "Of course not! He's a good man, Jakob. He's been generous to us, can't you see? He's backed me with his own money when no one else would offer me a dime. He's helped me publish. If it weren't for him I wouldn't have won that prize."

"You're wrong there."

I closed my eyes and counted. Jakob was like the male version of the girl in the nursery rhyme with the curl in the middle of her forehead. *When he was good, he was very, very good. But when he was bad, he was horrid.*

"He doesn't deserve the pedestal, Agnes." He made a face then rooted in his pocket and pulled out the half-smoked stub of another cigarette.

"Don't you dare."

Fortunately he didn't have a match. He contemplated it, turning it slowly in his fingers before addressing me again. "You're behaving like a child, Agnes. And it's not right. You'll be hurt in the end." He didn't look at me but twisted the stub so tightly that the paper tore. "You don't see it but it will happen. He doesn't care. Not about you and certainly not about this." He flung his arm at the room, now vastly improved from an hour's frantic sweeping and tidying.

"There's only one thing Dr. William E. Howlett cares about," said Jakob, spitting out each syllable of Howlett's name, "and that's William E. Howlett."

"That's enough," I said. All the happiness and energy I'd felt earlier that morning was leaking away. My head felt achy and tight.

But Jakob Hertzlich wasn't quite done. "Until yesterday I thought what we were doing here was worthwhile. This museum I mean. I didn't mind putting in the hours because we were serving people who were learning about medicine and disease. They need to see the organs and tissues first-hand so they'll be able to recognize them in their clinical practices. We're serving science, *ars medica* and all that edifying bunk. That's what I used to think.

"But now I see things more clearly. We're not serving science here, are we? We're serving William E. Howlett and his puffed bladder of an ego. This museum is his monument, isn't it? No wonder he sends money your way. They'll name it after him when he dies. There'll be no mention of Agnes White, you can be sure of that."

I stared at the scraps at my feet. My silence seemed to enrage Jakob, who slammed his hand on my desk. "And you're so ready to play his game. Open your eyes! Can't you see that everything he helps you with helps him? It's his career he's building, not yours, Agnes. Has he got you so mesmerized you've gone blind?"

In a quieter voice he announced that he needed a smoke. "Not here, don't worry. I won't disturb your preparations." He took up his coat and walked out.

As soon as he was gone I collapsed into the chair he'd just vacated — my chair, which happened still to be warm from him. His very particular smell — a mixture of cigarettes and the yeasty smell of his skin — lingered in the air. I couldn't think of what he'd said, couldn't bring myself to contemplate it.

Howlett did care, I told myself. He was looking out for me. Jakob Hertzlich was jealous, that was all. He was a bitter man with blighted prospects and I would have to be more circumspect with him in the future. I would discuss the matter with Dean Clarke. I hadn't feared Jakob during the confrontation but I'd been taken aback by the force of his anger.

Jakob knew nothing of the link between me and Howlett. All he saw was my adulation, which probably seemed pathetic, just as Rivers's did to me, watching from the outside. But Jakob had no idea that my father stood like a shadow behind Howlett whenever he and I met. I couldn't blame Jakob for this ignorance but the anger he'd shown was entirely unnecessary.

I was slicing cucumbers for sandwiches when Mrs. Greaves materialized in the doorway. Mrs. Greaves was the dean's secretary, a formidable woman whose blue-tinted hair was drawn back tightly from her forehead. The blue head rotated slowly, taking in the swept floor, the white cloth, the food laid out in an attempt to turn the museum into a banquet hall. When finally her eyes came to rest on me she gave a grim smile. "A call just came through for you, Miss White," she said.

Howlett had telephoned. The portrait sitting was taking longer than foreseen. High tea would have to be postponed until November at Oxford. He hoped there was no inconvenience. All of this was delivered in Mrs. Greaves's toneless voice. When she finished her lips flattened into a straight line. "Looks like there has been inconvenience," she said, tilting her head at the table. "What a lovely spread."

I couldn't speak.

"Do you want some help putting things away?" Mrs. Greaves offered, seeing how upset I was.

I shook my head and moved to my desk where I unbuttoned my lab coat. I did not look up again and at some point she took the hint and left. Half an hour later I was still sitting at my desk, chin propped on one palm. There were papers in front of me — Jakob Hertzlich's papers — so anyone who glanced in the door might think I was working. But my mind wouldn't focus. I was simply staring at the white sheets and the contrast they made with my green felt desk pad. My body felt almost numb.

Dugald Rivers stuck his head in the doorway. "I bumped into Greaves," he said quietly. "It's a shame about the party." His eyes made a tour of the room and returned to me. "Look at the trouble you went to, dear Agnes!"

To my intense annoyance my chin began to quiver.

"There, there," said Dugald, standing awkwardly beside me, his eyes big with sympathy.

"I'm sorry," I said, drying my eyes on my new dress. "It's not important, really."

He gave me an awkward pat on the back. His face was flushed and shiny. "It is," he said, his voice mounting even higher than normal with the difficulty of this intimacy. "Believe me, Agnes, I understand."

I nodded and pointed at the platter of sandwiches. "You want them?"

Dugald sniffed appreciatively. "Cucumber?"

I nodded again with more assurance. "Take them, Dugald. Please."

My reward was a peck on the cheek. "Stiff upper lip, White. You'll survive." He made off down the hall, the platter on his flattened, upturned palms.

After he had gone I began to sort through Jakob's notes. He'd done a considerable amount of work while I'd been navigating the fruit stands and I decided to pick up from where he had left off, copying Howlett's notes onto cards, which Jakob would eventually type for the catalogue. It was painstaking work, not creative in any way, but utterly consuming — exactly the antidote I needed. I barely noticed when the bell in the hall rang at three o'clock, then at four and again at five, the hour Jakob Hertzlich chose to return.

"I heard," he said simply, taking a sheaf of foolscap from my desk so that he too might help transpose. His tone was no longer hostile. "Too bad."

I said nothing. The work was carrying me and I didn't dare stop. I could not face further comments from Jakob. I kept scribbling and sorting, creating order out of the mess in front of me. It kept me from thinking and, most importantly, from feeling. Every so often I let out a sigh.

Jakob shut the window and turned on more lights. I realized I'd been working in near darkness. Outside I could see the wavering reflection of a gas jet. The building was silent. Not a single step echoed in the hallway. After a considerable time a bell rang, making me start. I pulled out my pocket watch and saw to my astonishment that it was eight o'clock.

Jakob had sat down at the table again and taken up his pen. His eyes were on his pages but I had a feeling he wasn't reading. His skin looked yellow in the glare from the overhead light and there were dark smudges under both his eyes. His shirt was so big I couldn't make out the contours of the body inside it. He probably hadn't eaten today but had smoked those damned cigarettes.

"What do you say to some food?"

He watched neutrally as I unwrapped the cheese and crackers. There were no plates but we used the starched linen napkins inherited from my grandmother. Jakob spread his out to its full size on the table and began stacking.

We did not speak. I hadn't eaten that day, not even breakfast as I'd left the flat so early. The inside of the brie flowed out the moment Jakob pierced the rind with his knife. We scooped spoonfuls onto crackers and ate them down. After his fourth or fifth cracker Jakob paused, scanned the room and went over to the sink. He didn't even ask, just pulled the bottle from the pail of mostly melted ice and unscrewed its wire top. Seconds later the cork sailed over our heads, smacking the wall above the door, rustling the streamers of decorative crepe I'd tacked there as it dropped to the floor. There was a spout of froth and I ran to him with teacups.

"Cheers," he said, spilling some of the champagne. "It's a little more lively than tea."

I raised my cup and we clinked. Jakob Hertzlich had never drunk champagne before. He told me this later, after we'd eaten our fill of cheese and preserves and imported crackers. Jakob Hertzlich had never drunk anything alcoholic, he confessed. Jews didn't as a rule, except for the wine they served on the Sabbath. That sickly sweet stuff could turn a person off spirits for life. "But this," he said, raising his teacup dramatically, "is the stuff of life."

I had drunk it only once before myself, and then barely a sip, when Dean Clarke had invited me to his home on New Year's Eve for a party. All I remembered were bubbles going up my nose and making me itch. I jiggled my cup, creating a golden maelstrom. The taste was so light it didn't seem of this world. I poured us a second round.

Jakob told his story, which stretched back to include tales of his father Otto Hertzlich and his mother Craina. "We lived in Berlin," Jakob explained, "where the Hertzlichs had been in the tobacco trade for several generations. My father manufactured fine cigars and sold them throughout the Continent. He was a big success, but then something happened."

Jakob was not entirely clear on the details but somehow Otto Hertzlich had lost a great deal of money and creditors began hounding him. "I was only three at the time," said Jakob. "I remember leaving our house in the middle of the night, sneaking away down to the docks like thieves so that we could board a ship. On the way down there someone recognized us. My first real memory is of a man running toward our cab in a dark Berlin street, his face blazing with anger, shouting insults."

I was engrossed by the tale. Many immigrants had stories like this tucked away in their trunks in the attic — stories of leaving the old country, usually in haste and physical danger. It informed the people who lived here, made them perhaps a little hardier than elsewhere and certainly more appreciative.

From the very start Otto Hertzlich had loved his new home. The land on the south shore of the St. Lawrence River was ideal for tobacco farming, and with Montreal's port and a burgeoning population he knew he had stumbled onto a very good thing.

"My father is a clever man, Agnes. He learned English quickly, even if he never completely got the accent down. He's charming. He uses old-world expressions and kisses women's hands. He was never entirely accepted by the Montreal elite, but he certainly was noticed. My mother too. She was beautiful, dark and petite. My parents," Jakob concluded, pausing for a sip of champagne, "had everything in their new life that a young couple could wish for." He put his cup on the table and looked at me. "Everything, that is, except a suitable son."

I didn't know what to say. This was clearly painful but it was equally clear he wished to talk. All I could do was listen.

"When I was born my father had counted on a son like himself, someone to follow in his footsteps, to take over the business when he grew old. I was a timid child and a dreamer. My father and I were very different in temperament. He and Craina tried to have more children but for some reason they couldn't. When I was seven or eight my father turned his attentions fully on me.

"I suppose I ought to treat it as a compliment. He refused to give up hope that I could become what he envisioned. But the hope had very little to do with who I was. My father was a businessman, Agnes, and if his work had taught him anything it was that obstinacy paid off. He made me work summers at the factory, trying to inculcate some sort of practical sense in me. He paid for boxing lessons. Boxing lessons, Agnes! Can you imagine me in a ring? I must have looked like a character from the funny papers with those gloves hanging from my wrists. When all of this failed, as was inevitable, he pushed me to study science. Medicine was a field in which a Jew might get ahead, just as my father had in business."

As it turned out medicine was a profession Jakob Hertzlich could handle. Despite the quotas for Jews at McGill he was accepted into the faculty. He worked hard, winning prizes and the respect of all his teachers. He fulfilled his father's expectations to the letter, but no matter how hard he worked, no matter how many plaques or specially bound books he accumulated, Otto Hertzlich was not satisfied.

"One morning I woke up," said Jakob. "It was as if a blind inside me suddenly snapped open. My father would never be pleased." He took another sip of champagne. "That day I slept in, and the day after. A doctor came and prescribed sedatives and told my parents how the strain of study might be too much for a boy as delicate as I. My mother believed it was a breakdown. My father, obstinacy. But I," said Jakob with a measure of pride, "know it as the day I finally woke up. The day my life began."

I could not imagine giving up medicine, especially when one had been accepted at McGill. "You would have made a brilliant doctor. You were almost through."

Jakob Hertzlich laughed, draining the drops from his cup. "It wasn't the path I was supposed to be on," he said quietly. "I rather think it's for the best, even if others don't see it that way. I wouldn't have ended up where I am today." He was staring at me with intensity, his face suddenly serious. "And you, Dr. White? What stories do you hide under that cloak of efficiency? You owe me one."

"I'm a terrible storyteller."

Jakob's mouth pulled down in neat folds and I had to laugh. The champagne was making us both silly. I placed the teacup on the table, moving with exaggerated care as I no longer quite trusted my hands.

"There's no story of a father or a mother?" he persisted.

I shook my head. "I am an orphan."

"There's drama in that, surely!" Jakob exclaimed. "Tell me the story of a parentless child." He was leaning forward, eyes gleaming.

Before I knew it I was spilling secrets. Not spilling, exactly, but releasing them one by one as champagne releases its bubbles. I found myself talking about my father, how he had been a doctor, brilliant by all accounts. I did not say where he had worked, nor did I give away his name. I described his departure when I was very small. I told Jakob about my mother, who had died of grief and pulmonary tuberculosis soon after the abandonment; and about my sister, who was physically beautiful but frail. Jakob's face was so close that I could smell his breath — sweet and at the same time sour from the wine. A bead of champagne clung to a bristle on his lip and I had an impulse to stick out my tongue and lick it clean. The thought vaguely horrified me. I realized I was drunk.

In my mind's eye was another face with bristles on its upper lip — my father's face, with his mouth pulled down by sadness. It was so close, so real, that I reached out and pulled it toward me. Part of me knew that it was not my father. Part of me knew this could not be but still I pulled the scruffy head toward me.

Jakob was unsurprised. That was what woke me up. His eyes remained cool, watching mine until finally I stopped his scrutiny by kissing him on the mouth. His lips were as sweet and sour as his breath had been, but also comforting in a way I would not have suspected from looking at him. Our lips remained together. My eyes stayed closed and there was a sudden surge, like electricity.

But then it changed. My eyes sprang open as I felt the thrust of his tongue in my mouth. I stepped back but he stepped with me, his mouth still on mine. His eyes were closed now as if he were asleep, yet his tongue probed, and suddenly I was afraid. Is this what people did? He was like a fish trying to swim inside me. I clamped down and pushed him off.

I stood there, weaving my fingers in embarrassment, unable to look at him. "I'm sorry."

"Don't be." He reached for me and this time I didn't resist. I hadn't been touched, I realized, not ever. I'd been starving and never known it until that day. The champagne I had bought for Howlett sang in my veins. Jakob's hand moved up beneath my dress, beneath the bodice, fumbling with the complex, interlocking system of buttons and hooks.

To my astonishment I felt no shame. I had spent a lifetime regretting my stubby body, hiding it away beneath dissimulating layers, but I no longer cared. I helped him release the hooks. His fingers closed around a nipple and it was as if he had opened a switch. Swept away was my awareness of the hand, of the face bending over me, and of any regrets I might have in the future.

19

Despite the title given him by the British king Sir William Howlett was not a real Englishman. His house in Oxford attested to the fact. He had installed central heating, a luxury unheard of in even the wealthiest neighbourhoods of London, let alone a university town. Since the afternoon three days back when I had descended the ship's gangplank and touched solid land I had not been warm. Not once in three days. A permanent frigid cloud seemed to have settled over England. Sir William said it would not budge for at least four months so he and Lady Kitty might as well accommodate themselves.

I had been staying at an inn because the day my ship docked Sir William's house had been full. Lady Kitty's brother and his family were visiting from Boston. Sir William had shown his customary grace about the inconvenience, choosing a hotel for me, picking up the tab and even sending a maid to inquire whether the rooms were adequate. I really hadn't anything to complain about. But the inn was damp, my sheets as slippery and as cold as ice. The coal fire lit every even-ing by a servant gave off much smoke but little warmth.

This was winter in England. I caught a head cold. I had felt it coming on right after my first night in the slippery sheets. At Sir William's home, however, it was warm. I dropped my valise in the hallway and a manservant carried it away to an upper storey. I hugged my arms and shivered with pleasure.

"Welcome to Open Arms," Sir William said with a smile, flinging his own arms out.

I had noticed the sign on his lawn cut in the shape of a shield with those two words, "Open Arms," painted ornately. Clever mockery. Every second home in Oxford had the word "arms" appended to it. Pickwick Arms, Fenwood Arms. The town seemed overrun with them. In his not-quite British way Sir William Howlett had joined the trend.

The great man hung my coat in the closet himself then led me to the room that had been allotted to me. Open Arms was even bigger than his house in Baltimore. The ceilings were higher and the rooms more spacious. I glimpsed Lady Kitty in the dining room as we passed it, giving orders to a servant.

"She's preparing," said Sir William. "Otherwise she would come and greet you. You know how women get with their parties." Howlett sometimes addressed me like this, as if I was not quite one of the female race and it confused me. On the one hand I appreciated the implicit inclusion in the masculine circle but on the other I felt a slight sting of insult. I was a woman after all. Was it so difficult to see?

The staircase wound upwards in a graceful spiral with a polished oak banister. Up its middle was a carpet with a delicate rosebud motif. On the first landing, gathered on a wide, low window seat, were the dolls. I recognized the one with the fan, though she was now dressed differently and her face was greyer than I remembered. Sir William passed the display without a word. He didn't seem embarrassed or shy. These were his wife's dolls. Judge Lady Kitty if I must, but leave him out of it.

My room was one of the smaller ones. It had a bed, a chair, a small table; but it was lined with bookcases. The name Open Arms was appropriate; the house welcomed many visitors. Lady Kitty's brother had left but Sir William's publisher from London had just arrived, as well as a former colleague from Johns Hopkins. They too were staying at the house, likely in rooms more lavish than the one offered to me. Not that I minded. My little corner was welcoming and warm. My bones had finally begun to thaw. I told Sir William I couldn't have been happier.

He went over the day's itinerary with me. The prize-giving ceremony would take place that afternoon at two, after which we would return to the house for a tea prepared in our honour by Lady Kitty. I thanked him and then began examining the bookshelves. Most of his library was medical. My room, Sir William explained, was a storage space for the overflow from his office. He gestured to the shelves. "Help yourself, Agnes. Take whatever suits you. But if I were you I'd save some time for resting. The day ahead will be quite long."

As it turned out "long" was an understatement. I'd had my rest in the upstairs room at Open Arms; Sir William and I had attended the prize-giving; and now I was standing beside Lady Kitty's mahogany table, the very same one at which I had sat in Baltimore while Revere hid underneath and filched my heart.

The prize-giving ceremony had been like a dream. Sir William and I mounted the stage arm in arm in one of Oxford's churches, and everyone stood and clapped. He took the envelope with the cheque, but this was as it should be. I knew he wouldn't deny me my proper share. Some of the funds would eventually wend their way to me. After the ceremony I was surrounded by crowds. The press had been alerted along with a host of British physicians and academics. Everyone, it appeared, was intrigued that I was not a man. The newspapers took my photograph. Half a dozen reporters requested interviews. By the time we left for Open Arms I was trembling with exhaustion. A combination of travel fatigue, nerves and a nasty British microbe were threatening to topple me.

The table was covered with doilies. Atop these were three-tiered plates with pastries in pastel shades: ballerina pink, lime green, sunshine yellow. There were also party sandwiches — neat triangles stuffed with creamed cheese or egg. I was drinking tea, holding the cup near my chin so as not to spill. My throat was hot, but not from the tea. My cheeks glowed with a low-grade fever.

"Who is the mystery man hiding away in your museum?" The man who had published our textbook peered at me through spectacles so thick they gave his eyes a bulging, fishy look.

I took a sip of tea. He was referring to Jakob Hertzlich, the last person I wanted to talk about at that moment.

"His work is terrific. You must bring him with you the next time you cross."

I continued to sip resolutely.

"He's too gifted to be working as a technician, if you don't mind my saying so. If he were in London I'd steal him away."

I produced a tight smile. Perhaps that was the solution. Back in Montreal things had reached a point of almost unbearable tension. The publisher, whose name I couldn't recall, had no idea what a sensitive spot he'd just touched. For seven months now, ever since the aborted tea party in April, there had been tension between Jakob and me. I had committed a huge blunder in becoming intimate with Jakob and there seemed no way to fix it. Of course he was doing nothing himself to help the situation.

The morning after our encounter we hardly spoke. But then, as he'd realized there would be no further intimacies, Jakob dropped all pretence of politeness. He'd been surly all autumn, to me and to everyone else at the faculty. My strategy at the moment was avoidance, which wasn't easy in our cramped working quarters. We had divided the specimens for cataloguing and were currently working in opposite corners of the room. Neither of us addressed the other unless it was absolutely necessary. We were like monks toiling on parallel tasks, scrupulously observing vows of silence.

My strategy worked for a while, but just before my trip overseas he'd turned vicious, declaring me to be the blindest woman he'd ever met and implying I was nothing more than Howlett's lackey.

There had been no time for reprimands, but I'd left the museum and the country with my mind made up. When I returned I would inform Dean Clarke that Mr. Hertzlich had to go.

"Sweet?" The publisher was pointing at the pastries.

If I refused I risked more of his talk so I took one. The icing was as hard and smooth as plaster. Sugar pearls dotted its surface. I had never seen anything quite like it.

A persistent tinkle became audible and the doctors, publishers, journalists and Oxford professors all turned to its source, the noise of their conversation declining. Sir William was tapping an empty champagne glass with a spoon. As soon as the room settled he put the glass down on the table and filled it.

"A toast, ladies and gentlemen," he said solemnly, holding up the frothing drink. The "ladies" was a bit much. Apart from Kitty, several maids and me the party was entirely male. Sir William walked over to me and to the astonishment of everyone in the room, myself included, handed me the glass. I blushed. I never wanted to taste that drink again, least of all in a crowd.

"You deserve it!" he cried, even though I was shaking my head in confusion. Women didn't drink. If I took the glass it might be the end of my already rather tenuous reputation.

"When your work is as good as a man's, Dr. White, you must accept the privileges that accrue to us."

There was a burst of laughter followed by applause. The men in the crowd had been drinking since the party began and probably would have cheered at anything he had said. Sir William raised my hand in the air so the glass was visible to everyone present. "To our partnership," he said. Turning my way and looking me straight in the eye he lowered the glass and took a sip. Then he offered it to me.

I had no choice. His dark eyes willed it. It was his party. His champagne. His toast. As I raised the glass the room went silent. And then there was a cheer. The taste was exactly as I remembered: sweet and sour, with bubbles that seemed to grab hold of my nasal hairs. Jakob Hertzlich's face floated into my mind, sneering and melancholy, and for a fraction of a second, before I could shut off the thoughts, his hands were on me, moving beneath my clothes.

Sir William took my glass back and drained it in one swallow. The spell was broken and I was back in the real world, in a place called Open Arms with all these people wishing me well. I gazed gratefully at my benefactor, stepped closer to thank him for the toast and promptly collapsed into his arms.

When I opened my eyes I was in bed in an unfamiliar room. There was little light but it was surprisingly warm. The sheets and bedding were thick.

"'The maid is not dead, but sleepeth ...'"

I turned my head to the left. Sir William was sitting in an armchair, hands folded, watching me. I tried to sit up but my head began to pound.

"You'd best remain horizontal," Sir William said, getting up and placing a cool, dry hand on my forehead.

I covered it with both of my own hands and lay back, shutting my eyes.

"There, there," he said. "You'll be all right."

My last moments of consciousness were returning. The toast and the champagne. "I fainted," I said, horrified.

"It seems to be a regular occurrence with you." His tone was strictly professional.

I shook my head, which made me feel more dizzy and sick.

"If I were you," Sir William cautioned, "I'd limit movement. You've a fever of a hundred and two." He dipped a cloth in water and placed it on my burning skin. "Is it only around me that you swoon, Dr. White?"

"I am so sorry," I said sniffling. The cloth felt good.

"There, there," he said again. His hand was on my shoulder. "You're going to be fine, Agnes. You're in good hands."

I smiled and nodded. Even nodding hurt. I was such a hopeless case. Fainting at a party in my own honour. And this wasn't the first time Sir William had been forced to tend to me. I wondered fleetingly what Freud would have said. Hysteria. Unacknowledged yearning for love. Not entirely unacknowledged I thought wryly. I looked up at him from under heavy lids. Sir William was still bending over me. I liked the warmth of his hand, but then I realized that my dress was gone. All I had on was a shift. Had Sir William undressed me? I half hoped so. I felt strangely unalarmed, probably because I was so drowsy. My eyes closed and I drifted to sleep.

When I awoke again it was still dark and the house was silent except for the occasional metal bang of a radiator. My head was clear and free of pain now and my feet were blissfully warm. I reached beneath the flannel sheets and touched them. Such comfort this place called Open Arms could bring. My pocket watch glinted on the little table beside the bed. Sir William had electric lighting, which was a good thing because I had no matches. I flicked on the lamp and the room illuminated, bringing all of his bookshelves into relief.

It was four thirty a.m. Too late to sleep any more, but too early to get up and start the day. I rose unsteadily and padded to the shelves at the foot of my bed. There were books on anatomy and physiology and pathology. Half a shelf was occupied alone by copies of the textbook we had written. My eye snagged on a title one shelf higher. *The Sexual Life of Our Time*. I had to stand on my toes to reach it. It was a thick book bound in a black cloth cover published in the 1880s, translated from the German. The author was a Viennese physician, Iwan Bloch.

I had read manuals on intimate relations before. The one used most widely in Canada was *Light on Dark Corners*, which had a lantern on its cover glimmering against a shadowy background. Despite the title and suggestive artwork it divulged little about sex, focusing more on proper attitudes and comportment for Victorian women when they were in mixed company.

The Sexual Life of our Time was different. Its thickness and serious scientific tone promised more substance. I carried it to the bed and thumbed through the pages to the chapter on virginity. Ever since my encounter with Jakob Hertzlich in April a question had been nagging at me. Jakob Hertzlich had not ventured inside my skirts. His hands had remained firmly on my breasts, but his restraint had made little difference. I'd had an orgasm in his arms. I had recognized it at once.

It astounded me that this could happen without genital contact. His hips had remained a chaste distance from my own. It was just the fingers on my breast, and yet it had happened. He must have realized when I slumped against him.

To his credit he had not taken advantage, even though at one point after my slump I'd felt the hard length of him pressing from inside his trousers. What I wished to know were the implications. We certainly hadn't been intimate in the usual sense. Yet I had surrendered. Did that count? Did I still qualify, at least technically, as a virgin? Bloch was mute on the subject. For this expert from Vienna sex was synonymous with penetration. Nowhere was the possibility raised that a woman might find release simply through the stimulation of a nipple.

The chapter after "Virginity" was "Auto-eroticism." Here the pages fell open easily. Howlett seemed to have consulted them a few times. What I read here also came as a relief. Touching oneself, which Grandmother had once hinted could damage the brain, was not dangerous after all. "In healthy persons," Bloch wrote, "moderate masturbation has no bad results at all." Bloch described how self-arousal was widespread in the animal kingdom. Monkeys in the zoological gardens masturbated freely, "*coram publico*." Horses shook their members to and fro until seminal emission occurred and mares rubbed themselves "against any available firm object." The mares comforted me somewhat. Bloch said the same had been observed in wild deer and in elephants. If it was this common, I decided, it could not be bad.

The big book was weighing on my chest so I got up again and replaced it on the shelf. I was almost certainly still a virgin. I must be one of a very select group of women to be sexually experienced yet chaste. A vision of Miss Skerry lying alone in her little room off the Priory kitchen came to me then. Perhaps she was a sister in this respect. My eyelids began to grow heavy and I undid the top two hooks of my shift. It was a lonely business this auto-eroticism. Lonely and lovely. My fingers closed on my nipple, exactly as Jakob Hertzlich's had done that night in the museum seven months ago.

V
FIRE

Sometimes a very small hole may be
accompanied by a very loud murmur.

— MAUDE ABBOTT, "CONGENITAL CARDIAC DISEASE"

20

DECEMBER 1905

I could smell burning all the way from my rooms on Union Street to the McGill campus. It was December, three weeks since I had last set foot in Montreal, a short enough period by any standards but long enough to decimate a life. My ship had docked at two o'clock that afternoon, but it had taken a maddening amount of time for the passengers to disembark. By the time I made it to the pier it was past three and daylight was fading. I'd gone straight to my apartment building, dropped my bags and dashed out the door again.

I spent the entire return trip sequestered in my cabin worrying. I had no idea what I would find when I reached the museum. Jakob Hertzlich had telegraphed me the day it happened, although he hadn't divulged any detail. "Fire at faculty" was all the telegraph had said. "Come home at once." That was it. His name had appeared in bold typeface at the bottom of the sheet.

I had telegraphed Dean Clarke immediately to ask if anyone had been hurt. His negative reply was the one piece of heartening news. The fire had struck at night when the building was empty. Faculty and staff were all fine. The only casualty seemed to be the janitor's cat. On the subject of the museum, however, Clarke had been as restrained as Jakob Hertzlich. "Picking up the pieces" were the words he had used.

Picking up the pieces. Twice aboard ship I'd awoken in a sweat, my heart pitching, a leaf on the waves. I'd wondered if I was going into cardiac arrest but each time I had survived into the morning. I was in the grip of dread I finally realized.

I entered campus through the main gates and could now see the medical faculty across the open field. I felt like Jane Eyre returning to Thornfield Manor after the madwoman had torched it. The facade of the building was still intact but through the upper windows I could see patches of sky. Flames must have ripped right through the roof. Even at a distance the air was heavy with the dark, charred odour of ruin. As I got closer I could also see that someone was out front, sitting on the stairs. It was so dark by this time that I had to get quite close to make him out. All I saw was a dark lump huddled in the cold, the glow of a cigarette lifting occasionally like a beacon.

I recognized his voice before I could make out his face. He had heard my ship had landed he said as soon as I was close. He had known I would come immediately to the medical faculty.

"How bad is it?" I was still weak from my illness. My whole body was trembling.

Jakob paused, considering. "You might say hello."

"Hello," I said quickly. "I'm sorry." I wasn't really.

"Apology accepted." He tossed his cigarette into the snow and ground it beneath his heel. "Come," he said, sticking out his hand for me to hold as if I were a child. "I'll show you." The hand was bandaged I noticed with alarm, bound in gauze from fingertip to wrist.

"You're hurt?"

He nodded. "The jars exploded in the heat. I got cut up."

I clung tightly to the gauze. The walkway was treacherous from the water used to put out the fire, now frozen into an irregular slippery sheet.

"There's only one entrance," he said, leading me around to the back of the building to a basement door. The stairs were covered with a thick layer of bumpy ice. "Hang on to the railing and go slowly," Jakob warned, releasing my hand and stepping down himself.

The smell was so strong I had the urge to flee. It was like stepping into a crypt. I didn't think I had the strength, but then Jakob encouraged me, telling me it was all right and I must continue. The darkness swallowed him whole but his voice was there as a guide. Unable to stand the thought of being left alone in the ruins I grabbed the railing and plunged downward.

"You've got to proceed slowly." He caught me as I slid down the last steps.

This time it was I who reached for his hand without any invitation. I clutched at the rough gauze.

Jakob Hertzlich allowed himself to be clutched and we shuffled forward blindly, stumbling through the debris. I was unfamiliar with this part of the medical building. What would I have done, I wondered, had Jakob not been waiting here to meet me? He led me to a large room, which, I finally realized, must be the main storeroom, a place I had visited many times. It was here we kept all the materials for the labs — test tubes, specimen bottles, preservative, Bunsen burners and sealant. I came down here often to replenish my supplies.

A match scraped on brick and suddenly Jakob's face wavered in front of me. He lit the wick of a lantern and the room filled with the thick smell of oil. The light spread an uneven glow. Jakob Hertzlich was smiling but for the first time I saw how exhausted he was. He looked pale and ghostly, spreading his arms in sad humour. "Welcome home."

Something wet dropped on my head. I ducked, brushing it from my hair before I discovered that it was only snow. There was no roof to protect us. In certain spots I glimpsed the sky.

The storeroom seemed to be the only part of the place still moderately intact. As my eyes grew accustomed to the light I saw that much work had been done here to re-establish order. The shelves were lined not with supplies but with jars — brand new intact specimen jars filled with formaldehyde and carefully sealed. Some of them were labelled.

"It's the best I could do," said Jakob Hertzlich. "A surprising number of your specimens were salvageable."

"So you got through to the museum?"

Jakob nodded warily. "I did," he said slowly, "but it's not easy. Officially we're not allowed. The floors are bad."

"But it's possible?"

He nodded. "Although for a lot of the stuff I didn't have to climb at all. Things fell through from the upper floors. I just rummaged around down here and gathered them for rebottling."

Later, from Dugald Rivers and Mastro, I learned the true story. How Jakob Hertzlich had not slept for three entire days following the fire; how he'd been the first person other than firefighters to enter the building; how he'd toiled without respite, defying orders to stay out of the upper storeys; how he had continued to salvage the museum throughout the week, working on adrenalin after everyone else had given up, refusing to sleep or slow his pace. Dugald said he was like a man possessed. Mastro spoke of him with awe, especially after he'd dared to climb up to a second-floor office and retrieve a soggy, carbon-stained manuscript, the fruit of years of Mastro's research, which would otherwise have been lost.

Wind pushed in through holes in the walls above us. A sprinkling of snow and soot fell, dusting our heads. I could see my breath. "It's freezing in here, Jakob. It's a wonder you haven't fallen sick."

"I've got Bunsen burners," he said. "I've become quite adept at brewing test-tube tea."

I smiled at him, even though my heart was breaking. A quick scan of the shelves showed that much of the collection had been lost. Jakob Hertzlich had worked valiantly but he'd managed to salvage perhaps a quarter of the specimens. I couldn't believe so much was gone.

"You must take me upstairs," I said.

He peered at me, the whites of his eyes flashing in his dark face. "I knew you'd say that."

"I have to see it, Jakob."

"Things could fall," he said, then paused. "We could fall."

In the end he kept me right behind him, showing me where to place my feet at every step. He held the lantern in front, then swung it back so I could see. It took half an hour to mount three flights.

The firefighters had smashed most of the windows with their axes, and what man and fire hadn't destroyed wind and snow were now at work on. A large, charred hole had been blown through the roof, leaving a third of the museum exposed. I looked up to see stars glittering in a vast, uncaring sky. The floor, or what was left of it, was strewn with shards of glass and shrivelled human remains. I poked around, feeling the boards with my toes to make sure the way was solid before transferring my weight.

Jakob stood near the doorway watching me. "I believe I've taken everything there is to take, Dr. White."

In places flames had stripped the paint off the walls. Jakob's drawings were nowhere to be seen. "Good thing we sent your sketches off to Howlett," I said, running my hand down the wall where several of his works had once been tacked. "We lost only a few."

He shrugged.

My favourite one — the earliest sketch I'd commissioned just after Jakob Hertzlich had joined me at the museum — was hanging safely on my bedroom wall. I smiled as I thought of it, but the smile dissolved as I glanced over at my desk. That corner of the room was relatively undamaged. The ceiling above it was still intact, as were the floorboards. I made my way toward it. The blotter was still in one piece. It was covered with ash and looked more grey now than green, but the flames had not touched it. I pulled open the main drawer. A stack of paper sat inside unsinged. My pens were still there. I wrote my name on an unblemished sheet. It was probably all right then. If pens and paper had survived, surely it had survived too. I cleared my throat. "You found the Howlett Heart?"

Instead of answering Jakob Hertzlich looked away.

"My pens still work!" I laughed, showing him my name on the sheet. "But the heart, Jakob. Surely it's still intact."

"A lot was lost," Jakob said vaguely, refusing to look at me.

I had a sudden urge to march over and twist his head my way, but given the state of the floor marching was out of the question.

"The heat was too much," Jakob explained. "Many of the jars burst." He waved his bandaged hand as a reminder.

He was telling me it was gone. I took a deep breath. Then another. It was only after we had regained the relative safety of the basement that he gave me the other piece of news. By that time I was so disoriented I could barely take it in. I listened in a kind of daze, as if he were telling me what tomorrow's weather would be like.

"I guess this marks the end of things."

I nodded, not at all sure of his meaning but sensing something important crouching behind the words.

"I've done all that I can," he said, gazing at me.

"You've done so much, Jakob," I said, "far beyond the call of duty." It was true. He'd spared nothing, risking his health and his life in the effort.

"I don't see what else I could possibly do." And then it spilled out, all in a rush. "It's over, isn't it? There's nothing left but to resign."

When I said nothing he looked startled. Then his face closed with resolve. "You can be cold, Dr. White."

I was indeed cold. It was as if winter had climbed under my skin and was now sitting inside me. The museum was in ruins, my life's work destroyed. My mind was reeling with this and also with a smaller thought, the irony of which had not escaped me. I had left for England determined to fire Jakob Hertzlich and purge him from my life. This disaster had revealed my short-sightedness. He was absolutely dedicated to me and to the work I held so dear. The lantern's flame trembled, but when I looked up from my thoughts I was alone.

VI
WAR

Short days ago
We lived, felt dawn, saw sunset glow,
Loved and were loved ...

— JOHN MCCRAE, "IN FLANDERS FIELDS"

21

The pier, to which the black hull of the *Metagama* was roped, was crowded with people. I was standing on my toes, trying vainly to see over the ocean of brightly coloured bonnets. Dugald Rivers, who was standing with Dr. Mastro and a boy I did not recognize, shouted my name and waved. He looked as if at any moment he might lift off the ground. He broke from the group of men and made his way toward me. When he reached my side, arms still thrashing, he bent forward and grazed my cheek with his lips. It wasn't a kiss exactly because his lips were closed and flat. More like a collision, as if his mind and body could not agree on a common intention.

I tried to smile. He had been acting strangely for the past few weeks, which I had dismissed as nerves. I had decided it wasn't my place to judge and that I would not take his actions or words personally in the days leading up to his departure. This would be Dugald's first military stint since South Africa. It would stir memories, I was sure. The news from Europe was not good. Last autumn, when the first Canadian contingent had left, there had been such euphoria. Everyone had been convinced of a speedy victory and quick return, but the Canadian boys, many of whom were from McGill, had spent the freezing winter in a camp on Salisbury Plain in southern England. It had rained for three full months, which had lowered morale and brought on a meningitis epidemic. Several young men from McGill had died without reaching the battlefield. Across the Channel in Belgium and France the news was worse. The Germans were killing the British infantry in horrifying numbers.

Into this nightmare was Dugald sailing. The others too, but they were younger and without experience. For them war was still abstract, a boys' adventure tale.

Two nights before, Dugald had invited me to dine at the University Club. When we arrived at the grey stone building on Mansfield Street across from campus I had hung my coat and proceeded up the back stairway as usual, the one reserved for waiters and women. I resented this stairway. It was as if the men wished to deny my existence. When I reached the second floor and the main dining hall Dugald was waiting for me. Without so much as a hello he took my hand and pulled me into an alcove near the lavatory.

My relationship with Dugald had never been physical; his reaching for my hand felt unnatural. He sat me down on a window seat. There was nothing spontaneous about the action, which I suspected he had plotted. Before I knew what was happening he presented me with a ring. It was his school ring I realized after the shock had settled, the one he wore on the little finger of his right hand, never removing it for dissections or scrubs.

"As you are aware, Agnes," he said, avoiding my eyes and speaking in a stilted style, "I must soon leave you. On Monday we set sail." He held my hand, trying to fit the ring on my finger. "I want you to have this," he said, straining slightly for it was a size too small for me. "To help you remember me while I'm gone."

I was taken aback. The last thing I wished to do was insult him. He was a dear friend about to leave for the front. His ring was obviously not intended for engagement. Perhaps it was a sign of his friendship?

Dugald Rivers was one of the most sought-after bachelors in the city. Despite his forty-five years he was really quite handsome and youthful. He had a successful practice and had won four medals in the Boer War. He was an excellent dancer.

But since his arrival in Montreal no woman had managed to captivate him. The previous summer a girl named Barbara, daughter of the railway magnate Dr. Owens, had drawn his fancy for a time. He had danced with her at parties and her father had let it be known that he favoured the match, but nothing had come of it. I was one of the few who had not been surprised. Privately Dugald referred to Barbara Owens as *Babs the Bacillus* and hinted that she was dull, but I suspected Babs's lacklustre personality wasn't the real issue. Dugald simply preferred the bachelor life. He was not looking for a woman.

I was one of the few females of the species he tolerated, but this I'd always thought was because I posed no threat. I inhabited a kind of no man's land separating the territories of the sexes. My training and work made me very much like him. Dugald could talk to me in ways he wouldn't dream of talking to other women. My emotional accessibility and eagerness to provide tea and food were traits he also enjoyed and had difficulty finding in men. In me Dugald had the best of both worlds. I clearly did not want him for my marriage bed. Until that night at the club I had thought we had a solid friendship.

After the fire Dugald had become an almost daily visitor to the museum. I was all alone now, for Jakob Hertzlich had left. Dr. Clarke was preoccupied with rebuilding McGill's medical school and had no time to worry about my lost specimens; we spoke less frequently than before. Dr. Mastro spent much of his time with his wife in New York state, as her health continued to decline. Dugald had become my confidant, slipping effortlessly into the position Jakob had once filled. He had been a supportive friend in my time of need, writing to Howlett and then, on Howlett's recommendation, to the War Museum in Washington to discuss the plight of the McGill Pathology Museum. A donation to McGill of over a thousand specimens had been the result. Dugald's military background had been of great advantage in this regard. He had opened doors that would not have budged for me. I was indebted to him and I liked him. I had never dreamed he would be interested in a woman, let alone in me.

Now on the pier he was holding my hand and towing me like a reluctant ship through the crowd. He was so glad I had come, he said, his eyes lingering on mine longer than necessary. It was flattering to have this big, lovely man suddenly and publicly attentive, but I didn't trust it for a second. The whole thing felt artificial, as if Dugald were engaging in a staged performance.

He tugged me right up to Dr. Mastro and lifted my hand. My face went instantly hot. We must have looked ridiculous standing with our hands locked — an absurd permutation of Beauty and his red-faced Beast. At the University Club he'd acted out his little folly in private. Now he seemed determined to flaunt it. Dr. Mastro looked at me with wide, unblinking eyes. A few yards behind us Barbara Owens, who was at the pier seeing off an older brother, stared.

I pulled my hand away and tried to restore normalcy by chatting with Dr. Mastro. He was sailing today as McGill Hospital Unit's commanding officer and looked more energetic than he had for months. I complimented him and his wide eyes softened. His wife had died and he was hoping the voyage would help him through his bereavement. We began to speak about the faculty but Dugald cut in, tugging me in an awful, proprietary way he had recently developed. I turned, annoyed.

"You will never guess who is here," he said, eyes darting to the young man standing next to Mastro.

The person in question was no older than sixteen or seventeen. He wore his uniform with the careless abandon of a boy still at school. The buttons were mostly undone and his collar was unfastened. His skin was the colour of milk.

"You've met," Dugald said.

The boy put his hand out but did not smile or raise his eyes. If we had met as Dugald claimed it obviously hadn't been memorable for either of us.

Dugald could not contain himself any longer. "Revere Howlett."

The black hair of his father. His mother's milky skin. I could see it now quite plainly. I did a quick calculation. He would be nineteen years old. Nineteen! I'd last seen him in Baltimore when he was still a child. In Oxford I had missed him, as he'd been away at boarding school when I visited. Now he was going to Picardy as Mastro's private orderly. Sir William must have arranged it when he heard about McGill's plan for a hospital unit. It was a convenient, face saving way to avoid conscription into the British infantry, where men were dying in numbers; and Dr. Mastro and the others would keep an eye on him.

"Dr. White is an old friend of your father's," Dugald explained.

I blushed. The boy must be subjected to such comments every waking moment of his life. "I came to your home in Baltimore once, years ago," I said, trying to engage him, "where you promptly did me in with a six-shooter."

Revere's face became smooth and thoughtful and I wondered if he were recalling the episode with the heart under the table. It had probably been as traumatic for him as for me. I certainly wasn't about to bring it up now.

"You came to Oxford too," he said slowly, "only I was away. You got sick or something." His accent was more Oxford than Baltimore.

I nodded, embarrassed. I was probably something of a family legend. The ship's horn blew, making us all jump. Men in naval uniform were ordering the women to move back. Boarding would soon commence.

Dugald Rivers made a final, mortifying lunge at my hand, which he lifted to his lips in full view of all. I pulled away from him and neglected to say a proper goodbye to Mastro or Revere Howlett in my haste. I didn't get far, for a solid wall of women blocked my way. There was no way to break through or to get around so I was forced to join the bonneted throng.

It seemed like the entire university was shipping out that day on the *Metagama*: three medical classes and just about every faculty member who hadn't signed up with the First Canadian Contingent when the initial call for troops had come the previous autumn. I would be the only one left. Well not the only one. I glanced around me. The women would stay. Some were crossing as nurses but their numbers were small.

Again the ship's horn blared. A hush fell over the crowd as the men began to climb single file up the boarding plank. I felt like weeping. It was a mistake to be standing here on shore waving my colleagues goodbye. There were a dozen practical reasons why I could not go. The city had been emptied of medical practitioners. The only doctors left were either French or long past their prime. My services had been sought out by the Children's Memorial Hospital and also by the Montreal General. And there was Laure. Who would care for her if I went to France? Miss Skerry was a stalwart, but she couldn't pay our bills. My salary from McGill might have been laughable but it was better than soldier's pay. If one were a family man, one had to have means like Dr. Mastro to enlist.

My gaze found another face in the winding line of men. Huntley Stewart, laughing with a gang of newspaper cronies. They were not paying attention and a hole opened as the line moved forward without them. Huntley was the first to see it. He pointed, making a cartoon face of horror then rushed ahead to rectify things. His newspaper cronies followed like sheep.

Huntley Stewart had enlisted. Already I'd noticed there were fewer men in Montreal. On a streetcar the other day the driver had her hair done up with pins. Women driving streetcars — what would be next? In Verdun a munitions plant had recently opened and the *Herald* reported most of its workers were women. The pay was thirty-five cents an hour, a better wage than I was getting at McGill.

Laure had no idea Huntley was leaving. In theory they were still married. In practice they hadn't spoken in years.

A photographer from the *Herald* was taking pictures of the waving women. He picked out one especially pretty girl in a bright yellow frock standing right beside me and came over for an interview. "What do you feel," he asked, shouting above the noise, "watching the men pull out?"

The girl came up with some banality about the king and the sacrifices people had to make. Such were the platitudes people spouted — lines straight from the newspapers or lifted from politicians' speeches. The girl was now speaking about her knitting club. Since October she'd finished twenty pairs of socks for the men overseas. Every person had to do his bit, she said.

"Are you here for someone special?" the reporter asked.

The girl blushed. She nodded.

"You're not afraid for him?" He was flirting with her, setting her up so the right words would come tumbling out.

Fear was not the point, said the girl, as if on cue. She was so sure of her rote pronouncements, so naive, she couldn't imagine the young man she fancied maimed or dead.

The reporter swung in my direction. "And you ... do you have someone in the line?"

The ship's horn sounded, sparing me the need to answer. With the rest of the crowd I looked toward where the last of the men were boarding. A familiar hunched back stopped me short. He was dressed like the others — army-issue boots and a mud-coloured jacket — but even in uniform he did not blend. At the moment he seemed utterly concentrated upon his cigarette. The others were bantering, talking with animation as they waited in turn to lug their kits up the gangplank. Jakob Hertzlich stood among them still and silent, but not of them.

I closed my eyes. It had been a decade. I was forty-six now so he must be thirty-eight. Old for a soldier, but a surprising number of the recruits were past their prime — even Dugald. Jakob and I hadn't spoken in years. He was working in a different building at McGill. Our paths rarely crossed.

I tried to imagine Jakob Hertzlich with a gun in his hands. Perhaps he would not touch one if he stayed inside a hospital. Some men were made for the battlefield, others most decidedly not. I wished I'd seen him earlier; even though we'd avoided each other for so long I would have liked to say goodbye and wish him safety.

"Ma'am?" The reporter was still at my elbow.

I shook my head. On the dock Jakob Hertzlich was grinding his cigarette under the heel of his shiny boot. He shouldered his bag and then unexpectedly looked out at the crowd. For a fraction of a second our eyes met. I broke away first, turning briefly left and right to see if there was anyone else at whom he could be looking. But to my left was the slogan girl in yellow and to my right was the reporter. By the time I found Jakob again his back was to me and he'd begun the slow climb up the gangplank.

22

DECEMBER 1915

The Priory parlour had not changed since my childhood. The upholstery on the chesterfield and armchair was more threadbare and there were more cracks in the plaster, but essentially the room was the same. I had come out to St. Andrews East for the Christmas holidays that second winter of the war as I always did, carting gifts and store-bought treats from Montreal. Miss Skerry said that this winter visit and the two weeks I spent with them each summer were the highlights of the year. She and my sister led their lives sequestered from society. Women from the older, English-speaking families still looked in on them occasionally, bringing compotes and pies, but the French, who had not known our family in previous generations, were not as accommodating. They were frightened of Laure, nicknaming her *"la folle de St. André."*

Laure was at her best when I came to visit. There was no sign of the rage that Miss Skerry described in her weekly letters. She considered the letters a duty — reports from the front, a precise tracking of the progression of my sister's illness and her daily battles to contain it. She described in detail the nosebleeds and facial discoloration that accompanied Laure's fits, the periodic flights into town and ensuing humiliation when Laure was recaptured and returned to the Priory. I had long stopped reading them they were so painful, preferring to let them accumulate on my dresser. When the stack grew too large I put them in a box in my closet. Their real function, I suspected, was to give Miss Skerry the illusion of company.

Miss Skerry had lit a fire in the hearth and she, Laure and I were huddled around it, wrapped in rugs. Over the last decade she had put on weight. Miss Skerry had never been pretty but there had been a time when she had seemed proud of her trim little body. It was as if she'd ceased to care. Her hair, once brushed and glossy, was unkempt. These changes would have worried me had her mind not remained sharp. In the evenings it was a pleasure to sit and converse with her.

But with Laure in the room conversing was not always easy. Tonight we were concentrating on work, not words. The only sounds in the parlour were the periodic hisses and crackles of logs on the fire and the click of our knitting needles. I flipped the toe of the sock on which I was working and laid it flat on my lap. I was slower than Miss Skerry, who had practically finished a thick beige pair. Laure, whose concentration was so frayed she had difficulties finishing a sentence, was nearly done hers as well. Working with her hands seemed to calm her, bringing back a semblance of her former grace. They knitted. They embroidered sheets and tablecloths. They sewed dresses and capes. Prior to the war I had been the beneficiary of their industriousness.

These days, however, the work was socks. For Laure it had developed into an obsession. Since the autumn of 1914, when the knitting drive had begun, she had completed three hundred pairs.

I had little of my sister's talent. I waved my stump of tangled wool before the governess and laughed. "I'm all thumbs, George." I felt awkward using this name but Miss Skerry had insisted. We had known each other far too long for me to continue calling her

"Miss," she said. She had been christened Georgina and chopped off the last two syllables. "Like George Eliot," she'd explained, "and George Sand. As clubs go, Agnes, it's one of the few I wouldn't mind belonging to."

George smiled at my knitting. "You're already doing your bit, Agnes. Socks aren't the only way to help."

It was true. I was doing my bit, though in less direct fashion than keeping the feet of Canadian boys warm in the trenches. I was employed at two Montreal hospitals and my private clinic was overflowing with patients. I had visited Harvard University that fall to give a talk on congenital heart disorders. In the United States the medical schools were flourishing, America being not yet at war. I was one of a handful of foreign scholars still available for American tours. So far Harvard, Johns Hopkins and Philadelphia had sent me invitations. I had refused everyone but Harvard, as I was too busy with my clinical work.

"Socks are a local specialty," George said, reaching forward and patting Laure's leg.

Laure looked up with such pride that I had to laugh. There was great comfort here at the Priory, sitting with my sister and our former governess, concentrating on simple things. It reminded me of the Brontë sisters, shut away on the heath, engaging in domestic work and then rewarding themselves with books and talk in the evening. Perhaps this would be my old age, sitting at the Priory's hearth, knitting with Laure and discussing with George Skerry. I had hoped for a more expansive life, for relationships extending beyond the circle of my girlhood, but there were worse fates.

Miss Skerry was translating *The Aeneid*, continuing the work in Latin on which her father had commenced her. She enjoyed the language, she said, although she confessed that she had mixed feelings about Virgil. "Too fond of war," she'd said the night before as we watched embers glowing on the hearth.

I was more like Virgil than I would have cared to admit. Not that I was in favour of killing, but I certainly did yearn to be with the men in the arena of war. I envied my colleagues at the front. I regretted not being in Europe. Dugald wrote weekly, describing scenes of camp life on the outskirts of Dannes-Camiers in northern France, where he and the others from McGill were stationed.

All through that summer and autumn I had received first-hand reports. Fighting on the Western Front had tapered off. The main theatre of action was Turkey. France was relatively quiet. The summer of 1915 had been the driest in living memory. Dugald described long days of sunshine. For me "war" conjured scenes of young men lying half-naked on riverbanks. How I envied them their comradeship beneath the Picardy sun.

McGill's was one of seven temporary tent hospitals set up on a plain above Dannes-Camiers. It had close to one thousand beds, roughly the same number as those of England, Scotland and France. They had set up in the late spring, just after the Battle of Ypres. Everyone was eager to see action, but beyond a few sniper casualties action did not come. A sort of standoff situation developed, and there was nothing for the hospital staff to do but wait.

According to Dugald Revere Howlett was like a schoolboy on holiday. He sent home almost immediately for his bicycle and spent most days fishing in the streams and rivers near their camp. Jakob Hertzlich was also enjoying himself. He and Revere had become friends. I reread this section of Dugald's letter with fascination. With regular meals and exercise Jakob Hertzlich had apparently blossomed. He had purchased a rusty bicycle in the village so he could accompany Revere into the countryside.

In September Howlett Senior had crossed the Channel to visit the McGill outfit and see his son. That was the final straw for me. Dugald's descriptions made me envious. He wrote that Howlett had organized a tour of the front for himself and Revere in a Red Cross car.

The last couple of letters I had received, however, had been more sombre in tone. Over a thousand soldiers from the Battle of Loos had arrived, suddenly the McGill camp was overrun. Dugald worked the first half of October without sleep, treating soldiers whose limbs had been shattered by shrapnel. It tore at the flesh, he wrote, creating jagged, irregular wounds that invited infection. In the filthy, close conditions of war, sepsis was ubiquitous. Patients were dying from the dirt.

This morning I'd received Dugald's latest letter, which I had yet to open. I pulled it out of my pocket and showed it to George.

She put her knitting down and rubbed her glasses with her hem. "I'd say that man is either in love with you or hasn't many friends."

"He's lots of friends," I said, and it was true.

"Women friends," said George, pointedly. "You know what I'm getting at."

"Well he's not in love with me," I said. "He's not the type."

Miss Skerry slipped her glasses back on. "Is that so? One has to be a certain type to fall in love?"

My words had come out wrong. "I mean," I said, "Dugald Rivers is not actually interested in women."

George's eyes narrowed.

"He likes me, George. He's sincere enough about that. But it goes no further."

"You said he gave you his ring."

"Yes, but only because all the men were doing it — giving rings and photos with endearments scribbled on the back to their girlfriends. If the others hadn't done it the thought wouldn't have entered his mind."

"So he's a conformist?"

"No. Just the opposite in fact."

"I'm afraid I'm not following."

I inhaled and tried again. "Most of the time Dugald Rivers is himself. And that self is perfectly content to converse and eat tarts in the museum. But the war brought certain pressures. Many of the men have sweethearts to write to. Dugald decided to fit me into the mould of a sweetheart. There's a certain logic to it. He has such trouble fitting the conventions that he felt obliged to give me that ring. It was so awkward. It felt like play-acting."

George Skerry raised her eyebrows. "He sounds like an invert," she said quietly.

Inversion: the crime of sexual love between men. The medical profession considered it a pathology. Yet the book I'd read over in Oxford, the one by Iwan Bloch, had been tolerant of the practice.

"I am not sure what Dugald is," I said finally. I had never discussed Dugald's sexual life with him and felt uncomfortable speculating about it, even with an intelligent and sympathetic person such as my old governess. "He's just himself, George."

Miss Skerry smiled. "Fair enough. Besides, he writes gems of letters." She made a few more stitches before looking up again. "Aren't you going to read it?"

I opened the envelope, which bore a November postmark. Mail took excruciating lengths of time to reach Montreal, having first to cross the U-boat-infested Atlantic and then be put on a train in Halifax. The letter began "My beloved," a fact I decided not to share with Miss Skerry or my sister, who was beside us on the sofa clicking steadily with her needles.

Dugald's first paragraph was devoted to rain. The Picardy sun was apparently in retreat. The most pressing medical challenges now were rheumatic fever and pneumonia, which had ravaged the beleaguered hospital staff. Dugald himself was suffering from asthma. Although the hospital was now empty of wounded soldiers the medical staff had been instructed to stay on until further notice, no matter how bad conditions became.

Their tents were in tatters. They had been a gift from India, a country whose tent makers had no idea how dismal a French autumn could be. They had begun to disintegrate in the first autumn rains. The cotton ropes anchoring them shrank, pulling the pegs out of the earth. The canvas split. Mud oozed through the floorboards and rain poured in, soaking bedding and clothes. "They've closed the hospital!" I exclaimed, looking up. "It was deemed unfit for habitation!"

Dugald had decided to leave for the front. Most of the young men, including Revere Howlett, wanted to do the same. Jakob Hertzlich, who was older, had opted for England, where he was trying to get work as a hospital orderly. No one, it seemed, considered the possibility of returning home.

"They're throwing away their lives," said George Skerry.

I stared at her. Hers could be an irritating frankness.

"It's true," she continued. "Bad enough some countries force their men to fight. These young men are leaping to their deaths of their own free will."

"I'd leap too if I could," I replied.

George Skerry looked at me. "Nonsense. Don't you see how blessed we are? Don't you see that war is one of those rare times when womanhood is a privilege, not a curse?"

She gave me pause. The war had been good to me professionally, it was true, but it had almost destroyed my personal life. Aside from George Skerry there weren't many women whose company I enjoyed. I was often lonely. I missed Dugald Rivers, Dr. Clarke, even Mastro. I missed my students, and — I couldn't believe I had been so reduced — I would even have been pleased to see Jakob Hertzlich again.

"Look at us," George went on, "warming our feet by the grate while our young men are dying on foreign soil."

Laure looked up blankly from her stocking. I had to smile.

"Agnes," Miss Skerry said briskly. "Our work is for the first time in history valued and in demand. Look at yourself, my dear. Think of all you have accomplished in the past year. Without the war Harvard would not have invited you." She paused, seeing the look on my face. "Not for want of talent. You know that. But under normal circumstances Harvard would invite a man. The war has offered you opportunities. You have seized them and shone."

I glanced at the socks lying on George's lap. They were expertly knitted, not a stitch loose or out of place. Some boy George Skerry had never met would likely die in them. She rewound what was left of the skein to replace it in the knitting box. Her argument fell down with her own life. She couldn't claim that the war had benefited her in any way. She was living out her best years in seclusion with Laure, knitting socks for corpses.

That night after we had put Laure to bed I stopped her, putting my hand on her sleeve. "You're not bored here, are you George?"

We were in the upstairs hall outside Laure's room. George drew back physically. Bathing Laure or even restraining her was one thing — it was part of her job — but a gesture of intimacy between equals was a different story. "Boredom is for boring people," she said hastily.

I sighed. She occasionally slipped back into being my governess, distancing herself with aphorisms. I tried one last time as we headed down the stairs. "Don't you dream of more?"

She looked up, eyes magnified by her lenses. Her gaze was so direct I had to drop my own. I moved toward the stairs, giving my old friend a moment to collect herself. In the parlour the fire had shrunk to a heap of ash-covered coals. George Skerry knelt beside it and blew, coaxing out a flame. It was obvious that she did not wish to speak so I went to the bookshelf. The number of books had grown since Miss Skerry had moved back. My old governess picked up her edition of Virgil and sat down on the sofa. She was wading through Book IV, the incendiary passions of Queen Dido.

About half an hour later the fire again began to dim and George rose to her feet. "You must have learned by now, Agnes, that it's not possible to judge a life from the outside," she said. Her voice had an edge. "One inevitably gets it wrong." Miss Skerry's face was half-turned from me and tinted by the firelight, making her expression difficult to read.

"I didn't mean to criticize you," I said. "Just the opposite."

There was a long pause and when George spoke again her voice was gentler. "I'm happy here, Agnes. I have my pleasures." She patted the worn cover of her book. "I am among people to whom I feel close." Her voice wavered slightly. It might have been fatigue or smoke in her throat, or it might have been emotion.

23

Afternoon light poured in through the window. It lit up the papers arranged on the floor around me. It spread over the table cluttered with jars and wax reconstructions, X-rays and charts. It coloured the skin of my hands and neck, and my forehead etched from hours of classifying. The heat was strong; I rocked back on my heels and leaned into the shade.

I stood to pull the blind and my knees almost buckled. While I worked I often forgot about my legs tucked beneath me. They felt dead. I propped my bottom on the rim of a lab stool and unbuttoned my collar. The little room on the top floor of the new Medical Arts Building was directly beneath the copper roof. It trapped the heat.

No one else was so obstinate as to work on campus through the months of July and August. Most of my colleagues were overseas, but even those who had remained in Montreal fled the city for the summer. Awful old Dr. Daimler, who had replaced Dr. Clarke as acting head of the medical faculty, hadn't shown his beaky face all July. I should count my blessings, but the secretaries were gone too, which I regretted. I liked to visit them and chat on breaks. At the moment even the janitor, a man named Cook whom we all called "the King" because of his self-possessed airs, was on holiday. People would start returning in a week or two, although there was hardly any urgency. The incoming class was tiny. If the war dragged on much longer, which it gave every indication of doing, the medical faculty would be forced to let in women. Perhaps there had been something after all to Miss Skerry's opinions.

I made it a point of honour to arrive at McGill each morning at eight o'clock and put in a full day's work. It lent shape to my life. There was plenty to do. I had just completed a pamphlet on Florence Nightingale, who had died recently at the age of ninety. A publishing house in London had shown interest, especially after I suggested that all the proceeds could go to the Red Cross. I'd accepted an invitation from the New York Academy of Medicine to give a talk at the end of the month. In the United States I had become something of a celebrity. My fame had spread, I suspected, largely by default. There were few scientists left on Canadian soil and I stood out as one of a handful of people continuing to do original research.

The talk I had planned was ambitious, the culmination of my years of research. I had gathered the specimens I used in my teaching and for publications. I was planning something entirely new. The traditional reading of dusty reports no longer interested me. I wanted to shake my audience and make them sit up.

What I had fashioned was a travelling show about the heart, designed to appeal to the senses instead of merely the mind. I had material to fill eight sheets of grey millboard, occupying wallspace four feet by thirty-two feet high. Awkward for travel, but once I'd set up it would take the breath away.

Strewn at my feet were my treasures: a collection of Jakob Hertzlich's sketches of cardiac anomalies, forty-two photographs of specimens, twenty-four radiographs, a number of tracings, seventeen charts and twice that number of diagrams. On the table were fifty specimens suspended in their jars, showing the most common defects and anomalies, as well as a handful of reptilian and piscine hearts to show the evolutionary and ontological course of development. In cases where I had no specimens I had made wax reconstructions.

Leaning against my desk was a chart of statistics indicating the special features of a thousand cases of congenital heart disease and necropsies. This material had originally been published in Howlett's textbook and was the cornerstone of my fame. But now I would build further. I was not simply a researcher — "Howlett's lackey" Jakob Hertzlich had once called me — compiling the results of his work in his shadow. Now I would step out on my own. I would do so in style.

Among the sheets scattered on the floor was a flyer announcing my talk. *Heart Specialist*, it read, giving my name and academic degrees. The advertisement would be published in major American newspapers on the eastern seaboard. Thousands of people would receive copies, one of whom might be my own missing father. Of course my name had changed, but surely he would recognize his wife's maiden name and the Christian one he had given me. I had no idea where he was living. I had inquired about him at the medical schools in Canada and at the major ones in the United States, but without result. He had probably set up a practice in a small town in the Boston states, to which many French-Canadians had migrated. I believed he was still practising. Medicine had been his life.

Whenever I published an article or saw my name in print like this on the flyer I felt a surge of hope. Honoré Bourret might see it. It was my life's dream.

On the table beside me were a collection of case studies, neatly typed and ordered. I would take my audience by the hand and lead them through the process of a diagnosis. Doctors were still astonishingly ignorant when it came to deciphering murmurs and trills. In my years of clinical practice and observation I had discovered that the path to understanding the heart lay in its sounds. Finer diagnostic tools would one day be developed, but right now the best I could do was listen. Of course the electrocardiogram was making headway. There was one at the Montreal General Hospital — but for the moment not a single doctor there knew how to use it. The human ear was still the best tool. If a person took the time to listen the heart would eventually offer up its secrets.

My first case study was a boy of six, admitted to hospital with a swelling in his neck. The swelling had had nothing to do with his heart — it turned out to be a tubercular node — but the instant I had placed my ear on his chest I had known. There were no outward signs. No clubbing of fingers, no tint of skin. His lung fields were clear and the blood pressure normal. But as soon as my stethoscope touched him it revealed the terrible verdict. The murmur was harsh, echoing against his narrow ribs. It reverberated over the entire pericardium and both scapulae. Upon his death two years later my diagnosis was confirmed. The hole in his ventricular septum was the size of a nickel.

The second case involved a girl of fourteen whose parents had consulted me. She had visible birth deformities: a bent spine and clubbing of one foot. Her early development had been normal but shortly before their consultation with me the parents had noticed that the girl's lips turned blue when she ran or walked vigorously. She was a small child, underdeveloped for her age and still prepubescent. There was no generalized cyanosis, no clubbing of the fingers or difficulties with breath. Midchest, however, I heard the clicking and diagnosed her on the spot.

The nurses at the hospital called me a witch; little was known about the heart and my diagnoses seemed like sorcery to them. All I did was to look and to listen. What others called magic was the careful, practised use of my ears and eyes.

Once a diagnosis was made, of course, there was nothing I could do. Such was the problem with cardiac anomalies. Cures were nonexistent. My patients were doomed to short lives of pain. The boy with the ventricular septal defect had been eight years of age when he died. His heart was now bottled and shelved. In time, provided her family consented, I would take the girl's.

I looked briefly up from my notes. I was surrounded by hearts, sectioned and preserved. Hearts with holes. Hearts with leaking valves or thickened walls. Hearts with narrow or transposed aortas. I closed my eyes.

When I opened them the dean's secretary was standing in the doorway. Over the last few years I had come to know Mrs. Greaves more intimately. She was a widow whose husband had died years ago during the infancy of their only child, a red-haired boy named Alexander. Now Alexander was in Flanders. He had been part of the victory at Vimy Ridge in April. More recently he had fought at Messines. He was still alive. Apart from Alexander Mrs. Greaves had but one sister who was a nun. She was alone like me. And like me she had shown up for work every day of this hot summer. She had not, to my knowledge, indulged in one day of sick leave. Every time she received a letter from her boy she climbed the stairs to the museum to share it. Alexander didn't write half as well as Dugald Rivers, but I rejoiced over his letters just the same, encouraging his mother to share the four or five scrawled lines with me over a cup of tea.

Today Mrs. Greaves was wearing a blue smock-like dress. Her face was puffy. "Mail's arrived," she announced, holding out a letter.

I made out foreign stamps and the looping script of Dugald Rivers. "Did you get one?" I asked, taking mine from her.

Mrs. Greaves shook her head.

I had not read Dugald's letters aloud to Mrs. Greaves but the woman in the doorway looked so forlorn I decided I should. I checked the postmark. The third of July. It had taken over a month to reach me.

"Terrible, the waiting," said Mrs. Greaves when I showed her. "Even when you get a letter you can't be sure if they're alive."

I nodded. This was something I didn't like to think about.

"My neighbour's boy was at Ypres. Second battle," Mrs. Greaves went on. "The Army sent a telegram informing her he'd been killed.

Two weeks after that a letter arrived from him announcing his good health." She paused. "It's enough to do a person in."

I put a hand on Mrs. Greaves's shoulder. Before the war I would not have invited this woman for tea, let alone touched her. Now she was a friend. "Let's see what dear old Dr. Rivers is up to," I said, diverting my guest by unfolding the onion-skin sheets. The letter was long, written in a hand that seemed spikier than Dugald's usual flowing script. At the moment, he wrote, he was in a hospital in London sleeping on an honest-to-God mattress between real cotton sheets, bathing in hot, clean water and eating food other than bully beef and wormy biscuits. That was the good news.

Mrs. Greaves's jaw sagged. "Don't tell me he's been hit."

He was intact, he wrote, but barely. His lungs were ruined. His battery had taken gas at Passchendaele, and that, combined with the interminable rain, had done him in. He'd suffered bouts of asthma so bad no one thought he would survive.

My own chest squeezed tight. For over a year Rivers had been divulging horrors so awful I had few remaining illusions about the sanity of war. He had described how German machine guns had mowed down battalion after battalion of Allied boys. The Canadian men had only rifles, and poor ones at that, with the fatal habit of jamming in damp weather. Our young men perished in rows, caught in the act of loading or cocking. In one unforgettable letter he described the gas used by the German Army. It hung over the trenches in a yellow cloud and shredded men's lungs. It blinded as well, but its primary target was the lungs, which filled with pus. Gas victims died horrendously, drowning in their own secretions. In all his years of practice, wrote Dugald, he'd never seen anything so ghastly.

Few letters of this kind were reaching people back in Canada. Dugald was a particularly candid correspondent with an artist's eye for detail. Although deeply patriotic and familiar with military culture he was a humanist before all else and the suffering to which men fighting on the Western Front were subjected appalled him. In the four years of the Boer War, he told me, a total of two hundred and twenty-four Canadians perished. The carnage of this current war was of a completely new order. Had his superiors ever suspected the contents of his letters I am certain he would have been censored. Fortunately for me he was clever enough not to give cause for suspicion. From the outside he appeared as quietly stoic as any other soldier.

He wrote that he himself had taken gas. His lungs had been weak to start with but now they barely functioned. He was able to hold a pen, which was encouraging, but I hoped he was not writing from his deathbed.

"Passchendaele," I read aloud to Mrs. Greaves, "was like the Somme all over again. It rained relentlessly, turning the fields into a swamp. It was as if not only the men's morale but the land itself had died. Everything was stripped bare. There were no longer trees or grasses or anything green, just mud rutted by shells, furrowed not for crops but for trenches."

"The man's a poet," Mrs. Greaves said, dabbing her eyes. "I never would have guessed he wrote like that." She uncrumpled her hanky and blew her nose.

As I read descriptions of men left to rot where they had fallen, prey to German bullets and shells, Mrs. Greaves became still. "Their flesh gradually drops away," I read aloud. "They sit or stand in the trenches amidst the rest of the battle wreckage — steel helmets, rifles, the husks of bombs."

Mrs. Greaves began to wave in agitation. "Stop, Dr. White. Please stop. It's too awful."

We finished our tea in silence. Mrs. Greaves had a tight, clenched look about her now for which I felt responsible. She rose as soon as her cup was done. "My Alex isn't gifted with the pen," she said suddenly. "Perhaps that's for the best."

I looked away. Dugald's letter had brought poor Mrs. Greaves no comfort. For some people knowledge is hard to bear. But how could one support one's son without knowing at least a little of what he was living through? The boys across the ocean could not simply block their ears and shut their eyes. Why should we?

I felt grateful. Through Dugald's letters I had been able to understand and experience the war imaginatively. Without his gifts of expression I could never have done this. Not all women were so lucky. But then again, I thought, watching Mrs. Greaves retreating out the door, not all women wanted to be.

I picked up Dugald's letter and continued where I'd left off.

Howlett had taken the train to London to see him. The old man had tried to keep a cheerful front but he'd looked awful. *Thin as a stick*, Dugald wrote, *with a grizzled complexion*. He'd been ill all winter with bronchitis. Dugald had been able to do him a good turn. He'd seen Revere just weeks before and could report on his well-being. *What a burly fellow he's become*, Dugald wrote. *Weather-beaten as an Indian after spending the entire winter and spring out of doors. He'd grown a moustache too, just like his father's, only less droopy. Howlett wept when I described him.*

The last lines of the letter were much darker. *Each of us has taken a hit, Agnes,* he wrote in his strange new spiky script. *Whether we're on the battlefield or safe in England we're all casualties. Poor Howlett is a husk of himself. I doubt Revere will return in one piece and I don't know if the old man will survive it.*

Nobody can make me go back across that Channel unless I choose to. I've got my ticket out, thanks to my lungs. But what is left, Agnes? France and Flanders weigh so heavily on me. I feel like Coleridge's Mariner, choking on horrors.

By the time I reached the last line I had lost my desire to be a man. That more than anything else was what war had done for me. From that day until I died I would offer up prayers of thanks for the good fortune of having been born a woman.

24

The skull seemed to smile in the hard April sunlight. I was sitting at my desk, trying to picture it as a human face with lips covering the misaligned teeth and eyes in its sockets. The bone structure was delicate; I was afraid it might snap. What would this boy have looked like? Handsome perhaps, but undersized — not fully out of childhood. This was not the only skull in the Canadian Army Medical Museum collection, of which I was now official custodian, but it was one of the more wrenching. Judging from punctures in the bone, death had been immediate. A bullet had entered the left temporal area of the head, ripped through both cerebral hemispheres and exited cleanly on the right. I stroked the smooth cranium; my vision blurred.

Age was making me soft. For twenty-five years I had resisted sentimentality and now I was shedding tears over my own specimens. A person would have to have a heart of stone not to be moved by the new collection, particularly this youthful skull. It could be Revere

Howlett, except that as far as I knew he was still fighting. It could be the son of Mrs. Greaves, who had died the previous summer after taking shrapnel to the abdomen and head. Alexander Greaves had been nineteen when his life ended. Regardless of whose skull this was, I thought, feeling the contours and heft of the bone, he had been young. His last days of life had been spent in trenches: cold, wet and alone.

The April sun, which graced the museum throughout most of the afternoon, slipped suddenly behind the clouds. I stood up, straightening my crumpled coat. The skull would go on the shelf reserved for crania and I would get on with my day. I was exhausted. As usual there was too much to be done. In December I had been offered the commission to catalogue and mount the Army's medical collection, which I had accepted. It would be prestigious for me and for McGill, and government pay was higher than what the university could offer, even with the course in pathology I was now teaching. The workload was immense. Few of the Army's specimens had been labelled and many had been poorly stored. I'd had to toss out a good number and remount the rest. It was tedious work and it took a toll on my back and eyes. The Army's representative was helpful, but only up to a point. He was stationed in Ottawa and came to Montreal twice a month.

I had taken on the job in part because I had been promised a technician, but so far nothing had come of it. I was reminded of my first days at McGill, when the museum had seemed nothing more than a chaotic mess of bones and bottles. I had lost my courage then as well, but Howlett had urged me on. Now I had no one to guide me.

"Alas, poor Yorick."

I wheeled, the skull still in my hands. A man was standing in the doorway, wearing a long and stylish coat. His eyes, which were so black I couldn't see where the irises left off and the pupils began, were narrowed in a squint. His cheeks were thick with black bristles, while the hair on his head was shaved close. It was the ears that tipped me off when he finally removed his hat. They were red and cold looking.

For several seconds I could not speak. "I can't claim to have known him, Jakob," I finally said, lifting the skull high and turning its empty eyes toward him, "but the grin does suggest a fellow of infinite jest and most excellent fancy."

Jakob Hertzlich laughed. At least I think he did, though what came out sounded more like a groan. My former assistant's mouth twisted into an unconvincing smile. I couldn't believe he was standing before me, the first back. So eager for overseas news was I that Jacob Hertzlich, with his prickly complexities, was welcome. He looked good — paler than before, but stronger. The beard made his eyes seem bigger. If anything he seemed to have grown more youthful. If I was forty-nine, he was forty-one.

He crossed the room, laid his hat on a stool and, to my complete surprise, put his arms around me. I could feel his body, solid beneath his coat. My free hand wrapped around him too, moving up his back to trace the scapulae, the slightly curved thoracic vertebrae. Jakob Hertzlich was home, I thought, giving him a squeeze. He stood perfectly still, eyes shut and hips so close to mine that the skull of the unknown boy, which I was clutching with my other hand, ground into both our bellies.

"Let me look at you!" I exclaimed, an excuse to step back, which I instantly regretted. He would look at me too, of course, and I hated to think what he would see. My hair was now quite grey. I had celebrated my forty-ninth birthday a month ago, but unlike Jakob I had lost weight. Without teas to prepare for friends and students, and pastries brought into the museum for afternoon snacks, eating had lost much of its appeal. I rarely prepared a meal anymore, preferring to take sandwiches on the run and a piece of cheese or sausage without fuss at night in my kitchen. I must look like a grandmother, I thought with alarm. My skin was sallow from a winter of indoor toil. Fortunately I was wearing a lab coat because the dress I'd put on that morning hung on me like a sack.

"You look fine," he said after a moment's scrutiny. "A bit thinner, but fine." To my surprise there was no hint of irony. His face shone with a childlike look of appreciation. Nor was there any trace of an accent. Some of the men were returning with England in their speech, but Jakob Hertzlich sounded exactly like he had always sounded. "Suits you, Dr. White."

I smiled, even though I knew he was lying.

It's impossible to say who began. I was embarrassed to cry and in the confusion and blindness of tears didn't notice much. I knew how ridiculous I looked when I wept. My eyes swelled up, my nose ran, my face turned ugly and mottled. I was so concerned with myself that it was some time before I realized Jakob Hertzlich was crying too. He wasn't making any noise, which I found at once odd and endearing.

Afterward I made a pot of tea and as we waited for it to brew he told me he'd made a life for himself in England. For the last two years of the war he'd worked in a military hospital in Colchester. One of the doctors there had noticed his artistic skills and had introduced him to a publisher of medical texts. One thing had led to another and he'd quit his orderly work to establish himself as an anatomical illustrator.

"Don't tell me we've lost you," I said, arranging cups and saucers so I could pour our tea. The thought of his leaving Montreal for England was painful to me. It was an absurd reaction, of course, given that we had barely spoken for over ten years before he left, but he was the first man back, the first piece of my old life to return.

He looked at me through the steam rising out of the cup I had just handed him. "I still have ties to Canada," he said. "My father's ill. That's why I made the crossing."

"I'm sorry."

"I am too," he said. "He's worse in sickness than in health." He looked at me strangely. "Truthfully, Dr. White, don't be so polite. Losing me to England will not be so bad."

I had to place myself in his shoes to see things from a perspective other than my own. To answer truthfully would be selfish. "Perhaps not," I replied carefully. He had always dreamed of being an illustrator. Colchester sounded like an opportunity, even if it were an ocean away.

His expression changed. I had insulted him. I had tried to be sympathetic but as so often happened with Jakob I had failed.

We sipped our tea in silence, which I finally broke by apologizing for the lack of food. I was unused to company I explained. When McGill had emptied I had no reason to keep my cupboards stocked.

He shrugged and said it didn't matter. "You heard about Revere Howlett." Was it question or statement?

I shook my head.

"Howlett hasn't written you?"

I shook again, reddening slightly. For the past two years my letters to Sir William had gone unanswered. For reasons I couldn't fathom I seemed to have slipped from the great man's favour. I tried not to dwell on this fact, and most days I succeeded.

"He's dead," he said simply. "Not far from Ypres. His battery was moving onto a ridge and a shell got him."

I put down my cup.

"He took shrapnel in the chest but didn't die immediately. They got him to a field hospital."

I gestured to him to stop. "Jakob, please." Revere Howlett, the child who had played cowboys and Indians, was dead. I couldn't grasp it.

Jakob stared at me.

"Poor Sir William." As I said his name I began to cry.

Jakob Hertzlich's eyes were hard. Maybe he was ashamed of his initial outburst of emotion and now felt he had to compensate for it. Or perhaps he hated me for my softness. I made a half-hearted effort to dry my face and ask for more news.

At Jakob's feet was a satchel. "I visited the Howletts in Oxford before sailing home," he said, pulling out a pad of paper. "I wanted to give them these."

The paper was of high quality, but the sketches had an amateurish quality that surprised me. The first ones were of hands. One holding a fork, another a pen. Following these was a series of still-life drawings from the military barracks — a canteen on a table, a pair of boots drying in the sun. Then came portraits — boys' faces reading or napping. Sometimes their torsos were included, cross-hatched in areas of shadow. It was not unlike the portfolio from a beginner's art class.

Folded between the last pages were two sketches of a different quality altogether. The dead boy was immediately recognizable with his dark hair and secretive eyes. The style was assured and masterful.

"I was teaching Revere to sketch at Dannes-Camiers," said Jakob.

We gazed down at him. In one sketch he was standing in uniform, eyes hidden by an oversized military cap. In the other he was on a riverbank, half-naked. Dannes-Camiers, that first summer — I had been so jealous of them.

"The portraits are yours? They're wonderful, Jakob. You've captured him."

Jakob's fingers played with the edges of the fine paper. They were no longer stained with yellow, I noticed, and the smell of tobacco no longer clung to him. "He got rather good near the end," he said.

"Sir William didn't take this?" I said, tapping the sketch pad. It was hard to believe a father could refuse such a treasure.

"Just before my ship left I went up to Oxford but I never saw him. That wife of his is quite something. She wouldn't speak to me."

"Lady Kitty?" I said. "She's not so bad when you get to know her."

"She was like a watchdog. Apparently the old man is at death's door."

The smile froze on my face. A few months earlier I'd heard that he was ill, but I had discounted it as a winter grippe. I had been in England in the wintertime. I had picked up a grippe there myself. But an Oxford winter exacerbated by the news of Revere's death was probably more than he could bear.

Jakob watched me, smiling almost cruelly. "It's the fashion these days, Agnes."

I took off my glasses to wipe them but also to blur his face. "Please, Jakob."

"Howlett isn't the only man to have lost a son, nor will he be the last. The entire Western world is grieving, Agnes. It's like the last act of *Hamlet*," he said, jerking his chin in the direction of my specimen. "Corpses everywhere."

"For God's sake, Jakob," I pleaded.

He said nothing more. He rose to his feet and stood over me, shifting his weight from one boot to the other. The awful smile he wore to hide his feelings was gone. "You didn't know Howlett was ill?" he asked. "You've not been corresponding?"

Jakob's eyes glistened. "You're still stuck on him." He was staring at me hard. "After all these years you're still stuck."

He turned to go but I restrained him, asked him not to leave so soon after so long an absence. His face now wore a dangerous expression and his mouth remained clamped shut, but he stayed. I talked about my life in Montreal since the spring of 1915. I spoke of the deserted campus and city streets. I told him about knitting socks and my lectures in Boston and New York. I talked about Dugald Rivers and how his letters had been my only steady link to friends and colleagues overseas.

At length Jakob relaxed enough to tell me he had seen Dugald Rivers recently. He was in London and not doing well. This much I knew for he still wrote almost weekly, a habit begun at the start of the war, when they were all at Dannes-Camiers. "I envied you when you first went to Picardy," I confessed. I mentioned the bicycle he had bought.

Jakob laughed. His laugh was real this time, unlike his first attempt. "What a time we had," he said. "Revere used to take me cycling. I'd never done that before, you know. I'd never learned as a kid. We'd ride into the countryside. He was a fine young man. Better than his father," he added unnecessarily. "The old man came to visit us at Dannes-Camiers, you know. Did Rivers tell you that?"

I nodded. It had been September of 1915, when civilian travel across the Channel had still been possible.

"He came in sort of like the king, which I personally didn't care for, but it seemed to rally everyone else," Jakob said. "He did rounds in the morning with the entire McGill group trailing on his heels, lapping up his every word. Rivers led the pack, as you can imagine. Rivers has no idea how he diminishes himself. Not that Howlett notices as long as he gets his daily dose of reverence."

I didn't say anything. I couldn't afford to given Jakob's volatile humour and the fact that I wanted to hear more. Because he'd befriended Revere Jakob had apparently been invited to accompany father and son on a tour of the front lines. At first he had refused. He had thought it too dangerous. The towns near the front were under fire. Why seek out trouble in the middle of a war? Sir William explained they would do it safely. He arranged for a Red Cross car, which the Germans left alone, to carry them along secondary roads.

Jakob went along. It was harvest time. When they crossed to the Belgian side peasants were in the fields in great numbers, working between the trenches. The landscape was also full of graves — rows of crosses in country graveyards, standing in testament to the young men who had fallen. They doubled back to France to sleep that night, which Jakob could not understand as it took them out of their way. But Sir William had reasons. The inn at which they stopped in the town of Montreuil was where Laurence Sterne had slept on the first night of his *Sentimental Journey*. The next morning they resumed what Jakob had since come to realize was Howlett's own sentimental journey, and drove north to Calais.

"And here, Dr. White," Jakob said, "the expedition took a sentimental turn not just for William Howlett, but for you."

It turned out that Sir William knew someone living in Calais, a man he had befriended years ago while a student. The group went to an inn not far from the town's ramparts to meet him. "The world is small, Dr. White," Jakob said. "Can you guess who the man was?" He paused, but I could not guess. "Honoré Bourret."

My father, living in Calais. The bearer of this news, for which I had waited my whole life, was the unlikely Jakob Hertzlich.

"I spoke of you," Jakob said. "I told him about the heart you had found and also about your article — the one giving him credit for the heart's discovery."

As the initial shock passed I realized something was wrong with Jakob's account. Sir William knew where my father was. He had sat in Calais in the autumn of 1915 with Honoré Bourret and hadn't written a word to me. There had to be an explanation. "Are you sure it was the same Honoré Bourret?"

Jakob smiled unpleasantly. "How many can there be? Especially Honoré Bourrets who are doctors and who once taught in Montreal."

I took a deep breath, not wishing to give myself away. "Did he confirm who he was, Jakob? Did he remember the heart?"

Jakob thought for a second then shook his head. "The meeting was bizarre. He skirted the issue of the heart. He never came right out and said who he was. At the time I thought it was modesty, or perhaps embarrassment, because I recalled a scandal you said had ended his Montreal career. Howlett must have sensed his discomfort. He steered us away from further talk about hearts. Bourret had been his mentor. You'd think they'd have wanted to talk about past glories, but it wasn't the case at all. It was actually the first time I'd seen Howlett at a loss. He panicked, if you want my opinion."

Jakob's prickliness had given way to curiosity, but I didn't have the energy to think about him. In my imagination I was already sailing over the Atlantic to find my father. First I would visit England

and demand an explanation from Sir William. Then I'd cross the Channel. "I have to see him," I muttered, ignoring Jakob.

"You mean Bourret?" he asked, trying to catch my eye.

"Not Bourret." My tone was impatient. So much history was involved I wouldn't have known where to start.

"Howlett?"

I nodded. Sir William — the man I had trusted as I would a father.

Jakob Hertzlich's eyes emptied of expression. He rose, said nothing more, and before I could stop him was out the door.

25

The cold had come overnight to St. Andrews East, along with a first fine powdering of snow. I was sitting in my sister's rocking chair in the Priory, watching the pink light of dusk pooling on a horizon of barren fields. Through the autumn I had managed to shut my eyes to the signs of winter until November, when I was jolted awake. The air outside was cold now, my lungs seized when I inhaled. I had forgotten what this was like — the pure shock of it and the body's instinctive contraction. The house contracted too. Timber cracked, pipes banged in protest.

On the bed my sister had kicked free of her covers. It was cold enough in her bedroom that I had put on double socks and wrapped myself in a duvet, but Laure was flushed with heat. She had run a fever all week. For the last two days she'd been alternately delirious and unconscious. Her lips were cracked from dehydration. Her eyes, when she opened them, had a frightening, glassy look.

She was still alive, I told myself. Others had been cut down so quickly they had not had a chance to call a doctor. This disease progressed with frightening speed. Within hours of feeling unwell many lost the ability to walk. Their faces turned blue. They bled from the nose or ears and coughed up blood as if consumptive. Laure had been spared these horrors. In her the illness had progressed relatively slowly, and this fact gave me hope. She had survived the flu itself and was now suffering from a secondary bacterial pneumonia.

People were calling it the Spanish Flu, although it was unlike any influenza I had ever seen. The symptoms reminded me more of cholera or typhoid, and the rate of death seemed to be ten to twenty percent higher than that of ordinary flu strains. Mysteriously it tended to spare the old and the very young. Its most virulent attacks were reserved for those in the prime of life.

The clock in the hall chimed five. In an hour George Skerry would take over. We had divided the watch into six-hour shifts. At the moment George was downstairs preparing supper. I could smell onions frying. She placed a lot of faith in the healing properties of food and kept offering me pungent broths she swore would keep me well. Despite having been cloistered here throughout Laure's illness she was still healthy, so perhaps there was something to it.

More surprising was my own continuing health. It was exactly a month since the mayor of Montreal had declared a state of emergency. For thirty days all my waking hours, which included much of every night, had been spent tending to the sick. Because most patients were being quarantined at home I made house calls, trudging through Montreal's frozen, deserted streets with my black bag. Not that there was any magic pill or cure I could give people. I explained the principles of hand washing and hygiene to the mothers, sisters and aunts tending to ill family members and handed out face masks. I advised people to take cod-liver oil, to avoid crowds, to keep their homes clean and to stay inside. I held their hands. I offered solace. There was no way to prevent the Spanish Flu, nor was there a cure.

By the time I left for St. Andrews East, Montreal was a ghost town. The first cases of the disease had surfaced in late September; by October it was rampant. Schools shut down. Theatres went next, then churches. Shops had stayed open for a while but people began hoarding staples and soon the shelves were bare. Any house with an influenza victim was forced, on pain of a fine, to post a warning on the door. Within days notices were hanging at every address.

On the other side of the Atlantic the Spanish Flu was killing soldiers faster than German guns and gas had done. In London Dugald Rivers had succumbed. I received a wire from Dr. Mastro, who was overseas and had attended the funeral. I wired back but that was all I managed. I did not cry; there was no time. For weeks after I received the news Dugald's death remained abstract. I had been corresponding with him for three years. The face I held in memory was of a man much younger and more innocent than Dugald had been when he died. It was a face, I suspected, bearing little relation to his features in those final days.

Closer to home, Dr. Clarke was now ill. He had braved the front and returned home unhurt only to contract pneumonia. His wife had telephoned McGill to seek my assistance, but by then I had already left for St. Andrews East to tend to Laure. The day before I had received a wire from Jakob Hertzlich, informing me that Clarke would not survive the week and that if I wished to pay my last respects I should come at once. Clarke's wife must have begged him for aid when I'd been unavailable. I wired back that I could not travel. My own sister was dying.

As if she could feel my attention returning to her, Laure opened her eyes. Their colour, even in the fading light, was bright blue like Grandmother's had been, like the forget-me-nots Laure and I used to pick as girls on the banks of the North River. I said her name and she looked at me, then opened her mouth to speak. I dipped a cloth in water to moisten her lips. I helped her sit up and squeezed a few more drops into her. She took it down so well that I was actually able to offer a glass, holding it while she drank.

With each swallow my spirits lifted. It was a miracle, a reward for the days I'd spent waiting at this bedside, watching over her, wrestling with my sense of growing despair. She couldn't speak. Her lungs would not allow it, but she was lucid, remarkably alert. The time had come. I needed to unburden myself.

Years ago I had stepped into the role of Laure's protector, assuming responsibility for most aspects of her life. Because of her mental state and the natural docility of her spirit I soon lost the habit of consulting her. Laure did not seem able to discuss or plan or make decisions of any kind, so I felt entitled to proceed on my own. I discussed her needs with George Skerry, or simply forged ahead, doing whatever seemed in her best interests. For weeks now I had been in possession of information that was important to me and my sister. Whatever the result it would be unjust not to communicate it to her.

"I have found Father," I said, kneeling by the bed.

Laure's face showed no emotion. The blue eyes stared indifferently into mine.

"He is in France."

She blinked then shifted her glance.

When Jakob Hertzlich first imparted this news to me the world had stopped turning on its axis. I had been filled with such euphoria, such hope, I had barely been able to contain it.

"I am going to meet him."

A fit of coughing overtook my sister and she sank out of my grasp beneath the sheets. I tried to sit her up again but she kept sliding down like a sleepy child. Although she was still conscious her eyes refused to open.

"Laure," I whispered, holding her in my arms. She was impossibly light, her bones weightless as a bird's. She lived for three more days, but in that time not once did she open her eyes again or make any other gesture.

26

NOVEMBER 7, 1918

The news came while I was on the train at a station stop between St. Andrews East and Montreal. It had been anticipated for weeks, but war was a time of rumours and I paid it little attention. The war was over. As our train chugged into the city the Allies and the Germans had laid down arms. In the carriages people hugged each other and cheered. It was a party. So much good news in such a short space of time. First the end of the epidemic, and now, two days later, the end of war.

Windsor Station was jammed. I was squeezed between an old man ahead of me carrying a very large portmanteau and a harried woman behind me stepping on my heels. After the stillness of the Priory it was overwhelming. My feet were heavy and slow. Laure was dead. We had buried her the previous afternoon in the Presbyterian cemetery next to the graves of my mother and grandmother. The snow was gone but the ground had been so hard that the gravedigger broke his pickaxe. Besides the minister there had only been two people at her funeral: George Skerry and me.

The crowd pushed forward, carrying me in its current. I allowed myself to be swept through the station's central hall with its echoing spaces and the disembodied voice booming out gate numbers and departure times.

Outside the station the cold air was a relief, though it was still crowded and noisy. The entire city seemed to have congregated in the streets, even though a sharp wind was blowing from the north. I pulled my scarf over my mouth. On Peel Street traffic had ground to a halt. No one minded. Drivers were smiling and leaning on their horns. Some waved flags, the Red Ensign and the Royal Union. On the sidewalk people stopped to watch as at a parade.

It was the seventh of November, 1918. The war was finally over. Maybe it would be declared a holiday and named *War's End Day* or something equally hopeful and wrong. Wars would break out again. Violence was part of human nature as much as love and generosity.

In front of me a woman in a bright blue sweater leaned out of a car window to hug a man standing on the curb. He kissed her hands before the car lurched forward out of reach. Then he moved on and kissed another woman. Peel Street was now so jammed that cars and horses could no longer move. People eddied around them. A man tried to grab my hand but I pulled away. Someone else came up behind me and squeezed me but I ducked sideways and escaped. I had nothing to celebrate.

Laure's death was the latest blow. Dugald had gone days before her. There were the war dead, boys whose names appeared day after day in long lists in *The Gazette*. A dozen of my students were buried in France and Flanders. The Greaves boy, whom I had never actually met but knew from his mother's stories, was dead, as was Revere Howlett, whose sweet, pale face I would not soon forget. Huntley Stewart had made it back from the war intact, but Samuel Clarke was now on his deathbed. I was rushing to his home right now to say goodbye. How could I hug strangers in the street and wave flags in the midst of such loss?

Dr. Clarke's house was just below the wooded heights of Mount Royal Park. Jakob Hertzlich met me at the door. I was flushed from the walk and had unbuttoned my coat. Jakob was sitting on the step, smoking. He must have been there for some time, for he appeared half-frozen. The tips of his fingers were yellow again and he looked thin and unwell.

"There's no rush," he said, flicking ash over the railing onto a flowerbed rutted with ice. "The body's upstairs if you want to see it."

It had happened while I was on the train. As the porters had come through with news of the armistice Samuel Clarke had died. Jakob reported that it had not been painful. Our old friend had slipped into a coma and had simply not reawakened.

I wanted to reach out then, to feel the solidity of Jakob's body, but I could not move. I stood dumbly, inhaling in the bracing air.

"You're looking well," he said.

My cheeks were likely red from the climb to Dr. Clarke's house. I exhaled a sort of sob. "I don't think I could be worse."

"That makes two of us." He looked away and asked after Laure.

It was the first time I had actually said out loud that my sister was dead. Sadness swelled. When I could speak again I inquired about Jakob's ailing father.

He shrugged. "Dead," he answered. "Like everyone else. Although in his case cancer got him, not the flu." He was staring straight ahead into the darkness, and I was afraid for a second that he too might cry. He bent a knee up, bracing his foot on the wall. From far below on Sherbrooke Street came the incongruous, celebratory honking of car horns.

Mrs. Clarke was upstairs in her husband's bedroom, sitting with the body. She was a plump woman with the same kind warmth for which her husband was renowned, but with a deeper respect for Christian rites and practices than he had ever had. She rose to embrace me the moment I entered the bedroom. She held my hands as I told her how distressed I was not to have been present for Dr. Clarke. She calmed me, inquiring about Laure and then expressing gratitude that I had come in my own time of bereavement. She described Jakob Hertzlich as her guardian angel, the epitome of Christian charity, living in her home for the last week, tirelessly nursing her dying husband. Jakob had followed me into the room, and as Mrs. Clarke praised him she reached for one of his hands too, bringing him into our circle. "He is so special," she said in her kind, fluty voice. "My husband regarded him as a son."

Jakob did not smile. He looked uncomfortable and slipped out of Mrs. Clarke's grasp as soon as he could. The ease that he had brought home from overseas seemed to have disappeared almost completely. Mrs. Clarke and I watched him hurry awkwardly from the room.

"He's a good man," the widow said as the door closed behind him. "More tender than he would have us know." She shook her head sadly then turned her attention to me. "Go ahead and approach the body, Dr. White. Don't be shy. You were also one of my husband's favourites."

Samuel Clarke was laid out in a fresh nightshirt. He looked frailer than when I had last seen him, his hair so thin that a waxy scalp showed through the white wisps. His expression stopped me cold. He looked happy. Perhaps it was just the relaxation of his facial muscles or the way the light was falling, but in his expression was something approximating joy. Contrary to what I had expected it was a relief to be in the dead man's bedroom. The world seemed suddenly less bleak.

Jakob Hertzlich was on the front porch waiting for me when I came downstairs. Light was losing ground to darkness and with it had come silence. Horns no longer blared. In fact the roads seemed to be empty except for trolleys. Jakob had just lit up another of his pungent, hand-rolled cigarettes. He was bundled in his coat and hat now, although his long fingers were still bare. "Bad news," he said as I closed the door behind me.

I thought he was referring to Samuel Clarke and began to speak about the strange expression on our mentor's face and how, on the contrary, it had uplifted me.

"I mean the war," said Jakob.

There had been a mistake. The armistice had not been signed. Apparently the war was still on. I covered my face. I had been making plans, I realized. Even while I had sat upstairs with Samuel Clarke my brain had been almost unconsciously dividing the coming days into tasks to prepare for my crossing to Europe. For that was what the war's end meant to me — that I would be able to cross the Atlantic.

Jakob took a pensive drag on his cigarette. "Have to put off the crossing."

I stared at him as if he were a mind reader.

"As soon as the waters are safe," he said, exuding an acrid cloud, "I'll be gone."

He'd been talking about himself. "That makes two of us," I told him. What did it matter now if I told him my plans? It would probably do him good to be reminded that there were people other than himself in the world. I told him I was off to Oxford.

He cut me off. "To see Howlett?"

The porch was now in almost total darkness. All I could make out was his beard in the glow of his badly rolled cigarette. "Yes," I said.

Below us the city glittered, a patch of fallen stars. He made a guttural noise in his throat. The animosity he consistently showed Sir William was beyond reason — a primitive response. "There are things you don't know," I said quietly. "Sir William has been pivotal in my life."

"Oh, that I know," Jakob Hertzlich said. "Believe me, Dr. White. That I know."

"It's not what you think," I added.

"It's not a question of thinking. It's as plain as the nose on your face what you feel about him. It's also plain that there's no reciprocation. He exploits you and you don't even see it."

A cold, bright moon hung above us, winking down through partial clouds as if the whole scene were a joke. "There's more to it than that," I said. I was close enough to hear the agitation in his breath. The moon winked again, and then suddenly it hit me. Jakob Hertzlich was jealous.

I could not make him out in the darkness but it didn't matter. I could not believe I hadn't seen it before. It was not as if he'd hidden his feelings. For years he'd been trying to attract my attention. I had chosen not to see. I blushed, remembering the night of the aborted party; our unconsummated physical tryst had meant far more to him than I had ever imagined.

Jakob Hertzlich had loved me for years. It felt strange, realizing I was loved. So strange I had not recognized it. For the briefest moment tenderness welled inside me. The skin around my eyes went tight.

In the darkness Jakob Hertzlich saw nothing of this. He picked up his satchel and before I could say a word marched down the icy walk to the street.

VII
THE CROSSING

Starting a long way off the true point,
and proceeding by loops and zigzags, we now and then
arrive just where we ought to be.

— GEORGE ELIOT, *MIDDLEMARCH*

27

DECEMBER 1918

It was the seventh day of the trip, a fact I'd learned in the mess hall that morning from one of the other passengers. Seven days of squall and storm, the ship tossed like a leaf on the swells. I felt like I had died. Seven days or weeks or months — I could no longer say how long I'd been at sea. The hours melted into each other, endlessly protracted and so cold that I couldn't stay outside for more than a few minutes. It was late December, the worst time of the year for an Atlantic crossing. I had taken a ship to England once before in winter, but the weather had co-operated and I'd been able to spend a good part of it on deck. This was a completely different experience. I'd been sick from the instant I stepped on board.

When I had told people about my plan to cross in December they tried to warn me. Miss Skerry thought winter crossings unsafe. Samuel Clarke's widow spent an entire morning attempting to dissuade me. The crossing would be hard, she said, but Europe would be worse. My former students, many of whom had only just returned from overseas, were more categorical. Winter crossings were to be avoided at any cost. I would be confined to my cabin by a cold more intense than any I had experienced in Canada. Europe was still reeling from the war. Even the ship's agent from whom I had purchased my ticket had said it would be wise to postpone my travels until the spring.

I could not wait. As soon as the armistice was signed on November 11, in a railway carriage in the forests of northern France, I began to mobilize. Passenger ships had started crossing again even before the ink was dry on the peace agreement and I was able to book a berth for the Christmas period. I was not scared off by the warnings of my students and friends. I thought I knew what winter crossings were like, and after four years of war-time confinement in Montreal I was itching to brave the open seas.

Open Arms was shuttered, its gate closed to visitors even though this was the Christmas season. The walk from the curb to the front door was icy, and I proceeded with care. I had taken the train from Portsmouth and found an inn not far from the Howletts' house, but even today, a full twenty-four hours after stepping onto dry land, I was still feeling the effect of the ship. I kept tilting to the left as though the world had skewed slightly and I was the only one to notice. The nausea had stopped. I must have lost a full stone in weight; my clothes hung off me. I was weak and exhausted, but I was here, safe and more or less sound.

I knocked on the Howletts' door and waited for a minute or so, peering through a little strip of frosted glass. I couldn't see anything inside the house except that it was dark. It was only ten o'clock in the morning, too early for Sir William to be out visiting. I got worried then. There had been so many deaths back in Montreal I suppose that worry was a natural response. I rapped again, more insistently, and kept rapping until a shadow filled the pane.

Lady Kitty poked her beautiful patrician head through the crack between the door and the door jamb. When she saw me she drew herself up like a long-necked bird and shook her elegant head. She still towered above me, but posture alone couldn't hide her alteration. Her mouth was pulled down almost clownishly and her eyes, once so bold and unblinking, would not meet mine. Although she was attempting to stand tall her shoulders appeared hunched; she was carrying a load so heavy it was about to break her back. She shook my hand, saying what a pleasant surprise it was to see me so soon after the armistice.

Now it was my turn to be surprised. "You didn't receive my letters?"

Lady Kitty was no master at dissembling. Her eyebrows lifted convincingly enough, but her eyes gave her instantly away. "Letters?" She didn't move or offer me any gesture of encouragement.

"I sent you several. The last one announced that I would arrive today." My toes had begun to burn with the cold. The walk from the inn had been too much, I realized, looking over Lady Kitty's shoulder into her heated hall.

"Perhaps you've not heard," said Lady Kitty, "but Sir William is gravely ill."

The porch lurched slightly underneath me. "I'm afraid I have to sit."

Lady Kitty looked at me in alarm, likely remembering my last two visits and the fainting fits she and her husband had been forced to nurse me through.

"I'm so sorry," I said, steadying myself on her wall. "The trip has been difficult. I haven't been especially well."

Lady Kitty's hands dropped to her sides. She glared at me but did allow me inside the door. "Come, Dr. White," she said, motioning to a bench strategically placed in the vestibule. "You may sit for a moment and warm yourself, but then I'm afraid I must ask you to leave. William is in no state to receive anyone. As a physician I'm sure you will understand."

Somewhere on the second floor of Open Arms the old man was lying on his deathbed. Jakob Hertzlich had been right. Kitty Howlett's face was etched with grief. A few months ago she had lost her only child to the war and now she would lose her husband. There was no common ground for us in terms of interest or outlook; but for the first time I felt what it must be like to be this woman. The immensity of her pain suddenly became real. Without even pausing to think I reached out and took her long, cool fingers in my own. A radiator banged beside us, making us both jump. Lady Kitty recovered first, laughing, and shyly retrieved her hand.

"Wait," I said, rooting in my bag, for I had brought along Jakob's sketches. It was he who had suggested I pack them. I would need some tasty bone, he said, to throw to Lady Kitty if I wanted to get past her to her husband. He had been right I now saw. But I also felt quite sincerely that she should have them. They were wonderful pieces and might bring her a little joy in a very bleak time. "There's something you must see, Lady Kitty. They've come from France to Montreal and now back across the ocean to you."

We sat on Lady Kitty's hall bench with the sketch pad between us. For some time Lady Kitty flipped the pages in silence, but the mo-ment she came to the portraits by Jakob Hertzlich her hands became still. When she looked up her eyes were full of tears. "Thank you, Agnes. I believe it will do William a great deal of good to see these."

The house seemed deserted. She and Sir William were on their own for one more week until the new year, Lady Kitty explained, with the servants gone for the holidays. Friends came by regularly to check on them. In fact every single day someone or other rang, but Sir William was too weak to receive them. Lady Kitty had sent word out that the doors of Open Arms were closed. There was no trace of Christmas anywhere, I noticed. No tree or sprig of holly. The main hall was dark, as was the dining room where a reception had once been held in my honour. A faint odour of disinfectant was the only smell.

The dolls sat placidly on the second-floor landing in exactly the same spot they'd occupied over a decade ago when I'd last been here. I surprised myself by feeling grateful for this one particularly female touch as I climbed the stairs behind Lady Kitty. She was not such a bad woman. Like my sister Laure she had probably dreamed of mothering a houseful of children. And also like my sister she had been unlucky enough to see that dream shattered.

I had thought that the last few months in Montreal and St. Andrews East would have steeled me for anything, but when we finally arrived at the bedroom door and I saw Sir William I realized I was not steeled at all. His skin was the colour of old parchment. Lying there on his back he looked diminished, already a corpse.

Lady Kitty entered first, calling out cheerfully and stepping forward to plump his pillows. He stayed her hands. "Who have you brought to me?" He nodded at the door where I was standing, rooted in shock.

I took a step forward out of the shadows and said my name.

"A pleasure." It was difficult for him to speak. By the time he reached the last syllable he was gasping.

"I heard you were ill," I told him.

His mouth formed an alarming smile, making me think of my skull samples back at the museum. "So many people have come to pay their respects," he said. "You'd think I was dying."

It was supposed to be a joke, a sardonic wink at the truth, but it made me want to weep. Sir William's vigour had leaked away. He gave an old man's cough to clear his throat. "You don't need to play-act, Dr. White," he said finally. "I've been following this case for months. I know there is no hope."

Lady Kitty fluttered beside him like a bird. "You mustn't speak like that, William. You'll frighten poor Dr. White." Then she told me how awful her husband was as a patient. She did this theatrically, trying to inject levity into the conversation. "He's constantly defying the doctors' orders and overexerting himself. The physicians are optimistic, though, aren't they, dear? Dr. Doyle thinks you're on the mend. Just yesterday he said you'll soon be fit as a fiddle."

"Fit to play a funeral dirge."

"William," Lady Kitty pleaded. "This isn't what Dr. White came for."

Sir William shut his eyes. He sighed; the exchange had completely exhausted him. "She should enlighten me then," he sighed, "as to why she did come."

I took a couple of steps forward and held out the sketch pad. "To bring you this."

Sir William took it. He was all right until he came to Jakob Hertzlich's portrait of Revere standing in military dress. At that point he rolled over. Kitty sprang from her chair and ran to him. I did not move. I watched this man whom I had once held so dear mourn his only son. At that moment my feelings for the man were mixed. I loved him more than I think I had loved any man except my father. He was my link to childhood, to Honoré Bourret. There was even a physical resemblance between the two men; and like my father Sir William had cut me from his life suddenly and without explanation.

When Sir William had recovered sufficiently I spoke again. "There is one other matter I wished to discuss with you, if I may."

Lady Kitty stepped forward, ready to fend me off, but her husband held up his hand.

"In private, if possible," I said quietly.

Strangely enough the tension in the room eased then, as if all three of us had been waiting for this moment. Sir William made another movement with his hand, indicating that his wife should leave, which she did without comment. It was clear to me now that my letters had been received and read. My visit had been anticipated by the Howletts. I had obviously been discussed.

"I learned about the trip you took," I said, "with Revere, early in the war." I mentioned Montreuil and Calais to prompt him, for he was looking away from me.

Eventually he turned to face me. "I thought that might be it." He paused to let us both collect ourselves. "Jakob Hertzlich told you?"

When I nodded he nodded too and pinched the bridge of his nose. "I thought you two were no longer in communication."

"We are in touch," I said a little sharply. I had not come all this way to discuss my relations with Jakob Hertzlich.

Sir William's breathing was clearer now and his words seemed to come more easily. "Your father and I were close once, Agnes. Very close. He was a man I revered at an early point in my life."

I knew this much already. We had spoken about it at length years ago in Baltimore. To be honest I was no longer interested in their shared past. "What I need to know," I said, "is your current relationship, Sir William. You told me you had no idea of his whereabouts. You told me he'd disappeared." My voice began to shake.

Sir William continued to look out the window. When he turned back to me his eyes were clear and kind. "It's complicated, Agnes." He stopped again, searching for his words. "I have tried to act properly here, both to you and to him. And I would defend my actions even though they have hurt you."

"So you admit you know him. And you admit that you concealed it from me." The words came out in a sort of throttled whisper. I could not have spoken normally to save my life. Sir William had misled me. He would mislead me still, given the chance.

"Agnes, dear," he said, reaching for me with his wasted hand. There was a hint of the old Howlett in this gesture, the charming, wooing figure of the past, but I was no longer under his spell. "I've wronged you," he said. "I am sorry."

I had not expected this. The apology was frank and simple; it stopped my anger. A slew of questions came rushing in its stead. "Have you two talked about me?" I asked. "Does he know of our connection?"

Sir William shook his head. "He knows nothing, Agnes."

I sat back, stunned. "But you have seen him. You have talked to him."

Sir William's voice remained kind. "I don't see him anymore. The visit to Calais was exceptional." He paused and then began again. "Listen, my dear Agnes. I know this must be painful. I did not wish you to find out."

I was cut to the quick. I could not believe he did not grasp my situation even now. "You mean you would still be lying to me if

Jakob Hertzlich had not told me about that visit to Calais?"

"It's not a lie."

"Oh no?" I had found my voice again. I was practically shouting. "What is it then?" Never had I spoken to him with such boldness.

He looked up then narrowed his eyes. "An omission," he said finally. "You never asked. Neither, for that matter, did he. The wrong done here, Agnes White, was for your own good."

"But I've searched for him my entire life. Finding my father is all I have ever wanted." I started to cry. "I thought you knew that. You did know it. I told you."

"Dear Agnes," Sir William said, stroking my hand. "My poor, poor dear. I couldn't tell you about your father. I know it seems harsh, but understand. Honoré Bourret is not a simple man. He wanted all ties cut." He paused here to watch me. "Every last one."

"He didn't cut the tie with you."

Sir William shook his tired head. "I'm different, Agnes. And even with me there were conditions."

It felt as if a giant hand were crushing my chest, breaking my ribs like match sticks. What was he saying? Somehow he was more deserving than I, more than my poor mother and sister?

"I did something for him once that he cannot forget," said Sir William in explanation. "In his mind there is a debt."

The story came out at last. It was a particular version of events told from a very particular point of view, but at last I had the pieces. Sir William's account began with a question that took me by surprise. "Do you remember my visit to your museum right before the fire? I was in Montreal to sit for a portrait organized by McGill's chancellor." When I nodded he continued. "During that visit you asked about my journals."

"The autopsy journals," I said, remembering the way Jakob had hounded him. "Jakob Hertzlich challenged you, as I recall."

"Over the Howlett Heart," said Sir William.

"Your journal said you'd presided over the autopsy, but you'd told me previously that the presiding doctor was my father."

"Yes," he said. He looked to the window, "You weren't the only one I told."

In 1873 he had perjured himself in a Montreal court of law to provide an alibi for his mentor Honoré Bourret. The heart had been excised in October of 1872, the exact month and year that Marie Bourret went missing. I had been aware of these dates but somehow had held them separate in my mind, managing to block out the connection. "So my father was not at the Dead House with you that night when you extracted the heart? It was you after all who did the work?"

Sir William inclined his chin upon his chest.

"Where was my father?" I asked, starting to panic.

Sir William shrugged. "Your father was a good man, Agnes. He was my teacher and he was my friend. That was all I was concerned with. I had enormous respect for him, but he was by no means universally loved. He was a French-Canadian and Catholic, don't forget, and he had strong views about a whole range of topics that he was not shy to express. When the murder charges were laid he had few allies."

"Except for you."

Sir William Howlett nodded.

"I see," I said after a pause. Sir William seemed utterly convinced he had done the right thing, and I was not about to argue. He had saved my father at some risk to himself. He had upheld values of loyalty and friendship.

"I need his address," I said in a voice now back to normal.

Sir William tore a corner off a page of his son's sketch pad and scribbled something on it. It was as easy as that. As I took the scrap from him our fingers touched and we both looked away, embarrassed. But that touch made me wonder. I felt nothing this time, unlike every other time our bodies had made contact. There was no current, not even simple heat. My break with him that day was so complete I had to ask myself what kind of bond we once had shared.

28

I stepped off the ferry in Calais in a downpour. This dismal town on the northwest coast of France was in many ways an obvious choice for a man like Honoré Bourret. It is a port city and also known as the most English of all the towns in France. During the Middle Ages Calais was under British rule. The British Army captured it in the fourteenth century, forcing the French out and implanting British settlers. But on New Year's Eve in 1588 the French Army launched a surprise attack and won it back. The occupiers had been revelling, and could not defend it.

So my father was living in a town similar to Montreal, and I had arrived on New Year's Eve to take him by storm. The date had been unintentional. I had only learned about Calais's military history in a chance conversation with the captain of the channel ferry.

My hotel was in the old section of Calais, just off Place d'Armes, the town's main square. The air smelled of salt and sleet showered me as I descended from the cab. Auberge des Flots, the inn where William Howlett had dined with my father, stood before me. From the outside it seemed as dismal as the other buildings that lined the street like crowded teeth, but the interior was surprisingly warm.

A woman with a child of about two years in tow, her belly big with another, welcomed me. "Entrez, entrez," she said, taking my umbrella and showing the driver where to put my bag. "It is no day for travel."

She and her little boy, Charles, accompanied me to the front desk where her husband was waiting. Judging from the proliferation of keys hanging on the wall behind him I was the only guest that night, though the tavern in the next room was full of talk and laughter. After the hard Atlantic trip and ferry crossing I treated myself to a room with a view of the harbour and a private bath. The husband himself carried my bags upstairs and lit the coal fire in the grate.

My little room was soon warm. It had been decorated simply, in colours bright enough to offset the weather, and soon I felt quite cheered. The trip and the meeting with Howlett had depleted me. When the innkeeper's wife came upstairs with a plate of soup I inquired about the address Howlett had scribbled out for me.

"Rue de Verel," she said, squinting in the gas light. "*Bien sûr je la connais*. It is a bit of a walk from the *auberge*, down in the *quartier* Courgain-Maritime where the fishermen live. Who is it you are seeking?"

"Dr. Bourret." I marvelled at how easily the name came out. I felt no shame anymore, just a slight quickening of my pulse, which settled almost immediately.

"The doctor. Yes, that is where he is located. I am not good with directions but my husband will indicate the way for you. You are planning to go tomorrow?"

Instinctively I liked this young woman, with her ready smile and hospitality, but I did not wish to talk. Calais was a foreign place but it was still a town. Having grown up in St. Andrews East I knew how fast news travelled, and also how it could distort. I thanked my hostess for her kindness and concentrated on my soup, nudging the conversation to more neutral topics.

As soon as she had gone back downstairs I unpacked my bags. Not my clothes — for apart from the ones I had on I had just one other outfit — but the bag full of things I had brought for my father. Choosing them had been difficult for it had forced me to put myself in his shoes and imagine what he might wish to see of my life. It had made me realize how little I actually knew about him. Forty-four years ago, my eyes had been those of a child. Appropriately, perhaps, the first items I had chosen were photographs of me and Laure as children, posing in pinafores in a photographer's studio. There was a picture of Laure on her wedding day. My father had never known her, but at least now he would see what a beauty his second daughter had been. The remaining photograph was of me receiving my Arts diploma from McGill.

In addition to family photographs I had packed the textbook by William Howlett containing my chapter on congenital heart defects. This he would also appreciate — his own daughter working for the man he once had mentored. I had also selected other academic papers I'd written, for the father of my memory had delighted in science and research. There were pamphlets announcing talks I had given at Harvard and Johns Hopkins and newspaper clippings reporting them. There were also articles on the museum and a flattering profile of my work at McGill in *The Gazette*.

Accompanying these items in a separate file folder was my first publication. I wanted to present this and the drawing by Jakob Hertzlich as special gifts to him. They both concerned *Cor biatriatrum triloculare*, the three-chambered heart with the little pocket compensating for the absent ventricle supposedly discovered by my father in 1872.

Several other three-chambered hearts with the compensatory pocket had been discovered after 1872, but the one at McGill was the first. In the article I had floated the term "the Bourret anomaly," which I had hoped would please him as much as it pleased me.

Now of course I blushed to read what I had written. The heart was bound up in my father's history, but differently from the way I had imagined. If what William Howlett had confessed were true his link with that heart was the last thing my father would want to be reminded of.

Then again he might be gratified to see the alibi he'd presented so many years ago corroborated by me in a reputable medical journal. I repacked it and Jakob's drawing with the other items in the bag. When I reached 27 rue de Verel I would decide what to do with them, not before. It was best to be prepared for anything.

There was one possibility that I could not envisage — that my father might simply not open the door. William Howlett had implied this could happen, but I did not accept it. Shame had kept my father away from me all these years, I was sure of it. What man wouldn't want to see his child — a child who cared so much she had crossed the Atlantic in midwinter to be with him? How could he not be pleased to learn she had recreated herself in his image, building a career that mirrored his own?

I slept better that night than I had in weeks. When I emerged from my room the following day full of hope and eagerness it was nearly ten o'clock. The innkeeper was at his bar, wiping glasses with a towel. He was a good-natured sort, with the red and bumpy nose of a brandy drinker. I guessed my red-nosed host was a few years younger than I, in his early forties. He invited me to sit down and his wife Eugenie soon came in with bread and a bowl of milky coffee.

"Eugenie says you are looking for Dr. Bourret," he said as I started to eat.

I nodded. The bread was very fresh. I spread it with sweet butter and a delicious plum compote. As I ate the innkeeper entertained me with talk. Apparently my father had been a regular at the inn until quite recently. He had health problems now, the innkeeper said, but for years he had dropped by a couple of times a week. His work made him well-known to the townspeople. In fact, the innkeeper added proudly, Bourret had assisted at his own birth. "I was a breech baby, born ass-backward as the doctor never fails to remind me." He winked and laughed.

So my father took a drink now and then with his neighbours. He had a sense of humour. The innkeeper had no idea what nuggets he was offering me. Honoré Bourret had become a country doctor, the kind he would once have disdained, contenting himself to deliver babies and nurse them through the ordinary maladies of childhood.

"Does he live alone?" I asked, draining my bowl. The bartender looked over at his wife then picked up a new glass. "Depends on what you mean by that word."

"Does he have a wife?"

The bartender laughed. "He's not exactly the marrying type, although women certainly like him."

His wife shifted beside me. She had lingered in the bar to listen to our conversation. "This is his business, Gilles, not ours."

"You are right, my dear." He turned to me. "She is my conscience, dear Eugenie. But it hurts no one, least of all Dr. Bourret, to say he has success with women."

"But there is no wife?" I asked again.

"Many have tried," laughed the innkeeper. "There is someone with him now, even at his age. Mind you he's probably sitting on a fortune."

His wife shook her head at him. "He was married once a long time ago. In England, if I remember."

"England?" I said, startled.

"She's right," said the bartender. He happened to be reaching for another glass and didn't notice my surprise. "I had forgotten that, but it's true. He was born in England. It's why he speaks in that peculiar way, with an accent and English turns of phrase. He had an English wife and child, but they died in a boating accident." He paused to study me. "You are from England too, are you not?"

I shook my head. "Canada," I said, although my mind was still with the wife and child drowned in England. It could have happened, I supposed. There were plenty of years in his life unaccounted for — half a century. But then I remembered that my father had been here in Calais over forty years ago, overseeing the innkeeper's ass-backwards birth. That didn't leave much time for a romantic interlude across the Channel, especially one producing a new child. Perhaps England was a fabrication, "*une fausse piste*," as they called it here. The drownings might be an allusion to things that had happened in an entirely different place and time.

"Canada," the bartender repeated thoughtfully. "But what are you to him, if I may ask, a relative? A friend?" He was observing me closely, rubbing the glass.

"A colleague," I said quickly. "Our connection is professional." It was partially true and I was not about to divulge anything more to them or to anyone else until I had spoken with my father.

Before I left the innkeeper drew me a map. Penmanship was not his strongest suit, and even before I left the inn I foresaw trouble. He apologized for the mess of lines but kept insisting it wouldn't be hard to decipher. The old town was small, he said. I knew this to be true. Calais was a walled medieval city surrounded by moats and canals. "*Ce n'est pas compliqué*," he kept assuring me, his maze of chicken scratches suggesting just the opposite.

Initially the map led me through Place d'Armes with its wide-open space and watchtower dating back to the thirteenth century. But soon the streets grew increasingly intertwined. The freezing rain of the previous day had stopped, but the temperature was still cold; the cobblestones were sheathed in ice. I hadn't walked for ten minutes when I slipped and fell, crushing the bag full of things for my father. I sat on the curb and looked through it, ensuring the papers and photographs were undamaged.

The smell of fish was stronger here than in the main square. The gutters were full of refuse that looked like it had been there long before winter began. I resumed my walk. Following the innkeeper's chicken scratches I turned left, then right, as I thought the map indicated. Then I turned right again. In Calais, like in the old sections of Montreal, street names were nailed to exterior walls. The one directly in front of me was nowhere on my map.

There was not a soul in sight. No shops, no cafés, no signs of life.

Stevedores and sailors lived in this *quartier*, and for them the day before New Year's was certainly a day of rest. They were probably sleeping, or perhaps the stillness suggested something more devastating and sad.

I walked down a deserted street, picked at random this time, following instinct instead of the map, which was not only unreliable but smudged after my fall. My boots slapped the cobblestones, creating an echo that gave me the sensation of being followed. I looked back over my shoulder until I realized that I myself was making the sound. A small white sign was screwed into a stone building in front of me, but again the street name meant nothing to me. I walked on, turning this way and that, abandoning myself to the feeling of being utterly lost.

The cold that had settled over this northern French city was bitter, unlike the cold of Montreal. When I had left that city I'd had to cover my face, and even then it had been hard to inhale. Frost had coated my eyelashes and exposed locks of hair. Calais, in contrast, had seemed warm when I arrived. Gradually, however, the damp had wormed its way inside my clothes. The town was built on a marsh; I was chilled to the bone.

Another street name was nailed into the wall of a building in front of me, but the lenses of my glasses had fogged and I couldn't make it out right away. I removed them for a quick rub and it was then that I discerned the "V." A few steps more and I was able to read the magic words. I stopped, shut my eyes and took a deep breath. I had arrived, walking in circles through the frozen streets with only a makeshift map and my instincts as guides. I rechecked the map one last time for the address. *Rue de Verel,* 27. The bartender had written the last digit the French way, like a crooked cross.

It was one of the bigger houses on the street, but even so it looked much more forlorn than I'd expected. The grey facade was almost indistinguishable in colour from the sky. Bars lined the lower windows. This was common in Calais, but it made the house seem guarded and suspicious.

There were no boards for pedestrians to walk on, just a strip of mud beside the cobblestones with boot prints frozen in it. I made my way to my father's gate. A small front garden had been prepared for the winter, its bushes tied in burlap and string. I imagined Honoré Bourret attending to these details. By the looks of it he was a meticulous man.

The woman who came to the door was younger than I, although not by much, dressed casually in crocheted slippers and an old skirt. Her hair was a burnt orange colour with grey showing at the part line and temples. Her face was not friendly.

"I am looking for Dr. Bourret," I said in French.

"*Il ne travaille plus*," she said. Without even inquiring as to my needs she directed me to another physician, someone called Babin, who had apparently bought my father's practice. His office was several streets to the south, she explained, but it was sure to be closed for the holidays.

I shook my head and told her I had not come for medical help. It was cold at the door. She hooked a slippered foot around her standing leg and folded her arms, waiting for me to say more.

"I need to see the doctor," I said again. "My reasons are personal."

This last remark made her angry. She had a square jaw, which she thrust out at me now, although frankly I couldn't have looked like much of a threat. I had deduced she was my father's companion — *la femme qui n'était pas sa femme*. Her attitude certainly made it clear that she wasn't a cook or a housekeeper.

To put her at ease I said I was a colleague. "We knew each other long ago."

We were both freezing by this time, so she allowed me inside while she went down the hall to announce me to Dr. Bourret. "I promise you nothing," she tossed over her shoulder as she left. "He seldom receives visitors."

The house was dark and smaller than it seemed from the outside. Its few windows were narrow, more suitable for a military fort than a home. The walls were painted white, which brightened it a little, and the gas lamps were lit, but the atmosphere was generally dreary.

The orange-haired woman eventually returned and led me to a living room at the back of the house. Now that the door was shut, closing off the salty smell of the sea, other odours took over. My hostess, I soon noticed, smelled of alcohol. We walked wordlessly to a den. Inside this room my father was sitting on a couch with his legs up, wrapped in a rug. He didn't get up when I walked in, just turned to me and squinted. And what a shock that gave me, for the face he turned in my direction was nothing like the one I'd held for years inside me. His upper lip was shaved clean. His hair was completely white. He still had a quantity of it. He was wearing glasses with lenses so thick they magnified his eyes to twice their normal size, making him look at once angry and amazed.

I stood in the doorway staring until finally he called me inside. "You will excuse me if I do not rise," he said in a French that was clearly not local. "My joints are painful with the wet weather." He motioned me forward. "Enter," he said. "Come into the light where I can see you."

The request surprised me for I was already in the light at a distance of only five feet. The orange-haired woman gave me a push. "Go on," she whispered. "His eyes are bad. You have to go right up close."

"I can hear you," said the old man. "My eyes may be weak but there is nothing wrong with my ears." He took off his glasses to reveal pupils the colour of milk. "I can't even read the papers now," he said, folding up an old copy of *Le Monde* and sticking it between his body and a cushion. "Solange has to read me the news." He motioned with his hands again. "Come closer! You are a blur!"

I had to walk right up to the couch. I felt like a little girl about to receive either a slap or a kiss. He stared for some time then finally looked away. "No," he said, as if answering a question. "I have never laid eyes on you."

A brandy bottle sat on a low table with two glasses. The old man must have seen where I was looking for he started chuckling. "I guess I must offer you a drink. We were toasting the end of this particularly awful year. You will join us?" He held up a glass for me. "I've always felt it's more important to bury the old year with a little pomp than to throw a party for the new one." He pointed to a chair opposite his couch where he wanted me to sit. "Now tell me who you are. You say that we have met."

He filled three glasses, handing one to me and another to Solange, who was standing nearby. "Come, my dear," he said. "Help me welcome our guest." He patted the free end of the couch and she sat down, reminding me of a tabby curling at its master's feet.

"It was years ago," I said. "I was just a child." These were my first words to him, and I spoke them in English. Surprise registered on his face that I was not French.

He sat forward, trying to bring me into focus. For a moment he dropped his casual air. He turned on Solange. "I thought you said she was a colleague."

Solange shrugged. "It's what she said."

"I did say that," I said in French. I didn't want to be the cause of a fight, and I certainly didn't want to turn Solange into any more of an enemy to me than she already was. "I am a colleague now, a doctor like you."

"You speak in riddles," said my father. He was still looking in my direction, but the cloudy lenses made it difficult to know exactly what he was seeing. "You are English?"

I nodded.

"And a doctor."

I nodded again.

"And where did you say we met?"

I steeled myself, half-expecting the floor to split open. "In Montreal."

Honoré Bourret shrugged. "Then it is certain you are mistaken, for Montreal is a place I have never had the pleasure of visiting."

His strange, milky eyes looked straight at me. It was the oddest sensation to have this father who wasn't quite my father deny me so brazenly.

"But you were born there," I said.

"I come from England," said Bourret. Solange watched me with sleepy, catlike eyes. The two of them were so insistent I began to waver. The face was different from the one I remembered. It wasn't inconceivable that this Honoré Bourret was a stranger. I began to consider this possibility, but then caught myself. Three years ago William Howlett had sat with him in the Auberge des flots. Jakob Hertzlich had been a witness. He was lying. Looking me straight in the eye and lying.

"I have just sailed from England," I said, "from the home of a friend of yours."

He had relaxed somewhat, leaning back on the couch, but at the mention of Sir William he sat up again. He turned to Solange and ordered her to leave the room. When she saw that he was serious she objected. Why should she leave because of a stranger? This was her home too, in case he hadn't noticed. What kind of a way was this to treat people? She heaped abuse on me too for disrupting her morning.

The old man had to shoo her out. It was an embarrassing spectacle that spoke volumes about their relations, or lack of them. "Women!" he said in English when he finally got the door shut. "Always such a handful." He sat down opposite me again. "So Dr. Howlett sent you here?" He continued in English, probably to prevent his girlfriend from listening in.

I told him that Sir William had done everything in his power to dissuade me from coming, that he'd called the situation "complex" and tried to warn me away.

"But you came nonetheless."

There was a pause during which we studied each other. I had no idea what he was thinking. Perhaps he was considering his options, trying to figure out his next move and just how much he wanted to reveal. Or perhaps he was considering me. The inscrutable eyes blinked shut. "I don't know you," he said for the second time that day.

I said my name — not the English one that my grandmother had given me but the older French one chosen by him. I said I was his daughter.

He did not respond for some time. He crossed one leg over the other and reached for a box of cigarettes. He offered me one. When I shook my head he lit one for himself. "I have never been to Montreal," he said, exhaling. "William Howlett tried to dissuade you from coming here for a reason. It is a waste of time."

I left soon after. Solange was in the kitchen, preparing lunch. She did not even look up as I passed in the hall. The old man had to accompany me to the door himself and hand me my coat and boots. The vestibule was quite small and he and I had to stand perhaps a foot apart as I dressed myself.

"You must not speak of this to anyone," he said quietly.

By that time I had collected myself a little, or at least I thought I had. "What is there to speak of?" I said, also low-voiced, as if we shared a secret. "We do not know each other."

"That is right," he said and smiled.

Those were our final words. I was shaking as he closed the door behind me. He was closing me out now just as years ago he had closed out my mother and a much younger version of myself, and even before that as he'd closed out his crippled sister. It was only when I reached the street that I realized my hands were empty. I had forgotten the bag with my gifts in the house. I could picture exactly where I had left it beside the chair on which I'd sat, but nothing in this world could have induced me to go back inside to retrieve it.

A light snow had begun to fall over la rue de Verel and all the other streets of Calais. My father was probably in his kitchen now, trying to make peace with Solange. They would sit down to their noonday meal and eventually one or the other of them would return to the den and discover my bag. There was no chance that

Solange would be able to decipher the materials I had so carefully packed and carried all this way, and no chance that my father would be able to read them even if he did get his hands on them.

29

When morning broke on New Year's Day it was barely distinguishable from night. The cocks crowed despite the heavy black sky. I had not slept much, in part because of my father, in part because of the noise from the bar, which happened to be located directly beneath my room. The New Year's Eve *réveillon* was an event at the Auberge des flots. Their annual party was renowned in Calais, and judging from the decibel volume half the town had dropped in to raise a glass.

I had stayed upstairs despite invitations from my hosts. When Eugenie heard me refuse her husband's offer of complimentary champagne she invited me to sit with her and Charles in their rooms and share a hot milk. Even this I could not manage. All night I sat alone and wept. Just before dawn I dressed and went downstairs. The bar looked like a storm had blown through it. Glasses and bottles cluttered the tables. Two bodies lay prone on the floor. I tiptoed past them, found my boots, and slipped out the door.

This time I needed no map from the innkeeper to direct me. I simply followed my nose down avenue de la Mer to the water. The sky lightened as I walked, but aside from gulls and cormorants circling above the town and calling with their piercing cries I seemed to be the only living creature. I walked at a good pace, the wind at my back, breathing in the fecund, salty odours. Calais was fronted by an enormous beach, la plage Blériot, which I had glimpsed from the ferry when we landed. A large hotel had been built overlooking it, but this was now closed for the season, its doors and windows boarded.

I crossed the beach, whose sands were rippled by the wind, and made it to a pier with a little tower at the end. There I stopped. The tide was on its way out, which I didn't realize right away. Rivers were what I had grown up with — the fast-flowing North River fronting my grandmother's property in St. Andrews East, the St. Lawrence after I moved to Montreal. The ocean smelled different, of salt and seaweed and creatures in its depths. I stood there for a long time, staring out at the water.

In a single week I had lost the two most important men in my life. Yet the word "lost" was misleading. Neither had died and it had been years since either had played any outwardly discernible role in my life. Internally, however, they had been pivotal, at the centre of everything. Now that centre, my centre, had slipped. Sir William Howlett had lied to me. I didn't care that the situation with Honoré Bourret was complex, or even that the lie in Howlett's estimation was in my best interests. My father was no better. For years I had believed him to be a victim, an innocent man vilified by the small-minded Scottish community in Montreal for daring to be ambitious and different. As a woman with the same qualities I had identified with him.

My father had left a wife in the final stages of pregnancy without a thought for the consequences to her or to the child yet to be born. He had abandoned me when I was not yet five. And when I turned up on his doorstep forty-four years later he had turned away again, lying to protect himself. Such a man, I now realized, might be capable of disposing of a crippled sister who made heavy claims on him. The clues to my father had been there but I had shut my eyes to them.

The French word *fille* means "girl" as well as "daughter." Yesterday at this hour I had still been a girl, with my hopes largely intact. I had been excited, wending my way through the streets to meet him, following the ridiculous hand-drawn map. I had pinned much on that meeting. The truth was, of course, I had left girlhood behind years ago. I wasn't the *fille* of Honoré Bourret or of anyone else. I was forty-nine and the bottom had fallen out of my life. I thought back to the scraps of my existence I had collected for him. I had been like a schoolgirl, toting home prizes from class. Only now could I see how pathetic I was. He would no doubt toss out the bag unexamined.

The voices of children roused me and I realized I had been standing on the pier for some time. The beach was now wider and slick from the receding water. Sunlight was beating down strongly enough to have broken through the clouds. Sea birds were basking in it on the still-wet sand. A group of children had come to play by the water's edge — two boys of eight or nine and a little girl. The boys were skimming stones and shouting, calling out the number of dips before the stones disappeared from view. They greeted me as I stepped down onto the beach. The oldest one wished me a Happy New Year and I reciprocated.

I did not know what the coming year would bring, but happiness did not seem highly likely. As I headed back toward town I came upon my own footprints going in the opposite direction, already half-erased.

VIII
RETURN

*The condition does not admit of cure,
but permits of amelioration and of arrest of
the downward trend of the disease.*

— MAUDE ABBOTT, "CONGENITAL CARDIAC DISEASE"

30

JANUARY 20, 1919

Tomorrow would be fine, the sailors had predicted, which I had trouble believing after weeks of poor weather. It appeared that my voyage home might be quite different from the one that had initially brought me to Europe. This time the wind was at our backs and the water was flat and blue, without a single squall in sight. Waves lapped at the ship's hull and the sky was clear except for a few cotton puffs gleaming in the setting sun.

I could still see the shoreline, although it was no longer possible to make out the buildings and houses of Brest, the port to which I had come from Calais and had been staying in for almost three weeks, waiting for a passage home. The coast of France had blurred into an indistinct line. Soon even this would disappear. I did not want to miss the moment when it vanished altogether, even though the strain of watching, of trying to hold onto it as long as humanly possible, was taking its toll. I had waited more years than I cared to count to get here, and now I was leaving it behind.

My journey had been demanding. Had I any sense at all I would be inside with a hot drink and a book, like a normal woman my age, not out on this deck in January staring over the frigid waters. I took off my glasses, flecked with the sea, and gave them a quick rub.

I had no idea what I would do once I got back to Canada. My professional accomplishments felt completely useless, like medals pinned on the chest of an invalid soldier. What did any of it matter? Most of the people I loved were either dead or gone. All my reference points had shifted. I was quite literally at sea, with days aboard ship before I reached land again, seven days in which to think. In part my delayed departure had been a blessing, for I had spent the last weeks wandering the streets of Brest, not talking to a soul. Solitude was what I had needed, time to permit myself to heal.

Several yards down the deck a girl tossed a chunk of bread out over the water for a hovering gull that swooped and caught it. The girl shrieked and pointed for the benefit of a second young woman standing beside her. I had noticed these two girls when I'd boarded. They were also Canadians, like several of the passengers on this Halifax-bound ship. Wearing the capes of Red Cross nurses they looked so similar they had to be sisters. My thoughts went immediately to Laure. Above the ship the gull hovered, jerking its neck and gulping.

AT DINNER THAT NIGHT I sat with them. Theirs was the first company I had allowed myself since the meeting with my father and I felt more than a little awkward. They were on their way to Halifax, they told me, after two years of service overseas. We were joined by a corporal from the Princess Patricia's Canadian Regiment, a handsome fellow with hair like wheat before the harvest who had lost the lower part of his right leg. He was on crutches, pants pinned at the knee. As soon as he returned to Canada, he said, the Army would fit him with a prosthetic.

I had been living a very simple life, on soups and bread from a bakery next to the gîte where I had been staying in Brest, and I was ready for a more elaborate meal. I was also hungrier than I knew for human contact. The laughter of the girls and their English chatter was a comfort. The blond sister informed us all that the ship's cook had an excellent reputation. The ship was French, which made all the difference. As if to prove her point a boy of about fourteen approached our table from the kitchen holding a bottle. He went straight to the corporal and bowed, displaying the label.

The light-haired nurse, whose name was Nora, laughed. "A sommelier! How civilized!"

The boy, who I suspected was the floor mopper, grinned and threw his shoulders back. He uncorked the bottle in front of us and poured a few dark drops into the corporal's glass. After the ritual swirling and swallowing, which everyone seemed to take very seriously, the corporal nodded. He also looked as if he hadn't sat down to a proper meal in ages; he savoured each moment.

The boy filled our glasses. We raised them. The wine was rich and warm. I was so grateful to be here with a glass of burgundy and company with whom to share it that my throat tightened. Such simple pleasures, but at that moment they meant the world.

The food arrived, borne by the same young man who had poured the wine. The dish was coq au vin, a favourite of mine. Tiny white onions shone like pearls in the lamplight and I closed my eyes, breathing in the smells. For most of the meal I did not speak, happy just to revel in my senses.

The Canadian sisters, in contrast, chattered blithely. The light-haired one named Nora was particularly lively, entertaining us with stories about her work at a Canadian Red Cross hospital that had been built on tennis courts belonging to a rich American who lived near London. Apparently the owner, Waldorf Astor, had offered the site to the British Army. When the Brits refused it it had gone to the Canadians. The dark sister spoke less than Nora, but had a lovely laugh. The corporal concentrated on his food, but whenever he heard the laugh he looked up and smiled.

Outside the wind was picking up, pushing against the portholes and causing the silverware to tremble. It was not strong enough yet to rock us, but every now and again the wine in our glasses sloshed. "Don't worry," said the corporal. "The weather will be fine."

I told them how terrible my trip over had been in mid-December. I didn't think I could survive another experience like that. The corporal asked what had induced me to travel in midwinter, so soon after the war's end.

"A friend who was ill," I told him. It wasn't a complete lie. Sir William's health had, after all, precipitated the trip.

"A soldier?" asked the corporal.

I had not wanted to talk about myself. I craved anonymity and did not feel I should let strangers get too close, but the wine had warmed and opened me. Surely it wouldn't make a difference if I mentioned Howlett.

The corporal looked at me with sudden interest. "Howlett?" he repeated. "You mean *the* Howlett? The physician from Oxford?"

The sisters were also staring. "We knew him too," said the fair-haired one. "He came to the hospital on Mondays."

"We attended the funeral," added the dark one.

It was my turn to stare. The news left me speechless.

"I went too," said the corporal. He was so involved in the topic that he didn't notice my silence. "He assisted at my amputation. He looked out for the Canadians."

"How strange we should all know him," said Nora. She turned to me. "What did you say your association with him was?"

I looked at my lap. I hadn't said and I wasn't about to. I could not have formulated a straightforward answer had I wanted to. "We're both doctors," I said after a pause.

"You are a doctor!" said Nora, admiration shining in her eyes. Fortunately she probed no further about my link to Sir William. She did describe the funeral, though, which had apparently been immense. Half of London had shown up as well as most of Oxford. Over the years Sir William had treated the prime minister and much of the cabinet, so a good number of England's politicians had been there too.

I listened, but only distractedly. Howlett was dead. The thought was difficult to grasp.

The corporal was now talking of his amputation. One third of his battalion had lost their lives, he told us without expression. Another third had lost limbs. He spoke slowly, as if the effort of stringing thoughts together was beyond him. "Sometimes I ask myself whether I ended in the right group."

"Come, Corporal," said Nora kindly. "Talk like that does no good to anyone. There's no going back so you might as well step forward." She paused and reddened, realizing the inappropriateness of the metaphor.

Her dark-haired sister came to her rescue. "Nora's right, Corporal. It's a lovely evening, the first of our voyage. We've been exquisitely fed," she paused and smiled. "Exquisitely watered too. It's worth giving thanks for."

I watched this little scene as if I were watching a play. The sisters were right; their advice wise. Yet how did people go on in the wake of such imponderable loss?

Nora raised her glass. "I want to give thanks for this night." She reflected for a moment. "Beth," she said to her sister, "I've just realized the date."

The dark one thought for a moment and then brightened "January twentieth."

"The Eve of Saint Agnes," I said.

Nora turned to me, surprised. "You know it?" Then she remembered my name.

"Do you know the poem?" asked Beth.

The corporal looked at us blankly. I thought back to Januaries in St. Andrews East with Laure and Grandmother, reading *Poems of Our Land* before the fire.

Nora stood and then dropped back down as the ship lurched

sideways. The Corporal reached out to steady her but she declined the help, gripping the back of her chair on her second attempt. The boat swayed, but not enough to shake her, and she began to recite:

> *Saint Agnes's Eve — Ah, bitter chill it was!*
> *The owl, for all his feathers, was a-cold;*
> *The hare limped trembling through the frozen grass ...*

She stopped. "That's all I can remember." She turned to her sister. "Help me out, Beth."

But Beth was also stumped. "There's something about sheep," she said vaguely. "And a rosary."

I laid my hands flat on the table and shut my eyes. The illustration from *Poems of Our Land* rose instantly in my mind: the skinny beadsman sitting on the steps, his white hair flowing, breath rising like incense. I took up where Nora had left off, reciting all the way to the sixth stanza, the one about the rituals girls must practise in order to dream about romance.

As we got up from the table after dinner the corporal made an attempt at a formal bow. "May your dreams be sweet tonight, ladies."

Beth laughed. It was clear the corporal liked her, but the way he was looking at her made me melancholy. My own loneliness and the news of Howlett's death had cooled the warmth of the wine. It was time for bed.

Before I left the dining room, however, Nora touched my arm. "You of all people must dream tonight, dear Agnes. It's your name day after all." She smiled, but her sister, who was standing beside her, looked embarrassed. The poem was about *young* virgins, after all.

That night, however, I did dream. The face that came to me was unexpected. It did not belong to my father or to poor dead William Howlett. I was no longer aboard ship but back in Montreal at the museum, surrounded by shelves of specimen bottles. This was the old museum I realized even as I was dreaming, before the fire had demolished it. Miraculously everything was intact. The bones were whole and white. The bottles were in one piece, standing upright in rows. Even my favourite specimen, the Howlett Heart, was there, sitting on the corner of my desk where I used to keep it. And there too was Jakob Hertzlich.

I must have tried to speak because I was awakened by my own moan. I lay still for several seconds, remembering the dream and thinking of blond Nora at dinner insisting that I have a vision. It must have been the wine affecting my fragile nerves, I thought, swinging myself upright and reaching for a sweater. My eyes moved around the cabin, taking in details as consciousness returned — the pale green walls, the fat pipe curving along the ceiling, the fogged porthole. I sighed and lay back on the bunk. Here I was at sea, three thousand miles from home, and whom should I find but Jakob Hertzlich?

31

The morning after I arrived in Montreal I took a train to St. Andrews
East. Between ship and rail I had been in perpetual motion for a
week and a half. I was looking forward to stopping. From outside
the Priory looked as it had when I had left, if perhaps a little shabbier. When I walked in, however, it was warm and welcoming.

George came from the kitchen. "It's you!" she said.

I hadn't told her I was coming. I hadn't known myself that I
would board the train to see her first thing. Since going overseas
I seemed to be living on impulse, following instinct rather than
reason. I walked up to her and gave her a prolonged hug. The
embrace wasn't entirely comfortable. I had trapped her arms with
my own, which she didn't appreciate. But as she backed away from
me I could see that she was happy.

I walked into the parlour. The room was bathed in late-January
sunshine. Outside the temperature was still below zero, but in here
there was comfort. George had taken the curtains off the windows.
Light was pouring in, making the room seem large and airy. She

had taken away my grandmother's rugs, exposing the floorboards, which she'd scrubbed and polished. The whole house seemed to have been scoured from top to bottom and all its contents sorted. The material accumulation of three generations of White family life lay in bags and boxes waiting for my permission to be delivered to needy families in the parish.

When I told her how wonderful the place looked she frowned. "I didn't do it for you," she said archly. "Or at least," she added, realizing how mean she sounded, "it was only indirectly for your benefit. I thought you wouldn't be home for months."

IN THE BAY WINDOW, three jars of paperwhites were sitting, their stems waving like long green fingers.

"That smell," I said, inhaling. "It's like springtime."

"Narcissus," she said. "Some people can't abide them but I'm partial to them. They're the only flower that blooms this early in the year."

The narcissus bulbs were fat and dark, scabbing slightly in the water and providing a startling contrast to the graceful shoots and flowers. "I did not plant them just for me, although they do cheer me up. They were also motivated by Jaime MacDonnell."

"Jaime MacDonnell?" The only Jaime MacDonnell I knew was a boy, son of the richest man in St. Andrews East, who happened to live two doors down from the Priory. For a crazy moment I pictured Miss Skerry going a-courting at the MacDonnell house, narcissus blooms in hand.

"He has come by here several times in your absence."

"He's all of seventeen!" I said, by this time completely baffled.

"Twenty-four, actually. He fought in Flanders but now he's home and recently married to a lovely girl from Lachute. A French one," she added as if this made things clearer.

"And why, may I ask, is he visiting you?"

George Skerry laughed and gave me a look as if to say that *some* people appreciated her, even if I did not. "It was really you he came to see, but you were away so he spoke to me instead. He has been living at his parents' home, but the wife, whose name is France, is pregnant now and they want a place of their own."

"And they're interested in the Priory?"

Miss Skerry did not respond at once. "You would like France," she said, looking out the window. "She's sweet but also practical. What is that French expression? *Terre à terre.* I expect she'll make a first-rate mother. She is having quite a time with her mother-in-law."

"She told you this?"

"She comes over too," said Miss Skerry. "We have both been in need of company."

"Of course," I said, for the first time picturing how hard it must have been for Miss Skerry when I set off for Europe immediately after Laure's death. "I wasn't here to help you, George. Forgive me."

"There is nothing to forgive. You had to make that journey."

I nodded. I hadn't said a word yet about my father, nor had Miss Skerry asked. It would all come out soon enough. "What did you tell Jaime MacDonnell?"

She took off her glasses and held them up to the light, checking for smudges. "I said that you were very attached to the place," she said, "and that you probably would not want to part with it."

This was only partly true. The Priory held many memories. It was where my mother had died and where Laure and I had spent the bulk of our childhood. But it was also a terrible drain on my finances and my time. My home was in Montreal now. There was nothing but nostalgia and my sister's grave to keep me here.

Before I could put any of this into words Miss Skerry resumed her story. "This only seemed to make Jaime MacDonnell more determined. He is like his father, Agnes. When he gets something in his head nothing on this earth will stop him. His wife is absolutely in love with the place."

There was something sly in Miss Skerry's manner. I had known her long enough to recognize when she was withholding a piece of news. "What are you saying, George?" I asked. "What exactly have you done?"

"Me?" said Miss Skerry, hooking her glasses behind her ears and turning to me with a look of exaggerated innocence. "I'm only the messenger, Agnes."

A bit more prodding eventually produced it. Jaime MacDonnell and his wife had made a handsome offer on the house. The amount Miss Skerry quoted was enough for me to retire comfortably and secure Miss Skerry's old age. My mind was all but made up, but I was afraid of being impulsive, so I asked what she would do in my shoes.

"What a question," she laughed. "I can't imagine what your shoes are like and I wouldn't presume to try them on. But I can tell you one thing. When opportunity knocks it's generally a good idea to open the door."

AFTER SHE HAD FED me a lunch of soup and fresh bread she suggested that we take a walk. But first she cut half a dozen narcissus blooms, wrapped them in newspaper, and put them in her satchel. I knew better than to ask what she was up to.

The section of the North River that flows in front of the Priory is not particularly wide, but the current is sufficiently strong that it does not freeze. Today great patches of blue were visible through the snow. The sun had been beating down so fiercely that some of the ice cover near the banks had begun to break off in chunks. It was by the river that I told George about the meeting with Sir William and about my reunion with my father in Calais. She was the first person I had told and the story came out awkwardly. I was glad we were outside. It seemed right as well to be telling this to her in wintertime in St. Andrews East — the same season and place in which my father had last lived with me. This time it was George who encircled me with her arms, clumsily because of her coat and mittens. She did not offer advice or try to cheer me up. She let me tell the story, and she held me.

We walked down the main road after that in the direction of Christ Church, which my great grandfather had founded nearly a century before. The Priory hadn't been sold yet and I was beginning to view it nostalgically as a place left behind. George led me down the street abutting the church and then stopped. Someone had dug a little path through the snowbank to the churchyard in back, which was surprisingly well-trodden and packed.

"Come then," she said, hoisting her skirts and stepping across the ditch. I was reminded of the year I turned thirteen when George Skerry first entered my life. She had hoisted her skirts in exactly the same way on our treks through the woods in search of microscope specimens. My eyes brimmed again. I was going soft with age and the funny thing was I didn't mind at all.

We climbed over the log fence, which was easy to do as it was half-sunk in snow, and entered the church's property. By this time I had figured out what my old friend was up to and wasn't surprised when she knelt down in the snow and opened her satchel. There were other offerings — a sprig of holly and the bright petals of a frozen amaryllis. On top of these she laid the sweet-smelling narcissus.

"I loved Laure," she said simply. "Your grandmother too."

The churchyard was lovely. I had only ever come here for funerals, never to sit, but now I had a chance to appreciate its beauty. It was sheltered by pine trees in whose branches chickadees had gathered. The snow was deep and clean, unmarred by any footprints but our own. We sat in silence for several minutes, thinking of my sister, buried under her cross. Her name — Laure Frances Stewart White — was chiselled in the stone.

"When I die," I said, "I shall be buried here." In my mind's eye I saw the stone. For the first time in my life I accepted the fact that it would bear the name of my grandmother, the brave woman who had loved and raised me.

As we walked homeward I recounted my dream.

"You did it!" George cried, startling me. "You actually conjured him on your name day! Well that is something, Agnes White."

I had expected her to say it was nonsense, but she did nothing of the sort. She started laughing, and with such unrestrained and simple mirth that soon I was laughing too.

32

A blister was forming on my right heel. I could feel it rubbing against my boot with every step I took. My stockings were wet, that was the problem. It was the second day of a thaw and the gutters were rushing with water. I had been out since early morning, walking the entire length of St. Denis Street, stopping at just about every door-way from Dorchester north to Mount Royal Boulevard.

I paused on the doorstep of a tall, grey, stone apartment building and unbuckled my boot to check the damage. This was the fifteenth rooming house I had visited. Tea was in order, I promised myself, ringing for the concierge. I was parched. If this one proved as futile as all the others I would stop. My heel was beginning to throb.

An old man in suspenders came to the door and I repeated the name I had been saying to concierges on St. Denis Street all morning. It was a hard one for French speakers, who struggled with the aspirated "H." I was expecting another negative response but the old man gave a little cry. "*Urts-ligue. Mais bien sûr. C'est un*

Anglais, n'est-ce pas?" He looked me over and said he couldn't let a woman up the stairs.

I was dressed that day in an old coat and boots that wouldn't last another year. In a month I would turn fifty. Clearly the reputation of the establishment was not in peril. "I have to see him," I said in my best French. "It is urgent." He relented and told me the room number.

Tracking down Jakob Hertzlich had not been easy. He had last been spotted at McGill, not long after I left for England. He had dropped in to visit Dr. Mastro, who reported that he looked dreadful, rake-thin and more unkempt than ever. He had mentioned something about renting rooms on St. Denis Street and talked about moving permanently to England.

Dr. Mastro had told me this the previous afternoon. He had also passed along news about Sir William Howlett. Apparently he had left instructions in his will that his body was to be autopsied, the brain donated to an institution of higher learning. Hopes had been raised in Montreal that that institution might be McGill University. They were dashed when the announcement came that the University of Pennsylvania would receive the honour. "Just think, Dr. White," Mastro had said. "You would have been custodian."

To Mastro's surprise I had shown no disappointment. I had dedicated so many years to serving Sir William in life, I told him, that I was more than ready to let others step in.

The climb up the rooming-house stairs was steep and I paused to rest. By the time I reached the top landing I was breathing hard. There were only two rooms up here. One was empty, its door open, revealing a mattress stripped of bedding and a low, sloped ceiling. This was an attic, decorated to hide the fact, but an attic just the same. The eaves of the roof were visible through the window. I could hear water dripping from a rainspout.

The second door was closed. Behind it someone was smoking. I stood staring at this door, which was white with a crack running the length of it and paint chipping at its edges. The tobacco smell was strong. What would I do if it turned out to be him? What would I say? Bedsprings creaked. Whoever was in there knew that someone was out here. I raised my hand and knocked.

There was a tentative reply in French, in a voice that seemed too small for Jakob Hertzlich's. The bedsprings creaked and then there was a bang, followed by scuffling. "*Une minute*," said the voice. A drawer was pulled open and shut and footsteps approached the door.

He was visibly surprised to see me. He was wearing only work pants and an undershirt, from which dark hair poked at the armpits and chest. His feet were bare. I looked away. The window was wide open. That had probably been the bang — wood slamming against brick as he tried to air out the room. The sunlight poured in, softening his astonished face.

The room was like a monk's cell. Jakob's folding cot was unmade with a novel lying face down on its sheets. Beside it was a cheap wooden chest of drawers. In a corner clothes spilled from a battered old valise.

"I thought you were the concierge," Jakob said. His voice was gravelly with tobacco. "He hates it when we smoke." He pulled the bedcovers hastily over the mattress, knocking his book to the floor. It was *Père Goriot*. He grabbed a shirt out of his suitcase. "To what do I owe the honour?" He had put his shirt on and was buttoning rapidly.

I swallowed and wet my lips. "I heard that you were leaving."

"You heard right."

"London?"

"Colchester, actually. That illustration work I told you about." He was sitting on the side of the bed now, pulling on socks. As soon as he finished he reached for his boots.

"That's wonderful news." My voice cracked.

"It's the only offer I've got," he said. "Mastro has nothing, what with the veterans returning. And everyone else I knew at McGill is dead or retired."

"I'm still here."

Jakob Hertzlich made no answer, but his expression hardened.

"If it's work you want," I said, loosening my scarf, "there's more than I know what to do with at the museum. I'd have you back gladly. We have received the Army's war specimens and they have said I can hire a technician. The Army pays splendidly," I added inanely.

His look made me wince. He had backed away at my approach, literally recoiled along the mattress. It was as if we were doing a dance but I had no idea what the steps were.

He jumped up and grabbed his coat from a hook on the door. "I don't wish to be rude, Dr. White, but I was on my way out." He was unshaven and unwashed. It was quite obvious that he had never intended to leave his bed that day, yet his hand was on the doorknob. "Keep your goddamn charity," he said over his shoulder. "Save it for someone who asks for it."

I didn't hear anything more, not the sound of ice dropping from the branches or the water rushing in the gutters outside. Not my breath, which seemed to have stopped altogether. Not even the beating of my own heart. Sun was pouring in the window and the heat was suddenly too much to bear. I lay down on his bed. I was trying to fill my lungs but each time I inhaled there was a stabbing pain. I watched, unable to move as Jakob Hertzlich turned and walked away.

His footsteps crossed the landing. He was walking out of my life just as my father had so many years before. It was such an old, familiar pain that I could do nothing but surrender. My voice failed now just as it had when I was four years old. My mouth was open but nothing came out. Inside me, however, every single cell was crying. My skin, my bones, my blood screamed in the silence.

I was so caught up with myself, lying there with my face in his pillow, that I failed to notice when the footsteps on the landing halted, or when they retraced the path along the carpet to the bedroom.

I did not notice the door open or Jakob's head peer in. In my despair I saw nothing until he was standing so close that I caught a whiff of cigarettes and dark licorice from Holland.

He knelt down on the floor. His gaze was strange, as if he wasn't sure who I was. "You can't go," I said, crying hard. "You mustn't leave me."

Jakob raised his eyes to the ceiling and took a breath. After what seemed an eternity he looked at me. "You are some woman, Dr. White. As perverse as they come."

I nodded and wiped my nose. "I've treated you so badly."

He shrugged and was about to say something when we heard the landlord's step upon the stairs. He called up, no doubt hoping for scenes of dissipation.

Jakob passed me a handkerchief. By the time the landlord got his head through the door I was halfway presentable. "We were on our way out," I said as he stared with suspicion. The room was cooler now and full of sunshine, but it was clearly time to leave. Despite the open window the landlord was sniffing for proof of Jakob's cigarettes.

"Come, Mr. Hertzlich," I said, taking his arm. "You'll be my guest for tea."

"YOU MEAN THAT OLD man I met was your father?"

"Honoré Linière Bourret," I said, stirring the cloud of milk in my cup.

"After you journeyed all the way to Calais he would not acknowledge you?"

A young waitress wiped down the tables at the front of the café. She hummed to herself, taking pleasure in the simple task, a sight that for some reason I found comforting.

"He's a scoundrel, Agnes. There's no other word for it."

"It's not that simple," I said, my eyes following the girl as she reached and cleaned. "The townspeople like him well enough. He built a life over there. He won their respect."

Jakob reached over and placed his hand on mine. "Scoundrel," he mouthed silently.

I shook my head. "Thinking that way doesn't help. Vilifying a person is the obverse of the coin of idealizing him. That is a lesson I have had to learn."

Jakob took my hand and gazed at it. After a moment he looked up. "What do you intend to do now?"

I shrugged. "The only plan I had was to track you down. Beyond that I have no idea. It feels a little like the earth has cracked open. The things I used to be certain of have suddenly ceased to be."

Jakob smiled. "Sounds practically mystical."

"Hardly," I laughed. "I just opened my eyes for the first time in fifty years. It certainly took me long enough. I had built my life on a dream. My picture of my father and of Sir William Howlett had little to do with reality."

He made a face. "We all have blind spots. And who is to say what is real?"

"My blindness wasn't a spot, Jakob. It was the whole picture. I built my entire life, don't you see, to please a man who did not exist." I was shy to admit this, but Jakob seemed neutral. There were no signs of judgment.

We sat in silence for a minute or two, simply looking at each other. Jakob Hertzlich's eyes were particularly warm and dark that day, set off against his full brown beard. I reached out and stroked the wiry bristles. He responded by taking my hand in his and kissing the palm. Then he smiled and signalled the waitress to bring more hot water for our tea.

❧
AFTERWORD

Although this novel takes its inspiration from the work and professional life of one of Montreal's first female physicians, Dr. Maude Elizabeth Seymour Abbott (1869–1940), the characters and events imagined here are purely fictional.

❖
ACKNOWLEDGEMENTS

I would like to thank the Conseil des arts et des lettres du Québec and the Banff Centre (specifically Fred Stenson and the Banff Wired Writing Program) for generous support while I wrote this novel. Caroline Adderson, Linda Leith (who came up with the title), my gifted and dedicated editor Marc Côté and my closest, most constant reader, Arthur Holden, made invaluable contributions for which I am deeply grateful. To these and other friends and family who read the manuscript in early form, my heartfelt thanks.

Conseil des arts et des lettres
Québec ❖❖